Lynda Page was born and brought up in Leicester. The eldest of four daughters, she left home at seventeen and has had a wide variety of office jobs. She lives in a village near Leicester.

Don't miss her previous novels:

'Inspirational and heart-warming' *Sun*

'When Lynda Page pulls the heart-strings, you won't fail to be moved' *Northern Echo*

Lynda PAGE

The Price to Pay

headline

First published in 2011 by
HEADLINE PUBLISHING GROUP

First published in paperback in 2012 by
HEADLINE PUBLISHING GROUP

3

Cataloguing in Publication Data is available from the British Library

ISBN 978 0 7553 8058 9

Typeset in Stempel Garamond by
Palimpsest Book Production Limited, Falkirk, Stirlingshire

Printed and bound by CPI Group (UK) Ltd, Croydon, CR0 4YY

Headline's policy is to use papers that are natural, renewable and
recyclable products and made from wood grown in sustainable forests.
The logging and manufacturing processes are expected to conform to the
environmental regulations of the country of origin.

HEADLINE PUBLISHING GROUP
An Hachette UK Company
338 Euston Road
London NW1 3BH

www.headline.co.uk
www.hachette.co.uk

It is said that behind every great man is a great woman. Equally so, behind every author is a team of unsung heroes. This book is dedicated with thanks to the team behind me.

To Darley Anderson and his wonderful staff at the Darley Anderson Literary Agency. I have never had cause to doubt that my career as an author has been in the safest of hands. It is said that you are the best in the business and I know that is true.

To Clare Foss, the most loyal and supportive editor an author could wish to have. As with Darley, in the twenty years we've been together, I have never had cause to doubt my work is safe in your hands.

To Lynn Curtis, whose expert editorial skills make my rambling manuscripts readable.

And to all the staff at Headline Publishing Group who beaver away to ensure that my manuscripts are transformed from type-written pages into beautiful books.

Thank you to all of you.

ACKNOWLEDGEMENTS

Thanks to Jonathan Harrison of Harrison Cameras, Sheffield. I much appreciate the time you gave up to answer my never-ending questions on the photographic industry. The information you provided was invaluable when bringing this story to life.

CHAPTER ONE

The eyes of the woman blazed with a look of desperate longing as she gazed at the child sleeping in its pram. She stood statue-still but her emotions were raging. Her heart felt as though it was being squeezed in a vice; the ache in the pit of her stomach hurt like sharp clawing talons.

These feelings were nothing new to Erica Dunmore. They were something she frequently experienced when caught off guard, as she had been now, happening upon the child outside a shop. Before she could prevent it she was tormented all over again by the knowledge that the one thing she desired most in life was unattainable to her. She had been prodded and poked, given every test known by the top gynaecologist in the county, and there seemed to be no reason why she was unable to conceive. He had advised her to be patient, let nature take its course, but after fifteen years of an otherwise happy and fulfilling marriage, her hopes of ever holding her own child in her arms were rapidly fading. She was grateful that Simon had made it very clear to her that she herself was more important to him than having children, and had not left her to find someone else who could bear him a child.

Several years ago she had approached him with the idea of applying to adopt. She had thought that at least he would discuss the idea with her, the same as they had always discussed anything important to them both, but on this occasion Simon shocked her by seeming unwilling to discuss this particular topic, just blustered that he'd give it some thought and let her know how he felt about it later.

Out of respect for her husband she had waited for him to raise the subject again after he'd had time to consider it, but to this day he never had. She could only assume that, when it came down to it, he didn't feel he could take on someone's else's child and raise it as his own, and felt unable to admit that to her in case she should see him as a lesser person because of it. She lived in hope for a while that he would come to change his mind, but as time wore on that hope too was beginning to evaporate, like the hope of ever bearing her own child.

Waking from its slumber, the infant began to whimper. Instinctively Erica reached for the pram's handlebar, her intention being to walk up and down outside the shop to lull it back to sleep. She had only taken half a dozen steps when she almost jumped out of her skin as a voice screamed behind her: '*Help!* A woman's trying to steal my baby. Someone call the police . . . *Help! Help!*'

Automatically Rica, as she was known, having given herself the nickname as a young child when she was unable to say the E in her name and pronouced the rest 'Reeka', spun around, prepared to do her bit to apprehend whoever was carrying out such a despicable act, only for her eyes to land on a young woman standing in the entrance to the shop and staring at her accusingly. Before Rica could prevent it, the woman had launched herself at her, was gripping her arm tightly and bellowing at the top of her voice.

'Will someone fetch the police! This woman's trying to take my baby.'

Rica's emotions were somersaulting. She felt torn between outrage at being accused of a terrible crime and mortified at being stared at by the crowd that was now gathering around them. 'No, no, you're mistaken . . .' she protested.

The frenzied woman cut her short. 'You were walking off with my child until I stopped you! I know what I saw. Good job I came out of the shop when I did.' She turned her head and addressed an assistant who had come out to see what all the commotion was about. 'Stop standing there like an idiot. Go and call the police and have this woman arrested.'

A voice from the crowd angrily cried out, 'She wants lynching, not pampering in a police cell!'

A wave of terror engulfed Rica as she imagined herself at the mercy of a crowd who believed her to be guilty of child snatching.

Just then a woman came pushing herself through the press of onlookers and demanded, 'What on earth is going on here?'

Rica had never in her life been so grateful to see her sister. 'Oh, Fran, this young lady thinks I was about to steal her baby! Of course I wasn't. I was only going to walk it up and down outside the shop, to get it back to sleep. It was crying, you see.'

Francine Derwent looked at Rica questioningly for a moment before she turned her attention to the scowling young mother. 'My sister was trying to do you a good turn and you repay her by branding her a criminal?' she snapped in reproving tones. Her eyes narrowed darkly before she added, 'It's *you* who wants charges brought against you . . . for leaving your child outside a shop unattended. What if it'd choked or something and you not there to deal with it? Or what if a real child snatcher had come along?' Without waiting for a response from the gawping young woman, shocked to find herself the accused now and not the accuser, Francine gave Rica a push in the small of her back, urging her to get clear of the onlookers.

She was only too happy to obey.

A short while later Rica and Fran were seated opposite each other in a tea shop. It was the kind of quaint establishment that was dying out now that more modern milk and coffee bars, with their juke boxes and espresso machines, were opening up to cater for younger members of society in the early-1960s who had plenty of disposable cash to spend. Rica would have much preferred to have visited one of the newer types of establishment, where the lively atmosphere created by the vibrant young clientele would at least make her feel she was still among the living, unlike the establishment they were in now where the rest of the customers appeared only a step or two away from death's door. Knowing her sister as well as she did, Rica was aware Fran thought milk and coffee bars were dens of iniquity, so hadn't even suggested it.

By any onlookers who didn't know them, it would have been assumed Rica was the younger of the two by quite a margin, when in fact she was the elder by two years. Fran was thirty-three but could have been mistaken for someone in her fifties, thanks to the way she dressed and acted. Fran had always been old for her years. Rica remembered their mother on numerous occasions stating that she thought her youngest daughter had been born after her time. She should have been born in 1835, not 1935, as her outlook on life was early-Victorian. Nevertheless she was an attractive woman, one whom Rica felt would be quite a head turner if she stopped making herself look so severe and brought herself up to date, even just a little.

The work suit she wore today was not at all flattering. It was dark grey in colour, the loose-fitting jacket hiding the shapely figure underneath. The skirt ended well below her knees, a long-sleeved white blouse was buttoned high at the neck, and the only adornment she wore was a cameo brooch pinned to one lapel. She wore sensible low-heeled court shoes, her dark hair scraped back into a severe French roll and no make-up.

Fran lived in a one-bedroomed flat which was furnished

with heavy dark-wood pieces that wouldn't have been out of place in a Victorian vicarage. Her idea of socialising was a visit to a museum or to attend an opera or classical music performance, with only a programme for company.

Rica, by contrast, was a very sociable person and liked nothing more than having friends around for dinner or else being part of a large group enjoying a lively night out. She was modern in her outlook and did her best to dress fashionably while always conscious it should be in keeping with her age. Today, under her woollen coat, she was wearing a short-sleeved geometric-patterned shift dress in shades of bright yellow and green, the hemline skimming the top of her knees. A hairband in the same material swept back her light brown, mid-length hair, which was worn bouffant for added volume and flicked up at the ends. Cuban-heeled black court shoes and a black shoulder bag completed the look.

The sisters hadn't spoken a word on their short walk to the tea shop. On arriving Fran had done the ordering . . . not because she was conscious that her sister was still reeling from the events of earlier, but because she always took charge and also assumed she knew what her sister wanted. Fran then thoughtfully watched Rica absently rearranging the silverware and small posy vase on their table while they waited for the elderly waitress in her smart black-and-white uniform to bring their order.

After the waitress had made her departure, Fran poured the tea from the patterned china pot and pulled a disapproving face as she watched Rica put three cubes of sugar into her cup. 'Sugar is bad for you,' she remarked.

Rica answered tartly, 'I understand that it's supposed to be good for you when you've had a shock. So is a stiff drink – and if I'm honest, I'd choose a large gin and tonic if I could.' Then a glint of tears pricked her eyes, her bottom lip trembled and she murmured, 'I can't believe that baby's mother really thought I was going to run off with it.'

Over the rim of her cup. Fran looked at her sister searchingly for several long moments. Finally putting the cup back in its saucer, she fixed Rica with her eyes and asked her, 'You *were* falsely accused, weren't you?'

'Are you asking me if my intention really was to kidnap that baby?' Rica couldn't quite believe what she was hearing.

Fran's reply was matter-of-fact. 'I know how desperate you are for one. When people are desperate, they sometimes resort to desperate measures.'

Rica's jaw dropped. 'I may be desperate for a child, but one of my own, not someone else's. How could you even think I would stoop so low as to steal another woman's child, Fran? How *could* you?'

Fran leaned over and selected a ham sandwich from the bottom tier of a cake stand, and put it on her plate together with a French fancy. She then looked at Rica and asked, 'How is Mother?'

Her abrupt change of topic signalled the fact that she did not deign to reply to her sister's question. Rica heaved a deep sigh. 'The same as usual.' And then asked Fran the same question she'd asked her on numerous occasions before. 'Why don't you visit her and find out for yourself?'

Her sister's face hardened as she said abruptly, 'You know I can't.' She picked up the delicate crustless sandwich. 'Aren't you going to eat anything?'

Rica shook her head. 'I'm not hungry.'

Fran disdainfully clicked her tongue. 'Oh, such a waste of good food, and money too. I wouldn't have ordered it if you had told me.'

Rica might have reminded her that she had not been consulted. But how could Fran ever have thought she'd be able to stomach food after what she had just been through?

For several moments silence stretched between them while Fran ate her fill and Rica sipped her tea, then to Rica's surprise her sister abruptly dabbed a napkin around her mouth to catch any stray crumbs. She gathered her things and rose to her feet, announcing, 'I need to get off; I have an errand to run before I go back to work. You'll take care of the bill, won't you? I'll settle up with you next week.'

As she watched her depart, Rica wondered just what errand was urgent enough to cut short their weekly get together. Fran ran the office for a local Chartered Accountant. She had worked for Reginald Moffett since leaving school. Reginald himself was a staid bachelor of fifty-five, a tall, thin man with a shock of steel-grey hair, a neatly trimmed moustache, and very conservative taste in his dress. Until her death three years ago he had lived with his mother; still did live in her house, in fact, which he had duly inherited as her only child. Rica had met the man informally on a couple of occasions over the seventeen years Fran had worked for him, when she'd needed to call in at the office. From what she had deduced on those visits it seemed that Fran and Reginald harboured a great liking and respect for one another, but neither of them would be the first to make a move for fear of making a fool of themselves. Rica felt this was a shame as the pair of them had a lot in common.

The conversations of her fellow customers intruded on her thoughts. Two old biddies behind her were discussing their funeral arrangements, which Rica felt would take place shortly judging by the age and fragility of both. Others were decrying the appearance of the mini-skirt, young women showing parts of their body that should only be viewed in private by one man, and then only after they had married him. A party of four were proclaiming their outrage at the decline in domestic servants since the war, now women had been lured into factories and were earning a substantially better wage than could be offered within private households.

Rica was still feeling the after-effects of shock, her mood

low enough without these conversations further depressing her. She needed to get out of here. Her plan had been to go shopping after she and Fran had parted. She'd had a dress made for a spring ball her husband Simon was taking her to and needed accessories to go with it. But now was not the right time. She could go home. All her housework was up-to-date, but she could find something to occupy her in the garden until Simon came home. She would tell him what had happened so that he could put her mind at rest that he believed in her innocence, even if her own sister couldn't find it within herself to do the same.

But it was five hours at least until Simon would return and Rica didn't like the thought of being on her own in the meantime. She had friends she could visit, several close ones, but wanted no one else but Fran and Simon to know what had happened today. All her friends were very aware of her longing for a child and when they learned what she had been accused of today, although outwardly expressing their belief in her innocence, she worried if privately they would wonder if there was no smoke without fire, and worry she could even become desperate enough to turn her attention to one of their young children. She couldn't bear the thought of that.

So Rica knew where she would go: to visit her mother. She would be free to spill out all her woes to her, with no fear whatsoever of being judged or condemned.

CHAPTER TWO

Rica leaned forward and took her mother's aged hands tenderly in hers as she concluded her tale. 'So you see, Mam, I only wanted to soothe the baby back to sleep in its mother's absence. Our Fran obviously has her doubts or she wouldn't have asked me what she did, but you believe I never intended to take the baby, don't you?'

Rica was looking into rheumy eyes that held no hint of recognition in them. It had been a long time since she had witnessed any sign of intelligent life in her mother's eyes. Altzheimer's disease had reduced this once-vibrant woman slumped in the chair before her to a lifeless shell. It had tightened its grip on Iris Derwent two years ago, after her beloved husband had unexpectedly died in his sleep from natural causes. The doctor had diagnosed heart failure.

Owen Derwent had been only fifty-five years of age when he died. Never had a day's serious illness in his life. He and Iris had been in the same class together at school and there had never been anyone else for either of them. They had married at eighteen and, except for Owen's time in the army during the war, facing action in Italy and France from which mercifully he returned unscathed in mind or body, the pair of them had never been apart.

Owen had been a patient and easy-going man with a dry sense of humour. On leaving school, he'd started work at a local factory as an apprentice tool-maker, and was still working for them when he had died. His life had centred around his wife and two daughters, and he was a loving husband and father. Rica could never remember either of her parents raising a hand to their daughters, even when in truth they had been more than deserving of a hard smack for something they had done. The punishment for any misdemeanour in the Derwent household was for a privilege to be denied, and how long that privilege was withheld depended on the severity of the misdeed in their parents' eyes. Both Rica and Fran were the envy of their friends in the neighbourhood. The other children all regularly sported handprints on the top of their legs, on their backsides or even their faces, or were locked in the dark, dank cupboard under the stairs for several hours at a time. Some received even worse punishments than those in reprisal for any misbehaviour – or simply because their parents had chosen to lash out at them because they felt like it.

The Derwents had lived in a two-bedroomed terraced house in a working-class area. Owen had maintained it as best he could, while Iris had kept it clean and comfortable, and put appetising meals on the table. Although holidays were beyond their means, the Derwents would save what they could after their dues had been paid to take their daughters for day trips to the seaside during the school summer holidays, either to Skegness or to Mablethorpe. Owen's only vice was a couple of pints in the local on a Friday night; Iris's was her penchant for a bottle of stout while they both played games of cards with close neighbours on a Saturday night – only for matches, though, as neither of them was a gambler.

Rica and Fran agreed about one thing: they had had a very happy upbringing.

The abrupt loss of the man she had shared all but a few years of her life with had hit Iris badly and her decline immediately began. At first she just seemed forgetful and vague, which was put down to grief, but when she began to wander outside in the middle of the night dressed only in her nightdress, it was apparent that there was something far more serious going on. Within a year she had deteriorated so badly that Rica and Fran were left with no alternative but to put her into a nursing home, to be looked after by people trained to do so. Six months ago the disease had robbed Iris of the last of her memory. She didn't even know who she was now, could do nothing for herself. Except when she was in bed, she would be seated in a chair to stare vacantly out of a window in the day room, where they were now, amidst a dozen or so other residents in varying stages of terminal illness, all waiting for death to release them from their living hell.

Fran had ended her visits to the home several months ago. She'd told Rica she couldn't see the point when their mother had no clue who she was. Rica could fully understand her feelings, but she herself kept visiting because she couldn't bear the thought of her mother having no visitors and believing no one cared for her, when they did, very dearly. Every Wednesday afternoon without fail Rica journeyed to the home, where she would sit and tell her mother all that had happened in the intervening week – regardless of the fact that not one word of what she was saying was registering with Iris. Without fail, every Thursday lunchtime she would meet Fran in the tea shop and update her on any changes in their mother's condition. If Iris was in need of anything that would make her existence just a little more comfortable, the sisters would discuss it and share the cost.

It was emotionally draining for Rica each time she made a departure from the nursing home, as she never knew whether this visit would be her last.

She was just wiping away a dribble of saliva that was escaping from the side of her mother's mouth when she heard the rumble of the tea trolley coming through the door,

11

and turned her head to look over. The woman pushing the trolley was homely and middle-aged with a cheery nature. Mary Abbot's job was to aid the nurses on duty, helping to feed and keep clean those unable to tend to those tasks for themselves. She was the type who would go out of her way to make the remaining days of those she helped care for as comfortable as she was able. In the time between chores, unlike the other two nurses' aides employed at the home, Mary was never found idly thumbing through a magazine until she was needed again, but would always take an able patient for a gentle stroll around the garden, wash their hair, play a game of cards, or just sit quietly chatting to them.

Spotting Rica, she looked at her quizzically for a moment before giving a broad smile and pushing the trolley over to her. There was amusement in her voice when she told her, 'When I saw you with Iris just now, I thought me mind was playing tricks on me . . . that it wasn't Thursday but Wednesday . . . and I was worried I would be joining the patients in here meself very shortly. Then I remembered seeing you here yesterday. I hadn't got me days mixed up after all.'

Rica smiled warmly at her. 'I just felt the need to come and see Mother again today.'

Mary placed one plump hand on her shoulder and gave it a friendly squeeze. 'Well, Iris is a lucky woman getting a visit from her daughter once a week, let alone twice. Most of the other old dears never get any visitors at all – family, neighbours or friends.' Genuine sadness filled her eyes. 'Their ailments may be terminal, but apart from the ones suffering from the likes of what your mother has, their minds are as sharp as they've always been. It breaks my heart to see their eyes dart to the door every time it opens, hoping to see a loved one's face once more before their time comes, only to be continually disappointed. I bet those same thoughtless relatives will soon crawl out of their holes to find out what's been left to them once their old folk pop their clogs. Anyway, are yer happy giving yer mam her tea or would you like me to do it?'

Rica told her she would.

Mary poured tea from a large aluminium pot into a special spouted cup, adding plenty of milk so it wouldn't burn Iris's mouth, and handed it to Rica. She then poured Rica herself some tea in a normal cup, which she placed on the small table at the side of the chair. Rica smiled her thanks. After saying her goodbyes, Mary continued serving cups of tea to the rest of the patients in the day room and lending a hand to those who couldn't manage unassisted.

A hour later, Rica gave the parchment-like skin of her mother's cheek an affectionate kiss, looked into her lifeless eyes and told Iris she would see her next Wednesday – inwardly praying that she would indeed – and then took her leave.

CHAPTER THREE

Home to Rica for the past ten years had been a 1920s three-bedroomed semi in a pleasant, leafy suburb a couple of miles from the centre of the city of Leicester. When the pair of them had moved in, the house had not been improved in any way or redecorated by the previous occupants since they had bought it new forty years before. It had been dark and dingy, and not at all inviting. The Dunmores had seen the house's potential at once, however, and now the previous owners wouldn't have recognised their old abode. All the rooms had been transformed. The dingy old wallpaper had been stripped off and replaced with modern geometric-patterned paper in bright colours. The curtains hanging at the windows complemented the wallpaper in each room. All the floors, apart from the bathroom and kitchen, were covered in good-quality carpeting, and the shabby, dated furniture had been replaced with modern stylish pieces.

In the living room the three-piece suite was long and low, with light wooden arms and legs and pale powder blue upholstery. Assorted brightly coloured cushions were scattered over it. Like the suite, the coffee table was long and low, of Scandinavian design and in light wood. The formerly open fireplace had been boarded up and a modern gas fire now warmed the room. On the wall above hung a starburst-design wall clock. In the corner was a free-standing colour television set. A holiday to Venice several years ago had introduced Rica to the beauty of Murano glass and she had returned home with several pieces which were now displayed on the sideboard. There was a Sommerso vase in reds and oranges, a multi-coloured clown figurine, and a heavy bowl-shaped ashtray in shades of blue and green. She hoped to return to Venice and add to her collection some time in the future.

Much to the envy of some of the neighbours, the Dunmores' tiny kitchen had been extended and was now large and spacious, fitted with an array of units in red-and-white Formica finish. It boasted a fridge with a large freezer box, a twin-tub washing machine, along with assorted kitchen aids such as a food mixer and toaster.

The two main bedrooms had fitted wardrobes and comfortable divan-style beds. The smaller third bedroom was where Rica did her ironing and sewing and Simon stored records pertaining to the business. Although if he'd had his way he would have used the room to lay out the cherished Hornby train set his father had bought him as a child, and which he was constantly adding to when he had time to visit junk shops and rummage around in dusty boxes in the hope of discovering pieces he hadn't yet collected.

The long garden at the back of the house was mostly lawned, edged around with flowerbeds and shrubs, and Rica took care of it. There was a small vegetable patch and a greenhouse at the bottom which Simon oversaw, Rica harvesting the results for their table.

When she arrived before the house, Rica stopped short in surprise to see their two-year-old black Humber Sceptre already parked in the driveway at the side of the house. It was only just gone four and Simon was rarely home before six-thirty during the week. He didn't shut the shop until five-thirty and usually there was something which needed to be done before he could leave.

Simon had inherited his father's enthusiasm for photography and had readily joined him in his business on leaving school, taking over on his father's accidental death twelve years ago. Richard Dunmore had been the official photographer at a society wedding when the flash from his camera had startled the horse pulling the carriage carrying the bride and her father. The frightened beast had reared up and the carriage had overturned. The bride and her father had escaped with a few cuts and bruises and the ruining of their clothes. Richard hadn't been so lucky. A hoof hit him full force on the side of his temple, fracturing his skull and killing him instantly.

Simon's mother had died in childbirth with her second child when he was five. The child had died too. Richard had been a devoted father to him and they had grown even closer on the death of the most important woman in their lives. Simon had been totally devastated by his father's unexpected demise; even his own beloved wife Rica couldn't console him. For several weeks the business was abandoned while he fought with his deep sadness and great anger over the bereavement. Finally Rica was able to get through to him that he wasn't honouring his father's memory by letting himself and the business they had worked so hard to build up fall into ruin. It had taken Simon a while to win back the customers who had taken their business elsewhere while he'd been in mourning, but eventually he did and over the following years the business had prospered to the extent that it now not only afforded them the means to buy their own house, but such luxuries as a car and a holiday abroad each year.

Extremely concerned as to just what it could be that had brought her husband home so early from work, Rica hurried to the front door and let herself in. Before she could call out to announce her arrival, a deeply troubled-looking Simon was in the hallway, demanding, 'Where have you been? I've been really worried.'

Her husband was just under six foot tall, with broad shoulders and slim hips. His straw-coloured hair, thick and wavy, was worn fashionably long below his ears. He was boyishly good-looking, with a strong square jaw. Rica felt he looked like an older version of Brian Jones of the Rolling Stones.

Like her father had been, Simon was easygoing, with a good sense of humour. They had met when Rica had been sixteen, on her first visit to the local youth club. Already a regular himself, Simon had spotted the pretty young girl the moment she had walked in and immediately approached her to ask if she fancied a game of table tennis. He later told her that he'd wasted no time in making his presence known to her as he didn't want to risk another chap getting in before him. They'd soon become inseparable. Richard Dunmore was more than happy with his son's choice of future wife. The Derwents thought Simon perfect for their daughter. They married four years later, when they were earning enough between them to afford the rent on a little terraced house near their parents'.

At the moment Simon was soberly dressed in a dark blue suit and white shirt worn with a plain light blue tie, albeit he had taken his jacket off on arriving home earlier. During his leisure time, though, he liked to keep up with the latest trends, although he drew the line at ruffled shirt fronts and glaring colours and trousers so tight they looked like they'd been sprayed on.

'I don't know why you would be worried about me,' Rica observed. 'You know I meet Fran for lunch every Thursday. Today, though, she needed to get off sharp as she said she had an errand to run before she went back to work. And as I didn't fancy going into town shopping for accessories for my new dress after all, I decided to go and see my mother again. If I'd known you would be home early, I would have come straight back after parting from Fran.' She then looked

17

at him questioningly. 'It's very unusual for you to be home so early, Simon. There's nothing wrong, is there?'

'No, no, everything is fine. I just thought it'd be nice to finish early for a change. I've left Jason to lock up at closing time.'

Rica hadn't been with Simon all these years without knowing when he wasn't being truthful with her. Even had she not known him that well, she would still have known he was prevaricating now. He wasn't a natural liar. Whatever had brought him home early, it wasn't because it would be a nice change for him. Then the truth suddenly dawned on her and she exclaimed, 'Oh, so that was Fran's urgent errand? She needed to see you at the shop, didn't she, Simon, to tell you what happened this morning?'

He looked at her for several long moments before he confessed, 'Yes, she did.'

Rica's face twisted with hurt. 'So, despite me telling her I would never, ever contemplate doing such a thing, she believed I was about to run off with a baby before its mother challenged me?' A glint of tears sparkled in her eyes then and there was a quiver in her voice when she added, 'You never leave the shop early except in an emergency. In all the time we've been together, I can only remember two such occasions. When your father was killed, and the time I tripped and sprained my ankle and you took me to the hospital to have it checked. You have just lied to me, haven't you?

'You haven't come home because you fancied finishing early. Like Fran, you believe I would have run off with that child if I hadn't been stopped. It's hurtful enough knowing she believes I'm so desperate for a baby that I'd resort to stealing someone else's, but you too . . . Have you any idea how that makes me feel? So come on, tell me, Simon, just what have you decided to do about me between you? Lock me in the house? Forbid me to go out on my own unless either you or Fran can accompany me?'

He blurted, 'Oh, darling, you've got it wrong! Neither Fran nor I think for a minute you were actually planning to take a baby and saw your chance today. Just that when you unexpectedly came across an abandoned, upset child, desperation took over and you didn't quite know what you were doing . . . We feel you need to talk to a professional. Let them decide if you need their help or not.'

Rica narrowed her eyes quizzically at him. 'A psychiatrist? That sort of professional, you mean?'

He nodded.

Her jaw dropped and she shook her head in disbelief. 'If my own husband and sister, the two people who are supposed to know me best, don't believe that I'm totally innocent of what that woman was accusing me of, then what chance have I of convincing anyone else?' With that Rica rushed past Simon and into the kitchen, slamming shut the door behind her. Standing at the sink, she leaned against it and cradled her head in her hands.

Back in the hall, Simon stood staring helplessly at the closed door. Matters hadn't gone the way he'd planned at all. When his sister-in-law had arrived unexpectedly in the shop and explained the reason for her visit, he'd been utterly stunned but had immediately jumped to his wife's defence. No one was more aware of her desperate longing for a child than he was, but he was adamant that Rica was neither stupid nor callous enough to deprive another woman of her baby.

Fran said she wholeheartedly agreed with him. But, as she'd explained it, there was still that nagging element of doubt. Perhaps when confronted with a child who was apparently abandoned, Rica's mothering instinct had momentarily overcome her usual good sense, and she had decided to take it before its mother stopped her. If this were the case, what if she tried again when the next opportunity came along? Simon had reluctantly agreed she had a point. It became apparent to both of them that professional help was

19

called for. An expert ought to verify whether Rica was in need of specialist treatment or not. They just had to get her to agree with them.

After due deliberation Simon had decided to go home early, suggest to Rica they have a bottle of wine with their dinner, then once she was in a mellow mood, casually bring up the events of that morning and guide the conversation so that it appeared that Rica herself had come up with the idea of seeking professional help.

His plan had completely failed as he had bargained without his astute wife querying his lame reason for finishing work early. Fran would not be backwards in coming forwards with criticism when he let her know how badly he had fared. But of far more concern to him was the fact that he had unwittingly managed to deeply upset his beloved wife. He couldn't blame Rica for how she was feeling. How would he react if the tables were turned, and it was she telling him she feared he could be mentally unstable and in need of professional help?

He raked his hand through his thatch of hair. As matters stood at the moment, he had no idea if she would ever talk to him again.

He was very annoyed with himself for messing things up, but that was overridden by a surge of acute guilt.

His wife was under the impression that she knew all there was to about her husband; that there were absolutely no secrets between them. But she was wrong. Simon had a secret that he feared could cause his marriage to crumble if his wife ever discovered it. He should have divulged it when her maternal instincts first rose to the fore; she had made no secret of the fact that, having landed the man of her dreams, nothing was more important to her than becoming the mother of his children. At the age of fifteen, however, Simon had been unfortunate enough to suffer a serious attack of mumps and had been told by the no-nonsense doctor who confirmed his illness that one of the known side-effects was the risk of being rendered sterile. That was not something that had caused him any sleepless nights at an age when becoming a father was the last thing on his mind. The fact was lost somewhere at the back of his mind, along with all the other matters he saw as of no importance to him then. He had been extremely happily married to Rica for twelve years, and they had been seriously trying for a baby for ten. After years of disappointment, Rica had started to voice her worries that maybe there was something wrong with her; that she couldn't conceive. That was when the forgotten prophecy that his childhood illness could leave its legacy had burst to the forefront of his mind, to nag him like chronic toothache.

Although he had no doubt his wife adored him, Simon just couldn't bring himself to tell her that the problem was more likely to lie with him. He was not prepared to risk losing her to someone who could father children. He constantly kept telling her that having children would be wonderful, but he didn't need them to complete his life as that had happened the day she had entered it. He even went so far as to pretend to attend the hospital for fertility tests and then fabricated a clean bill of health in that department. Ten years later, he still couldn't come clean to her. He had nearly had a heart attack when she had approached him about their applying to adopt a child several years ago. He wasn't, in truth, against the idea, would readily give a child in need a home and raise it as his own, but he feared that the adoption process could involve the authorities possibly checking their health records. His adolescent bout of mumps was bound to come to light, and then Rica would discover that he had been aware for years that it was almost certainly his fault she had not conceived, not hers as she'd assumed. He could lose her for ever.

He had managed to quash the idea of adoption . . . for

the time being at any rate . . . by telling Rica they shouldn't lose hope of having their own child. If nothing had happened for them in another few years then they would give it serious thought. By then he hoped to have a water-tight excuse as to why they shouldn't proceed down the adoption route.

But now her need for a child was apparently so great it could have affected her mentally. As selfish as it was of him, though, he would sooner help Rica through a period of receiving psychiatric treatment over her presumed barrenness than risk losing her after his deception was revealed.

He really should go and plead with her now to calm down. Maybe then she would be more receptive to hearing him out and believe that he and Fran had only her best interests at heart. Even if he had lied to her . . .

He would go for a walk first, he decided. Taking his casual jacket off the coat rack in the hall, he quietly let himself out of the front door and set off.

With his mind full of today's events, he just put one foot in front of the other and carried on doing so. It was with a sense of shock that he suddenly realised the March evening had drawn in and he took a look at his watch to find that it was half-past six. He been walking for over two hours. At least his walk had afforded him time to think deeply. Part of him still believed that Rica would never take another woman's child merely to satisfy her own needs, but the other part was preoccupied with Fran's worry that maybe she hadn't known what she was doing and needed help before she found herself in serious trouble.

Simon felt as if he was stuck between the devil and the deep blue sea. Then an idea struck him as to how he could handle this matter in a way that resolved both issues. He could convince Rica that he and Fran had been wrong to think the young woman's accusation had had any substance to it, and beg her forgiveness. But, secretly, they could keep a sharp eye on her for any signs that she was becoming mentally unstable. Should they witness them, then they would have no alternative but to take matters into their own hands.

Satisfied that this was the way forward, he took a look around. He was in a street that was unfamiliar to him. He could have been in one of several large areas of back-to-back terraces that housed the lower-working-class population of the city. Just ahead of him on a street corner he noticed a public house called The Grapes. Judging by its shabby exterior it looked to be a rundown establishment. The sign was faded, the paintwork on the doors and window frames chipped and flaking, and the frosted-glass windows in dire need of a wash. Litter was heaped around the front step, and looked as though it had been there for weeks. It didn't seem to Simon that the landlord was the conscientious sort. But his long walk had made him thirsty and a pint of best bitter would quench it, besides giving him the Dutch courage to return home and carry out his plan.

Simon made his way over to the door, pushed it open and went inside. A further two half-glazed doors faced him. One had 'Snug' etched into the glass, the other 'Bar'. Many back-street pubs had by now been modernised by the breweries in the hope of attracting the younger clientele. This pub, for whatever reason, had been overlooked and its interior was still largely as it would have been in the thirties. There was one room, the snug, where men could entertain their ladies, and a workaday bar complete with sawdust on the floor and several strategically placed spittoons, exclusively for male drinkers. Simon chose the door to the bar, opened it and went through. To his surprise, considering it was not long past opening time, the place was heaving with men, mostly wearing grubby work clothes, obviously having a pint to wash the dust from their throats before they went home for their dinner.

Edging his way through groups of milling drinkers to the

bar, Simon waited his turn to order from a portly, ruddy-faced man he assumed was the landlord. Finally armed with his drink, he took a sip. The beer was good. In fact, this landlord could teach the one who ran his upmarket local a thing or two about beer-keeping as it was the best Simon had tasted for a long while. It seemed he was going to have to drink it standing up as all the tables lining the sides of the room were fully occupied.

Then he saw a vacant seat at a table in the farthest corner. A young man was already sitting at it, cradling a half-empty pint of mild. His head was bent down. He had an air of doom about him. It didn't appear he was looking for conversation and that suited Simon fine as neither was he, his mind far too preoccupied with how he was going to make things up with Rica. He made his way over to the table and sat down. The other occupant didn't even seem to notice him.

It was two hours later when Simon left The Grapes, his thoughts leaping around like jumping beans in his head. Inside the grim interior of the backstreet public house, a way had come to him of satisfactorily resolving the problem that had been plaguing him for the last twelve years; a way to give his beloved wife what she most craved. Simon was beside himself with joy. He needed to keep a check on himself, though, over the next few weeks. It wouldn't do for Rica to suspect he was up to something and demand he tell her before his plan had come to fruition.

He was desperate now to get home and make his peace with his wife, but he needed to visit her sister first, to update her on what had transpired. She'd go along with his plan, he'd insist on that.

CHAPTER FOUR

Standing at the kitchen sink, Rica was staring out of the window into the garden beyond. But she wasn't seeing the freshly mown lawn, the variety of colourful flowers nodding their heads in the warm early-June breeze or the abundance of Bramleys slowly ripening to maturity on the tree. Instead her thoughts drifted back to that night, three months earlier, when Simon had accused her of attempting to kidnap a baby.

After crying herself dry in the kitchen the evening it had happened her common sense had reasserted itself. She had thought long and hard about whether she really ought to take notice of her husband's and sister's opinion that she needed specialist help, in case her underlying intention really had been to take the child without her conscious self realising it. After some deep soul-searching she'd decided, however, that neither wittingly nor unwittingly had her intention been to do anything other than rock it back to sleep. To take anything that didn't belong to her was totally against Rica's moral code. After she'd lived with her husband so long, Simon should be well aware of that trait in her. It seemed he had forgotten the sort of woman she was and needed reminding . . . as did her sister.

Rica had gone in search of Simon and had been most surprised to find he'd gone out. In her earlier distress she hadn't heard him leave the house. She had wondered where he had gone. Possibly to visit Fran, to tell her of Rica's reaction to their renewed suggestion that she needed psychiatric help. Were they trying to cook up another plan between them, to get her to comply? She felt she was being conspired against. Well, one way or another she would make sure she got through to them both that their concern for her was unfounded.

She had gone into the lounge where she'd poured herself a gin and tonic and had sat down in an armchair to await Simon's return. She hadn't bothered switching on the television, knowing that however entertaining the programmes being broadcast were, she wouldn't be able to concentrate on anything but straightening matters out with Simon and Fran.

It had been getting on for four hours later when she'd heard a key in the front-door lock. It had certainly taken a long time for him and Fran to come up with another plan to get her to agree to see a shrink after their last one had failed. It would be interesting to see what they had come up with now. During her long wait she had become more and more aggrieved that she was being discussed behind her back, even though she knew those discussing her believed they had her best interests at heart.

She'd stood up to address Simon as soon as he'd come in, feeling so tense that she felt sure she'd snap in two should anyone give her just the slightest poke with a finger.

In her anxiety it had seemed to Rica to take an age for her husband to come into the lounge. As soon as he had entered he'd spotted her, and for a moment they'd stood and stared at each other. It was Rica who had made the first move by saying in a stilted tone, 'Look, Simon . . .'

Before she could say another word he had approached and thrown his arms around her, pulling her close.

He could not have failed to notice how stiffly she'd held herself in his embrace.

26

Simon had been by no means drunk, but the fact he'd been drinking had not escaped Rica's notice.

Urgently, and in a pleading tone, he'd said to her, 'Please forgive me, darling. I know you would never do what that woman accused you of. Never in a million years would you! You've got to believe that I mean that, love.' To his relief he'd felt the stiffness leave Rica's body as she'd relaxed against him. 'You will forgive me and not let this foolishness on my part come between us?' he'd implored.

She had wanted nothing more. 'Yes, of course I'll forgive you,' she'd whispered. She had eased herself away from him, looked up and asked, 'What about my sister? Does she still believe I tried to take a child and that I need help?'

'Now she's had time to think about it all properly, no, she doesn't.'

Rica had let out a sigh of relief. It had been a nightmare of a day. She just wanted to put this all behind them and get back to normal.

Three months later, as Rica busied herself with her housework, it was as if nothing out of the ordinary had happened. The incident had not been referred to again by either Rica, Simon or Fran. But, regardless, since that evening Rica had gained the distinct impression that there was something going on with Simon. Exactly what she could not put her finger on, but there was an anxiety about him which seemed to be escalating as the days went by. He would seem very preoccupied and she needed to speak to him several times before he would finally respond to her. He usually slept soundly, often joking that a burglar could steal the bed from beneath him and he'd not wake, but recently he had become very restless and was constantly waking Rica up with his tossing and turning.

Several times she had asked him what was going on. He had just looked at her, bemused, and professed not to know what she was talking about. She wasn't convinced but had no choice but to put these observations down to her own over-active imagination. She wasn't, though, imagining that they hadn't been out socially together for weeks. Usually they went out at least twice a week, either to the cinema, on visits to friends, or to the local for a drink. Whenever she had suggested to him they should go out lately, he'd put on a tired look and claimed not to be in the mood.

Several reasons for his strange behaviour had presented themselves to her, and after deep deliberation she had narrowed them down to two . . . he was either suffering from a terminal disease or else the business was foundering and he couldn't bring himself to tell her. But she was his wife, supposed to share the good and the bad things with him. She'd made up her mind to tackle him again this evening and not let him fob her off. She must learn the reason for his erratic behaviour in recent weeks.

A knock on the back door made her jump in surprise and then heave a fed-up sigh. She didn't need to wonder who her caller was. It was the same person who called at this time every Monday, Tuesday, Friday and Saturday morning. They didn't call on Wednesday because that was the day she visited her mother, or Thursday either due to her long-standing arrangement to meet her sister for lunch. It would be Dorothy Wainwright from next-door, checking to see if she was going out that day, and if so what time she was planning to leave so she could be ready and not keep her waiting.

Rica wasn't sure how this state of affairs had actually come about. If memory served her correctly, it seemed to have started the day after she had been accused of trying to kidnap the baby. Dorothy, a matronly middle-aged widow, who until then in all the years they had lived next-door to each other had never exchanged any more than polite conversation with Rica, had started to call upon her to ask if she was going to the shops that morning, and if so would she mind Dorothy accompanying her?

As the social sort she was, Rica had made numerous attempts in the past to acquaint herself better with her neighbour, but each time Dorothy had rebuffed those attempts, making it very plain she was the sort who liked to keep herself to herself, so this request for company now came as a surprise. Nevertheless Rica was more than happy at last to have the opportunity to be on more than nodding terms with her. After all, you never knew when the help of a neighbour could make the difference between life or death. From that day on, though, Dorothy seemed to be under the impression that she was welcome to accompany Rica every time she ventured out to the shops. It wasn't that she minded Dorothy accompanying her sometimes, just not on every occasion. She hadn't yet come up with a way of telling the other woman, though, and dreaded hurting her feelings.

Planting a smile on her face, Rica went to answer the door.

Her plan for that evening was already laid. She had made two of Simon's favourites for dinner: liver and onions with creamy mashed potatoes covered in lashings of thick tasty gravy, then treacle tart and custard for pudding. After Rica had cleared away and watered the garden, and Simon was settled comfortably in his armchair, either catching up on the day's news in the evening paper or watching the television, she would pour them both a drink, a whisky for Simon, a Martini Bianco for her, switch off the television so she had his undivided attention, then confront him . . .

That evening Simon accepted the Edinburgh cut-glass tumbler his wife handed him, and smiled appreciatively up at her. 'Thanks, love. Just what the doctor ordered.'

Her eyes flashed with concern. 'What do you mean by that, Simon?'

He looked at her, bemused. 'I suppose I could just as well have said, "A bit of what you fancy does you good." I'm just saying, this drink is the perfect way to finish off that tasty meal you made us, that's all.'

Rica wondered if she was becoming paranoid, looking closely into everything for an underlying meaning. She went over to the settee. Kicking off her mules, she sat down, tucking her legs comfortably under her. She took a sip of her drink, then cradling the glass between her hands, said, 'Simon, we need to talk.'

He frowned at her, perplexed. 'About what?'

'About what you're trying to hide from me.'

He pulled a bemused expression. 'I'm not hiding anything from you, love.' He took a long swallow of his drink. 'Put the television on or you'll miss the start of *Coronation Street*.'

'Simon, you've got to stop fobbing me off and be honest with me about what's going on. We've never kept secrets from each other, and because you are now you're worrying me. I'm thinking the worst . . . that either you've a terminal illness or else the business is going under.' The flash of guilt in his eyes was unmistakable. Rica gasped, clasping her hand to her mouth, her eyes fearful. 'Oh, Simon, which is it?'

There was a hint of annoyance in his voice when he said sharply, 'It's neither. I've told you, nothing is wrong with me. I don't know where you've got the idea from.' He tossed back the remainder of his drink and made to get up.

'Simon, I know something isn't right. You're not sleeping properly . . . tossing and turning most of the night. I'm constantly catching you staring into space. These days you never want to go out in the evening, always saying you're too tired when I suggest it . . .'

He snapped back at her, 'And just because of that you've decided I'm either on my deathbed or the business is going under?'

'I know you better than I know myself, Simon, and those things tell me you're worried about something.'

He scraped his hand through his hair in exasperation. 'For the last time, Rica, there's . . .' He was interrupted then by a loud rap on the front door. He started and then fixed Rica with his eyes. 'You stay there,' he commanded. 'I'll get it.'

As he rushed from the room, a puzzled Rica stared after him. Someone knocking at their door was not unusual . . . this time of an evening it was more than likely a door-to-door salesman. Simon's reaction to this visit tonight was strange to say the least. As if he'd been waiting for it to come, but now that it had was terrified, which didn't make sense to her. Then it struck her that this wasn't the first time he had reacted strangely to an unexpected knock at the door during the evening. Several times over the past couple of weeks he'd almost leaped out of his skin and hastened to answer it before she could. Who exactly was he expecting to call that he didn't want her to see?

The murmur of voices cut through her thoughts. She strained her ears. Their caller sounded like an adolescent boy to her. One of their neighbours' children come to borrow something or ask for their help in some way, she assumed. She heard the front door shut and Simon immediately returned, looking extremely flustered. He was urgently pulling on his coat.

'I have to go out,' he blurted.

He was heading out of the door when she called to him, 'Out where, Simon?'

He turned to face her. 'Eh! Oh, er . . . to the studio.'

'At this time of night?'

He was heading out in a hurry. 'I'll explain when I get back.'

Before she could challenge him further, she heard the front door slam shut.

Rica stared blindly after him, her thoughts racing wildly. He had lied to her. Wherever he was headed it wasn't the studio. That was just the first place that had entered his head when she'd asked him where he was off to. So where was he going? And why was he being so secretive about it? There was only one answer she could think of for his evasiveness. He had to be meeting someone. Their caller just now was the go-between. But who could he be meeting, and why the need for such a cloak-and-dagger way of arranging things?

Her heart began to beat thunderously inside her chest as dreadful fear flooded her. She could think of only one answer that would plausibly answer her question: Simon had met another woman. That was where he had rushed off to now – to see her. She must be married herself for their meeting to be so clandestine. Tears of distress pricked Rica's eyes. The thought of the man she adored with all her being wrapped in another woman's arms, kissing her, making love to her, formulating plans for their future together, was just too much for her to bear.

No, she told herself, she would not believe that. Simon was her husband. He wasn't capable of the level of deceit necessary to conduct an affair under her nose.

Rica froze then as she heard the front door open and close again. She glanced at the clock ticking away on the gas-fire surround. He had been gone barely an hour. What on earth was he up to?

With her heart in her mouth, she gazed at the lounge door as it opened and then at Simon's face. There was worry in his eyes but also an air of excitement about him.

Before he could say a word, Rica jumped up from her chair. 'Simon, I can't stand this any longer,' she announced. 'Please tell me what's going on?'

He opened his mouth to speak but was cut short by a mewing sound that appeared to be coming from over by the doorway. For the first time Rica spotted the lidded basket he had put down on first entering. Was that what he had rushed off to do, collect a cat?

Rica looked at him quizzically. 'You know I'm not fond of cats, Simon.'

He glanced at her in confusion, clearly wondering why she'd said that. 'Yes, I do.'

'Then why have you brought one home?'

He gave a shrug. 'I haven't.'

'Well, that sounds just like a kitten to me.'

'Does it?' He took a deep breath and took her hand. 'Let me show you what it is.'

Bemused, she allowed him to lead her over to the door, where he let go of her hand so that he could pick up the covered basket. With its handle over the crook of one arm, he flipped open a flap and motioned her to take a look inside.

Curious, Rica stepped to one side of him and peered inside. The sight that met her eyes made her gasp in shock. Fighting her overwhelming desire to reach into the basket and scoop up its contents, she tore her eyes away and looked at Simon. It was several moments before she could find her voice. 'But it's . . . it's . . . a baby! A newborn baby, by the look of it! Whose baby is it? How come . . .'

He cut in, 'It's our baby, darling.'

She stared at him, astounded. 'Ours! But . . . but how can it be ours?' Her face then filled with horror. 'Oh, my God, you haven't done what I was accused of doing? Kidnapped it?'

'No, of course I haven't. We've adopted this baby.'

Rica was staring at him wildly. 'But I don't understand. I mean, we haven't applied to adopt. Besides, when I approached you about adopting a couple of years back, you said we shouldn't consider it until we'd given it a few more years of trying for our own.'

He grabbed her hand. 'Look, come and sit down and I'll tell you all.'

In a trance, Rica moved over to the settee and sank down.

Simon sat beside her. Putting the basket down by their feet, he took her hands in his, drew in a deep breath and began. 'It was that night when . . .' a look of shame filled his face before he continued '. . . well, when we had words and I went off. I knew I'd really hurt you and felt it best I should go out to let you calm down, so that when I came back you might be more receptive to my apologies.

'I walked around for ages, but before I came home I needed some Dutch courage to face you so I went into a pub for a drink. I wasn't at all in the mood for making conversation with anyone so I'm not sure how I got talking to a bloke, but before I knew it he was telling me that he was out wetting his new baby's head, was just waiting for his brother and a few close mates to join him. I congratulated him on his new arrival and then tried to move away. As I've already told you I wasn't in the mood for company. He didn't give me a chance to, though. Started to ask me how old my children were. I told him that unfortunately we hadn't been blessed with any yet, but hadn't given up hope. That's when he told me that, after trying for nearly twenty years, he and his wife had given up and applied to adopt.

'He asked me if we'd considered going down that route. I told him that my wife was thinking along those lines and I wasn't against the idea myself, but that I had delayed as I was so frightened of my wife having her hopes built up in vain.

'He told me his wife knew of a private adoption agency who were very good and reliable. It cost to use the agency's services but it was worth the price. He told me the details in case we decided to pursue this avenue. The man's brother arrived then, and after wishing me good luck, he left me to drink the rest of my pint in peace. After thinking about it for a while, I decided it wouldn't hurt to pay the agency a visit and find how for myself how they went about matters.'

He paused for a moment to give Rica a concerned look.

He was conscious she hadn't said a word or moved even a muscle since he'd begun his story, and wondered how she was taking it all . . . he might not have been deceiving her with another woman as she had assumed due to his odd behaviour, but regardless he'd still been deceiving her. She was giving him no indication how she was feeling, but at the same time he was glad she was allowing him to relay it all without interruption. He continued.

'I found the owner of the agency to be just the way the man in the pub had described her. Very sympathetic towards our childless situation, but also understanding of my concerns over how this could affect you should either one of us not meet the adoption criteria for some reason. Obviously she wanted to assure herself that we would make suitable parents for any child she matched to us, but she assured me that if I wanted to go ahead, she could vet your suitability without your needing to be aware of it. I told her that I would willingly go ahead on those terms. I gave her all the personal details she wanted to know about us and we discussed her fee. She told me to return in a fortnight to learn whether we'd been accepted to adopt a child or not.'

He paused again to shoot a glance at Rica, trying to get an idea of how she was reacting, but still she was giving nothing away. He pressed on. 'Meantime I did my damnedest to carry on as normal and not alert you to the fact that I was up to anything. I didn't succeed as well as I'd intended. I didn't at all like making out that you were imagining things, but I felt I was doing it for the best. After we'd been passed as suitable, I was in such a quandary over whether to tell you or not . . . but then I realised it was hard enough for me getting off to sleep at night, wondering if we'd be parents by the end of the next day, so how would it be if we were both on tenterhooks? I decided I would shoulder the anxiety of the wait for both of us.

'Well, I know it'll be obvious to you now that our caller tonight was a messenger from the agency to say that our baby had arrived. And that's where I went off to, to sign the documentation and collect it.' Now he had finished his story he looked at her tentatively for several moments, looking for any tell-tale signs of what she was making of it all, but still Rica remained a closed book to him. Finally he ventured, 'So . . . er . . . I expect you're in shock from all this?'

Rica felt that this assumption was an understatement! As she had listened to Simon, many emotions had flooded through her. At first she had had difficulty accepting that this was not some elaborate joke. Then she had felt anger that he had carried on such a deceit behind her back over a matter of such monumental importance. They should have journeyed through it together, despite his good intentions. But then anger was swept aside as she felt overwhelmed with love for him, for going to such lengths in order to fulfil her dearest desire.

Right now she was torn as to what to do first. Show her gratitude to Simon for what he had done for her, or introduce herself to the baby.

The latter won by a large margin. She had waited so long to hold her own child, had so long ago concluded it was not going to happen for her, that she wasn't prepared to wait any longer. She would show Simon her gratitude later.

She didn't even have to see the child to know that she loved it. It didn't matter to her what gender it was, the colour of its hair or eyes, whether it was chubby and cute or had yet to fill out. She would nurture and protect it as devotedly as if she had carried and given birth to it herself. She leaned over, stretching out her arms to reach into the basket and scoop the child up, but then a dreadful fear manifested itself within her and she yanked back her arms as though she'd been scalded.

Simon frowned in bewilderment. 'What's wrong, love?'

'The mother . . .' she began.

'You're the baby's mother, Rica,' he told her firmly.

'The baby's natural mother.'

'What about her?'

'Oh, Simon, what if she changes her mind and wants her baby back?'

He placed a reassuring hand on hers. 'She can't change her mind, love. I was assured by the agency that before she agreed to give the baby away, she was well aware that there was no going back once she had signed the papers.'

Rica visibly relaxed on learning this information, but still needed confirmation that she wasn't going to be living in fear that at any time in the future she could hear a knock on the door and a demand for her to return the child. 'No one can take it away from us then? Not ever?'

Simon shook his head. 'The child is ours in every way. Only to the obvious people . . . your sister, our close friends, those locals who know we don't have any children and will wonder where we've suddenly produced one from . . . need we say we've adopted. To the rest of the world, the child is our natural one. We have six weeks to register the baby but I'll go down tomorrow and get it done, if that will put your mind at rest?'

She squeezed his hand, her eyes telling him that it would. Her eyes then darted down to the basket by their feet. Filled with emotions she would never have found words to describe, Rica reached down and, with great tenderness, lifted out the bundle inside the basket. She cradled it protectively in her arms. Tenderly she pulled open the folds of blanket to fully reveal the child, then leaned over and brushed its pudgy cheeks with her lips, before whispering, 'I promise to be the best mother I can to you, my darling.'

Simon wasn't looking at the child; his attention was fixed on his wife. He had never seen such a look of pure euphoria before. At this moment in time he knew nothing else existed for Rica, including himself, but the child in her arms. She had waited a long time for this and deserved to be left to savour it. He eased himself off the settee and left the room to have a cup of tea, waiting for her to join him when she was ready.

He also had an errand to run. He no longer needed the services of their neighbour, Dorothy Wainwright, whom he had been paying to accompany Rica whenever she went out shopping, so that any repetition of the incident when she'd been accused of trying to kidnap a child could not occur. The elderly woman had not been at all keen to accept Simon's assignment until payment for her services had been mentioned. He knew she'd be glad to return to calling her time her own, but would miss the remuneration she had received each week. He had chosen Mrs Wainwright for the job as he knew that she liked to keep herself to herself and was not a gossip, so Rica need never find out what he'd done. And his worries were at an end now. Rica finally had her own baby to care for.

CHAPTER FIVE

Rica was at the sink, washing her hands after peeling potatoes, when she felt something pulling at her skirt. She swivelled the top half of her body around so she could look behind her and see what was causing it . . . as if she didn't know! She chuckled to see her eighteen-month-old son wobbling unsteadily on his feet, clinging to the hem of her skirt as though his life depended on it and looking up at her with a gap-toothed grin.

Remembering the night Simon had brought him home never failed to produce a rush of emotion in Rica. It wasn't until the baby had started to whimper, letting it be known he was getting hungry, that she had been brought out of her euphoric joy to realise they hadn't even so much as a bottle to feed their new family member with. Simon hadn't given any thought to the array of items a new baby needed to aid its care, so consumed with excitement at actually being given a child had he been. Rica had packed him off on a mad dash around the neighbours with young children, to ask for a loan of items to tide them over until she could shop the next day for all they required. The name of their new baby had come easily to them: Richard Owen, after both of their much-missed deceased fathers. Ricky for short.

If Rica had been able to specify in advance her requirements for the perfect child and to place an order with Mother Nature, Ricky would have been the child delivered to her.

He had never given her a moment of worry or a sleepless night; never thrown a tantrum, and only ever became mildly tetchy when he had just cause to be, such as if he was teething or running a temperature, and that very seldom as he was a robust child. It had been apparent to Rica right from the first moment she had looked at him that he was destined to be an attractive child who would develop into a very handsome man, and her prophecy was proving to be correct.

At eighteen months of age Ricky had the face of a cherub, large blue eyes and a head of thick curly white-blond hair. He possessed a very engaging personality and a quick brain. The first understandable word he had said at the age of eleven months was 'Dada', which delighted his besotted father. Since then he had added 'No', which he said whether he meant no or yes; 'Mamma', 'car' 'woof-woof' for dog, 'ninna' for dinner and 'coc coc' for chocolate, which always raised infectious laughter from anyone who heard him saying it as he would point a tiny finger towards the tin on the sideboard where he knew his mother stored treats for him.

The once immaculately kept Dunmore home was still kept clean but was nowhere near as tidy. Toys and children's paraphernalia had to be stepped over when moving from one room to another or shifted off seats in order to sit down. Whatever needed doing at work had to wait outside shop hours as Simon had more important things to do, like helping to bath his son then playing for an hour with him before bedtime.

Rica had not been able to wait to tell her sister such exciting news by going around to her flat the next evening. Fran was not connected to the telephone unlike themselves so Rica telephoned her at work the next morning as soon as she knew she would be there, despite her boss frowning on personal calls except in an emergency . . . to Rica this *was* an emergency. Her sister had to know she was an aunt. After telling Fran just what her emergency was and a brief outline of how it had come about, there was silence from the other end of the line for several long seconds and Rica could have sworn she had heard an exhalation of relief. Was that because there was no longer any need for Fran to worry Rica could end up stealing someone else's child? Fran did say she was pleased for her, and that was the most Rica could expect since she was aware that Fran had never been able to understand her sister's yearning to become a mother. She herself had never hidden the fact that it was the last thing she wanted to be. She found children a nuisance and didn't believe they should be allowed out in public until they had learned they should be seen and not heard.

The Dunmores' previous nights out had become a thing of the past, to be replaced by taking Ricky for a stroll in the park after dinner, weather permitting. For the first six months of being a mother, Rica would not entertain the idea of going out and leaving her child in the hands of someone else, no matter how capable they were or how much she trusted them, so consequently the friendships they had had with the couples they had previously socialised with had petered out. Since his arrival she had only been persuaded to leave Ricky on one occasion, and only then because it was their wedding anniversary and Fran had been pressed into watching over her nephew, on proviso that he was in bed before the couple left the house. Even then they had been back at home before two hours had passed. Not only Rica had been unable to relax and enjoy herself, but Simon also. Fran was relieved to be spared from her babysitting duties. This served to prove to both Simon and Rica that there were three of them in the family now, and it didn't feel right for two of them to be out without the third with them.

Rica still went to see her mother in the nursing home every Wednesday afternoon but now she had company: Iris's grandson. Rica was just sad that her mother had no idea the child was her grandson and could not share the joy he brought to other residents who still had all their faculties intact. Being entertained by the child's playful antics during the weekly visits gave them something to look forward to, breaking the boredom of their otherwise monotonous lives.

Fran and Rica no longer had a weekly appointment for lunch so that Rica could update her sister on their mother's condition. Rica had no problem whatsoever with taking Ricky to the tea rooms with her, but Fran wouldn't entertain the idea. She wouldn't like having her meal disturbed by the presence of a baby as there was never any guarantee the child would stay asleep for the duration. So instead Fran visited the Dunmores' home every Saturday afternoon, to catch up on their mother's condition and needs. Over a pot of tea and plate of biscuits, the two sisters would chat, Rica relaxed on the settee with her legs curled under her, Fran perched primly in an armchair, her skirt pulled well down over her knees, while Ricky would be playing happily with his toys on the carpet.

Fran had held her nephew just once. Sensitive to how Fran felt about children – not that she could understand herself how any woman could fail to possess a morsel of maternal feeling – Rica would never put her in a compromising situation, leaving it up to her to say if she wanted to hold the child or not. That was until Ricky was about three months old. Fran had arrived for what was by now her routine Saturday afternoon visit to find Rica had just finishing bathing her son. Lifting him out of the baby bath, Rica realised she had left the clean towel she'd intended to dry him with warming on the radiator in another room. Concerned about her son catching cold, she hurriedly plonked him in her sister's lap, not giving her a chance to protest, and rushed off to collect the towel.

Not only did the wet child drip water all over Fran's new skirt, he also emptied his bladder and bowels into her lap. Rica thought the incident hysterically funny; Simon too when he arrived home and learned of it. Fran was not at all amused and made it clear that that was the first and last time she would be so close to a child, whether it be her nephew or anyone else's. She might not have wanted physical contact with Ricky, but otherwise she proved herself a faultless aunt and never arrived without a treat for him in her handbag. She was always buying him a new outfit or toy and never left without putting a few coppers in his piggy bank.

Rica no longer had her neighbour Dorothy Wainwright's company on shopping trips. The parting of their ways had puzzled Rica for a time, but then she had far more important matters to occupy her mind so did not dwell on it and was only reminded of it now and again when she spotted her neighbour going about her business. The very morning after Simon had granted Rica's deepest wish, Dorothy had not called to check if she was going to the shops. Nor had she since. In fact, she had reverted to keeping herself to herself. It was very strange. As her neighbour had never attempted to offer any explanation for her behaviour, Rica could only assume that she herself had offended the elderly woman in some way, although she couldn't think how. She had been disappointed that Dorothy hadn't called that first morning as she had been desperate to introduce her new son to those he was living amongst, and them to him. The other neighbours and friends more than made up for it, however, when they learned of the new arrival. For days afterwards a steady stream of visitors called at the house, armed with gifts and offers to babysit.

Now and again Rica did find herself thinking of Ricky's natural mother. Whatever the reason the woman had come to part from her child, Rica believed she wouldn't escape this episode in her life unscathed. She sincerely hoped, though, that the unknown woman had managed to put it all behind her and was making a good life for herself. Rica felt so strongly that she was indebted to this woman for a sacrifice which had brought Rica herself such joy, but they would never meet, never in fact even know each other's names or anything about each other, so the only way she could repay that debt was to endeavour to make sure another woman's child was loved, happy, and grew up to be a good man and a valued member of society.

She leaned over now to reach for one of Ricky's hands and, once she had got hold of it, gently guided him around so that he was in front of her. Then she scooped him up to give him a big kiss, making the loud smacking noise which always caused him to giggle. Ricky's chuckles never failed to make his mother laugh. They were both laughing and giggling when the sound of the front door opening put a stop to Rica's display of mirth and set her eyes darting questioningly to the kitchen door. It was far too early for Fran so this could only be Simon, and she wondered what had brought him home so early on a Saturday. It was only half-past one and closing time on a Saturday was usually four.

Rica frowned as her thoughts returned to the previous evening. Simon had not been his usual cheery self when he'd returned from work, but instead had greeted her with a distracted kiss on the cheek. He hadn't bothered to change out of his work clothes into something more casual, and while he'd played with his son it had been clear his mind was elsewhere. Rica had waited until Ricky was in bed and they were both settled in the lounge before she'd raised the subject.

'What's going on, Simon?' she'd asked. 'You're not yourself at all today. Has something happened at work?'

Simon's eyes had been focused on the television, but Rica had been sure that he wouldn't be able to tell her what he was watching. He'd turned and looked at her blankly for what seemed like an age before he'd answered, 'Oh, it's just the mystery of the disappearing cleaner that's giving me a headache. You remember that we advertised for a replacement for old Mrs Evans a couple of weeks back and a Mrs Smith applied and was really pleased to be given the position.'

Rica couldn't remember him telling her this but she'd nodded nonetheless.

'Well, she worked the week and did a very good job. She seemed to like it, but the following Monday she didn't appear and she hasn't been seen since. If she hadn't enjoyed the job then that's fair enough but it's good manners to give notice. It seems strange that she didn't even come to collect the pay for the work she'd already done. I tried to take her wage around to her personally and check that she was all right, but I must have had the wrong address because the old man who lived there had never heard of her. The whole thing is very strange.'

Simon had folded up his newspaper and stood up saying, 'I'm going to bed, love. I've got a headache and I feel done in. Hopefully a good night's sleep will sort me out.' He'd left the room before Rica could even offer him an aspirin. She had frowned. The story he had told her about the cleaner was indeed baffling, but could not excuse her husband's behaviour. Whatever the cause of his mood, Rica had hoped it would have resolved itself by the morning, so that life could go back to normal.

Now, as Simon stepped into the kitchen, Rica smiled welcomingly at him, and addressed Ricky in her arms. 'Look who's home, sweetheart. It's Daddy.' Then she asked Simon, 'Feeling better today, love?'

'To the best of my knowledge I haven't been ill,' he snapped.

'Well, maybe not ill, but you certainly haven't been yourself for a day or so. Look how snappy you are now and . . .'

He cut her short. 'Yes, all right, Rica. So I've not been myself, but everyone is allowed an off day now and again, aren't they?'

'Yes, of course. But it's what is causing you to be off colour that is bothering me. Just what is troubling you, Simon?'

A flash of annoyance appeared in his eyes. 'You never give up when you've got the bit between your teeth, do you? Nothing is troubling me. I had a touch of indigestion and it's making me irritable, that's all. I'm going to get something from the chemist for it. I came home early to collect Ricky. I want to take him to the park for a play on the swings . . . be good to spend some father and son time with him.'

She frowned at him quizzically. It was unlike him to abandon the shop on its busiest day of the week, leaving just his young apprentice to deal with the customers. Rica wasn't fooled by Simon's explanation for his bad mood. Something was going on, but it seemed that for the moment he wasn't ready to take her into his confidence. 'Ricky would love a trip to the park with you but it's hardly the best day for it, Simon. It's nippy out there and it's starting to spit.'

'A bit of rain won't hurt the boy, Rica.'

She was shocked by his dismissal of her objection. Why was he so desperate to take Ricky out when he could play with him here in the warmth? Simon had every right to his son's company, but to make sure he wasn't out too long with Ricky on this chilly day, she said, 'Will you have him back by the time his aunty comes to see him? Fran usually gets here about three.'

'Your sister doesn't call to see her nephew, Rica. She can't stand kids. She'll more than likely be glad he's not here, then you can both have a conversation without him interrupting.' There was an angry tone in Simon's voice when he added, 'For God's sake, Rica, can't I take my son out for a while without you putting obstacles in the way? Just get him ready else it will be his bedtime by the time we've argued the toss.'

46

She was astonished by his short temper. She wanted to demand he tell her what was behind his aggressive mood, but instinct told her to leave it. For now.

Before she could say she would go and get Ricky ready, Simon stepped over and took him from her arms, saying, 'I'll do it then.' He strode out of the kitchen while she stood rooted to the spot. She could hear Simon dressing Ricky for outdoors . . . the child chuckling excitedly as his coat was put on . . . then the click of the pushchair straps, and the front door shutting behind then as they left. Rica felt hurt. Simon had gone off without saying goodbye or allowing her to kiss Ricky. He never usually left the house without giving her a kiss and a hug!

She went over to the sink and leaned against it, staring thoughtfully into space. This behaviour from her husband was most uncharacteristic. Why was he being so hostile to her? It wasn't as though they'd recently had cross words. Rica couldn't remember the last time they had, in fact.

Half an hour later she heard a tap on the back door. It opened and Fran came in, hurriedly shutting the door behind her and propping up her dripping umbrella in the sink.

Wiping her wet shoes on the door mat, whilst unbuttoning her coat, she said, 'Winter is definitely on its way: it's turning colder.'

A distracted Rica answered, 'Mmm, yes, it is.'

Her sister eyed her sharply as she draped her damp coat over the back of a pine kitchen chair and put her handbag on the table. 'What's eating you?'

'Oh, it's Simon. He's obviously got something on his mind but he won't talk to me about it.'

Fran pulled a face. 'You two don't usually keep things from each other. Oh, except for the time he kept you in the dark over applying to adopt. He was acting out of character then, wasn't he? Maybe he's applied to the agency on the QT again and shortly Ricky will have a brother or sister.'

Rica shook her head. 'We had a discussion about that after he'd brought Ricky home. I told him that I fully appreciated why he'd decided not to tell me, but that in future when it came to something as momentous as adopting a child, we should see it through together. He agreed so I know it's nothing like that on his mind. He's not worried about the business either as he told me only last week it was doing so well he was thinking of moving to bigger, more up-to-date premises. I can only think that he's ill with something dreadful and can't bring himself to tell me.'

Fran looked worried by that remark. 'Has he complained of any pains or anything that would make you think that?'

Rica shook her head. 'No. Apart from his mood and not sleeping at all well, he seems to be just as he always is.'

'Well, I'm no doctor but if he was suffering from some serious life-threatening disease, he would surely show outward signs that you would notice?'

'Yes, you'd have thought so. Oh, I can't for the life of me think what lies behind the mood he's in.'

Fran said matter-of-factly, 'I'm no authority on men so I can't advise you. I'm sure whatever is ailing him, he'll get over it soon. Any chance of a cup of tea?'

Normally Rica would have had the kettle boiling ready for when she arrived. 'Oh, I'm sorry, Fran. I'll have one made in a jiffy.' Rica moved over to the stove and turned on the plate under the kettle. While she busied herself making a pot of tea, Fran hung up her coat in the hall, then came back into the kitchen and took a seat at the table. She sat down stiffly, knees pressed demurely together. 'How did you find Mother on Wednesday?' she asked.

'The same as last week. No better, no worse,' Rica responded, going over to the table to deposit on it two Denby Pottery mugs with matching milk jug and sugar bowl, despite Fran's opinion that tea should be drunk in nothing but bone china. Before she returned to get the rest

48

of the things, she paused and looked meaningfully at Fran. Her sister held up a hand in warning.

'Are you never going to tire of asking me that question? I wish you'd *stop* asking it. I don't see any point at all in spending at least three hours every week getting to and from the home, just to sit twiddling my thumbs while knowing Mother hasn't a clue that I'm there, or who in fact I am. The best thing that could happen would be for her to go to sleep one night and not wake up.'

Rica gasped in shock. 'Fran, how could you wish your own mother dead?'

'For goodness' sake, face facts, Rica. Our mother died the day she lost the last of her memory, well over two years ago. Now, you deal with this awful situation in your own way and leave me to deal with it in mine.'

Rica sighed. Fran was right. They were each coping with it in the way that felt right for them individually. They shouldn't be thinking the worst of the other for not acting the same way.

The kettle started to boil. Rica went over and took it off the plate, filled the teapot and took it back to the table to sit it on a mat.

Meanwhile Fran was opening her handbag and taking out a white paper bag which she put on the table. 'Some jelly babies for Ricky. He's very quiet, by the way. Having a nap?'

Rica was pouring out the tea. 'He's out with his father. Simon came home unexpectedly about half an hour ago, wanting to take him to the park.'

Simon was right. Fran didn't seem at all put out that she might not see her nephew today, Rica noticed.

'It's not like him to leave the shop during business hours,' she mused.

'No, but then, like I told you earlier, he's not been acting like himself for a day or so.' She pushed a cup of tea in front

49

of Fran then picked up her own mug. 'Maybe spending time with his son will soften Simon's mood and he'll tell me what is troubling him when he comes home.' She turned her head and looked out of the kitchen window. 'It's raining more heavily now so I should think they'll be back any minute.' She smiled warmly at her sister. 'So, how are things with you, Fran?'

'Things?'

Rica tutted in frustration. Her sister knew exactly what she meant. 'Life in general then. Have you been up to anything groovy since I last saw you?'

Fran cocked an eyebrow at her. 'Groovy? Just what does that word imply, may I ask? It's certainly not one I learned at school.'

Rica tutted disdainfully again. Their mother was right. Her sister really was a prim Victorian spinster type, her ways not at all suited to the swinging sixties when the language used by youngsters was peppered with such words as 'fab' and 'groovy'. You were considered square nowadays if you didn't use such words or at least understand what they meant, and Rica wasn't ready to be perceived by the younger generation as belonging to the doddery old dears brigade just yet. 'It means have you done anything that was fun?'

Fran gave a haughty sniff. 'Well, your idea of fun is not the same as mine. But as it happens I have had what I call fun.'

Rica eyed her keenly. 'Oh?'

'I attended an exhibition of Tapestry through the Ages at the museum in New Walk last Monday evening.'

'Sounds riveting.'

Fran shot her a withering look, knowing her sister thought it anything but. 'I found it so,' she said sharply. 'Tonight I'm off to a concert at the De Montfort Hall given by the Huddersfield Philharmonic. They're playing a selection of

50

Tchaikovsky's works. I'm particularly looking forward to the *1812 Overture*. Such stirring music . . . it fairly makes the hairs on the back of my neck stand up.'

It might have surprised Fran to know that Rica didn't just listen to the latest pop tunes on Radio 1, a station recently created by the BBC to cater for the younger set, but that her taste in music encompassed big-band sounds too, the likes of Glen Miller and Artie Shaw, as well as the more popular classical pieces such as the *1812 Overture* and Rossini's Overture to *William Tell*. These were broadcast by the BBC on what used to be their Light Programme but which was now Radio 2, on shows such as *Bandstand*, *Family Favourites* and *Million Dollar Bill*. It was all background music, of course, as most of Rica's concentration was taken up by caring for the family. Anyway, if Fran had mentioned she was going to the concert when she had first booked a ticket, Rica would have offered to accompany her.

But then, on second thoughts, Fran would have been uncomfortable with the style of clothes her sister would have worn, possibly a long flowing gypsy dress worn with wedge-heeled shoes. Fran herself would no doubt dress in a severe below-the-knee black dress and cardigan, more like widow's weeds than something to wear for a social outing.

Fran didn't wear make-up and would have pursed her lips in disapproval of Rica's doing so, even though it was only lightly applied considering the fashion at the moment was for it to be worn caked on. False eyelashes like spiders' legs were very popular too, worn covered in so much black mascara it was a wonder the wearer could keep her eyes open.

Fran didn't drink anything stronger than orange juice, and in the interval Rica would not have enjoyed her gin and tonic with her sister casting reproachful glances at her. She gave a wistful sigh. There was no question but that they cared deeply about each other, but neither of them understood what made the other one tick. Rica thought it a shame that she and Fran weren't more alike in their outlook on life, sharing more interests instead of going their totally separate ways on that front.

Her sister was busily gathering her things together, saying to her, 'I'd best be off. I've grocery shopping to do before I go home and get ready for my outing tonight.'

Rica was genuinely disappointed that she was leaving so soon. 'Oh, I was going to ask if you'd like some lunch?'

'Thank you but not today. I'll see you next week then.'

Rica walked with her to the front door where the sisters pecked each other affectionately on the cheek. Out on the step, Fran put up her umbrella and Rica watched her hurry down the path. As she shut the gate behind her, they gave each other a wave before Fran headed off down the street and Rica back inside the house.

The light rain had grown much heavier. As they weren't home, Rica assumed Simon and Ricky had taken shelter somewhere to wait. She knew her husband would not risk giving Ricky a soaking, and the prospect of him going down with something nasty because of it.

She had plenty of things to do meantime.

An hour later she had tidied Ricky's toys but not put them away as no doubt he would want to play with them again before his bedtime; had finished her preparations for the evening meal; folded and added to the ironing pile clothes that were drying on the airer in the kitchen. Rica glanced at the kitchen wall clock. It was just coming up to three. The Saturday afternoon film was about to start. Not that she was complaining one iota, but it had been eighteen months since she had watched a film on a Saturday afternoon uninterrupted. She went into the lounge and selected the *Radio Times* from the magazine rack, looking up the television programme guide for that afternoon, hoping the film was the sort she liked. She was pleased to see it was Lana

Turner in *Imitation of Life*. Rica hadn't seen this particular picture before but had heard it was a weepie. Collecting her darning bag and some clothing that needed attention, a fresh cup of tea on the coffee table along with a plate containing four Bourbon biscuits, after making sure she had the tissue box to hand, Rica switched on the television set then settled herself down in her armchair just as the film was beginning.

Nearly two hours later she laid aside the sock she was in the middle of darning, gave her wet eyes a wipe and her runny nose a blow. The film had been very emotional, the ending particularly so, and Rica had cried unashamedly several times during its showing. Having composed herself, she looked up at the star-burst clock on the wall. It was four-forty. She got up and went over to the window to look out. The rain had stopped and the sun was now out. Due to her being engrossed in the film she didn't know when that had happened but hopefully it had been a while ago and Simon and Ricky had had some sunshine. They should be home any minute now. Ricky would be in need of a nappy change and would also be getting hungry for his dinner. Simon himself never voluntarily missed the football results on *Grandstand*, which he marked down to check on his Littlewood's pools coupon, and that programme started shortly. She felt it was safe to start cooking the dinner.

A while later Rica's face was screwed up in concern. Still no sign of Simon and their son, and it was now gone six o'clock. The cooked sausages had grown cold and so had the chips; in fact, they were ruined and she'd have to make fresh. She wasn't sure whether to be worried that something had happened to them or annoyed that Simon had lost track of time as they were enjoying themselves so much.

She decided to take a walk to the park and remind her husband what the time was. Hopefully she would meet them as they were making their way back.

Rica passed plenty of pedestrians on her journey but there was no sign of her husband and son. She arrived at the park to find it almost deserted. At this time most people were eating their evening meal, except for a couple of older children sitting on the roundabout smoking a cigarette between them, and a couple of adults walking dogs, enjoying the late-evening sunshine. There was no sign at all of her family.

Across a wide expanse of grass she spotted the park keeper emerging from his hut, and ran across to address him.

He had just locked up his shed when she caught up with him and said, 'Excuse me, but can you help me, please?'

There was irritation in his eyes when he turned to answer her. 'You just caught me, I'm off home for me dinner. Wife don't like it if I'm late and it goes cold.'

'Well, I won't keep you any longer than to ask if you've seen my husband and son? They came to the park this afternoon only they haven't come home yet.' Rica gave a brief description of them both.

The man gave a helpless shrug. 'That could describe most of the men who come here with their kiddies, and most kids look like angels to their mothers, don't they?' There was a hint of sarcasm in his voice when he made his last remark.

Rica supposed he had a point.

The keeper was saying, 'The cafe closes at four, so if yer can't see 'em in the park grounds then they've obviously left and are on their way home. Maybe they went a different way and you missed them. Sorry I couldn't help yer, love. Now yer will excuse me, won't yer?' Without waiting for her response, he turned away from Rica and headed off across the grass.

Of course he was right. Simon had taken Ricky home by a different route and that's why she hadn't bumped into them. They would be home by now, wondering where she was.

She kicked up her heels and ran after the park keeper towards the gates.

But there was still no sign of her husband and son back at home when she breathlessly arrived after running all the way. A niggle of worry began to gnaw at the pit of Rica's stomach. Maybe one of them had met with an accident . . .

With her heart thudding, she rushed into the hall and grabbed the telephone book to look up the number of the Royal Infirmary. Twenty minutes later, having telephoned the Royal along with the General Hospital and also the local police station, she put down the receiver, her face drawn with worry.

No patients answering their description had been brought into the Accident and Emergency department of either hospital, and the police had no record of any incident involving them either. Rica was enormously relieved to hear this but the question of where they were remained unanswered.

Then a thought struck her. After leaving the park, had Simon decided to go by the shop to check that all was well? And, as far-fetched as it sounded, had they somehow got locked inside? There were frequent problems with their home line so if Simon had telephoned she might not have received the call. Grabbing up her coat again, Rica dashed from the house.

The shop was a good two miles away in the middle of a very busy thoroughfare. She arrived outside it panting heavily, having run all the way. To her dismay the shop was in complete darkness, the door locked securely. Leaving nothing to chance, she made her way down the street to where there was an alleyway that led around the back of the premises. She had to stand on a dustbin to see over the high wall behind the row of shops. Peering over, her heart sank to see that the back of their premises was in complete darkness. Her husband and son could not be inside.

Having exhausted all the avenues she could think of, there was nothing Rica could do now but wait back at home. She hoped they would come back soon as worry over their unexplained absence was making her feel sick.

Rica woke with a start. It took her several moments to work out where she was, and several moments more to realise she must have fallen asleep in the armchair and that was why her neck was aching. The hissing sound was coming from the television set, the star-burst clock telling her that transmission had ceased hours ago as it was now after five o'clock in the morning. But how had she come to fall asleep in the armchair and not in bed?

Then, like a floodgate opening, it all came back to her. Her husband had taken their son out yesterday afternoon and they hadn't been seen or heard from since. They obviously hadn't returned while she was asleep or she'd have heard them.

Sitting upright in the armchair, Rica rubbed her aching neck. She was completely at a loss as to where to start looking for them. Should she call the hospitals again, to check they hadn't been admitted since she'd last called? Then a different thought struck her. Were they perhaps with Fran? It seemed unlikely as they had so little in common but the way Rica was feeling now anything seemed possible.

Heedless of the early hour or of the dishevelled state she was in, Rica heaved herself wearily from her chair and went into the hall to grab her coat off the rack.

The streets she hurried through were deserted. Most people would still be in bed for a few hours yet, savouring their day of rest. It had rained in the night and she barely noticed the muddy water that splattered the back of her legs as she rushed carelessly through puddles. She was going to see Simon and Ricky. They'd both be with Fran. They *had* to be. There was nowhere else left for Rica to try.

Fran's one-bedroomed flat was on the second floor of an imposing Victorian villa. Rica arrived at the front door and pressed the button of flat number two. She stood and waited only a moment. When her summons was not immediately answered, she impatiently pressed the button again and again, until eventually the front door opened a crack and a bleary-eyed, tousled-haired Fran peeped out. She looked absolutely shocked to see who her caller was.

'Rica! But what on earth brings you here at this time of . . .'

She got to say no more. Rica was pushing the door wider so she could get inside and saying in a far from happy tone, 'I've been going out of my mind with worry, Fran. You could have gone to the telephone box, surely.'

A bewildered Fran was shutting the door behind her. She exclaimed, 'Telephoned to tell you what exactly?'

The door of the downstairs flat opened and an annoyed elderly face looked out. 'What's going on?' a disgruntled voice asked.

Fran looked over apologetically. 'I'm deeply sorry, Mr Barker. I didn't mean to disturb you.'

'I should think not, at this time on a Sunday morning. Now could you take your discussion up to your own flat and let me get back to sleep?'

'Yes, of course, Mr Barker. Again I'm . . .'

She never finished because he had disappeared back inside his flat and slammed the door.

Fran flashed Rica a dark glare and hissed, 'Thank you very much, Rica. I've told you often enough how difficult Mr Barker is. If I don't put the lid back on the dustbin in the way he feels it should go on, he reports me to the land-lord. He won't waste a minute reporting me for causing a disturbance at this time on a Sunday morning. If I get evicted, it will be *your* fault.'

With that she stormed off up the stairs and Rica had no

choice but to follow. She did not feel at all remorseful for possibly causing Fran trouble. All she could think of was discovering the whereabouts of her husband and son.

Inside the flat, Fran shut the door behind them and demanded, 'Why are you here at this time, Rica? Just who do you think is here?'

'Why, Simon and Ricky, of course.' Then Rica's eyes filled with a pleading expression. 'They are here, aren't they, Fran? Please tell me they are, because if they aren't . . .'

Her sister looked astonished.

'No, of course they're not here. Why would they be?'

Rica's eyes were darting wildly. She caught hold of Fran's arm and frenziedly shook it. 'Are you sure Simon didn't bring Ricky here yesterday afternoon, to shelter from the rain, and they just spent the night for some reason?'

Even as she said the words she realised how lame they sounded. Simon would never have kept Ricky out overnight for such a trivial reason.

Fran shook her head in bewilderment. 'No. I haven't seen Simon for several weeks, and the last time I saw Ricky was last Saturday afternoon when I came for my usual visit. I was out at a concert last night, as I told you, and didn't get in until after eleven. So if Simon did call, I wasn't in anyway.'

Rica's face turned ashen and she slumped against the wall. 'Well, if they aren't here, then where are they? I've looked everywhere else I thought they might be. I rang the hospitals and the police . . . them being here with you was my last hope.' Tears filled her eyes as she frantically wailed, 'Oh, Fran, where on earth can they be?'

Her sister looked at her sharply. 'Well, wherever they are, wailing like a banshee and waking up all of my neighbours isn't the way to find them. Now, you look fit to drop, Rica. Go and sit in the living room while I make us a cup of tea. Put the gas fire on. Matches are on the mantle.' She saw her sister was about to protest and stopped her. 'I can't function in the morning until I've had a cup of tea, and you certainly could do with one. Please do as I say.'

Ten minutes later Fran was sitting opposite her sister in a wing-back leather armchair at the side of the lit gas fire. The high-ceilinged room was still chilly, not having had time to warm yet, and Fran pulled her dressing gown tighter around her before she picked up her mug of tea from the hearth. Looking enquiringly at Rica who thankfully had calmed down and seemed to be lost in her own thoughts, she said, 'When he took Ricky out yesterday, Simon gave you no indication he was thinking of going anywhere else but the park?' When Rica did not answer her, she raised her voice. 'Rica, did you hear me?'

'Sorry . . . No, he never mentioned going anywhere but the park.'

Fran fell silent for several moments before she said, 'You're not going to like what I'm going to ask you . . . but did Simon take anything with him?'

Rica frowned at her, bewildered. 'Such as?'

'Such as any personal belongings of his and Ricky's?'

'I don't know. I was in the kitchen when he left. Oh, my God, do you think he's left me and taken Ricky with him?' she exclaimed, mortified.

'Well, it would explain why he's been acting strangely these last couple of days, wouldn't it?'

Rica cried, 'But we're as happy together as we've ever been. He said to me only last week that he'd got everything a man could wish for, and how lucky he was. And he's been as loving towards me as always . . . I don't know why he's been acting oddly, but I'm sure it's got nothing to do with him planning to leave me.'

'All right, there's no need to raise your voice at me, I was only trying to explore every avenue.'

'Well, you can stop exploring that one!'

Fran took another sip of her tea. 'As you've tried

59

everything you can think of to find them, it seems to me that if they haven't returned under their own steam by dinnertime there's nothing else for it but to report them as missing to the police. Leave it to them to find out what's happened.

With a sinking heart, Rica knew that her sister was right.

CHAPTER SIX

Rica looked expectantly at the stocky, middle-aged policeman when she opened the door to him in the early evening three days later. Before he had chance to say anything to her she blurted out, 'You've come with news of my husband's and son's whereabouts, Constable. You've found them, haven't you? Please tell me you have. Oh, but where are my manners? Please . . . come in, come in,' she urged him.

After shutting the front door behind him, Rica was so desperate to hear what he had called to tell her that she virtually ran into the lounge, expecting him to follow as quickly. She had to wait several frustrating seconds for him while he plodded in to join her. Rica fought not to show her impatience as she gestured him to take a seat on the settee.

He'd hardly parked his backside and taken off his helmet before she was demanding again, 'You have found them, haven't you, Constable? Simon's lost his memory . . . people do suddenly lose their memories, don't they? And for no apparent reason. They're in hospital and the staff had no idea who he was so they didn't know who Ricky was either . . . that's what's happened to them, isn't it?'

The policeman swallowed hard as he stared at the frantic woman peering eagerly at him from the armchair opposite. She looked as bereft as anyone who had recently suffered a death in the family. It was apparent she'd not slept a wink since he'd last seen her three days ago, when he'd taken her missing persons report and informed her they'd be in touch as soon as they had any information. Her skin was the colour of parchment, eyes red and swollen, hair unbrushed. She didn't look as though she had attended to herself in any way since he'd last seen her; she was certainly wearing the same rumpled clothes as she'd worn at the station.

He solemnly shook his head. 'Mrs Dunmore, I want to assure you that we have done our best to locate your husband and son, but have turned up nothing as yet. No patient in any Leicestershire hospital matches their descriptions. I made enquiries with the keeper at the park you said you usually go to. He said you'd already asked him yourself, but I showed him the photograph you gave us of your husband and son and he didn't remember seeing them at all that afternoon. I then returned to the park several different times over the last three days in order to catch people who had been there on Saturday afternoon. None of them remembered seeing your husband and son at all. Most of them thought they'd certainly have remembered the little boy as he was so cute. It doesn't appear therefore as if your husband actually went to the park, Mrs Dunmore.

'Two of your neighbours said they saw Simon with Ricky in his pushchair around one o'clock on Saturday afternoon. He wasn't heading in the direction of the park but towards the bus stop on the main road.' The PC paused to consult his notes before he continued. 'A Mrs Fraser did say she stopped to speak to him but he carried on straight past, not seeming to see her. She said usually Mr Dunmore would always stop and say hello to her whenever she bumped into him, and especially when he was out with his son so she could make a fuss of him. She said Mr Dunmore definitely wasn't his usual self. He was usually such a friendly man but that afternoon he seemed very distracted . . . definitely looked to her like he'd a load on his mind. You've no idea what Mrs Fraser would have been referring to, Mrs Dunmore?'

'No, I haven't.'

He gave a sigh. 'Well, we've exhausted all our usual lines of enquiry and turned up nothing. We can only conclude that, wherever Mr Dunmore is, he doesn't want to be found.'

Rica's face had paled to a deathly white as the policeman told her the conclusion he'd come to. At his last sentence she eyed him frantically. 'What do you mean by "doesn't want to be found"? Why would Simon not want to be found?' Then her sister's suggestion occurred to her and she exclaimed, 'Oh . . . are you telling me that it is the police's opinion that my husband has left me and taken our son with him?'

He nodded. 'Yes, that's exactly the conclusion we've come to.'

Rica shook her head and frenziedly cried, 'No, he hasn't left me! We've a happy marriage, Constable. We're very close. If he was planning to leave me, I would have known.'

He eyed her sympathetically. 'With due respect, Mrs Dunmore, a wife is usually the last to know when her husband is planning to leave her.'

Rica was adamant when she responded, 'Not this wife. My husband might have had a problem on his mind that he wasn't ready to discuss with me, but him leaving me is out of the question. Besides, he took no personal belongings with him, nor any of our son's.'

'Maybe Mr Dunmore took nothing with him as he just wanted to leave his past life behind and start afresh?' the policeman suggested sheepishly.

But Rica was shaking her head vehemently. 'No. He has not left me, he has not. My husband is not a cruel or vindictive man, and would never willingly take my son away from

63

me like this. He wouldn't leave me not knowing if they were alive or dead. He knows without doubt my son is my world . . . and himself too . . . they're both my world. Besides that, he has a successful business that he and his father built up together. Simon would never just leave that behind to fall into ruin. The reason he's not home now is because something is preventing him. You can't give up looking for him and my son, you just can't.'

'But we've no leads to go on, Mrs Dunmore. Mr Dunmore could be anywhere by now. And you have to respect the fact that even had we discovered where he was with your son, unless he gave us his permission to, we couldn't tell you. Your husband is a grown man, quite at liberty to conduct his life in whatever way he wishes. We have no further reason to be involved in finding him as he's done nothing criminal so far as we're concerned.' The PC leaned forward and looked compassionately at her. 'I can see this has come as an awful shock to you and it's going to take you a while to come to terms with it. You came to the police station with another woman . . . your sister, I remember. Can I fetch her to be with you?'

Rica was fighting with all her might to keep her composure, not wanting to break down in front of this kindly man and embarrass him. She managed to tell him, 'Thank you, Constable, but I'll be fine.'

He picked up his helmet and got to his feet 'I hope things resolve themselves for you. I'll see myself out.'

Rica sat like a statue for an age, staring blindly at her hands clasped tightly in her lap, fighting to keep her mind free from any thoughts. She didn't want to think, dare not, because if she did she would have to face the fact that was glaring to everyone else but which she was unwilling to accept. Finally she lost the battle. Her mind was shouting, over and over, *Simon has left you. He's taken your son. They are not coming back.*

She let out a cry of anguish. For Rica life without Simon beside her, her rock, her soul mate, would no longer hold any meaning. Life devoid of the little boy who had captured her heart before she'd even set eyes on him was unthinkable. She saw life stretching before her like an empty black hole. A nothingness. She had nothing left to live for now the two people she cared for most were gone from her. And she couldn't bear any longer the intolerable pain she was feeling. It was as if someone had ripped her open with their bare hands and was tightly squeezing her heart.

An overwhelming tiredness came over her. She felt a desperate need to sleep, a dreamless sleep, to be released for a while from this terrible realisation. But then her suffering would only return when she woke. There was no telling when it would begin to subside, if it ever did. She still wished for sleep, desperately so, but waking up was another matter.

She wasn't aware that she'd even got out of her chair and returned to it until she realised she was holding an unopened bottle of gin in one hand, and in the other a full bottle of codeine tablets. All she had to do now to achieve her wish was to drink the gin and swallow the pills, lie back in her chair and let the alcohol and medicine work together to spare her from the years of torment and misery she knew were in store for her.

She was about to put the bottle temporarily on the floor by her feet so that she had both hands free to unscrew the top of the bottle of tablets, when suddenly both bottles were whipped away from her and a voice was saying, in a matter-of-fact tone, 'I see you're struggling to open that bottle of pills, so let me try for you.'

Rica's head jerked up and she saw her sister standing before her. She hadn't heard Fran come in, too intent on the task she was trying to accomplish. She could tell by the look in her sister's eyes that Fran was fully aware of what she had been about to do. Rica felt anger well up inside her that her sister's untimely arrival had stopped her from putting an end to her own misery. Only temporarily, though. As soon as she was gone Rica would carry on from where Fran had interrupted her.

The bottle of gin tucked under one arm, Fran was appearing to try and unscrew the top of the bottle. She heaved a sigh of exasperation at her failure to do so. 'The lid is stuck tight. I'll see if there's anything in the kitchen that'll release it. Mother used to use a wet cloth to get a grip on a tight bottle top, if I remember right. I'll try that. I'll bring you back a glass of water to take the pills with when I return, as I see you haven't got one.' She turned and made her way towards the door, stopping en route by the sideboard to open the cupboard where the bottles were kept and return the gin.

A minute or so later she came back, carrying a glass of water and two of the codeine tablets. She held them out to Rica, saying, 'These will soon ease your headache.' She then fixed Rica with her eyes and added meaningfully, 'I put the other tablets away as it's very easy to forget how many you've taken when you've a lot on your mind.'

Rica gave her sister a tight smile as she took the pills, swallowing them with water. Handing her sister the empty glass, she said to her, 'Not that it's not nice to see you, Fran, but shouldn't you be at work?'

'I had an errand to do so I finished early. My errand didn't take me as long as I thought it might so here I am.' She paused for a moment to draw in a deep breath before she continued. 'I know the police have been to see you, to update you on their search for Simon and Ricky. I realised that not hearing anything from them since you made your initial report was only adding to your distress, so I telephoned the station from work this morning and spoke to the man in charge, to find out if they'd had any news. He explained to me that their enquiries had resulted in no positive findings, but that they were satisfied that no harm had come to Simon or Ricky. They obviously believe Simon has left you of his own accord. The local beat bobby was on his way to inform you, they said. I'm very sorry, Rica, really I am, but now you have to accept this.'

It was all right for Fran to say she should just accept the fact that her marriage was over, with no word of explanation. Accept the fact that the child her husband had taken such pains to bring to her could just be taken away again, seemingly with no thought for the heartbreak it would cause her. She'd defy any loving wife and mother just to accept what she herself was being expected to, and get on with her life as though it was a minor setback and of no consequence. Rica couldn't.

Fran was asking her, 'Now have you eaten today?'

Rica couldn't remember whether she had or hadn't. She couldn't eat anyway as just the thought of food made her feel nauseous. 'Yes, I've had plenty,' she lied.

'Oh, what exactly? Only I had a quick check in the pantry when I was in the kitchen just now, and the same food that was there yesterday is still there today. Don't lie to me, Rica, I know you haven't eaten for three days now. You can't survive on cups of tea alone. I'm going to cook you a meal, and while I'm doing that you can go and have a long soak in the bath.'

Rica sighed. 'I do appreciate your offer to cook but I'm really not hungry and don't feel up to having a bath. Maybe I will tomorrow.'

'You haven't washed or changed out of those clothes for three days, Rica. You don't smell very nice! Your hair needs a wash, and a good brush too. I'll go and run the bath for you. All you have to do is strip off your clothes and get into it. I'll put your dressing gown on the radiator to warm.'

Frustrated, Rica sighed again as Fran turned away from her and left the room. Her sister meant well but how Rica wished she would go and leave her to get on with what she wanted to do. She supposed, though, that the sooner she did Fran's bidding, the sooner she would be rid of her.

A while later Fran was coming out of the kitchen carrying cutlery to set the table with as Rica appeared fresh from her bath.

Fran smiled at her and said, 'You look better. Did you enjoy your bath?'

She didn't feel any better but to humour her sister she responded, 'Yes, it was lovely.'

Fran handed her the cutlery. 'Well, you've timed it just right. I'm about to put dinner on the table, so go and sit down.'

Not giving Rica a chance to protest, she returned to the kitchen.

Normally Rica would have savoured the cottage pie Fran put before her. Today it was a struggle to eat it all, as she knew Fran expected. In fairness, though, Fran had only given her a small portion.

Pushing her empty plate away, she said, 'I enjoyed that, thank you.'

Fran looked at her as if to say, I know you did not. What she said though was, 'Go and relax by the fire while I clear away. I'll bring you through a cup of tea.'

Normally Rica would have offered to do the clearing away as Fran had cooked but she suddenly started to feel a little groggy, as if a fog were forming in her head. Her legs felt as if they were turning to jelly. The short walk to her armchair seemed like a mile and she fell down into it, resting her head against the chairback. Her eyelids suddenly felt very heavy and she had difficulty in keeping them from shutting. She felt a hand shaking her arm and forced her eyes open to see a blurry Fran, cup of tea in her hand, looking down at her in concern. When Rica spoke her words were as slurred as if she'd drunk alcohol. 'Oh, Fran, I can't understand why I feel so dopey all of a sudden. I can hardly keep my eyes open.'

'Oh, that'll be the sleeping tablets I crushed into your dinner taking effect,' her sister told her matter-of-factly. She put the cup down on the hearth, then eased her arm around Rica's back. 'Come on, I'm going to help you get to bed. You haven't slept for four nights so I made it my business to make sure you would tonight.'

By now the medication she'd involuntarily taken was overwhelming her and Rica was barely able to comprehend just what her sister was telling her. All she could think was that she needed to get to her bedroom as quickly as she could, before her legs completely failed her and she fell asleep where she was. As unprotesting as a lamb, she allowed her sister to guide her to bed.

CHAPTER SEVEN

The pounding in her head was what roused Rica. She lifted her arm free from the covers and gave her throbbing brow a rub as she forced her eyes to open. It took a moment for her vision to focus. She could tell by the gloom in the room that it was early morning. She turned her head and looked at the alarm clock, squinting hard in the poor light. It was half-past seven.

An immediate rush of panic swept through her. They had slept in. Why hadn't the alarm gone off as usual at six-thirty? Maybe she hadn't set it right before she had settled down last night. More to the point, Ricky was usually awake and demanding their attention long before now. But Simon had to leave the house at eight as he liked to be in the shop at eight-thirty, and if she didn't get a move on he wouldn't have time for any breakfast.

As she hurriedly sat upright, simultaneously pulling back the covers to swing her legs over the side of the bed, searching with her feet for her slippers, she urgently called out, 'Simon, Simon, wake up! We've overslept.' She was on her feet now, pulling on her dressing gown which she had grabbed off the hook on the back of the door, and turning back to face the bed. 'Simon . . .' His name died on her lips as her eyes fell on the empty space where he usually slept. The reason for that empty space came flooding back, along with the return of all the pain and anguish that sleep that temporarily released her from.

She jumped as she heard a noise and spun around to see Fran had come into the room. With tears in her grief-stricken eyes, Rica uttered, 'Oh, Fran . . .'

Taking her arm, her sister interjected, 'Come downstairs, I've a pot of tea mashed.'

Rica shook her head, pulling her arm free. 'I don't want to go downstairs. I want to go back to sleep and shut all this out.' A hazy memory suddenly flashed into her mind. She had been sitting in a chair, about to put an end to her misery, when Fran had interrupted her . . .

Her sister was looking at her hard and in a stern voice told her, 'Shutting it all out by sleeping is not dealing with it, Rica. You've already had twelve hours' sleep so I doubt you'd fall asleep again very easily. No point in lying here brooding and making yourself more depressed. That's not good for you. I have bacon keeping warm in the oven. If it isn't eaten soon it will ruin, and you know how I hate to waste food. Now downstairs, please. Come on,' she ordered.

Rica rubbed her still-throbbing brow and gave a deep sigh. She hadn't the fight in her to stand her ground with her sister. Fran would have to leave for work soon or she'd be late, so all Rica had to do was humour her for a short while and then she'd be free to get on with what she wanted to do.

Rica barely nibbled at her bacon sandwich. It tasted like cardboard to her. If Fran noticed the difficulty she was having eating her food then she didn't comment, but went about tidying up the kitchen and making a fresh pot of tea. Rica was clock-watching, willing the time to pass so she would be left on her own again. When eight o'clock came and went and Fran still did not make any move to leave, Rica said to her, 'You do know what time it is, Fran? I

71

appreciate you getting up early this morning to come and check on me, but you'll be late for work if you don't leave very soon.'

Putting the pot of tea on the table, Fran sat down and began refreshing their cups. 'Oh, I didn't go home last night, I stayed here. Well, I did pop back while you were asleep, to pack a bag and put out my rubbish while I'm away. I'm not going to work. I've got outstanding holiday to take, and I had a word with Mr Moffett yesterday. He was very understanding when I explained we'd had an upset in the family so I needed to take it all at once. He's arranged a temp to cover my work meantime so I'll be staying with you for the time being, to support you.'

This unexpected and not at all welcome announcement from her sister temporarily swept aside all the other emotions Rica was feeling. She was horrified. The last thing she wanted was company, and definitely not that of her forthright sister. They barely saw eye to eye on matters as simple as how to make a bed. Fran was never open to compromise; her way was always best, and she made that readily apparent in any discussion. Besides, with her beady eyes watching Rica's every move, how was she going to complete the task she had set herself last night? It was the only way to proceed, Rica was sure of it.

'I really appreciate you giving up your holiday time to be with me, Fran, but I'm fine, honestly. You only get two weeks' holiday a year as it is, you should be using it to . . .'

With a meaningful look on her face, Fran broke in to tell her, 'I'm staying with you until such time as I feel you can cope on your own.'

Rica put down the remains of her sandwich and said, 'Look, Fran, what you saw when you came in last night . . . well, I wasn't doing what it looked like. I was only going to take two of the tablets, and with water. I'd had a drink of gin the night before but hadn't put it back in the sideboard so it was . . .'

Fran held up a warning hand, eyeing her sharply. 'Please don't insult my intelligence, Rica. A village idiot couldn't have failed to miss what you were attempting.'

She snapped, 'Then I'm surprised you've not had me committed to the mental home as a danger to myself, considering you couldn't wait to get me in there when you thought I'd tried to steal a baby!'

'Oh, you do like to dramatise things, don't you, Rica? Trying to get you to agree to consult a mental health professional can hardly be considered in the same light as having you strapped into a straitjacket and locked up in a padded cell!' Cradling her cup between her hands, Fran continued, 'I respect the fact that you weren't thinking at all rationally last night, through lack of sleep. You didn't know what you were doing. Well, now you have slept I expect you to be rational again. I'm sure you won't be attempting anything so stupid a second time.'

Another memory stirred within Rica then and she challenged her sister with it. 'You drugged me with sleeping tablets, didn't you? That's why I've got such a pounding headache this morning.'

'Yes, I did,' Fran said, without an iota of shame. 'Before I came here yesterday I went to see your doctor, to ask him for something for you as I knew you hadn't slept since Saturday. And after speaking to the police and knowing what they were on the way to tell you, I was worried that you'd not sleep again last night. You can't make solid plans for your future when you've not had a decent sleep for days.'

Rica glared incredulously at her. 'You're expecting *me* to make plans for my future! Fran, don't you understand? I don't see any future for myself without Simon and Ricky.'

'Don't be so melodramatic! Of course you have a future,' her sister scolded her. 'I do understand that you can't be expected to get over what Simon's done to you overnight.

But neither can you allow yourself to become a martyr and wallow in self-pity for the rest of your days. Now, first things first, we need to find out what position you're in.'

Rica looked startled. 'What do you mean, what position I'm in?'

'Financially, Rica. We need to find out how Simon has left matters.'

Rica couldn't care less where she stood financially. Where she intended to go, she'd have no need for money. 'Please stop, Fran! I can't deal with this right now. My head is still throbbing after those sleeping tablets you gave me; I can't think straight.'

Without a word, Fran got up and went out of the room. Moments later she returned and put a glass of water in front of Rica along with two codeine tablets that she'd obviously taken from the bottle she had confiscated the previous night. She returned to her seat, saying, 'Those will soon start to ease your headache. I'll give them a minute or two to start working then we'll get back to making plans.'

Rica resignedly swallowed the pills and took a long draught of the water. Fran had made it clear she wasn't going anywhere, so unless she wanted to endure being relentlessly pressured by her to start addressing her future, Rica may as well get it over with. As annoying as her sister's bossiness was, Rica couldn't find it in herself actually to feel angry with her, as she knew Fran was worried for her and had only her best interests at heart.

After a minute or so had passed, Fran took up where she'd left off. 'I'm concerned that if Simon's capable of walking out on you and taking your son without warning, he may be capable of even worse.'

Rica frowned at her. 'What do you mean?'

'Well, what if he's left you destitute? If he's sold the house and business, and gone off with all the proceeds? The first you'd know he'd sold the house would be when the new owners came to take possession and ordered you out immediately.'

Rica stared at her blindly. It was hard enough for her, trying to come to terms with the fact that Simon had left her and taken Ricky with him. That he'd also sold all their assets and left her with nothing was something she hadn't even considered or could believe he would ever do; not the Simon that she knew and, despite everything, still loved. Her desire to stop the world and get off returned with a vengeance. All Fran was achieving by making her face these things was prolonging her agony and misery.

Jumping up from her chair, Rica cried at her, 'I want to be left alone! I know you mean well but I can't deal with this now. Please, go home . . . or to work . . . please, just *go*, Fran. Just give me a few days to get used to what's happened, then I'll discuss with you whatever you want me to and make whatever plans you want . . .'

Fran cut in, 'I told you that I'm not going anywhere until I'm satisfied you're safe to be left on your own. I cannot risk a repetition of what I came in here and caught you trying to do last night. I might not be here to stop you next time, and where would that leave you then?'

Rica frenziedly cried out, 'Free from this suffering, Fran. Saved from year after year spent not knowing why Simon stopped loving me, worrying that he's looking after Ricky properly, worried my son is missing me and can't understand where his mummy is, and me missing them both like hell . . . I can't live like that. I don't want to live like that.'

Fran ruefully shook her head and in her usual calm tone said, 'If everyone who suffered a blow in life like you have were to top themselves, then there'd hardly be anyone left in the world. Anyway, most people who try to do away with themselves end up maimed for life because they didn't do it right, so not only are they still left having to come to terms with what they were trying to escape from in the first place, they are also having to cope with whatever disability their failed attempt left them with. I suppose if you're lucky you could end up in a coma, and be out of it anyway. But then, you have to consider that you could come out of that eventually. Provided you weren't brain-damaged, you'd still be left with all the heartache you were originally trying to escape from.'

Rica was staring at her open-mouthed. Was this actually intended to make her feel better?

Fran was continuing, 'You don't really want to end your life, Rica, you just want the pain you're feeling to end. But you're not doing anything to help yourself, are you?'

She blurted out, 'But I don't know *how* to help myself, Fran. It's all right for you, sitting there in judgement on me, I'd like to see how you'd react if it had happened to you.'

'I'd be devastated, like you are, but I wouldn't see the answer as ending my own life. I don't expect you to get over Simon's betrayal of you overnight, it's going to take time. You can help yourself, though, by not allowing yourself to dwell constantly on what's happened. Instead you need to keep your mind occupied by working out things like what you're going to do now.'

Fran was making it sound so easy: just keep directing her thoughts on to other things . . . one of those things occurred to Rica now.

She resumed her seat and, with no enthusiasm whatsoever, said to Fran, 'Simon won't have sold the house from under me.'

Fran frowned. 'What makes you so positive?'

'Because I'd have had to countersign the deeds. We're joint owners. Right from when we first realised we were serious about each other, we've always made joint decisions and considered each other equal partners.'

Fran looked mortally relieved to learn this. 'Well, thank God for that! Apart from losing what you have already, the last thing you need is to find yourself homeless as well.' She then hopefully asked, 'Did that include the business when he inherited it from his father? Please tell me Simon made you a partner in that too?'

Rica nodded. 'He did. I told him he didn't need to have me down as joint owner, but he said that as far as he was concerned it was as much mine as it was his. And he was worried that if anything should happen to him, all his assets would be frozen while probate went through. In Simon's opinion, solicitors only have one pace of work: slow. So while all his affairs were being sorted out, he worried how I'd manage meantime, as well as how his staff were going to be paid. The bank accounts, both the personal and the business one, are in our joint names too.' Her bottom lip trembled then, eyes sparkling with tears. 'That's what I just can't understand, Fran. When a man loves you as much as Simon showed he did me, why should that love just die for no apparent reason? We hadn't been going through a bad time, we were getting on as well as we always have done. The only time in all our fifteen years of marriage we've had cross words was when I was accused of trying to take that baby . . . and, after all, you too doubted me then. But that didn't last more than a few hours before we sorted it out between us.

'Simon never gave me any reason recently to believe he wasn't happy or loved me any less than he's always done. In fact, only last week, when I was in the kitchen cooking the dinner, he came up behind me, put his arms around me and asked how many men were as lucky as him? That's not how a man who's planning to leave his wife in a few days acts towards her, is it? But what makes even less sense is Simon walking away from all he's worked so hard to build up . . . especially the business. He thought far too much of his father just to abandon their joint venture.'

'Well, he has, Rica, and you have to accept that or you're never going to get over this.'

She heaved a deep sigh. 'I'm trying to accept it, Fran, but it's hard when nothing about all this makes sense to me.' She frowned. 'And what is Simon doing for money? I know he had a couple of pounds and some loose change on him after he'd given me my housekeeping on Friday night, as he asked if I needed any extra for anything this week. And *that* doesn't make sense either. If he didn't care about me any more, why was he so concerned about me needing any extra money? Anyway, that couple of pounds he had left won't go far, will it?'

'Unless he cleared out the bank accounts before he left and that's how he's surviving, Rica. But you also have to face the fact that it's a strong possibility he left you for another woman,' said Fran.

Rica gazed back at her, horrified. 'Another woman! You think Simon has left me for another woman? But . . . but how would he have met her? He never went out without me. The last time I can remember him going out for a drink on his own was the night we had words over eighteen months ago, and then it was only for Dutch courage so he could come back and face me, to apologise for what he'd said.'

'Maybe this other woman was a customer and that's how he met her? She could be a rich widow, or well off in her own right . . . and that's how he's been able to walk away with just the clothes he's wearing. He's starting afresh with her.'

Rica's already pale face had by now drained to a deathly grey. That Simon had left her for another woman hadn't entered her mind. Until the police had made her face the probable fact of his desertion of her yesterday afternoon, the only explanation she could come up with was that he'd had an accident of some kind or lost his memory, and *that* had been the reason for him not coming home. In the few hours that had passed since then, considering she'd been asleep for twelve of them courtesy of her sister, Rica had been trying to accept that Simon had left her, assuming it was because he didn't love her any more or want to be married to her. How stupid she had been, not to realise that another woman had stolen his affections and lured him away from her. The thought of him with another woman in his arms, making love to her, planning his future with her, was more than Rica could bear. But not quite as dreadful as another thought that struck her now.

'Oh, Fran!' she cried, mortified. 'That would mean another woman is caring for my son. How long will it be before he's thinking she's his mummy? Ricky's *my* son. *I'm* his mother.'

Fran snapped, 'Rica, I was only pointing it out as a possibility. We don't yet know for sure. There's no point in getting yourself het up over something that could turn out to be untrue.'

Rica's eyes had lost their look of hopeless sorrow. Now anger glinted in them. 'But even so, Simon decided to leave me and take the coward's way out, by sneaking off without any hint to me that he was unhappy. He had no right to take Ricky with him! I want my son back, Fran. I won't rest until he's where he belongs, with me. I'll go to the ends of the earth to find out where Simon has taken him.' She stopped talking for a moment as a worried frown creased her brow. 'But if the police can't find any trace of Simon's whereabouts, where do I begin looking?'

Fran didn't openly show it but was gratified that her sister had found a new purpose for living in her need to get her son back. 'Rica, the police only asked the people who went to the park that afternoon if they'd seen Simon or Ricky, and a few of the neighbours – just to satisfy themselves that they did leave this house in good health, as you said they did. That and checking the hospitals was the extent of it. We could take it further. We could hire a private detective to find them.'

Rica's eyes lit up. 'Yes, we could.' She asked urgently, 'How do we go about finding one, Fran?'

Her sister shrugged. 'I have no idea. I've never had any need for one. But, of course, you do have to consider that should the private detective you hire find out where Simon and Ricky are, you'll have to decide in advance how to get Ricky back. Apart from kidnapping him, that is.'

'Then that's what I'll do,' Rica said with conviction. 'I'll instruct a solicitor to get me custody of Ricky, so Simon cannot take him off me ever again.'

'Well, first things first, Rica. We need to find out just what financial position you are in. You need to be able to pay for a detective's services. I just hope that if Simon has emptied your bank accounts, he's left enough in there for you to pay your immediate bills at least.'

'He would never be so thoughtless as to leave me with nothing, Fran,' she said reprovingly.

'You have to accept that the Simon you knew is not the same man he is now, Rica. Yesterday, until the police came to see you with their findings and made you face facts about him, you would never have believed he could be so cruel as to take your child from you with no warning whatsoever, but he has.'

Rica's shoulders slumped in defeat. 'Yes, you're right, I never would have.' She cradled her head in her hands for several long moments, before she gave herself a mental shake and told Fran, 'Simon kept all his documents and papers in an old briefcase on top of the wardrobe. I'll go and fetch it so I can check the balances of the last statements . . . find out where I stand.'

'Those statements might not be up-to-date if he went to the bank and made withdrawals after you received them. You'll need to visit the bank to get an accurate balance. Then we should visit the shop, to find out how matters stand there.'

'How do you mean, how matters stand at the shop?'

'Well, I'm concerned that Simon could have lost interest in the business when he lost interest in his marriage. It might not be worth the paper it's written on any longer. Hopefully, though, he didn't run it down and it is still a viable concern, which will provide you with an income.'

Rica looked worriedly at her sister. 'I hope so too. But with Simon gone, I'll have to find someone to replace him, won't I? As you know, I never had any real involvement there. I felt that the shop was Simon's domain and the house was mine. I do know a few things about it, but not nearly enough to say I'm clued up. I know he employed a young man who's around eighteen now as his apprentice, and an elderly man who's in truth well past retirement age. Simon hadn't the heart to finish him as he worked for his father first, then Simon himself, and is still doing his job well enough. As far as I remember, the old chap sees to the developing of the photographs that Simon takes and those rolls of film customers bring in. But with Simon gone, it's a photographer I'll need to employ, isn't it? I don't know anything about employing anyone, let alone going about finding a photographer and knowing whether he's any good at what he does.'

Fran was looking thoughtful. 'I know the business has given you and Simon a good standard of living to date, but I doubt it would give you much of one by the time you'd covered the wages of the old man, the apprentice and a professional photographer to manage it all. He'd be expecting a decent wage in exchange for his skills. As far as I can see, there's only one other way to go.'

'And what way is that?'

'You'll have to take Simon's place yourself.'

Rica gazed at her in surprise. 'What! Don't be ridiculous, Fran. I know nothing about running a shop or taking photographs. I can't remember if I've ever taken one, in fact. Simon took all of ours, for obvious reasons.'

Fran gave a disdainful tut. 'How difficult can it be to take a snap? You just point the camera at the object or person concerned, and press the button.'

'I'm sure there must be a bit more to it than that, Fran.'

'Well, you'd need to make sure you didn't move while taking the picture so as not to blur it. You might take a few out-of-focus shots to start with, but you'd soon get the hang of it.'

Rica laughed hollowly. 'I wish I had your confidence! But apart from taking the photographs, I don't know enough about cameras to be able to sell them to customers. And what about the office side? I was a copy typist in a typing pool. I know nothing about keeping accounts and whatever else I'd be required to do, to run the business as it should be run.'

'I can show you how to do the books. And until you're competent, I could keep a check on them to make sure they're all correct and above board to be given to the accountant at year end.'

Rica felt overwhelmed by the magnitude of what she was facing. Scraping a hand through her hair, a worried expression clouding her face, she told her sister, 'I don't think I can do it, Fran. I don't think I have it in me to learn all I have to in order to run the business successfully. And especially not in the short space of time I'd need to do it in.'

Fran eyed her crossly. 'I see. You're giving up without even trying. Well, I'm extremely disappointed in you, Rica. In that case, I can't see the point in your even attempting to find Ricky, let alone get him back, as you'll hardly be able to afford a half-decent roof over his head on the wages you can expect to earn as a clerk! I mean, I doubt you'd land yourself a job as a copy typist again, considering you haven't been near a typewriter for twenty years.'

Fran's words conjured up a vision of Rica and Ricky living in a hovel, barely able to afford to heat the place in winter, with scraps to eat and the poor little mite dressed in whatever hand-me-downs she was lucky enough to get for him. Like any mother, Rica wanted to give her child the best she could provide for him. Her sister was right to be disappointed in her, giving up before she even made an attempt to take over the business and assure herself of a future. Her son deserved more from her.

She fixed Fran with her eyes and said with conviction, 'You've no need to be disappointed in me. I will succeed in running the business as well as Simon did, so that I can hire the best private detective there is to find my son for me. And when I have, I'll give Ricky the best life I can.'

Fran didn't smile very often, being the serious sort that she was, but now she did. 'I'm glad to hear it. Well, why are you still sitting there, wasting time? Go and get yourself ready so we can get started on what we need to.'

CHAPTER EIGHT

Rica looked pensive when she came out of the bank manager's office to rejoin her sister.

Fran waited until they were outside in the street, making sure they weren't being overheard by any passing pedestrians, before she asked, 'Just how did Simon leave you off financially then?'

Rica heaved a sigh. 'Not quite penniless, but it won't be long before I am unless I start bringing some money in myself. You were right, the manager couldn't understand why I didn't already know the balances in the accounts as I am joint signatory. I told him the story you advised me to. That usually I leave the monetary side to Simon but that he's been called away unexpectedly on a family matter, isn't contactable, and is not expected back for a couple of weeks. As the latest statements weren't in the place he usually keeps them, they must be in the briefcase he's taken with him. I said I needed to know what is in the accounts as I have to draw out money to pay my household bills plus pay the staff's wages and settle outstanding bills for the shop out of the business account. He went off to find out for me.

'When he came back, he told me that the balance in our personal account was a few shillings short of thirty pounds. Simon gave me fifteen pounds a week for my housekeeping, so that amount I can manage on for a couple of weeks . . . more if I'm careful. There was only a little more than that in the business account. The manager knew from copies of the past statements roughly how much we require to cover the shop's outgoings, and it isn't enough. So unless money is taken over the counter to make up the shortfall before Friday, he advised me I'd need to transfer some money from our savings account to cover it. Fran, I had no idea we even had a savings account that I'm also joint signatory to! There was an awful lot of money in that account . . . over three thousand pounds.'

'Was?' Fran queried.

Rica looked at her for a moment before she continued. 'The manager checked the balance of that too and told me that Simon had drawn it all out last Friday afternoon, leaving just a couple of pounds in the account to keep it open.'

Both women fell silent, looking at each other as they contemplated the significance of what he had done.

It was Fran who voiced it aloud first. 'That would be more than enough for him to start again. He could put down a sizeable deposit on a house, pay for it outright in fact, and still leave himself enough to set up another photography business.'

Despite being out in public, Rica couldn't stem her flow of miserable tears. 'Oh, Fran, Simon was always telling me that he intended us to have a good old age, live as well as we had when he was working, and was making sure he was providing for that. Obviously he was building money up in that savings account. Now, though, he's found other uses for it . . . not to benefit me and him in our old age, but his new woman and his life with her instead!'

'We don't know that he has got himself a new woman,' Fran reminded her. 'I'm not condoning Simon's actions – he's certainly slipped off his pedestal in my eyes – but some men leave their wives with nothing when they desert them. At least he left you with a roof over your head and a little in the bank to tide you over. Plus there's the business to provide you with the means to earn yourself a living, even if he has left it in a bad state and you've the job of building it up again.'

'Provided I do have it in me to or I'll end up with nothing anyway,' Rica said worriedly.

'It's up to you to make sure that's not the case. If you go into this believing you're going to fail, then you will for certain. Isn't your need to get your son back and provide for him in the manner he's accustomed to enough of an incentive for you to succeed?'

Without hesitation, Rica responded, 'Yes, it is.'

'Good. Then let's get to the shop and find out what awaits us there, shall we?'

Rica couldn't remember the last time she had visited the shop. She used to be a regular caller when she and Simon had first become a serious item. His father had always made a fuss of her when she had come to meet Simon from work on a Saturday afternoon, making her feel more than welcome. He had made it apparent he thoroughly approved of his beloved son's choice of future wife. In turn, Rica couldn't have wished for a better father-in-law.

After their marriage there seemed to be no need for her to visit the shop. Had anything urgent arisen during the day, then she would have telephoned. She had perceived his place of work to be Simon's domain for so many years that it didn't seem right to Rica to be going there now, to poke and pry like an intruder. As she hurried to the shop alongside her sister, she kept having to remind herself that it was Simon's own decision to walk away from the business. As she needed it to function in order to earn herself a living and get her son back, then she had no choice but to step into his shoes.

The shop had been in the possession of the Dunmores for nearly forty years and had hardly changed since the day Richard Dunmore had first opened for business. The premises used to be tobacconist's until the son of the first owner had died and his widow had put the shop up for sale. The then thirty-year-old Richard had bought it with money he had saved up by taking photographs of local people with his ancient Kodak camera, charging less than half the price a professional photographer would have done at the time. Having taught himself the developing process, he would develop the negatives in the outhouse of the rented terraced house he shared with his wife and young son. When she used to visit the shop, Rica felt positive she could still smell the faint trace of tobacco mingling with the smells of age and must and chemicals in the shop's dark room.

In the main shop itself the original dark-wood panelling still lined the lower half of the walls. The plaster above was painted a dark cream colour, or possibly white when it was first done but age and cigarette smoke had darkened it. There were another five rooms besides this, the largest being the studio where all the sittings took place. Then there was the dark room, office, small store room and kitchen. All of them still had their original cast-iron fireplaces, although no fires had been lit in them for over two decades as the installation of electricity had afforded Richard the luxury of having heaters in each room to warm them in cold weather. Although much had been done by the odd job man Richard periodically called in to patch things up, the window-frames needed replacing, as did the patched-up back door. In the small yard outside there were two outbuildings, both in a dilapidated condition and no longer used except as a home by rodents and creepy crawlies. The fireplace in the main shop Richard had had removed and boarded up, and where the large hearth had been stood two old leather wing-back chairs for use by customers. Many wives had no interest at all in their husband's photography hobby and would sit there and look bored while the men deliberated over their purchases.

The counter in the shop was actually a large glass case, the sort pawnbrokers used to display their better quality wares. It had two glass shelves inside which held a display of cameras, their prices ranging from the cheapest basic models to the latest professional equipment commanding high sums. There was also a selection of camera accessories. On the wall behind the counter was an open wooden shelf unit that held all manner of stationery items. On the wall above several wooden shelves held replacement film cartridges, bottles of chemicals for those who chose to develop their own photographs at home, photographic paper, a choice of various photograph albums, camera cases, and other sundries. At the side of the room was a large wooden cabinet with four wider-than-normal drawers, which held the packets of developed film awaiting customer collection. Around the walls of the room hung a selection of framed photographs taken by either Richard or Simon, to show potential customers the standard they were capable of.

Rica remembered there always being a good layer of dust on the stock items when Richard's father had been alive as the old lady he'd employed to clean never seemed to get around to dusting during her daily two hours, it taking the old body all that time just to sweep and mop the floors. Richard's father was far too kind-hearted to replace her as he was aware she could end up in the workhouse without the money she earned off him. If Simon had to keep Rica waiting when she called for him while he finished off a job, she would keep herself occupied meantime doing the dusting herself, so that occasionally it did get done. The old lady wasn't replaced until she failed to turn up one morning, having died during the night. Since then he'd employed younger women, and Rica wondered what had happened after the lady who had mysteriously vanished and had failed to collect her wages. She'd find out soon enough if no one had replaced her.

Photography was not a cheap pastime. The price of even a basic camera along with all the necessary sundries and accessories when the shop first opened in the 1930s was well beyond the means of the average working man, so as a hobby it was only affordable by the more affluent members of society. These days it was still an expensive pursuit, though its popularity had mounted, given that the average factory worker's wage had risen sufficiently against the cost of living to allow for some spare cash to put towards leisure activity.

Rica knew that a reasonable profit was made from the sales of cameras, accessories, and from developing the customers' rolls of films, but the majority of the Dunmores' income still came from commissions they received to take photographs – from a single portrait shot to several dozen group shots capturing special events. Both Richard and Simon had had a penchant for outdoor photography, in particular landscape, and their prints were always in great demand by manufacturers of calendars, magazines, and producers of framed photographs for display, all of whom would pay a good price for the right to reproduce a suitable shot. No matter how many hundreds, if not thousands, of photographs both Dunmores had taken over the years, neither man ever failed to experience a thrill when setting up a new one or to feel nervous anticipation during the wait through the developing stage, to find out whether the finished photograph met their own high standards.

The reputation of both father and son for fine photography and a high quality of personal service had spread far and wide, and people would travel across town and from villages in the Shires to use their services.

As Rica walked alongside her sister, she found herself wishing she had taken much more of an interest in the shop so that she was more knowledgeable about even just the basics, better equipped to undertake what she knew she must now.

* * *

The shop was sandwiched between a chemist's and an iron-monger's, both businesses having been in operation for nearly as long as Dunmore's. On arriving Rica reached out to take hold of the shop door handle, but instead withdrew her hand. Fran and she had discussed what she would tell the staff, to excuse Simon's absence and herself taking over, but suddenly the thought of standing before them as an authority figure filled her with trepidation. She was so afraid of making a fool of herself in front of them and of them seeing her for the nervous novice that she actually was!

Fran looked at her, obviously wondering why she wasn't going inside, and immediately guessed the reason. 'Now isn't the time to lose your nerve,' she said sharply. 'If the staff get a hint that you are unsure of yourself, they'll ride rough-shod all over you and you'll have no control of them. It'll soon be them running this place, not you. You need them to be aware, in no uncertain terms, that you may need some time to learn the business, but regardless you expect the same loyalty and standard of work from them that they showed to your husband. You can do this, Rica. Whenever you start doubting yourself, just think of Ricky and what it means to you to be able to pay someone to find him and get him back.'

Her words were enough to kindle Rica's determination to make every effort to succeed. She took a deep calming breath then squeezed Fran's hand affectionately by way of thanking her for her support. Another deep breath and then she grasped hold of the door handle, turned it, and walked purposefully inside the shop, Fran following immediately behind.

She'd been hoping her confident entry would impress the staff. It did not. The shop was empty.

Fran was not impressed to find the shop unstaffed. She said to Rica, 'Doesn't make for a good impression on anyone who hasn't visited before, finding it as deserted as the *Mary*

Celeste. It's a good job we're not thieves either. In the time we've been here, we could have emptied the till and had our pick of the stock and be well away with our spoils . . . and you with a big financial loss to contend with!'

Nor was Rica herself impressed. As a customer in other shops, she expected to be received with courtesy, treated respectfully, and made to feel that her custom was important by the staff in any shop she chose to browse for wares in.

She started to ask Fran for her advice but her sister held her hand up to silence her and mouthed, 'Shush! Can you hear what I can?'

Fran was looking towards the door that led through to the back rooms. Automatically Rica looked in that direction herself and cocked an ear.

After a moment Fran said, 'Someone is having a jolly conversation, by the sound of it.'

Rica nodded. 'Yes, they are. But I can only hear one voice. A young man's.'

'It's my guess that's because the person he's talking to is on the other end of the telephone. Come on, let's go and break up the party.'

Rica looked hesitant. 'Do you think we should? Maybe it's a customer on the other end and the shop was abandoned so the telephone could be answered?'

'From the laughing and joking that seems to be going on he's talking to a close friend, in my opinion. My boss would sack our receptionist on the spot should he find she'd left the reception area and switchboard unmanned and was taking a personal call in another room. Your staff need to be made aware that you'll take serious action against them if this situation happens again.'

Giving Rica no chance to shrink from the confrontation, Fran grabbed hold of her arm and took her across to the closed door leading through to the back of the shop. They found themselves in a lengthy corridor, two doors on their

91

left side, two on the right, with a fifth door at the end of the corridor. All were closed. The young man's voice could be heard coming from behind the nearest door to the right. Rica remembered that Richard Dunmore had used that room as his office and assumed Simon had made no changes since. Urged on by Fran, she opened the door and walked inside.

Opposite them stood a desk cluttered with paperwork. Lounging back in a well-worn captain's chair on the other side of it, his feet on the desk, telephone receiver clamped to his ear, was a young man who appeared to be no older than fifteen, though Rica knew he had celebrated his eighteenth birthday last year, as Simon had asked for her advice on a suitable gift for his assistant. He was an ordinary-looking boy with a thatch of mouse-brown hair. His complexion was marred by a profusion of adolescent spots. He was tall and stick-thin. The brown tweed suit he was wearing was a little shabby, in the women's opinion. It did not quite fit in with an establishment of the calibre of Dunmore's.

For a moment the young man stared in surprise at the unexpected arrival in the office of two strange women. Then he said into the receiver, 'Hang on a minute.' Addressing the intruders, he snapped, 'Customers ain't allowed back here. Go back into the shop and take a seat in the chairs. I'll be with yer when I've finished.'

Fran bristled. Marching the short distance over to the desk, she slammed her hand down on the cradle of the telephone, cutting off the call, and said to the young man, her tone of voice leaving him in no doubt how annoyed she was, 'You'll deal with us *now*.'

He looked stunned. 'Oi, just who d'yer think you are, cutting off me call like that?'

Fran looked at Rica and said, 'Put him out of his misery.'

'Well?' he demanded, looking at each of the women in turn.

Rica gulped, but before she could speak, Fran said, 'Wait!

You might as well tell them both together so you'll only have to do it the once.' She then addressed the young man again. 'Where is the older employee?'

'Mr Fisher, yer mean? He was on his way into the kitchen to put the kettle on and have a fag when I last saw him. I had to come in here to answer the telephone.'

Fran replied, 'Go and fetch him. And hurry up about it!'

He gawped, stupified. 'But . . . customers haven't any right to come in here and order the staff about!'

'If you want to keep your job, I suggest you do as I've asked, and post haste.'

He opened his mouth to protest again then obviously thought better of it. He snapped it shut, and went off to do her bidding.

'I don't think he'll give you much trouble, Rica, but if he does just raise your voice to him and he'll be quaking in his boots,' Fran said to her. 'And he could do with a new suit. The one he has on might be good enough for the likes of other shops around here, but not for Dunmore's.'

Rica had no time to respond as the young assistant returned along with an elderly man who looked to be seventy if he was a day. He was small in stature, with a barrel-like girth and a domed head with not one hair growing on it. He reminded Rica of Humpty Dumpty. He was wearing a large stained white apron over his trousers and shirt, sleeves rolled up to his elbows. With his beady eyes beaming at them in annoyance, he growled, 'This better be good as I'm in the middle of a job which is more than likely ruined after young laddo here came barging in, telling me I was summoned to the office. Now who the hell are you two? And what is it yer want?'

Rica gulped before she said, 'Er . . . I'm Mrs Dunmore. From now on I'm . . . er . . . going to be taking the place of my husband and running this place.'

This news obviously came as a bolt from the blue. They

both stared at her for several long seconds before the old man demanded, 'Why?'

She gulped again. 'Er . . . well . . . er . . . because . . .'

'Mr Dunmore has been called away,' Fran finished for her.

'He said n'ote to us about having to go away,' the older man snapped. 'Why's he gone away? When will he be back?'

'What is your name?' Fran asked him.

'Eh?'

'Your name?' she reiterated.

'Mr Fisher.'

'Well, Mr Fisher, the reason for Mr Dunmore's having gone away is none of your business. Nor do you need to know when he will return. You are employed here to work, not to question the comings and goings of the owners.'

He obviously didn't like being reminded that he was only an employee here. Scowling darkly, he demanded of Fran, 'And just who are you when yer at home?'

She cocked an eyebrow in annoyance at his rude tone. 'I'm Mrs Dunmore's sister. You'll be seeing a lot of me as I'll be in and out of the office for the foreseeable future. Now, Mrs Dunmore will need both of you to help her settle in, and I'm sure she can rely on you to do that. I presume you'll be showing her the same loyalty and commitment as you showed Mr Dunmore.'

'You're sure of a lot, ain't yer? Women shouldn't meddle in a man's world. Their place is at home,' the older man muttered under his breath. 'I don't tek orders from no woman.'

Rica hadn't caught all the comments, but from his tone could tell he wasn't at all happy over the change at the helm. It didn't help her waning confidence.

Keen-eared Fran had heard every word. 'Do I understand right and you wish to give in your notice, Mr Fisher? If you really are against having a woman as your boss, we wouldn't like the thought of you working here against your will so we'll allow you to leave immediately.' She couldn't help but add, 'Though at your age, I doubt that securing another job will be too easy. But I'm sure Mrs Dunmore will give you a glowing reference.'

Rica gasped, grabbed Fran's hand and urgently whispered to her, 'But I need Mr Fisher to continue working here.'

Fran pursed her lips and nodded towards him. 'Don't worry,' she murmured. 'He was just trying to intimidate us, but by the look on his face, I think he's realised he's failed.'

Fisher stood staring at the two women for a moment, then started to shuffle his feet uncomfortably. Looking everywhere but at Rica and Fran, he stuttered, 'Er . . . no, no, I . . . Look, you misunderstood me. Whatever it is you thought I said, well, I didn't.'

Fran said blandly, 'In that case, I'd better get my ears checked. So I'm to understand you're quite happy to continue working here for Mrs Dunmore?'

It was apparent his response was sticking in his throat. 'Yes,' he mumbled, so low it was hardly audible.

'I didn't quite catch that, Mr Fisher?' Fran said to him.

He glared darkly at her before he raised his voice several decibels and repeated, 'Yes, quite happy.'

'That's good to hear. We know Mr Dunmore thought a lot of you and wouldn't have liked to see you go.' She then turned to the youth. 'And what about you, Mr . . . What exactly is your name?'

His face flushed the colour of beetroot as he stammered, 'Jason Pickles.'

'So what about you, Mr Pickles? Are you happy to continue working for Mrs Dunmore or are you going to be seeking employment elsewhere?'

A feeling of despondency was creeping over Rica. She hadn't expected the staff to take her sudden arrival and supplanting of their old boss with a pinch of salt. But nor had she expected that her gender would be such a stumbling block, as far as the old stalwart was concerned at any rate. The apprentice she wasn't quite sure of yet. Well, it was up to her to find out how he'd view having her as his boss.

She lifted her head and looked Jason in the eye. 'So . . . answer my sister, Mr Pickles. Are you happy to continue working with me as your employer or do you want to move on?'

He blurted out, 'Oh, I'm happy to stay, Mrs Dunmore, really I am. I'll work as hard for you as I did for Mr Dunmore.'

He came across as very genuine in his response, which was a relief to Rica. One bolshie member of staff was enough for her to deal with. She smiled warmly at him and said, 'I'm pleased to hear that, Mr Pickles. I'm sure we'll get on very well together.'

Out of the corner of her eye she caught Fran looking at her. For a moment Rica felt shocked as she was positive there'd been a look of admiration in her sister's eyes. Fran, proud of her? Never before had she openly showed that, no matter what Rica's achievements. Fran had always had this way with her that made Rica feel she was disappointed in her because she didn't respond to things in exactly the same way. But then, wasn't it a good thing they were so opposite in their natures? It was all due to Fran's bossiness, her no-nonsense, pick-yourself-up-and-dust-yourself-down approach, that Rica was here now, trying to forge ahead instead of sitting at home wallowing in misery. Even if her attempt to run the business failed, she would still be indebted to Fran for getting her this far.

Had Rica not had an audience she would have grabbed hold of her sister then and given her the biggest hug of gratitude she could, even though Fran would be mortified by such an open display of affection. Well, she'd give her a hug when they got home, whether Fran liked it or not, Rica decided.

CHAPTER NINE

Rica fought to ignore the look of pure contempt beaming at her from Sid Fisher's eyes. Her immediate reaction after introducing herself to the staff had been to leave them to digest what they'd been told. She'd been hoping, especially in the old man's case, they might thaw even just a little towards her as their new boss and then she would return in the morning to begin the task of getting to grips with the business.

Fran would not hear of that, though. To her there was no time like the present. The staff had already been left to keep the business going unsupervised for nearly a week. It was obvious that it would rapidly decline without being managed properly. Rica had reluctantly agreed with her. And there was a danger, she supposed, that she could lose her nerve overnight and then have to go through all the hard work of building it up again.

Fran shooed them all out of the office so that she could look through the books there undisturbed. After the two men had stepped out, she told Rica she'd expect an overview of what she had learned about the business so far when they met up again in a couple of hours' time.

Outside in the corridor, without giving Rica the chance to dismiss him, Sid Fisher disappeared back into the dark room, shutting the door none too gently behind him. Jason, though, waited respectfully for her to instruct him on what to do. Thinking she would get the worst interview over with first, she asked him to man the shop while she spent some time with Mr Fisher.

She tapped on the closed door of the dark room and opened it. But before she'd even set one foot over the threshold, Fisher was bellowing at her.

'Don't yer know that yer should never enter a dark room without being given the nod from whoever's inside? Well, I'm glad it ain't me that's gotta tell the customer whose photos these are that they're ruined!' He thrust a strip of negatives towards her and waved it menacingly.

Hand still on the door knob, Rica stiffened at the nasty tone of Fisher's voice. His bigoted opinion of women aside, she would not speak to a dog in the tone of voice he was using to her. It was apparent he had no intention of showing her any respect, either as a woman or as his boss. She knew she faced an uphill struggle here, but he had to be made to see that she would not tolerate his attitude.

If Fran had been proud of the way she had introduced herself to the staff, she would have been doubly so had she witnessed how Rica handled this tricky situation.

Taking a deep breath in an effort to calm her jangling nerves, she stepped inside the dark room and closed the door behind her. Then, very calmly, she said, 'No, I didn't know that I wasn't supposed to enter a dark room without permission, but I certainly do now. Thank you for informing me, Mr Fisher. But actually I doubt you'd already started developing a new roll of film as I was only a moment or two behind you. Anyway, I'm prepared to give you the benefit of my doubt on that. What I'm not prepared to do is to put up with your manner towards me any longer. I thought we'd settled this already, but obviously you have a short memory.

'Whether you like it or not, I am now running this business until my husband returns, and at the moment there is no telling when that will be. If you speak to me or my sister in that way again, I will be asking . . . no, telling . . . you to vacate the premises immediately, and your reference will not be favourable. Is that understood, Mr Fisher?' Through narrowed eyes, he was glaring darkly at her. He made no attempt to answer. She was quaking inside but determined not to let him see it. Calmly she reiterated, 'Is that understood, Mr Fisher?'

He continued staring at her for several more moments before he sullenly nodded and mumbled his agreement.

It was very tempting to do what Fran had done with him earlier and pretend she hadn't heard his response, in order to make him repeat it more loudly, but Rica thought better of it. She vehemently hoped that this whole situation was over with now; she didn't want to harp on about it any longer.

She cast her eyes around the windowless room. It was of a reasonable size and held a large bench along the length of the back wall on which stood several metal trays, most of them holding some sort of clear liquid. Strung overhead were several lines with pegs on them, some of them holding developed photographs in the process of drying. Shelves fixed to the back wall held an assortment of brown bottles and tubs – Rica assumed these held the different chemicals needed for the developing process. On a wall to the side of the bench was a sink. On the wall above this was a light socket holding a red bulb. In the ceiling above it hung another light socket, this one holding a clear light bulb. It was this that lit the room now. Considering she had never really had any more than a passing interest in the intricacies of photography before, Rica was surprised to find herself most intrigued to learn what went on in this room.

She directed her eyes back towards Sid, ignoring the resentful expression that was still lurking in his, and asked, 'So how exactly do you go about developing a roll of film, Mr Fisher?'

Two and a half minutes later Rica left the room, shutting the door firmly behind her and resting her back against it while she heaved a frustrated sigh. If she were not so dependent on his skills, she would have had no qualms about sending Fisher packing. He had grudgingly relayed all that his job entailed, but had told her no details on how exactly he went about it, so she was in fact no wiser than she had been before she asked him. It was as if he regarded the processing of films as his own closely guarded secret, one he would take to the grave with him, as a possessive cook would refuse to pass over a recipe they were famed for. Fran had explained to her, though, that she needed to know everything that went on in the shop, in order to be able to keep it running successfully and so as to fill in for the staff members should they be absent from work for any reason. Somehow Rica was going to have to get Fisher to divulge the ins and outs of his job to her, but at the moment the way to do that eluded her.

Hopefully Jason Pickles would prove more affable towards her and would readily impart his role in the firm. He was still learning the trade, in fact, so she was concerned that what he could tell her might be more limited, but as he had been employed by Simon for over three years she felt he must have picked up quite a bit during that time. More than Rica knew at any rate. Poised before the door leading into the shop, she took a very deep breath before she entered.

She saw Jason physically jump on seeing her arrive, his eyes alarmed. He was over at the cabinet where the packets of processed films were stored, awaiting customer collection, and appeared to be sorting through them. Rica wasn't sure if he was actually doing something or just making himself look busy for her sake. She didn't like the thought that he was fearful of her and felt she should really put him straight. She wasn't an ogre about to rule him with a rod of iron, but wanted them both – in fact, the three of them, though a question mark still remained over Sid Fisher – to get on amicably, so that they'd all enjoy coming to work, just as the staff had when Simon had been in charge of them.

Smiling at Jason, she said, 'I'm not disturbing you in the middle of something, am I? I can come back later.'

He nervously stuttered and stumbled over his words. 'No, no, Mrs Dunmore. I was just checking these packets were still in alphabetical order. I've been in the drawer quite a few times and added more since I last did a proper check.'

'My husband spoke very favourably of you to me, so I'm sure they are, Mr Pickles.'

His whole face lit up on hearing this. 'Did he? Really? I like Mr Dunmore. He's a good boss to work for.' He then added hurriedly, 'Not that I don't think you will be too, Mrs Dunmore. Not at all. I'll do me best for you, honest I will.' He suddenly stopped talking and looked at her worriedly. It was obvious he had something on his mind.

'Are you all right, Mr Pickles?' she asked.

He swallowed hard. 'Well, I . . . well, you see . . . it's just that what I was doing when you first arrived here this morning . . . it was wrong of me to have left the shop unattended but . . .'

'While the cat is away, the mouse will play?' Rica finished off for him.

He looked bemused. 'Eh?'

'Was it your girlfriend you were talking to?' she asked.

He reddened in acute embarrassment. 'Er . . . no. No, it wasn't. Anyway, I would never dream of using the telephone at work to make private calls. It's not allowed. Though actually, I don't know anyone who's on the telephone. Still, I heard it ringing, and Mr Fisher wouldn't answer it even if he wasn't in the middle of developing as he reckons it's not his job to, so that only left me. I had no choice but to leave the shop, and there was no one in anyway. The call was from a junior secretary at a firm that wants us to do

101

some work for them . . . take photographs for a brochure they're producing, to send round their customers. She'd called us up to make an appointment for Mr Dunmore to go and see the owner and discuss it.'

'Oh, I see. And with Mr Dunmore not being here himself, you were chatting up the young secretary and letting her believe you had been left in charge?' Rica could tell by the look on his face that that was exactly what Jason had been doing. She looked at him in concern. 'So when did you make the appointment for?'

He screwed up his face. 'What appointment?'

Rica hoped he wasn't as lacking in intelligence as he now seemed. 'The one you made for Mr Dunmore, to visit the owner of the firm and discuss the work they want doing?'

'Oh, er . . . I never made one. I told Janet . . . that's the name of the junior secretary . . . that Mr Dunmore was up to his eyes at the moment, but as soon as he was free, I would ask him to telephone them.'

Rica looked impressed, pleased to find he did have some common sense after all. 'Then I'll do that tomorrow. Today I just want to get a feel for the place.' With a twinkle in her eye, and by way of trying to put him at his ease with her, she asked him, 'And when are you taking Janet out then?'

Jason reddened in embarrassment again and looked down at his feet, mumbling, 'I'm not.'

'Oh, then you've already got a girlfriend? I should have guessed a good-looking boy like you would do.'

He continued to stare down at his feet and Rica was sorry to see his shoulders sag as if a great weight was pressing down on them. An air of despondency seemed to settle over him. She had obviously struck a nerve. Her maternal instincts rising, she wanted to question him, find out what the cause of his sadness was, offer her help. She had to remind herself that she wasn't his mother but his boss . . . or learning to be his boss. She needed to concentrate on that, make sure he had a decent working life and leave his personal problems to his own mother to help him with.

A sudden vision of Ricky danced before her and a sharp stab of pain pierced her heart. Was another woman offering him comfort now, soothing his cries for his absent mother? Was she already beginning to take Rica's own place in his affections? Would it be only a matter of time before he was calling her 'Mother', and his memories of Rica faded to nothing? The pain she was suffering at the thought was a sharp reminder of exactly why she was here, facing this arduous task. To get her son back where he belonged. With her.

Jason's voice, full of concern, cut into her thoughts. 'Are you all right, Mrs Dunmore, only you look . . . well, really upset?'

She told him hurriedly, 'I'm fine. Thank you for asking. Is a Thursday always as quiet as this? Since my sister and I arrived there hasn't been a single customer come in.'

'You never can tell through the week how business is going to be. We can have a really busy day, then slack the next. A whole busy week, hardly see a customer the next. We're always busy on a Saturday, whatever the weather. Interest in photography is growing ever so quickly, especially now it's cheaper to buy a camera with these new instamatics the big makers have brought out. And they're much easier to use too.' Jason paused as he realised his new boss was looking most impressed. His cheeks blazed to a beetroot colour for the fourth time in the space of less than an hour. 'Mr Dunmore told me all that,' he said bashfully.

'And obviously you listened to what he was telling you, and I'm glad you did or you wouldn't be able to instruct me now.' How I wish I'd listened more to Simon when he was talking about the shop, she thought. 'So . . . just what is an instamatic camera?'

Jason slid open one of the glass panels at the back of the counter and took out the smallest in the display, which he handed to her, saying. 'This little beauty has brought photography to the masses. It's light and compact, fits nicely into a pocket. Very reasonably priced, too.'

Rica hid a smile. He was treating her like a potential customer, giving her his practised sales pitch.

Jason went on, 'The films for it come in a specially contained cartridge, so you don't have to load them in the dark or have the fiddly job of feeding the film through the spools and getting them sat properly on the wheel cogs so that they feed through evenly after taking each shot. Once it's loaded, all you have to do with these cameras is point them at the subject, focus by turning the dial on the front . . . and then press the button on top. If it's a night-time shot or the light isn't very good, you just pop on a flash cube. We sell this model for three pounds, twelve shillings and sevenpence. We also sell the accessories to complement the camera . . . the case and wrist-strap as well as the flash cubes and the AAA batteries.'

Rica was thinking that maybe . . . hopefully . . . Fran hadn't been far off the mark when she had announced that all there was to taking a photograph was to point the camera at the chosen topic and press the button.

Jason was telling her, 'We also carry the Ilford Ilfomatic camera that came out last year. It's basically the same as the Kodak, as easy to load and use, but slightly cheaper. The quality of the photographs is about the same . . . not bad. But when you compare these to ones taken with an SLR camera, there's no comparison.'

He then took out another camera from the display case. A long lens protruded from the main body of the camera, with a pleated leather concertina housing enclosing its sides. It had several complicated-looking knobs and dials. Jason started going on about different shutter speeds, apertures and light meters . . . Rica soon became horribly confused and lost in the technicalities. Despite the fact that what he was telling her was not making any sense to her she listened politely, knowing that she was going to have to make sense of it all, and the sooner the better.

This became more apparent when he told her that the camera Simon used for his photography assignments was the same make, Pentax, as the model he was now showing her, but far superior with its wide angle and telephoto lens. If anyone wished to buy a camera of this calibre then it was ordered in especially as it was priced at over a hundred pounds, well beyond the pocket of the average working man whose weekly wage was around the fifteen to twenty pound mark. They would require payment for it in advance before it was ordered.

Jason returned that camera to the display case then made to take out another, but Rica felt she'd taken in as much as she could for now. Panic was manifesting itself. There was so much for her to learn! Hopefully by tomorrow it would all start to make some sort of sense.

She laid a hand on Jason's arm to stop him and said, 'We'll continue this tomorrow.'

She wanted to ask him if as part of his training he had got round to learning the developing side of the business yet, so he could tell her how it was done and save her the struggle of trying to get the information out of Sid. But he broke in, 'It's five-past one, Mrs Dunmore. We should have shut the shop five minutes ago.'

She hadn't realised it was that time already. Like the rest of the shops round here, they closed for business between one and two so the staff could eat their dinner. 'Oh, you're five minutes late. You'd better hurry or the meal your mother has laboured over all morning will be cold.' She added with a laugh, 'And then she'll be coming around here, brandishing her rolling pin, to warn me not to let this happen again or else.'

A look flashed into his eyes then but was gone before she could try and work out what it signified. If Rica had had to make a guess, she would have said that it had been a look of regret. Before she could wonder what he had got to be sad about, he was telling her, 'I don't go home for my dinner. I sit in the back and have a cuppa.'

'Oh, I see. You bring sandwiches with you?'

'Er . . . no. No, I don't. I never really get hungry in the day.'

Riva thought it odd for a young man of his age not to be ravenous at all times, let alone a designated mealtime. It took all sorts to make a world though, she thought.

Jason was telling her, 'If it's not raining or too cold I go out for a walk. Mr Fisher goes home for his dinner though. He leaves prompt at one, goes out the back way, and comes back on the dot at two. Would you like me to put the front door on the snib and turn over the sign before I go?'

Rica smiled at him. 'You've already lost over five minutes of your break, I'll see to it.' She would then go and collect Fran and they'd see if they could find a decent cafe nearby where they could have some lunch. There was a modern coffee bar several doors away but she knew Fran wouldn't set foot in the place to have her ears blasted by the latest pop music, let alone to eat the fare they served up of chips and hamburger in a bun with a splat of tomato ketchup on top. It would be a traditionally made sandwich for her sister or nothing.

As Jason disappeared through the door leading to the back, Rica made her way over to the front door. She was halfway there when it suddenly flew open and a man charged in. He was around her age, in his thirties, about five foot ten and handsome in a rugged way. He was wearing a grubby workman's overall and a well-worn donkey jacket, a Bob Dylan cap crammed on top of his dark unruly mop of wavy hair, which he wore fashionably long.

He blurted out in relief, 'Oh, thank goodness you're still open! I felt sure you'd be shut for lunch. I took some lovely shots last night of the sun setting over Burrough Hill in Rutland . . . well, I hope I've captured what I intended but I won't know until I've developed them tonight, only I can't as I've run out of developer.' He paused and an embarrassed expression filled his face. 'You must think I'm an escaped lunatic, talking to you like you work here.' He grinned at her and said jocularly, 'Don't worry, I'm just a simple plumber on his lunch break. Simon getting something for you out the back, is he? I hope he won't mind serving me too before he closes for lunch.'

Rica told him, 'I'm afraid Simon has been called away unexpectedly and it's not clear yet when he'll be back.' She held out her hand to him. 'I'm Erica Dunmore, his wife. I'm afraid you'll have to make do with me.' She just hoped she could help him. Thankfully Jason was still on the premises, though she didn't want to disturb his break. She would try to deal satisfactorily with their customer, a regular one it was obvious to her as he had referred to Simon by name.

He accepted her hand and they shook. 'I'm very pleased to meet you. I'm Bill Simpson.' His dark brown eyes twinkled mischievously. 'Simon can stay away as long as he likes, you're much prettier to look at than he is.'

Rica smiled at his compliment. 'What can I help you with, Mr Simpson?'

'On this visit, just a large bottle of developer. Oh, and I'd better take a pot of Hypam Fixer as I'm not sure if I've enough left for what I'll need tonight.'

She made her way behind the counter to scan the array of sundries the shelves held. All the different items were clearly labelled and priced and she thanked Simon's methodical ways as she quickly found what she was looking for. On the wooden unit at the back of the counter she found brown paper bags to put the purchases in. Once they were bagged up she put them on the counter and told Bill the combined price of two pounds, eleven shillings and sixpence. He handed her three pound notes. The till was the old-fashioned brass type with large lever keys. Rica had never used one before but it was easy to see how it worked. Placing her fingers on the appropriate round keys, she pressed them down hard. As they rose back into place, a bell rang out and the appropriate flags in the glass display strip at the top of the register shot up as, simultaneously, the drawer flew out to punch her hard in her stomach. Rica let out a yelp of shock as she jumped back. Hearing laughter, she spun around to see Bill Simpson in a fit of mirth.

Through his laughter he said to her, 'I'm sorry, I shouldn't be laughing at what happened, but I couldn't help it when it was so funny. Simon always says that till is the bane of his life and he should replace it with a new NCR electronic cash register. A rep keeps calling in, desperate to persuade him to buy one, but Simon just can't seem to part with that old register, for sentimental reasons.'

Rica gave a wan smile. 'His father got this till when he bought the shop in the thirties. It was part of the fixtures and fittings, and he reckoned it was his good luck charm as the shop prospered right from the off. It was nothing to do with this till, of course. Simon's father was a damned good photographer, and nothing was too much trouble so far as his customers were concerned. That's why the business prospered. The same reason it's still prospering under Simon . . . he's out of the same mould as Richard was.'

Bill Simpson said, 'I have to agree with you. There is another camera shop nearer to where I live, but the owner can't hold a candle to Simon.'

She thought, Well, let's hope you don't change your mind now I've taken over. As matters stand I can't offer you the same expertise as Richard or Simon did.

Rica turned back to the till, put in the notes and took out the correct change. After she had handed it to the customer and he had picked up his bags of purchases, she followed him to the door. 'Thank you for your custom. Look forward to seeing you again soon, Mr Simpson.'

As he walked through the door he said to her, 'And it will be soon, I'm always in need of something. Ta-ra for now.'

Rica closed the door after him. As she turned over the sign from Open to Closed she saw him running around the back of an old Fort Transit van with 'William Simpson, Plumber' painted in black lettering on the side, along with an address and telephone number. As she walked back into the premises to go and seek out her sister, she was thinking that she hoped all her customers were as nice and as easy to deal with as her first one had been.

In the office Fran was just closing a large ledger and stacking it on top of another of the same size. A proud Rica told her, 'I've just served my first customer and managed not to make a fool of myself. That bloody cash till belongs in a museum, though. It physically attacked me.'

If she was expecting praise from Fran then she was disappointed. 'You did log the sale in the book, to keep the records straight?'

Rica pulled a face. 'I know nothing about a book or even if I'm supposed to log all sales.'

'Didn't the apprentice tell you, when he was informing you what went on in the shop?'

'We never got round to that. He was too busy explaining to me how a camera works.' Rica anxiously gnawed her bottom lip and admitted, 'It sounded like gobbledegook to me. I'm worried I'll never pick enough up to come across as competent in front of the customers.'

Fran looked at her meaningfully, wagged a finger at her and in a severe tone said, 'With that attitude, you're setting yourself up to fail. You have to get to grips with it all – *yesterday* – if you want this business to keep earning you a decent living, and to stand a chance of finding Ricky. Customers will be looking to you for advice and will soon go elsewhere for it if you can't give it to them. Now, get that young lad to explain it to you again and again, until it does sink in. And you pay more attention! Don't forget to log those sales in the book either or the stock will be out when we do a stock take and the ledger won't balance either.'

Rica stiffened. Fran had made her feel like a naughty schoolgirl. She felt like reminding her that she was a grown woman and Fran's elder sister at that, not a young child to be bossed about. But she also knew that Fran was right to be ticking her off. Her attitude did leave a lot to be desired. She needed to stop letting this overwhelm her. Simon had known nothing until his father taught him. Everyone had to start somewhere. It was just that she couldn't take years over gaining this knowledge, or even months, but was going to have to find a way to become competent enough in the customers' eyes in a matter of days, before she lost their custom. To Rica at the moment it sounded like finding a way to achieve the impossible.

'I'll do it immediately we return from lunch,' she said.

Fran looked at her in surprise. 'Is it that time already?' She pushed back her chair and stood up. 'I won't say no to a cup of tea and a sandwich.'

They found an old-fashioned cafe in the same mould as their regular one. It was owned by two genteel elderly ladies, one of whom fussed over them, taking their coats and showing them to a vacant table. They both settled for a pot of tea and mixed sandwiches.

As soon as the fussy old dear had departed, Rica asked her sister a very important question. She hadn't felt it was right to do so back at the shop, in case any of the staff were lurking and could overhear. 'Have you managed to make sense of the books? How is the business looking financially?'

Fran thoughtfully stroked her chin. 'Simon kept meticulous records and did so right up until last Friday afternoon when he emptied the business account of all that was in it. That morning he'd put in orders with suppliers for developing chemicals, film cartridges and flash cubes. Not the actions of a man losing interest in his business and planning to walk away from it, in my opinion.'

Rica's face screwed up in puzzlement. 'You mean, he seems to have left me on impulse? But he wasn't the impulsive kind. Simon always thought long and hard, trying to be as certain as he could that it was the right thing to do before he acted. And he told me everything.' A tear glinted in her eye and there was a choking feeling in her throat when she added, 'At least, I always believed he never made any big decision without involving me, but obviously he couldn't consult me over this one, could he?'

Rica could feel a flood of tears welling up and knew they were in danger of bursting forth. Fran would be mortified if she made such a display of her emotions in a public place, so she snatched a handkerchief out of her handbag and fought to compose herself, taking several deep breaths under pretence of blowing her nose. Thankfully she succeeded in stemming the tears and managed to speak evenly. 'The Simon I knew would never have made such a change in his life, on a whim.'

Fran said matter-of-factly, 'I have to agree that the man I knew him to be wouldn't have, but it appears he has so we have no choice but to accept what the facts are telling us.'

Rica wished Fran would stop telling her to face facts and accept what Simon had done. She was doing her best. She was reminded then that Fran still had not completely answered the question she had put to her. Rica waited while

111

their food was offloaded from a tray and their waitress departed before she said, 'So did you manage to find out how the business is doing or do you need longer to go over the books?'

'I know exactly how the business is doing,' Fran told her. After pouring out their tea, she put the pot down on the table and filled it up with hot water from the jug. 'It's very profitable. Should keep you off the streets. Simon has actually left you in a good position. You have a virtually new car sitting on the drive of your three-bedroomed house, with only a few years left to pay off on the mortgage. You'll still be able to take a holiday abroad every year, should you wish; afford to shop for your clothes at the likes of Lena's Modes; still have best steak for dinner in the middle of the week, and manage to put something aside for a rainy day or your old age, like Simon did. Yes, I'd say it was doing very well indeed for a small business outside the centre of town.'

Although she knew she should have been very relieved to hear this, Rica sighed, heavily looking bothered.

Fran stared at her sharply and snapped, 'Obviously not doing well enough for you, though.'

Rica shot her an annoyed glance. 'You know I was worried that Simon had lost interest. Hearing that he hadn't is a relief . . .'

'So why the long face?'

'The business will only stay profitable so long as it's run properly. Apart from the fact that I'm going to have to come up with a cunning plan to get that old man to divulge the developing side of things, Jason told me that Saturday is always busy, so that means I have only today and tomorrow to become competent enough to convince customers I know what I'm talking about. All the cameras that we keep in stock are different, though, and I doubt even a genius would be able to learn how each of them operates in the short space of time I have, even if I am paying attention as hard as I can to what Jason is telling me. I don't like going into a shop and asking for advice, only to find they've no more idea than I have. I just hope I don't chase customers away by not knowing enough.'

Fran finished her sandwich before she responded. 'My advice is to forget that bigoted old man for the time being and concentrate on learning one thing at a time. We can deal with him later. As far as the cameras are concerned, I think you're getting yourself far too bothered about becoming an expert. I doubt even Simon knew the intricate details of the workings of every camera he kept in stock. He would have had to consult the manuals occasionally. Just apply yourself to learning the basics first, and once that all makes sense the rest will start to. Honesty is always the best policy, remember. If a customer asks you something and you have no idea, tell them your husband has been unexpectedly called away and you've been thrown in at the deep end, but you'll do your best to find out the answer.'

Rica's spirits lifted. She'd been contemplating trying to learn in a very short time . . . a day or so . . . what it had taken Simon years to learn from his father. At least by knowing the basic workings of a simple camera she wouldn't look a complete idiot in front of customers.

She told Fran, 'You're right. I'm trying to run before I can walk. I'll get Jason to explain the basics to me this afternoon.'

Her sister said wryly, 'That's more like the attitude you should be displaying. No more of that "O, woe is me" complaining.'

Rica felt her hackles rising at that. Fran could be so conde-scending sometimes, although she probably didn't mean to be. It was just the way she was born.

Her sister asked, 'Have you requested Mr Pickles to smarten himself up yet?'

'Oh, for goodness' sake, not yet, Fran. He's hardly had time to accept me as his new boss, and I want him to take to me, not see me as Mrs Hitler. I know that to us the suit he wears is on the shabby side, but he's just on an apprentice's wage so maybe he can't afford to splash out on a new one. For all we know he may be saving up for one. I need to pick the right moment to tackle him about that.'

'Hmm, well, getting that lad to smarten himself up and familiarising yourself with the stock are the least of your worries at the moment.'

A chill ran through Rica. 'What do you mean?'

Fran picked up the teapot. 'More tea?'

'Sod the tea, what did you mean by what you just said?'

Fran glared at her. 'I don't appreciate bad language, Rica, you know that.'

'Sod isn't actually a swear word, Fran, it's another word for grass.'

'Not in the way you intended it, it isn't.'

Rica had to admit she was right. 'All right, I apologise for my use of bad language. Now please explain what you meant.'

Fran took a sip of tea before she said, 'Simon kept the appointments book in the office. I checked through it. There are bookings for portrait photographs and family sittings plus a couple of weddings. You could cancel the portrait sittings until you feel confident enough to undertake them yourself. One wedding is for next year, but your immediate problem is the one set for this Saturday.'

Rica looked at her blankly for a moment until the significance of Fran's announcement registered. Her face paled as she exclaimed, 'And that telephone call we caught Jason on was from a firm asking us to take photographs for a brochure. We haven't got a photographer! Oh, Jesus Christ, what am I going to do?'

Fran pulled a peeved face. 'Now you're taking the Lord's

114

name in vain. You should have your mouth washed out with soap and water!'

'And you shouldn't be such a self-righteous prude! It's not like you're a practising Christian yourself,' Rica snapped back at her. Then gnawed her bottom lip anxiously, eyes fearful. 'Fran, those clients will be expecting a professional photographic record of their big day and I don't even know how to take a photo with a Box Brownie! This late on, it's doubtful they'd even get another company to take on a wedding.'

'Maybe Simon had someone he called on to cover for him when he couldn't fulfil a booking, due to illness or whatever. Mr Pickles will surely know.'

A little colour returned to Rica's cheeks. 'I hope that's the case, Fran, I really do, and that they are free to cover the booking. Otherwise ... well, I don't want to think about that. I'll have to hope ... pray ... cross everything ... that Simon did have someone he called on in emergencies.'

'There's another thing. Do you know anything about a Mrs Smith?' Fran asked. 'Only, I've found a wage packet with her name on it in one of the desk drawers.'

Rica looked at Fran blankly for a moment before she remembered. 'Oh, she's the mysterious cleaner Simon told me about the night before he left. He took Mrs Smith on to replace the old dear who died. She worked a week, and then he never saw her again. She didn't even call in to collect her wages. Simon tried to take them to her at the address she'd given him, but when he arrived it turned out she didn't live there, and the person who did had never heard of her. Odd, isn't it?'

Fran gave a dismissive shrug. 'She obviously had her reasons. She probably landed herself a more promising job. Anyway, under the circumstances you should consider doing the cleaning yourself until we know the business can support the extra wage. There's one more thing I think you should consider ...'

115

Rica's eyes filled with alarm. She stopped Fran in mid-flow by putting up her hand and saying, 'Don't you think I've enough on my plate as it is, without you heaping on more?'

Fran looked put out. 'I'll just keep my suggestion to myself then.'

Rica sighed. 'Suggestion? Oh, I thought you were going to drop another bombshell on me. What is this suggestion then?'

'That you should take driving lessons.' Fran could see by the look on her face that Rica couldn't for the life of her think why she was making such a suggestion, so she elaborated. 'You'll be having to make business calls on people who want to discuss hiring your services, and it doesn't look very professional or give the impression that you're running a successful business to turn up on public transport. And you can't very well lug around all the camera equipment you'll need, on and off the bus, and taxis could take a good chunk out of your profits over a year once you start doing the photographic assignments yourself. You've a car sitting idle in your drive, don't forget.'

Rica stared at her thoughtfully. She'd never had cause to consider learning to drive before. Simon had always taken the car to work, and whenever they had gone out together he had driven. She didn't know what she thought about learning to drive. Fran had a point, though, and it was something to which she should give serious consideration. But not right this minute. She had enough to be thinking about already.

Fran was saying to her, 'It's coming up for two so we'd better get back. Doesn't set a good example to the staff if the management are expecting them to operate good time-keeping while they themselves flaunt it.' She summoned over the waitress to ask for the bill.

CHAPTER TEN

A while later Rica replaced the telephone receiver in its cradle. Fran didn't need to ask her the outcome of the call. She had gathered it by hearing Rica's side of the conversation.

'He sounds a nice man,' she said to Fran.

'Sounds like an idiot to me! Who in their right mind climbs a lamp-post to get a close-up shot of Diana Dors as she opens a shop – only to lose his balance and end up with a broken leg, arm, and smashed camera? Plus no photographs to sell to the likes of the *Mercury* or even the nationals. You didn't ask him if he could recommend another photographer to you.'

'He was feeling so sorry for himself, I didn't have the heart.'

Fran tutted disdainfully. 'You're a businesswoman now, sentiment doesn't come into it.'

Rica sank down on the chair by the side of the desk and put her head in her hands. 'Oh, this is so awful, Fran. How am I going to sleep tonight, knowing I've ruined a couple's big day?'

'If anyone is to blame it's Simon. He's the one who's let them down. Look, the sooner you tell this couple – her parents, I should imagine, as it'll be them footing the bill – that we have no choice but to let them down, then the more time they'll have to try and find someone else. Maybe you could soften the blow by offering to do their first child's christening at a reduced price?' She scraped back her chair and stood up. 'I need to pay a call. I won't be a moment. Oh, by the way, the tap in the kitchen is dripping. We'll have to get someone in to fit a new washer. Simon probably had a man he would call in to do jobs such as that. There's a book in the middle drawer of the desk with details of suppliers. Hopefully he kept the details of any tradesmen he used in that. I'll have a look through it when I come back.'

Her words triggered a memory then and Rica exclaimed, 'Oh, Fran, you're a Godsend.' Then she hurriedly added, 'And I mean that in the religious sense.' Ignoring Fran's look of utter bewilderment she asked urgently, 'Have you come across a customers address book?'

She shook her head.

'Oh!' Rica exclaimed, mortally disappointed. 'How do I find out the address of a customer if Simon didn't keep a record?'

Fran was looking at her quizzically. 'Why do you need a customer's address?'

'Because I know one who just might prove to be our knight in shining armour.'

Fran was still none the wiser but told her, 'You could try the order book.' She pointed to it, sitting on top of a pile of papers. 'If the customer you're after has placed an order for anything in the past, their address would be in those details.'

Rica had already grabbed the book and was thumbing through it, saying to herself, 'Come on . . . please let me find him.'

'Just who is this customer?' Fran asked her.

'The one I told you about this morning. My first customer. He bought some developing stuff. I can't quite remember his name. Jack . . . Ben . . . no, Bill . . . it's Bill something. He told me he was a plumber. It was you mentioning the leaking tap that brought him to mind. He seemed an intelligent man . . . well, he's got to be to have his own business. He takes his own photographs and develops them himself. What he bought from us this morning cost him nearly three pounds. So to my mind he's not going to be throwing that kind of money down the drain. He must be quite good at it, mustn't he?'

'Oh, I see where you're heading with this. You're hoping he's good enough to take the wedding photographs.'

Rica stabbed her finger against a name in the book and exclaimed, 'Ah, yes, Bill Simpson, that's him. He bought a new camera at the beginning of the year and Simon had to order it in. The price was fifty-nine pounds. He's not going to be paying that kind of money out for a camera unless he's serious about photography. Oh, there's no telephone number down in the book for him . . . just his address. I'll have to pay him a visit this evening. Fran, keep your fingers crossed that he'll agree to help us out and is free to.'

Never one to keep her opinions to herself, she said, 'Well, I think you're taking one hell of a gamble. Spending a lot on his hobby doesn't mean he's any good at it.'

Rica fixed her eyes on her and said with conviction, 'Well, we've just got to hope he is. Because if he isn't any good it's us that'll be taking them. We've no other choice.'

Fran spent the rest of the afternoon finishing off her inspection of the books, checking and chasing any outstanding orders, paying a couple of bills and dealing with correspondence, using an ancient Remington typewriter that Simon and his father before him had typed on one-fingered.

Rica meanwhile asked Jason to explain to her in idiot's terms the basic principles of how a camera worked, in between serving any customers who came in. She found herself fascinated by his telling her that basically a camera captured the light reflecting off an object for a fraction of

119

a second while the shutter opened and closed. It then hit the film, a strip of plastic coated with emulsion, at the back of the camera, causing a chemical reaction to fix the image, which later became visible when it had been processed with chemicals. He told her the history of how it all began as related to him by Simon. That the word 'camera' meant 'chamber', and was first used by artists as long as four hundred years ago. They had used a cylindrical chamber with a pin hole in it to project an upside-down image of a brightly lit scene on to canvas. The artist would then trace the outline on to the canvas, ready to fill in paint with oils.

As Jason was relaying all this to her, Rica had the opportunity to form an impression of him as a person. From his patient delivery, she felt him to be a sensitive and caring young man, and had no doubt that the two of them were going to work well together. She wished she could feel the same about Sid Fisher. He was making it very obvious he had no intention of building a cordial relationship with his new boss, as from the moment he had disappeared back inside the dark room after their introductory meeting that morning, she hadn't seen hide nor hair of him. Any new film cassettes or canisters that had been brought in by customers were logged, labelled, then left in a box outside the dark room for him to collect, and any processed films were packeted by Fisher himself and left in another box for Jason to collect and file in the drawer awaiting the customer's arrival. At closing time Fisher disappeared via the back door before Jason had turned the sign over from Open to Closed and locked up at the front.

At the moment, though, Fisher's obnoxious behaviour was not of any consequence to Rica; in fact, she was relieved she did not have to deal with him, as long as he did his job, as she had far more serious things on her mind, the most important being finding someone to fulfil the wedding assignment on Saturday.

After a simple dinner of omelette and salad, Rica left Fran clearing away and set off for Bill Simpson's address. As she passed the car in the drive she was reminded of Fran's suggestion she should learn to drive. At that moment it did seem to make sense to her as, had she passed her test, she could have driven the six miles across town to Bill Simpson's house in about fifteen minutes, whereas it was going to take her at least an hour on two buses and the same again when she returned. And now it was beginning to rain.

An hour and a quarter later she found herself outside a neat-looking terraced house with a small well-kept garden at the front. The street wasn't in the best of areas, but there were far worse. She knew she had the right address as the white Transit van she had seen Bill Simpson get into as she was locking up at lunchtime was parked outside. At least he was home and she wouldn't have to hang around waiting for him. Rica opened the front gate and made her way up the short tiled path to rap purposefully on the front door.

It was opened by a blonde-haired, reasonably attractive woman in probably her late-thirties. She had a curvaceous figure beneath a pair of brown slacks worn with a tucked-in white blouse and a thick black belt. She looked a little agitated. Rica could hear the sound of a television and the strains of the Z Cars theme tune heralding the start of the programme. She guessed her arrival had disturbed the woman's viewing and that was what was causing her irritation.

'Yes?' she said shortly.

Rica smiled at her. 'Is it possible to have a word with Mr Simpson, please?'

'About a plumbing job?'

'No, I'm Erica Dunmore from Dunmore Photography. Mr Simpson is one of our customers. I have a proposition I'd like to put to him.'

The woman frowned quizzically. 'What proposition?'

Rica wasn't happy about discussing what she'd come to say on the doorstep with the man's wife. She wasn't sure how Bill Simpson would feel about that either. Ignoring the question she asked, 'Is it possible to have a word with Mr Simpson, please?'

The woman snorted indignantly, obviously displeased that Rica was not prepared to divulge to her what she had come to see her husband about. 'He was just off up to his dark room when you knocked. He might as well live in that dark room, considering the amount of time he spends in there. Since he got hooked on photography a few years back, I hardly see him. Neither will you if the door is shut as it means he's started developing and can't be disturbed. It could be hours before he comes out again.'

Just then the pounding of footsteps was heard on the stairs. Mrs Simpson turned around and said, 'There's a woman here to see you.'

Bill was heard to say, 'Oh, I hope it's not an emergency plumbing job . . . I really want to see how the photos I took last night turned out. I was just about to start when I realised I'd left one of my pans down here after washing it.'

Then he appeared at the side of his wife, smiled at Rica and said to her, 'What can I do for you, love?' Recognition struck. 'Oh, it's Mrs Dunmore, isn't it?' He frowned at her quizzically. 'What brings you here then?'

It was his wife who answered him. 'She's got a proposition for you.'

'A proposition? Oh.' He addressed his wife. 'Why haven't you asked Mrs Dunmore to come in, Freda?' He stepped aside, pulling his wife with him, to allow room for Rica to enter. He led her down the hall and into a room at the back, which they obviously used as their main family room. There was a comfortable-looking brown and cream checked moquette suite with, in Rica's view, old-fashioned embroidered antimacassars on the arms and backs, placed around a fifties-style tiled fireplace. A welcoming fire was burning in the grate.

On the mantle sat a jumble of knick-knacks obviously accumulated from trips to the seaside over the years. Above the fireplace hung a framed print of the 'Exotic Lady' by Ken Bates. A half-moon red hearth rug lay on top of a fitted carpet with a blue background covered in red swirls.

Behind the armchair to the left of the fireplace stood a standard lamp, its fringed shade a pale gold colour; by the side of the chair lay a folded newspaper. This was obviously the chair Bill sat in. In the middle of the room stood a glass-topped coffee table with a tropical beach scene painted on the surface under the glass. Against the wall by the kitchen door stood an oak dresser crammed full with all manner of bits and pieces, including several framed photographs of two children taken over a period of time as they were growing up. Against the side wall stood an oak gate-legged table and four matching chairs. There was a door at the back leading into the kitchen. The room had a homely feel to it, though Rica could sense the tension crackling between husband and wife.

Bill was asking her to sit down, which she did on the sofa, but when his wife was about to take her own armchair, he said to her, 'Aren't you going to offer our guest a cup of tea, Freda?'

She wasn't happy about being asked to leave. Her nostrils flared and she said tightly to Rica, 'Tea or coffee?'

Rica smiled back at her. 'Tea, please.'

'Milk and sugar?'

'Yes, please.'

She left the room to go into the kitchen.

Bill said, 'So, Mrs Dunmore, just what is this proposition you have for me?'

Out of the corner of her eye Rica could see Freda Simpson hovering by the door, pretending to be doing something though it was obvious she was listening to what was being said.

'I told you that my husband had been called away unexpectedly and it's not clear yet when he'll be back. His uncle has fallen ill and Simon is taking care of his business while I take care of ours. I found out this afternoon that we have an assignment on Saturday, to take the photographs for a wedding. Simon does have a man who covers for him in emergencies but he's out of commission at the moment.' She told Bill the story, and although he didn't laugh out loud, she could see he was amused by the tale.

'We photographers will go to any lengths to get a good shot. I ended up in a river once, trying to get one of a kingfisher as it flew off a branch. All I got was a ruined camera and a soaking for my trouble Anyway, why don't you take the wedding photographs yourself?' he asked her.

Rica chuckled. 'I have never taken a photograph in my life, Mr Simpson. I'd probably chop their heads off or they'd all be out of focus.'

He looked at her meaningfully. 'So that's the proposition you've come to put to me?'

She nodded. 'Would you please consider it? It's doubtful the couple would get another photographer this late in the day. I hate the thought of their happy day being ruined by us. I know it's an imposition, and of course I'd pay you. Whatever fee Simon was going to charge will be yours, less our costs for the films and whatever else we need to provide.'

Bill's wife virtually dived back into the room then and declared to her husband, 'You could use the money to put towards that special surprise for me you said you were saving up for.'

He shot her a look of reproof and said, very quietly, 'Freda, Mrs Dunmore hasn't come here to hear our business. Is that the kettle I hear boiling?' She shot him a tight look before disappearing back into the kitchen. Bill then turned his attention to Rica. 'I've taken shots at family gatherings but it's debatable whether they'd stand up to anything a professional like Simon would produce. It's landscape photography I specialise in, but I don't consider myself anywhere near professional standard.'

She looked at him pleadingly. 'Look, Mr Simpson . . .'

'Bill, please.'

'Look, Bill, this is going to come out all wrong but I can't think of a better way to put it. Any photographs of a couple's wedding day are better than none at all.'

She expected him to be mortally offended by her telling him that he was better than nothing, but to her surprise he started to laugh. 'Well, when you put it like that, how can I refuse?'

'You'll do it!' she exclaimed.

'I'll be happy to help you out but please understand that I won't expect any payment. Be my way of paying Simon back for all the encouragement and advice he's given me over the years I've been a customer. But I think you'd better have a look at some of my handiwork before we seal the deal. Once you see that, you might change your mind and decide that no photographs are better after all. I'll go and fetch some examples for you to look at.'

He got up and went off into the hall, heading for the stairs. He'd hardly been gone a second when his wife scurried in carrying a tray with three cups of tea on it. She placed it down on the coffee table and, her voice low, asked Rica as she handed her a cup of tea, 'So how much will Bill be getting for the job? I mean, it's a professional job you're asking him to do so he can expect a decent amount, can't he? A good few quid.'

Rica accepted the cup. 'Thank you,' she said politely. She felt that it was only right Bill should decide whether he told his wife or not what money he would receive. She fought for something to say to change the subject and found it when her eyes fell on the photographs on the dresser. She asked Freda, 'Are those your children? They are a good-looking pair.'

She looked irritated that Rica had not answered her question and snapped, 'Yes, they are. Paula and Kevin. So what will Bill . . .'

Rica cut her short. 'You must have been pleased to get one of each. How old are they now?'

She snapped, 'Kevin is twenty. Paula is eighteen. So what can Bill expect . . .'

Rica was looking at her in shock. 'My goodness, but you don't look old enough to have a twenty-year-old son.'

The compliment threw Freda. Looking coy, she patted her hair. 'Well, Bill and I were young when we married. I was only eighteen when I had Kevin. He's married himself now and they've a baby on the way, so I'll be a granny in a few months.'

'When you're out with the baby, people will think it's you that's its mother.'

She patted her hair again, looking pleased with herself. 'Well, I do try and take care of myself. I swear by Pond's Cold Cream. So, you were going to tell me . . .'

This time she was stopped in her tracks by Bill returning with a pile of photographs in his hands. Sitting down, he said to Freda, 'Thanks for the tea, love.' Then he said to Rica, 'Well, let me know what you make of these.' He spread the photos on the table between the tea things.

She put down her still half-filled cup on the tray and leaned over to study the dozen or so prints. All of them were in black-and-white, and the images were very clear and sharp. These obviously hadn't been taken with a cheap instamatic. They were mostly scenic views but amongst them were a couple of group shots. She was no expert but she knew a good photograph from a bad one. These were good. The scenic shots were as good as any Simon had taken. The two group pictures were what really caught her attention, though. These were far from the usual stiff rows of grim-faced individuals. The two shots had been taken of people who were unaware they were being photographed, so were acting naturally. They were busy pictures, the sort that could be looked at time and time again, and each time something new would be spotted that hadn't been noticed before.

The first picture had been taken from a doorway looking into the back room of a house. In the background, against the far wall, stood a table groaning under a display of food. Several people were filling their plates. Differently patterned tablecloths covered the table, reaching down nearly to the floor, and where they overlapped in the middle a mischievous young face was peeping out. At one side of the table two very old ladies, dressed from head to toe in black, capacious handbags clutched on their knees, their hair encased in nets, were sitting on straight-backed chairs gossiping together. One was wagging a finger at the other and had an *I told you so* look on her wrinkled face. At the other side of the buffet table was a smaller one on which stood a barrel of beer and several bottles of pale ale, port and sherry, together with a stack of beer glasses and several short glasses.

In the middle of the room a group of four men wearing suits, two with their jackets off and shirt sleeves rolled up, stood deep in conversation, more than likely about football. Each had a glass of beer in one hand, cigarette in the other. A cloud of smoke swirled above them. To the side of the men stood a group of women, dressed in their best frocks, two holding cups of tea, the others holding small glasses containing, she guessed, either port or sherry. One was obviously telling the others a humorous story as the other women's attention was focused on her and they were all laughing. In the foreground, only visible from the chest up and in profile, a man and woman in their early-twenties had their heads close together. They were obviously very much in love from the way they were looking at each other, it being apparent that at that moment no one else in the crowded room existed for them.

Rica stared at them transfixed. Pain stabbed her to the heart. She felt tears start to prick her eyes. That couple could have been herself and Simon at the same age. They used to look at each other then just like this young couple were. As far as she was concerned, she still had looked at Simon that way until the last time she had seen him. When had he stopped looking at her with love in his eyes? More importantly, how come she hadn't noticed?

She felt Bill's eyes on her and feared that he would ask her if something was the matter, then she'd not be able to control her emotions and would break down in front of him and his wife. It took her an effort of will to move her eyes off the happy couple and on to the second group photograph.

This one had obviously been taken much later that evening. The table now held only scraps of food, empty plates, glasses and dishes. The barrel was still on the small table at the side and had an empty look about it. All the glasses had gone and the bottles were drained. The two old dears were still sitting on chairs at the other side of the table, but one had fallen asleep, still clutching her handbag on her knee, and it was possible to see that the top half of her set of false teeth had slipped down in her mouth, making her look goofy. The other old dear was cradling a sleeping child on her knee . . . it looked to Rica like the one whose face had been peeping out through the tablecloths in the previous photograph. In the foreground all the men and women were now dancing, clinging together as if holding each other up, obviously the worse for drink. The young couple were not in the shot. Maybe they had sneaked off to a secluded place for a kiss and a cuddle.

Both photographs were so atmospheric Rica felt she could

actually hear the music in the background, the buzz of conversation, smell the cigarette smoke. She was no expert but it was glaringly obvious to her that Bill had a real eye for taking a shot that would capture the moment and the viewer's imagination. Simon possessed the same talent but tended to go for the more formal, posed approach, his philosophy being that if it was working well, why take risks and change things? But to Rica's mind, if she was having a special event captured for all time, she would want some of Bill's type of photograph as well as the more usual, specially posed sort.

'These photographs are . . . well, they're just captivating, Bill,' she told him.

He looked uncomfortable. It was apparent he found it difficult to accept praise for his work. 'Oh, do you think so?'

'I'm no expert, but I certainly do. I'm surprised Simon didn't suggest you try and sell some of them.'

'Well, actually, he did. He was always telling me I should send samples of my work to card manufacturers, especially the snow scenes, for them to use for Christmas cards. Calendar makers too.'

'Why haven't you then?'

He gave a shrug. 'I just haven't got around to it. I might pluck up courage one day.'

She didn't think he hadn't got round to it. It was more than likely that he wasn't confident that his photographic skills were of a professional standard, despite Simon telling him they were. 'Well, I think you should make that one day soon,' she urged him.

Freda was keenly listening to the conversation. Her eyes were alight and she exclaimed, 'Are you saying that Bill could make some real money from this photography lark?'

He shot her a hurt look. 'Freda, my photography is not a lark. You know how much enjoyment I get from it.'

129

She snapped back, 'Are you not listening to Mrs Dunmore, Bill? You could make money out of it. If you made enough we could . . .'

He cut her short in a meaningful tone. 'Freda, could I please finish my conversation with Mrs Dunmore? She doesn't want to hear us having a barney about money, now does she?' He flashed Rica an apologetic look before he took a deep breath and said to her, 'I'm not sure about this. I'm still not convinced I'm qualified, but I can see you're stuck so I'll take on the assignment for you. As I haven't tackled anything like this before, I think it would be a good idea for me to drop by the shop tomorrow between jobs, take a look at the sample books you show potential customers and get a feel for how Simon goes about it. I can also get all the details of the job from you then.'

Rica felt so relieved that Bill had agreed to take on the assignment. He might be nervous about it but her gut instincts were telling her that the end results would be well worth paying for. The tension between husband and wife was making her feel uncomfortable, though, so it was time she left.

Rica picked up her handbag and stood up. 'I've taken up enough of your evening. I'll see you tomorrow, Bill.' She turned to address Freda then, who was sitting stiffly in her chair, a tight expression on her face. 'It was very nice to meet you, Mrs Simpson. Thank you for the tea.'

Rica was extremely tired by the time she got home at just before ten o'clock. The only sound in the house was of classical music playing on the radiogram. Rica had no idea who the composer was but to her it sounded very dull and dreary, and the volume was turned down low so that it was just background noise. As she walked into the lounge Fran looked up from the book she was reading. Rica wasn't surprised to see it was the Victorian novel *Vanity Fair*, very apt considering Fran was so Victorian in her attitudes and would have been far better suited to those times than the 1960s.

Fran was about to ask her sister how she had got on, but thinking of her mother made Rica stop her by exclaiming in horror, 'Oh, Fran, how could I have?'

She frowned in bemusement as she closed the book and laid it in her lap. 'How could you have what?'

Rica sank down in her own armchair as she explained, 'Forgotten to visit Mother yesterday . . . Wednesday. How could I have forgotten something so important?'

Fran eyed her incredulously. 'Well, it's not like you had nothing else on your mind. And it's not like Mother is going to notice, is it?'

'That's not the point, Fran. I go because I want to know how she is . . . if she is in need of anything. We've had this discussion and I know your feelings on the matter, but we have no evidence that people who are suffering from Mother's condition are unaware of what's going on around them. It may just be that they can't show us they are. If that is the case, then the last thing I want is Mother thinking neither of us care for her.'

Fran gave a disdainful tut. 'I don't live in a fantasy world, Rica, but if you want to then that's up to you. The specialist told me that Mother isn't aware of who she is, let alone anything else, and I'm not going to question a man who's devoted his life to studying the human mind. You've never before missed a visit in all the two years Mother has been in the home, so once is quite forgivable, especially in these circumstances. Wednesday is half-day closing at the shop so you can still visit then like you've always done. So, was tonight's trip worthwhile?'

Rica told her that in her opinion it had been, and why.

'Well, let's hope this Bill person is as good as you claim he is and the business doesn't suffer.'

The music playing in the background really was proving

depressing to Rica. She had to stop herself getting up to change it for something more uplifting, or even put the television on for some light entertainment, but out of respect for her sister she couldn't bring herself to. Neither was she in the frame of mind to deal with Fran's disapproval of what she perceived were Rica's uncultured ways. She hoped this wasn't going to be the pattern of their evenings together while her sister was staying with her: both of them quietly reading with what was to Rica dirge-like music playing in the background. She could never see her spirits lifting in such a depressing atmosphere.

It was best for both of them that Fran should go home.

Rica firmed up in her mind how she would tackle it. The last thing she wanted was to hurt her sister's feelings. Then she took a deep breath and said, 'Fran, I want you to know how much I appreciate what you have done for me . . . are doing for me . . . but I'm feeling guilty now for keeping you away from your own home. I can manage on my own.'

Her sister responded blandly, 'I prefer to be the judge of that. I told you, I'm not leaving you until I'm satisfied you're coping. There's no need for you to feel any guilt; it's my choice to do what I'm doing. You have made great strides forward today. In another fortnight or so, if you continue like this, I shall be convinced I will never again find you in the situation I did.'

Rica knew she should be grateful for Fran's intervention, not feel resentful about it. She had no doubt she would still be locked inside this house, wallowing in self-pity, had she not. She was reminded then of her own promise to herself to give her sister a big hug, to show her how grateful she was, but she knew that would make Fran uneasy. Rica was going to have to find another way of thanking her difficult-to-please sister. Just what could she do for her that she would appreciate and accept in good grace?

Rica sat and pondered the problem for a while before an

idea began to take form. There was something that she knew Fran craved more than anything in the world. If Rica handled it right, she might be able to bring it about. She needed to make a plan, but she was too tired tonight and in truth had enough on her mind for now. But as soon as she did have the time and the strength available, she would put her mind to it. If she did pull off what she had in mind, Fran could never know that it was her behind it, so she would never know this was Rica's way of thanking her. Only Rica herself would.

Fran had picked up her book, put it on the arm of the chair and stood up. 'You've had a lot of excitement today, you look worn out. Why don't you go and have a hot bath and get into bed? I'll make us both a cup of hot chocolate.'

Rica inwardly groaned. Fran's suggestion was not open to negotiation. It was bath and bed for her. She resisted the urge to tell her sister to stop treating her like a little girl, but Fran was right. Rica was feeling dead on her feet and bed was the best place for her. She needed to be refreshed and fully alert for what she faced tomorrow.

The hot bath and cup of hot chocolate would normally have had her asleep moments after her head had touched the pillow, but tonight sleep would not come. Rica felt so lonely and lost in this big double bed. Now she was on her own in the darkness, all the pain and heartache that she had managed to contain for the best part of the day came flooding back to her and miserable tears began to flow, to roll down the sides of her face, soaking her pillow. How she wished she could hate Simon for what he had done to her, wish him ill, but she still could not accept that the man she had known and loved would do what he had to her. She knew she would have to, though, or she was never going to heal her wounds, never going to be able to trust another man again . . .

CHAPTER ELEVEN

When dinnertime came and went and there had been no sign of Bill a niggle of anxiety started to gnaw away at Rica. As the afternoon wore on and there was still no sign, the niggle turned to outright worry. He hadn't seemed at all the kind of man to make a promise and let her down. There was only one course of action open to her now, it seemed. She would have to take the photographs herself. She didn't as yet know how to operate the complicated Pentax Spotmatic camera Simon used for such jobs. Thankfully Jason did. She would have to get him to show her tomorrow. She could only hope they were not inundated with customers and she'd have time to learn enough to look professional, even if she was far from it, and produce some decent photographs.

Jason had gone through to the dark room to empty the box of the last of the films Sid Fisher had developed that afternoon and put them in the drawer for customer collection. Rica hadn't seen Sid all day and, quite honestly, was glad that she hadn't had to deal with his contemptuous manner towards her. As long as he did his job, she didn't care whether she never saw him again. Fran had, though. It was payday today and she had told Rica that if the man wanted his wages then he could come to the office and ask her nicely for them, because if he thought she was going to put them in the box of films outside his door then he had grossly misjudged her.

He had left it until twenty minutes past five before he had gone to the office and off-handedly demanded his pay, adding that Mr Dunmore had always made sure the staff had their wages at dinnertime. Fran had reminded him that she was not Mr Dunmore and told him he could have had his pay at dinnertime if he'd come to collect it instead of waiting for her to take it to him. Fran later said that photography wasn't of any interest to her normally but that she wished she'd had a camera to hand, to capture the expression on his face when he realised that a woman had got the better of him. Rica felt no guilt at all for being pleased by this small victory Fran had won over him, and hoped that he'd begun to realise that his surly attitude was having no effect on the new regime; was in fact only serving to make his own life more difficult.

Jason came back in with a pile of processed films in his hand and asked her, 'Is it all right if I put these away tomorrow, Mrs Dunmore? Only it's Friday night and I need to get home promptly.'

Despite her own overpowering worry she managed to smile at him. 'To get ready for a date tonight?'

It seemed to her that a look of sadness flashed into his eyes again before he shook his head and said, 'No. It's just that I have to meet my dad at six.'

'Oh, meeting him for a pint after work? That's nice, that you get on with your father so well.'

He didn't smile at the thought, but confirmed, 'So it's all right if I go then?'

'Yes, of course. Go out the front way and I'll lock up after you.'

After pushing down the snib on the Yale lock and turning the key in the lower one, she was making her way back to the counter to empty the till when she jumped at an unexpected urgent knocking on the front door. She spun around to see a face pressed up against the glass between the sign and several advertising stickers. Rica's spirits soared. It was

135

Bill. She had never been so overjoyed to see someone in all her life.

She dashed to the door and unlocked it, pulling it open and exclaiming, 'I thought you'd changed your mind.'

'I'd never renege on a deal without even having the courtesy to tell you.' He walked into the shop and she shut and locked the door behind him while he continued, 'I was all set to call in just before dinnertime in between jobs. I'd had a few small ones in the rundown area around Narborough Road, where the old terraced houses are in the process of being demolished – and not before time in my opinion. I'd just finished re-lagging a pipe for an old lady and forcing down what felt like the hundredth cup of tea she insisted I had while I was working when her neighbour came in and told me a young lad was urgently trying to find me. His mother had a burst pipe and water was pouring into her kitchen.

'I dashed around there – and what a pantomime! I've been in some dire houses in my time but this . . . well, I was risking my health, it was so filthy.

'I couldn't do anything about the burst pipe until I'd got permission from the landlord, else there was a chance that when I handed in the bill he'd say he never authorised me to do the work so wasn't at liberty to pay me. Thankfully the jobs I had lined up for this afternoon weren't anything that couldn't wait. Anyway, another hour had passed by the time the landlord's agent had been located on his rent round and then he had to go off to get me permission to carry out the work. Then I hadn't got the length of pipe I needed on the van so had to go off to the wholesaler's to get it. And all the time I was conscious of my promise to you and getting increasingly anxious as time wore on. Oh, you will excuse the state of me, won't you? I would have gone home to wash and change but I didn't have time.'

Rica had been enthralled by his story and hadn't noticed

the state of him. Only his remarking upon it made her notice. Bill's face was streaked with dirt, his overalls were stained with grease, and a nasty smell was coming off him. She didn't care what he looked or smelled like, though. He was here and still going to do the assignment tomorrow, and that was all that mattered to her.

She went behind the counter to collect two large portfolios of photographs to show Bill what sort of shots the bride and groom would be expecting as a record of their day. The fifty or so sample photographs were of several different weddings but all seemed to follow the same pattern: the bride going into church on the arm of her father, then the couple signing the register after the wedding and later standing on the church steps as they were leaving, along with the customary line-up of the bride with her bridesmaids, the groom with his best man and ushers, and various family groups before a shot of the wedding party all together. Bill hadn't made any comment as he had flipped through the albums and Rica politely didn't disturb him meanwhile, but as he was nearing the last few pages of the second album she couldn't contain herself any longer. She needed to know that he felt comfortable that he could achieve what the bride and groom would be expecting.

'Will you be able to handle it?' she asked him. Then hurriedly added, 'Not that I doubt your skill, after those stunning shots I saw last night.'

He closed the album and turned his attention to her. 'I can't say the job excites me. The thought of all the patience required to get everyone in place, then hope they keep still for a moment or two so the shot isn't blurred, is a bit daunting. But it'll be an experience for me.'

Rica heaved a sigh of relief to hear him say this. 'Well, maybe I can suggest a way to make the job a little more interesting to you.'

He eyed her enquiringly. 'How?'

'Well, those two photographs you showed me last night, where you'd captured everyone unaware. I wondered if you'd like to take a few like that during the wedding?'

He smiled, nodded and said enthusiastically, 'I'll do my best.'

Rica looked pleased he had agreed. She felt sure the bride and groom would be thrilled when they saw the extra trouble they had gone to, to capture the essence of their day. She had already written down the details of the job for Bill. All that remained was to hand him the case containing the camera, the rolls of film and the tripod to rest the camera on when he was taking the stills.

Automatically he opened the case, just to check that everything he would need was in there, nothing missing. His eyes gleamed when he saw the camera. He picked it up like a precious antique, carefully easing it out of the moulded slot in its case, and held it lovingly in his hands. 'What I'd give to be able to afford a camera like this! In my opinion, this is the bee's knees. It's got a centre-weighted meter to give better photos across the spectrum, and it's easy to set the shutter speed and focus. It has its own built-in light meter, too, so it's easy to operate where other models are fiddly and time-consuming. If the light changes . . .'

He abruptly stopped his flow when he realised that Rica was looking at him with an expression on her face that told him she hadn't got a clue what he was talking about. 'I'm sorry, I got carried away. I will take very great care of this equipment, please rest assured of that.'

Rica smiled at him. 'I'm in no doubt of it.' She eyed him thoughtfully. She needed to address her own lack of photography skills as a matter of urgency as she couldn't expect Bill to keep coming to her rescue or afford to pay a professional photographer his going rate to cover all their future portrait and wedding bookings. As she had been listening to him, the answer to her problem became clear. She just hoped he was willing to come to her aid . . . yet again.

Rica asked him, 'How long did it take you to master the art of taking a passable photograph, Bill? My sister says all there is to it is to point the camera at the object you want to capture, and press the shutter. But I think there's a bit more to it than that, from what I've gathered already in the couple of days I've been in the shop.'

He chuckled. 'Well, yes, there is a little more to it than just that, but it is the basic principle.' He then looked thoughtfully at her for a moment before he said, 'It's difficult to set a time limit on how long it takes to produce a decent photograph. I suppose it depends on the individual and what sort of eye they have for an interesting image. Also it depends on individual tastes, doesn't it? I mean, for me looking at landscape and wildlife photographs takes my mind off into the open spaces and out of this concrete jungle I'm really living in. My wife hates the countryside and isn't an animal lover, so photographs of those topics do nothing for her at all. She can spend hours looking at ones with family and friends, though. Even after the several years I've been at it now, I'm never completely happy with any photo I've taken. Always feel I could have done better. It took me a couple of years of snapping away to feel my efforts were good enough to show to anyone.'

'A couple of years? Oh! That long.' This was worrying news to Rica. She needed to be taking quality photographs that people would pay for, not in years or months even but in a few weeks maximum – that is, if the business could stand the loss of income even that long.

Bill couldn't understand why she seemed so upset. He shrugged. 'Well, I suppose it depends on the individual and how serious they are. It's like anything else, some people pick things up quicker than others. I wasn't serious about it when I first started, only taking a few snaps here and there when I was out walking on a Sunday morning. Then the bug got me and I started to take it more seriously. And, I have to say, it makes a big difference what camera you have. I only had an ancient Box Brownie when I started.'

Rica's spirits lifted slightly. She was fortunate that at her disposal she had one of the best cameras on the market, according to Jason. She had to hope that, because she was serious about learning, she would pick it up quickly. She had to, there were no two ways about that. She suddenly found herself intrigued as to how Bill first came to take up photography as a hobby, so she asked him.

'Well, it all began when I found my Box Brownie a few years back, in an old junk shop. The owner was only asking pennies for it. I was actually on the lookout for a sink for a customer who couldn't afford a new one when the camera caught my eye. It was all dusty and scuffed, tucked on a shelf behind other old items that looked like they'd been there for ever. On a Sunday morning then I'd take the kids for a walk along the canal bank near where I live while Freda cooked the dinner. She liked to get us all out from under her feet so she could get on with it without us all mithering her.

'My dad is a keen fisherman and, weather permitting, can usually be found in one of a couple of favourite spots. We'd find him and then me and the kids would have a catch up with him and a cup of tea out of his flask before we headed back. During the walks I'd often spot something that caught my attention: a lovely view through some trees on the opposite bank that I hadn't noticed before, a family of moorhens gliding through the water. Sometimes I'd even be lucky enough to see swans, that sort of thing. Although my wife is indifferent to the countryside I'd still try and describe what I'd seen to her when I got home, and as I stood in that junk shop with the camera in my hands I suddenly thought that with a photograph she could see for herself, instead of just trying to imagine it from my description.'

What a thoughtful man, Rica decided. 'Who taught you to use the camera?'

'A village idiot could use a Box Brownie, they're so simple. The first lot of photos I took were an utter waste of my time and the price of the film and getting them developed because I exposed the film to the light while I was trying to put it in. Of course, with these new instamatic cameras where the film comes in a cassette, you don't get that problem any longer. The second lot I took were a waste of time and money as well, as I took every one facing the sun so most of each photograph was obliterated by a huge white splat in the middle. All I can say is that I learned quickly from my mistakes.

'As I got more into it, I would study books of photographs and try and work out what made them special enough to be published. Mine weren't worthy of the paper they were printed on as yet. Gradually I improved enough to let a friend have a look at them, but it did take me a while to consult a professional like Simon. I wanted to start developing my own photographs because it was proving so expensive to keep having them done for me by professionals.'

Or was that because his wife had started to complain about the money he was squandering on his hobby? Rica thought.

'I had no idea how to go about developing. Then one day, as fate would have it, I was plumbing in a new sink for a customer and got talking to him. It transpired that the room I was working in was going to be his dark room as he was a keen amateur photographer. I told him I too was a keen amateur and wanted to learn how to develop my films myself. He offered to show me. The upshot was that I went around to his house a couple of nights a week and he took me through the process. He was the friend I mentioned, the first person I showed my work to. I kept in touch with Gerald until he died last year. His wife, bless her heart, gave me all his developing equipment as a memento of him.'

There was a hopeful look in Rica's eyes when she said to him, 'So really it didn't take you as long as you made out to take a decent photograph . . . just two years to have the confidence in yourself to show your work to the likes of my husband?'

Bill eyed her. 'Maybe I'm getting the wrong end of the stick, but why does it seem to me that you are desperate for me to tell you that it's possible to become a professional photographer virtually overnight?'

She took a deep breath and told him, 'Because I need to.'

His frown deepened. 'Need to?'

'Yes, if I'm to keep this business profitable enough to support me and my son, and pay the staff wages. And I need to find a photographer who's willing to teach me.' She looked at him pleadingly. 'You wouldn't consider it, would you?'

Alarm filled his face and he blurted out, 'What! Oh, I'm not sure I'm qualified to teach anyone . . . I'm just an amateur.' He looked at her quizzically. 'Look, I don't mean to pry, but just how sick is Simon's uncle if you're worried the business is going to suffer?'

She gulped, avoiding his eyes, not liking the fact that she was lying to him. 'I don't know. Very sick. Simon is very fond of him and won't leave until he's on his feet again.'

'Well, he'd *have* to be very fond of him, to leave you with the worry of keeping the business afloat when you're not experienced in this line of work.' Bill looked at her for a moment before he said, 'Why don't you come with me tomorrow? I'm a great believer in hands-on learning and, you never know, you might pick up something from watching me. Then you won't be such a complete novice when I try and help you take your own photographs.'

Rica's eyes lit up. She was so delighted he was agreeing to help her, she had to stop herself from rushing over and giving him a hug. 'Oh, Bill, thank you so much! I'd really like to come with you tomorrow. I'm sure Jason will be fine on his own. I know Simon has trusted him before now to lock up. Shall I meet you at the church? The service starts at three, so shall we say two-thirty?'

'Two-fifteen to be on the safe side, make sure we're set up and ready to go when the guests start arriving.'

'Two-fifteen it is then. And thank you again, Bill. I expect you'll be wanting to rush off home now as your wife will have your tea ready.'

'Well, actually, she'll be waiting for me to bring it home with me. Friday is fish and chip night and it's my job to collect them.' He picked up the case of camera equipment and smiled at her, saying, 'I'll see you tomorrow then.'

Rica had just locked up after him when she heard the door leading into the back open and, with a sense of shock, saw Fran walk through into the shop. Rica had completely forgotten she was still here, waiting for her to hand her the day's takings so she could tally up then put the money in the safe along with the rest that had accumulated during the week. Tomorrow's would then be added and the proceeds banked on Monday morning.

'Fran, I'm sorry. I was so relieved that Bill had finally arrived it slipped my mind you were waiting for me to bring the takings through.'

'I did actually come to fetch them about twenty to six. I'd just opened the door to come in when I saw you with your plumber photographer.' Fran pulled a face here, to indicate what she thought of that particular combination of skills. 'I didn't want to disturb you as you were deep in conversation so I went back to the office and kept myself busy while I waited. Now give me the takings. I'll put them in the safe and deal with them tomorrow morning. I don't know about you but I'm ready for my dinner.'

CHAPTER TWELVE

Bill was looking extremely nervous as he watched Rica work her way through the fifty or so photographs he had taken the week before and developed himself. He had called her on Friday to say that unless he had a dire emergency he would drop in at Saturday dinnertime to show her the results. Rica had asked Fran to bring her back a sandwich when she had gone out for her lunch and, after locking up, had sat in one of the armchairs by the old fireplace to thumb through a magazine while she waited for Bill. She was anxious to view the photographs herself, but even more anxious that the bride and groom should be delighted with them.

A while later Rica finally put the last of the photographs on the pile with the others and Bill tentatively asked, 'What do you think then?'

She turned her head and looked at him. 'What do I think! Bill, words cannot describe what I'm thinking right now.'

His face fell. 'Oh! Look, I'm so sorry . . .'

'Sorry?' she interjected. 'Why should you be sorry for what I've just looked at? You have done an excellent job. You really do undersell yourself and are wrong to. The formal line-ups are as good as Simon would have taken, but it's the candid snaps where no one was aware they were being photographed that really stand out for me. The one with the bride and groom stealing a kiss . . . the mother of the bride laughing with the father of the groom . . . the two little bridesmaids sitting in the corner eating cake. My favourite is the one of the little boy stealing a sip of his mother's wine when she's busy talking to the woman sitting next to her. You can actually see the naughty twinkle in his eye. You really are clever, Bill. I have no doubt the bride and groom are going to be delighted with the extras we've done for them.'

The relief he felt was written all over his face.

Rica told him, 'I asked my sister to check through the original order and find out how much Simon agreed to do the job for. It was twenty-one pounds, which included the cost of the films and the sample prints for everyone to choose which they want copies of.'

He eyed her resolutely. 'If this is leading towards you insisting I take payment for the job, then I already told you – I was happy to help you out.'

'You might have insisted on that, Bill, but I never agreed. You more than deserve paying for what you did. Not just for these wonderful photographs but because I learned such a lot from watching you on Saturday and all that you explained to me as you were doing it. You're saving to take your wife on holiday, aren't you? I hope the money goes some way towards that.' She saw his mouth open in protest but stopped him by raising her hand and telling him, 'I won't discuss this matter any further. Your share is thirteen pounds, four shillings and sevenpence.' She reached into her pocket and pulled out a bulky brown envelope. 'I had my sister make it up ready for you when you telephoned yesterday to say you'd be in with the prints for me to see.' She held it out for him to take but Bill made no move. She then noticed the shocked expression on his face and frowned worriedly. 'Oh, were you expecting more?'

He exclaimed, 'More!' and vehemently shook his head. 'I wasn't expecting anything as you already know. I'm just shocked by how much a professional photographer can earn in one afternoon . . . of course there was the work afterwards developing the films, but even so it's not to be sneezed at. It would take me a good twenty hours to make that sort of profit in my line of work.'

'It gave . . . gives . . . Simon and myself a good standard of living.' Rica looked at him for a moment, debating whether this was the right time to ask him a question that she was really hoping he'd be receptive to. Yes, now was as good a time as any. 'Look, Bill, I don't wish to put you in a compromising situation, but would you consider taking on other bookings we have already committed to doing before Simon had to go away? Of course you can fit them in with your own work commitments. I won't be offended if you say no, but I wanted to ask you first, before I advertise for a freelance photographer to take on the jobs for me. As you know, I'm going to work hard at becoming good enough to take on the work myself, but trying to guess how long that will take is like trying to guess how long is a piece of string.'

She watched in surprise as Bill opened up the battered old briefcase he'd taken the sample prints of the wedding from earlier and took out half a dozen more. He spread them in front of her on the shop counter. 'What do you think of these?' he asked.

Puzzled, Rica put the envelope holding his payment down on the counter and then studied each of the six photographs in turn. Finally she said, 'Well, if you want me to be honest, to me they aren't anywhere near as . . . well, perfect as the others you've shown me today.'

'Why don't you think they're as good?'

She thought, Oh, he's testing me, checking to see if I did indeed listen to him as he talked me through each shot he was setting up. She would show him she had paid attention. She pointed her finger at one of the photographs. It was of a woman arranging flowers in a vase by the side of a grave.

'This one is slightly blurred. Your hand must have moved when you pressed the shutter.' He seemed pleased with her diagnosis so Rica went on to the next. It was of a small spinney of trees over on the far side of the church grounds by the wall. She studied it for a moment before she said, 'It's a nice picture but there's something in the tree which I can't make out, and I'm distracted by trying to see what it is. This shot was taken from too far away.'

He nodded. 'What is your opinion of the next one?'

She looked at it. From what she could made out there was sky and grass, and the rest was blocked out by a big dark blob. She wasn't sure what had caused the dark void in the middle.

Bill could tell she was struggling and told her, 'That dark spot is a finger on the lens. And the next one?'

It was of the front of the church. Most of the composition was taken up by the steps; the ornate carved stone archway over the top of the door was missing. She said, 'The shot should have been more centred, to capture the whole of the door and archway.' Bill nodded his agreement with her opinion.

The last photograph was the easiest of all for her to diagnose. It was a double exposure. 'You didn't wind the film on after you'd taken the last photograph.'

Bill smiled. 'Yes, that's exactly what happened. But apart from the minor faults, the subject matters of the pictures are recognisable, so from their first effort, the photographer has great potential, don't you agree?'

Rica scanned her eyes over them again and nodded. 'Yes, I do.' Then she looked at him quizzically. 'But I thought you said your first efforts weren't worth the paper they were printed on? Didn't you say you threw them away?'

'Oh, I didn't take these photographs. You did.'

She gazed at him. 'I did! Oh, these are the ones I took after the wedding party had left for the reception. I'd forgotten you let me loose with the camera while you were packing the tripod and other stuff away in the case. I never thought for a minute you'd take the trouble to develop them.' She ran her eyes over them again, then looked at him questioningly. 'You really think I show potential?'

He nodded, smiling. 'For what my opinion is worth, yes, I do. Sometimes we don't realise we have a talent for something until we give it a go. You're a quick learner too. The camera you took those photos with is not easy to operate, and the shots you took might all be flawed in one way or another, but your mistakes are easy ones to correct. The best advice I can give you is to make sure you have a camera with you at all times. You need to go out and about as much as you can, and snap anything and everything. Then, after they're developed, we'll study every frame in minute detail . . . see where you could have improved the shot. The more practice you have, the quicker you'll be filling Simon's shoes and then you'll no longer need my help. Tell you what, why don't we meet up a couple of times a week and study the new photos that you've taken?'

'I'd really appreciate that, Bill.'

'In the meantime, I'll help you fulfil your obligations, my own work permitting, and you should only have to hire a professional now and again.'

'Oh, Bill, I really appreciate that too! But only on condition you take proper payment for each job you do.' She picked up the brown envelope again and handed it to him. 'Please accept it or I'll won't feel comfortable about taking you up on your offer. Then, if I don't find another professional to help me out, the business is going to suffer and could go under.'

He shook his head at her. 'Shame on you, that's blackmail.'

The look Rica gave him told him that she knew that very well. She thrust the envelope at him again. 'So will you take it now, please?'

He sighed. 'All right, this time I will. In future, though, we'll settle on an hourly rate that I feel is fitting for an amateur like me who's only trying to pass themself off as a professional. And that's not all. The time I spend helping you with your photography is me helping a friend, no payment involved. Do we have a deal or not?'

Rica smiled at him and held out her hand. 'We have a deal.'

He accepted it and they shook.

They then went through the appointments diary. Thankfully there were only a half dozen engagements Bill could not take care of as they were for studio sittings during weekdays when he would be carrying out his plumbing work. The rest, four weddings spread over the next three months, two bar mitzvahs, a society ball and six christenings, were all either on an evening or a Saturday or Sunday, so Bill could manage them. Rica was concerned that he might be called to attend to a plumbing emergency during the times he was filling in for her commissions, and that his business could suffer as a result. He told her that should that happen, he would instruct Freda to say he was already out on a job and give the caller the names of several other plumbers he was acquainted with, who would be pleased of the extra business coming their way.

After closing the door after him Rica returned behind the counter to put the sample wedding photographs back in the envelope. Jason would take them round that afternoon to the bride's parents so they could be perused at leisure, shown around family and friends, and orders for copies made. The door to the back of the shop opened then and Fran came in.

As Fran made her way over to the counter she spotted the photographs that Rica was in the process of putting into an envelope. She said, 'Bill managed to get here while I was out then. Are they the photos he took of the wedding? How did they turn out?'

She stood by the counter and put down a bulky white paper bag containing sandwiches that she had fetched from the baker's for their lunch. She also put down two brown carrier bags by her feet. One contained the food for their evening meal, the other toiletries for their mother and a new bed jacket, which the staff at the home said she needed.

Rica took the photographs back out of the envelope and handed them to her sister to look at. She waited until Fran got to the last one then asked her, 'What's your opinion of them?'

'As good as any I've seen Simon produce,' her sister proclaimed.

Rica couldn't resist saying, 'So you agree my gamble on using Bill paid off then?'

Fran was looking at the pile of photos Rica herself had taken. Ignoring her gibe, she asked, 'Are those some more of his? Why aren't they in this pile with the others?'

Rica hurriedly swept them up, turning them upside down and putting them on top of the stationery cabinet behind her. She now fully appreciated why Bill was loath to show anyone his early work. She wasn't ready to feel belittled by criticism of her efforts, and especially from someone like her sister who had never taken a photograph in her life but wouldn't hold back from offering her opinion on how Rica could have done better. She wouldn't let anyone but Bill see what she had produced until she was confident she had produced something of merit.

'Oh, they're just a few that we felt shouldn't be included as they have minor flaws. People moved when they were being taken . . . that sort of thing. They need to be thrown away.' She rapidly changed the subject in case Fran still insisted on looking at them. 'I'm glad to say that Bill has agreed to help me fulfil the other bookings. I'll still have to find a professional to cover the sittings in the studio, though, as they're scheduled for during the week when he'll be

150

attending to his own work. Maybe the man Simon used will know of someone else I can approach while he's out of commission.'

'I'm sure he will.' Fran looked at Rica meaningfully. 'So, just when are you going to start to learn one end of a camera from the other?'

She responded a mite smugly, 'I've already started. I learned quite a bit from Bill on Saturday afternoon. So, Fran, I certainly do know know one end of a camera from another – and quite a lot more besides that.'

'Good. You should give yourself a pat on the back,' said Fran in her usual matter-of-fact tone. 'I'll go and make us a cup of tea to go with our sandwiches. We've only ten minutes left before dinner hour is over.'

As she headed off to make the tea Rica stared thoughtfully after her sister. Less than a fortnight ago she had wanted to end her life, feeling she had nothing left to live for. Now she was striving to keep the business going and earning enough to search for her son and get him back with her. Yes, Fran was right, she should give herself a pat on the back. But then Fran herself deserved an even bigger pat. If it hadn't been for her perseverance in driving Rica to get her life back on track it was all too likely she'd still be moping around, feeling sorry for herself. Once again she was reminded of her idea for a way to repay her sister. As soon as Fran stopped watching her like a hawk, she would put it into practice.

CHAPTER THIRTEEN

It wasn't until another two weeks had passed that Fran broached the subject of returning home. They were sitting in the lounge after clearing away dinner. Fran was reading her book, Rica catching up with the local news in the *Mercury*. The only sound was of pages turning. Despite trying to concentrate on what she was reading, Rica couldn't drag her mind away from thoughts of Simon and Ricky. They'd be getting on with their new lives now while she was still trying to pick up the pieces and make the best of what she'd been left with. Fran had told her that time healed, but she couldn't see any evidence that it was healing her.

She looked up from the newspaper as Fran closed her book and said, 'That was such a good read, I'm sorry it has come to an end. You should read it, Rica.'

She enjoyed a good book but was in no doubt she would not find that one entertaining as their tastes in all things were poles apart. Regardless she said, 'When I'm in the mood to read a book, I'll give it a try.'

Fran looked across at her as though to say, I know damned well you won't because this book is definitely not the mass-produced trashy fiction you go in for but a literary classic. She then totally flummoxed Rica by saying, 'I think it's safe to say that I don't need to worry I'll find you again in the lamentable situation I did before, so maybe my time here has come to an end.'

Rica stared at her in confusion for several moments until what Fran had said made sense to her . . . well, she hoped her interpretation was the right one. She tried not to look hopeful when she asked, 'Are you thinking of going back to your own flat?'

'I've used all my holiday up so I'm due back to work on Monday. It makes sense for me to go home then as otherwise I'd have an extra half an hour's travelling and double the bus fare.'

Rica tried to keep the relief from her voice when she said, 'Well, yes, it does make sense in that case.' Then she lied, 'I shall miss your company though, Fran.'

Her sister just cocked an eyebrow at her, to let her know she knew Rica most certainly would not. 'I've worked out a plan for how I can handle the shop's books, until you're in a position to take them over yourself. I've shown you how to log all the sales and purchases, and how to fill in the bank slips, so I want you to bring the books and the bank slips over to me on Saturday evening, so that I can update the books on Sunday morning. Then you can send Jason round to my place of work on a Monday morning, and I will give them back to him. As for the wages, just let me know if either Jason or Fisher has been off sick or taken any time off for other reasons so that I can make the adjustments, and I will calculate their wages and make out the slips. All you have to do is put their money along with the slip into the wages envelopes . . . there's a stock of them in the middle drawer of my . . . the . . . desk in the office. Don't expect a thank you from Fisher, I don't think he knows the word.'

An annoyed frown appeared on Rica's face. 'I can't remember the last time I actually saw him. I wouldn't know he was on the premises if the rolls of film we put in the box outside his door didn't appear a couple of days later as actual photographs, and you saw him on Friday when he came to you for his pay.'

'Well, you will see him at least once a week in future as it'll be you he comes to for his money now. He thinks he's got one over on us by keeping his distance. Little does he know we prefer not to see him.'

'As long as he does his job, I don't care whether I never see him again,' Rica said with conviction. 'It's a shame he's hell-bent on not accepting me as his boss. I had hoped he'd come around to it, but it seems he's not going to. It appears he'd sooner have seen the shop go under and him lose his job than accept a woman as his boss. We could be a happy little band if it wasn't for his ridiculous behaviour. Jason is proving to be a nice lad and very willing . . . can't do enough for me. A good choice Simon made there, taking him on when his last apprentice finished with him and went to work for the *Mercury*. But there's something not quite right there . . .' She frowned as she realised she'd been worried about Jason for a while.

'What do you mean?

'That's just it, I don't know. Just . . . something.'

'You're not making much sense, Rica. You said you find him a nice lad, and I have to say I find him pleasant enough myself. You've no complaints about his work, so what is it that you feel isn't right about him? Is it something you feel will affect the business? Like you think deep down he's a thief . . .'

'No, no, no, it's nothing like that. It's something to do with his personal life. Sometimes I catch a look in his eye when we've mentioned in passing his life outside work.'

'What sort of look in his eye?'

'Sad.'

'Sad? You're bothered about him because sometimes you think you catch him with a sad look in his eye?' Fran tutted disdainfully. 'He's a young man with his whole life in front of him, a roof over his head and a job with good prospects. For the life of me I can't think of anything he need be sad about.' She then eyed Rica meaningfully. 'Don't you think you've enough to contend with at the moment, without concerning yourself with worries you've dreamed up? There is something that might prove more important that I should mention to you.'

Rica pulled a worried face. 'Oh, what's that?'

'We seem to have been going through far more processing chemicals these past two weeks, yet the number of films coming in haven't significantly increased. I can't for the life of me see why we're needing to order larger quantities.'

'Oh! Well, I don't know anything about the processing side and you know why that is, so I can't come up with any reason for it either. Unless Fisher is drinking it,' Rica said lightly.

Fran didn't find any reason for amusement in Rica's quip. 'I shall monitor the situation, and if it continues we will have to speak to him about it.'

Rica looked at her as though to say, I'll let you deal with that. 'And we need to talk about payment for you, Fran, for the work you're doing.' A thought suddenly struck her. She knew that her sister only got two weeks' holiday a year plus bank holidays. They had been working at the shop for a month. So Fran must have taken the last two weeks off without pay. She'd never mentioned it or asked for any compensation for the shortfall, and must therefore have funded herself for the last two weeks out of her savings. Rica's heart swelled with love for her. People who didn't know Fran would just see a humourless, austere individual, never knowing that beneath that veneer she was capable of acts of great unselfishness when it came to those she cared deeply for.

Fran responded, 'We'll talk about that when you have got your son back. Meanwhile any spare money needs to be put into the pocket of the private detective you're going to hire. How you go about finding one I have no idea, but you could start by checking the advertisements in the *Mercury*.'

Rica gasped with excitement. 'Are you telling me that the business is making enough of a profit for me to afford one?'

'Well, how else could what I've just said be interpreted?' Fran wasn't being sarcastic but serious. 'Of course the business is not a bottomless pit and I don't imagine a detective's time will come cheap, so just make sure you don't give him free rein.'

Rica clapped her hands in delight. 'Oh, Fran, you have just made my dreams come true! I shan't be dreaming tonight, though, as I won't sleep a wink. I can finally make a move towards getting Ricky back. I shall get a *Mercury* on my way home tomorrow.'

Then Rica suddenly didn't care what Fran thought. She jumped up from her seat and rushed over to her, flinging her arms tightly around her bemused sister's neck and then kissing her on the cheek, ignoring the fact that Fran immediately stiffened in her arms.

Finally her sister pushed her off and snapped, 'All right, Rica, that's enough.'

'Well, I'm going to celebrate this brilliant news with a gin and tonic. What about you?'

'Yes, this is indeed something to celebrate. A cup of tea would go down very well.'

CHAPTER FOURTEEN

The following Monday at midday Rica was sitting on a well-worn but comfortable chair in a shabby office over a chip shop on London Road, near the city centre. She had thought it might take her a while to locate what she was after, but to her surprise almost immediately she'd found not one but three small adverts in the *Mercury* offering private detective services. The one that caught her eye was small and simple, offering a professional, discreet and fully confidential service. Rica decided to give that agency a try first.

She very much enjoyed Hollywood private eye films but wasn't naive enough to expect to be greeted by a brassy blonde receptionist chewing gum while filing her nails, and a Robert Mitchum or Humphrey Bogart wearing a shoulder holster with the handle of a gun poking out. But then neither did she expect to be greeted by a very pleasant middle-aged receptionist, who looked like the matronly chairwoman of the local Women's Institute. The man she introduced Rica to, sitting behind his desk in the inner office, turned out to be an ordinary-looking, tubby person of about sixty, dressed in a well-worn pair of brown cords, off-white shirt and olive green hand-knitted cardigan. The crown of his round head was as bald as a coot's apart from a strip of hair running around from ear to ear, as white as snow and neatly trimmed.

Rica doubted with the weight he was carrying and in respect of his age that he'd prove any sort of a match for a furious husband caught out in adultery . . . maybe he gave divorce work a miss. The office didn't give the impression that business was flourishing. It was badly in need of a fresh coat of paint and some new furniture. There was a smell of pipe tobacco in the air.

He stood up and held out his hand to her, introducing himself as Cyril Jackson. He indicated a seat before his desk, then for a moment Rica sat and watched him as he tapped out the old ash in his pipe and repacked it with fresh tobacco from a pouch. Finally he rested a pair of kindly but very shrewd eyes on Rica, and said to her, 'In answer to your question, this place isn't plush like London agencies or the other two outfits that operate in Leicester. If it was you'd end up paying through the nose to cover the cost of the luxury surroundings. I could make this office exactly like those, but to give it a makeover or move to better premises would cost me dearly. To pay for that I'd have to put my prices up, then some people who are really in desperate need of my services wouldn't be able to afford them. Most people who come to see me are more interested in me getting the job done for them than in whether or not they sink into the carpet when they walk on it.'

Rica was looking at him in surprise. 'But I hadn't actually asked you any question.'

Cyril smiled. 'Your expression told me just what you were thinking when you first walked in, Mrs Dunmore. In my line of work, I have to read body language and minds to see if what I'm being told is truth or lie. Now, your next question is what qualifies me to do what I do. I'm a retired detective sergeant. I was in the police force for thirty years, so I do know just a little bit about detection.'

He paused for a moment to point to the wall to one side of him. Rica could see at least a dozen pictures of him there, showing him in uniform as a young man then progressing through the years to one showing him at his retirement party, being presented with a gift by the then Chief Constable of Leicester.

Cyril continued, 'I was looking forward to a retirement spent working on my allotment, growing my own fruit and veg and entering competitions for the biggest marrow. Dreaming about it was one thing, but the reality was entirely different. I soon grew bored. My dear wife Mary . . . you met her when you first arrived . . . grew fed up with me grumbling about being fed up, so she took it upon herself to place an advert in the *Mercury*, offering my services as a private detective.'

He paused at a tap on the door. It opened and the homely woman who had first greeted Rica, whom she now knew to be Cyril's wife Mary, arrived carrying a tray with two cups of tea, milk jug and sugar basin, and a plate of custard creams on it. She gave Rica a smile before she turned and walked out, her husband saying to her, 'Thank you, dear.'

Cyril then took up his tale again. 'The very next day a middle-aged but still very beautiful widow, who was far from short of a bob or two, telephoned asking for an appointment to see me. She wanted me to check out the credentials of a man who had asked her to marry him. He was her age, a retired army major, very distinguished-looking and with money of his own. She'd fallen head over heels for him, but her instincts were telling her that something wasn't right about him. She was right to listen to those instincts. The man was telling the truth – he was a retired army major and did have a healthy bank balance. It was *how* he'd got his healthy bank balance that was the problem. He was in fact a serial bigamist six times over, only married his wives to bleed them dry before he disappeared to find his next victim. He was absolutely furious that he'd been sussed! Well, that was six years ago. Business has been steady since. We worked out of our home for the first three years, then the carpets were wearing thin with the extra traffic on them and the suite getting threadbare too, so I felt it would be cheaper for us to rent an office than keep refurbishing our home. So that's how we came here.

'Now I'll answer your next question while I'm at it. No, I cannot guarantee you a hundred per cent success on the job you wish to hire me to do, I'd be taking your money under false pretences if I did, but I have an eighty per cent success rate and you get my promise I will do my best to solve your case for you. You've come to see me at a good time. I've just concluded a job . . . yes, it was a good outcome . . . and I've nothing else in the pipeline at the moment, so I can concentrate all my efforts on your case alone. Now I have a question for you. What is it you wish me to try and do for you?'

Rica had taken a liking to the man seated before her. He came across as scrupulously honest and made her feel confident that if anyone could find the whereabouts of Ricky and bring him home to her, then he could. There were tears glinting in Rica's eyes when she said softly, 'Find my little boy for me.'

Cyril looked at her as he picked up his packed pipe and said, 'Do you mind if I smoke? It helps me concentrate better.'

She told him she didn't mind at all.

Cyril lit the packed pipe, blowing out several short bursts of smoke from the sides of his mouth. It smelled quite pleasant to Rica, unlike the sweaty-sock smell some tobaccos emitted. Then, clamping the pipe between his teeth, he pulled an unused spiral-bound notepad in front of him, flipped over the cover page and took a Biro out of a pot holding several pens and pencils. Then he prompted her, 'Why don't you start from the beginning?'

He took extensive notes as Rica told him her story. When she had finished, he leaned back in his chair and said to her, 'Do you have any photographs of your son?'

'Oh, yes, that's something I have plenty of.' She pulled an envelope out of her handbag and slid it across the desk to him.

He took the prints out of the envelope and looked through the four she had brought. 'He's a good-looking little lad.'

Rica fought back tears. 'Yes, he is,' she murmured. Then asked, 'Do you think you can find him for me, Mr Jackson?'

Cyril looked at her steadily. 'Like I said earlier, I can't guarantee anything, but you have my promise I will leave no stone unturned.'

That was good enough for Rica.

She had just got off the bus at a stop further down the road from the shop and was waiting for the steady stream of traffic to allow her to cross over when a car passed by. It was the same make, model and colour as the one Simon drove. By the time this had registered with Rica it had gone by, not giving her the chance to view the driver. For a moment her heart leaped, her hopes soared that he had come back, was parking the car and then coming to seek her out in the shop. But as quickly as her heart and hopes had risen, they sank without trace as she remembered that the car couldn't be theirs, or the driver Simon, as their car was sitting on the drive back at home. The traffic thinned then and, with a heavy heart, she made her way to the shop.

But the memory of the car standing idle in the drive back at home reminded her of Fran's suggestion that she should learn to drive. The idea seemed as preposterous to her now as it had done when her sister had first proposed it. What did she in fact know about cars? The *Highway Code* too was a complete enigma to her. But then, hadn't Fran's suggestion that she should replace Simon in the shop seemed as ridiculous when she had first put it to Rica?

If she could drive then how much time would be saved, not having to walk or travel by bus to and from work or out on errands? Her energy too could be put to much better use. There was also the fact that when attending assignments currently they journeyed to them in Bill's old Transit van, which should their clients see them arriving couldn't be doing the reputation of the business any good. As she arrived at the shop, Rica made a decision. She was going to take driving lessons. And she'd made another decision too. In the meantime, Bill could use their car to travel to the shoots. She couldn't see him raising any objections to that.

She arrived in the shop to find Jason dealing with a customer. Not wanting to interrupt him, she made her way over to the door leading into the back and went through. As she arrived in the passage she saw Sid Fisher coming out of the kitchen with a mug of tea in his hand. They stood and stared at each other for a moment, Rica fighting to find something to say to him, like a boss would to an employee, but that fight was rapidly superseded by another. She had to fight not to flee from the expression of pure loathing for her that was beaming from his eyes.

It was Fisher who made the first move by continuing on his way back to the dark room and firmly shutting the door behind him.

Rica went into the office to take off her coat, with fury building inside her. It wasn't right that the behaviour of an employee was making her feel so uncomfortable; that she would catch herself peeping through the door into the corridor to make sure he wasn't in sight before she went to the office, or to the kitchen to make a cup of tea. She wasn't prepared to let this state of affairs go on any longer. Fisher's hatred of women in superior positions and inability to hide those feelings were going to lose him his job, despite the fact he was under the impression his position was secure as he'd worked for the Dunmore family since he was a young man. If Simon did return and want to reinstate him, that was up to him. Rica would begin her search forthwith for someone to replace him, and when she succeeded it would give her great pleasure to see Sid Fisher's expression as she sent him packing.

CHAPTER FIFTEEN

Fran had warned Rica not to put all her hopes on Cyril Jackson tracing Simon and Ricky, not wanting her to suffer further from disappointment if he failed. Rica had to agree that Fran did have a valid point, and did her best to keep her mind off the enquiry by continuing her efforts to prove herself worthy to be the owner of a photography shop. Regardless, though, deep down she was pinning all her expectations on Cyril finding her child. He had to as life without ever seeing her son again was unimaginable to Rica. That hope never faded over the next three weeks. Every Friday evening at six-thirty Cyril would telephone her at home to update her on his progress, but as yet could not give her the news she was desperate to hear. She chose to believe, though, that no news was good news.

On the fourth Friday evening, when six-thirty came and went and Cyril hadn't telephoned her with his usual update, Rica wasn't unduly concerned. He had informed her two weeks previously that he'd accepted several new commissions and was working on them alongside her case, which was normal practice. She'd assumed he had just been held up on one of his other cases. But when eight o'clock came and went she started seriously to wonder why he hadn't called her. He would know she would be eagerly waiting to hear from him, even if he hadn't anything to tell her. Then a reason for her not hearing from him occurred to her. He had uncovered Ricky's whereabouts and wanted to break the news to her in person.

As she paced the lounge, waiting for his knock on the front door, she wondered what he drank, hoping that whatever his preference was, she had a bottle of it in her cabinet so they could toast his success. Had Fran been on the telephone at her flat Rica would have called her to come over and share this special moment. And there'd be plans to make, too, as to how exactly she was going to get Ricky back with her. She'd need Fran to help her formulate those and carry them out.

Finally at eight-thirty the knock came. An excited Rica dashed to the door and yanked it open, beaming in delight to see that her caller was indeed Cyril. She stood aside to allow him entry, urging him, 'Come in, come in.'

As soon as he'd sat down in the chair she'd indicated, she could no longer contain herself and blurted out, 'Did you actually see him? Did he look all right to you? Where exactly has Simon been hiding him?' It was only then that she noticed the grave expression on the detective's face. Rica gasped, clamping her hand to her mouth before she moaned, 'Please tell me nothing has happened to my son? Please tell me he's all right?'

Cyril took a deep breath. 'That I can't tell you, Mrs Dunmore. In fact, I can't tell you anything about him. I've never had a case with so many dead ends as this one. It wouldn't be fair of me to continue taking your money when I have absolutely no fresh leads to pursue.'

Rica was staring at him wildly, heart hammering. She cried hysterically, 'But no one can just disappear off the face of the earth! You can't stop looking, you can't, Mr Jackson! Simon has got to be out there somewhere, and Ricky with him.'

'Wherever he is, Mrs Dunmore, he's obviously done everything he can to cover his own tracks.'

'But there's got to be something you haven't tried yet . . .'

He cut in, 'Mrs Dunmore, I've exhausted every means I know of. The last positive sighting of your husband and son was by the conductor whose bus they caught that Saturday afternoon. The conductor recognised Mr Dunmore and Ricky as soon as I showed him the photographs. Ricky stood out in his mind because of his almost-white, curly hair. He remembered thinking at the time that it was unusual for a man to be out on his own with a child in a pushchair. It had to be folded up and stored in the luggage space during the journey and Mr Dunmore was holding your son on his knee, sitting on one of the long bench seats just inside the bus, so that when the conductor wasn't collecting fares he had a constant view of them from where he stood on the platform. He had no doubt that the child was the man's, and that there was no funny business going on, as the child seemed very happy with him and did on a couple of occasions call him Daddy . . . well, Dada was actually what he said.

'The conductor also told me that in his opinion Mr Dunmore seemed very preoccupied, worried, like he'd the weight of the world on his shoulders. Anyway, he can't remember in which direction Mr Dunmore set off when he got off the bus in Charles Street as his attention was then on the queue of passengers getting on. I've spoken to every other conductor for both the Corporation and the Midland Red bus companies, and not just for the city routes but those that go outside and into the Shires too, and not one can remember having them as passengers on that Saturday afternoon. I tried the coach companies and the train stations next, but no joy either. I've tried all the taxi and car-rental firms but Mr Dunmore did not use them. I still have contacts in the police force and no unidentified bodies have been found. I checked the hospitals again, and no one of Mr Dunmore's or your son's name or description has been admitted since the police checked.

'You asked me not to call on the proprietors of the five other photography shops in Leicester as you didn't want it known in the trade that your husband has gone missing with your son. I therefore visited the shops in the guise of a customer and it was the staff I obtained my information from. No new staff members have been taken on in the past couple of months at any of the establishments, and neither has any business changed hands. No new photography establishments have opened up recently in Leicester or in any towns or villages in the Shires, nor are there rumours in the trade of any about to be. I've checked all the hotels and boarding houses and none have had a Mr Dunmore and his son or anyone of their description staying with them, and no estate agents have had him enquiring about properties to buy or rent locally.'

Cyril Jackson paused for a moment before he said to her, 'Mrs Dunmore, it's my opinion that Mr Dunmore and your son are no longer in this city. How they left it . . . well, I can only conclude that they were met by someone who drove them to wherever it is they have gone to start their new lives, probably under new identities.'

She cried, 'No, no! This can't be the case, it can't! I know I have to accept that Simon doesn't want to be with me and it was his right to leave, but he'd no right to take my son with him.'

Very quietly Cyril said, 'He does have a right, Mrs Dunmore. He is the boy's father.'

Rica's whole body sagged, the pain she was suffering etched on her face. 'You promised me you wouldn't leave any stone unturned, and you haven't. For that I thank you, but I have to find my son, Mr Jackson. I won't rest until Ricky's back where he belongs, with me.' She looked at him imploringly. 'You must widen your search.'

He smiled at her sympathetically. 'You have already told me that Mr Dunmore has no living family, and to your knowledge no friends or acquaintances outside his home town. Have you any suggestion as to where I could make a start?' The look on her face told him that she hadn't. 'Mrs Dunmore, the only thing we can hope for now is that your husband's conscience pricks him and he will get in touch with you, if only to let you know that your son is well and happy. And please rest assured that although I won't be taking any more of your money, I will not stop keeping my ear to the ground for any news at all of the whereabouts of your son. Should I hear the slightest thing, I will check it out and let you know my findings.'

Wringing her hands, distraught, Rica whispered, 'Thank you, Mr Jackson, I appreciate that.'

She couldn't remember Cyril Jackson leaving and had no idea how long she sat in the armchair after he had gone; neither was she aware of going upstairs, taking off her clothes and getting into bed.

Fran found her on Sunday morning when she called round to find out why Rica had not delivered the books to her the previous evening, for her to update.

She found the house deathly silent and freezing cold. Fran's concern for her sister immediately mounted. After finding no trace of her downstairs, she hurried up to Rica's bedroom. It was a dull winter's day outside and as the curtains were drawn tight the room was gloomy. She automatically switched on the light by the door to illuminate it, her eyes directed to the bed. She was relieved to see a huddled shape under the covers. Thinking that Rica was sick she went over to the bed, wrinkling her nose at the stale smell that permeated the air. She laid her hand on the shrouded outline and gently shook it, saying, 'Rica, it's me, Fran. Are you in need of a doctor?' She received no answer so she tried again. 'Rica, do you want me to fetch a doctor to you?'

From under the covers a muffled voice croaked, 'No doctor can help me. Broken hearts can't be fixed, can they?'

It took Fran a moment to comprehend why Rica would come out with such a statement, then she realised. 'Are you telling me that the private detective you hired has had no success in finding Ricky?'

'No trace at all. No one has seen Simon or him since they got off the bus that Saturday afternoon in town. It's like they've both vanished in a puff of smoke. Now please just go, Fran. I want to be left alone.'

She heaved a sigh. 'I'm so sorry to hear this, Rica, truly I am. I did tell you not to pin all your hopes on the detective.'

'Yes, you did, and as usual you were right, Fran.'

Fran ignored the sarcasm and told her, 'I'll go and make you a cup of tea.'

From under the covers came the retort, 'I don't want a bloody cup of tea. I want to be left alone. Please go home, Fran.'

In her usual unflustered monotone she replied, 'You know I don't appreciate that kind of language in my presence, Rica. And don't try and tell me that word you used isn't swearing, as it was in the context you were using it. Now you might not want a cup of tea, but I do. Maybe by the time I've made it, you'll have changed your mind.'

The bedcovers Rica was cocooned in were suddenly heaved aside to reveal her face. She glared up at Fran. 'Haven't I made it plain enough? *I want you to go.* I want to be left alone. How much clearer can I make that to you?'

'Oh, I hear loud and clear what you want, Rica. How selfish you are not to consider what *I* want! I want to stay with you and unless you throw me out bodily, which would mean your getting out of bed, then I'm not going anywhere until I'm ready to.'

Rica looked at her knowingly. 'Oh, I see, you think I'm in danger of doing away with myself, don't you? Well, I can do that whether you're here or not. Don't bother hiding my bottle of headache pills or the bottles of drink as there are other ways of doing it. I can always throw myself out of the window.'

Fran pulled a face. 'Oh, dear, we've talked about this before. Just think of the consequences should you not succeed in killing yourself. You could break bones, be left crippled for life. Think of that, Rica. You'd be stuck constantly with me having to do everything for you. Actually, your doing away with yourself hasn't entered my head recently. You can act selfishly sometimes, Rica, but I can't imagine you'd be selfish enough not to consider how that could affect your son. You don't know what tale Simon will tell him to excuse the way he left you and took him away from you, so don't you want the opportunity to make sure Ricky eventually knows the truth? That you never abandoned him, but that he was taken from you?'

Leaving Rica to think about that, Fran went downstairs.

From under the covers Rica let out a loud groan. Her domineering sister as usual was right. She did sometimes want her life to be over, but only in order to bring to an end the unbearable pain of the loss she was suffering. At the moment she could see no end to it, and she defied anyone in the same circumstances as she was not to feel the same. But now Fran had given her a good reason not to wish for death to release her from her agony. She hadn't considered that Ricky would come looking for her when he eventually found out about her existence, which he was bound to one day on seeing his birth certificate.

Even if Simon hadn't left her for someone else, just left because he didn't want to be married to her any longer, Rica couldn't be sure what story he would tell their son to excuse the fact of taking him away from his mother, and it was important to her that Ricky should one day know the truth from her side. And when he did seek her out, it was of

169

paramount importance to her that he found a mother he could be proud of, not a pathetic individual who had crumbled and wasted her life because she'd not the strength of character to build herself a new one. In the meantime she still had the faint hope that Cyril Jackson may yet discover her son's whereabouts.

Fran returned a short while later armed with a cup of sweet tea which she placed on Rica's bedside cabinet beside the alarm clock and lamp. Rica had once again cocooned herself inside the bedclothes, curled up in a foetal position. Fran leaned over and placed her hand gently on what she assumed to be her sister's shoulder. 'I can imagine how much you're hurting but . . .'

She jumped as, unexpectedly, the bedcovers shot back again to reveal Rica's eyes blazing up at her. She barked angrily, 'No, you can't. How can you? You've never been married or had children and then lost them.'

Calmly Fran responded, 'No, I haven't, but I have lost people I loved and cared for. Like Father and Mother.'

Rica hissed at her contemptuously, 'Your father only. Your mother is still alive, despite the fact that you consider her dead to you.'

Matter-of-factly Fran answered, 'We all have our own way of dealing with painful matters, Rica. I've already explained to you that I believe that awful disease has killed the person she was, the spirit of her. Just because I don't wear my heart on my sleeve like you do, doesn't mean I don't have feelings. I deal with them in a different way from you, that's all. Now please drink your tea, it will make you feel better.'

Rica looked at her incredulously. 'You think a cup of tea will actually help me!'

'Yes, I do. The body cannot function without liquid and solid food, and it's my guess you haven't had either since you received Mr Jackson's conclusions. If he ran true to form then it was on Friday evening he delivered them to you, so I assume that that was the last time anything passed your lips. While you drink your tea, I'll go and run you a hot bath.'

Rica furiously cried, 'I don't want a bath!'

But Fran had already disappeared, and Rica knew there was nothing for it but to get into that bath – whether she wanted to or not. Her only consolation lay in day dreaming about the way, one day, she'd turn the tables on Fran and wrongfoot her by interfering in *her* life. See how she liked that!

CHAPTER SIXTEEN

'This is most unusual. In all the years I've been practising as an accountant, I've never had a client thank me for doing work they'd paid me for, not in such a way. There's no address on the letter and for the life of me I can't make out the signature or recognise it, so I have no idea who is behind this. Can you recognise the signature, Miss Derwent?'

Fran was sitting in the chair on the other side of Reginald Moffett's desk, pad and pencil in hand, going through the morning post with him, making notes on what he wished her to do. Although she was usually very focused on the task in hand, her mind at that moment was not on her work but had strayed on to her sister.

She admired Rica so much for the way she had found the strength of mind to put her double loss aside, show a brave face to the world, and throw herself into proving her worth. She was determined to be a mother Ricky would be proud of when they were eventually reunited. But Fran suspected that in the privacy of her home, where the ghosts of her husband and son haunted every room, she was still mourning their absence. It was of great concern to Fran that Christmas would be upon them shortly. It was going to be a very difficult time for Rica and she would need Fran's support to get through it . . .

She was jolted out of her thoughts by a commanding voice. 'Miss Derwent?'

She said evenly, 'Yes, Mr Moffett?'

'I have asked you a question twice and you haven't answered me.' He frowned at her quizzically 'It's not like you to be distracted, Miss Derwent. Is it your sister that's the cause? You took unpaid leave to help her through her traumatic time, and should you need more . . .'

She insisted, 'No, no, Mr Moffett. I apologise for losing concentration but you have my full attention now.'

He seemed mollified by her assurance. 'Do you happen to recognise this handwriting as that of one of our clients?' He nodded his head to indicate the letter he was referring to.

She looked down, picked it up and studied it for a moment before shaking her head. 'No, I don't.'

'What about the signature. Can you make it out?'

Fran considered for a while then again shook her head. 'It just looks like a squiggle to me.'

'Yes, me too.' Reginald looked awkwardly at her. 'Well, er . . . what do you think?'

It was her turn to frown at him. 'About what, Mr Moffett?'

'Oh, did you not read the letter?'

'No, I didn't. I just looked at it to see if I recognised the handwriting, like you asked me to.'

Reginald took a deep breath before falteringly telling her, 'Well . . . it . . . er . . . says . . . er . . . that the enclosed tickets for the production of *The Pirates of Penzance* by the Leicester Operatic Society at the De Montfort Hall this coming Saturday are . . . er . . . for us both, by way of a thank you for the work we've done on their behalf. They are aware apparently that we're both fond of light opera.'

In all the years Fran had worked for Reginald Moffett she had never seen him display any emotion, his mood always the same calm and collected one, except for once when she'd gone into his office with some letters for him to sign and caught him quietly sobbing into his handkerchief, totally unaware he was being observed by her. It was the day before his mother's funeral. He was a very private man. So to see him so flustered now came as a shock to her.

Her stomach was starting to turn somersaults. She had never told a living soul the dearest dream she had harboured for close on seventeen years, not even her sister. Fran longed for Reginald Moffett to see her in the same light as she did him. Over her years spent working for him, what had begun as liking had grown into deep regard and respect, which then had turned to love. It was of no significance to Fran that he was more than twenty years her senior.

Over the years there had been several occasions she had thought her dream might be about to come true when she had caught him looking at her with a wistful look in his eyes, but as soon as he had realised she had noticed it was gone, leaving her doubting her own impressions. She was aware Reginald felt great respect for her from the way he treated her, but if he felt any more for her than that, he was keeping it to himself. Now a grateful client was presenting her with a chance to find out whether the thought of a night in her company in a social setting was appealing to him or not. Just how the grateful client could have known such personal information about them both was a mystery though, as Fran never spoke to any of the clients in a familiar way and very much doubted Reginald did either, knowing him as she did.

She noticed that he was looking at her awkwardly. Disappointment filled her. He was going to offer a reason for not taking up the client's generous offer, and she would then find out after all these years that her fondest hopes for a relationship with him had been futile. But to her surprise he said, 'I . . . er . . . suppose it would be rude of us to not accept the gift of the tickets. What is your opinion on that, Miss Derwent?'

Though inwardly joyous, Fran appeared as composed as

she always did. 'I agree with you, Mr Moffett. It would be very rude of us.'

The look on his face told her that a new thought had struck him. 'You do realise the concert is for this Saturday evening? Only you may already have made arrangements.'

'No, no, I hadn't anything planned. Have you other plans, Mr Moffett?' She vehemently hoped that he hadn't.

'No, no, I've nothing planned either.' He looked at her hesitantly for a moment before he ventured, 'So, there's nothing preventing us from attending the concert. Oh, but of course, as long as you have no objection to my company, Miss Derwent? I shall not be offended if you have.'

'I have no objection at all, Mr Moffett.'

'Well then, the tickets state that the curtain goes up at seven-thirty, so shall I meet you in the foyer at seven-fifteen? That should give us plenty of time to be settled in our seats before the start. Is that agreeable to you?'

Mixed emotions were now seething inside Fran. She still could not quite believe that her long-cherished wish had at last been granted. She was excited as well as apprehensive over what was to come, fearful that something might happen between now and Saturday night to prevent either of them from turning up, and at the same time mentally sorting through her wardrobe for something suitable to wear. She wanted Reginald to feel proud to have her by his side.

Though daring to hope that this evening out together might result in the start of a personal relationship between them, she was too sensible to set much store by it. She was already imagining the huge disappointment she knew she would feel if he didn't ask her to accompany him again some time in the future.

'That would be most suitable, Mr Moffett,' she responded to him formally.

Rica had no idea whether her plan had been successful or had fallen foul. By closing time on Saturday she was

175

champing at the bit to find out. She arrived at Fran's flat at just after six to drop off the books and whatever else Fran needed to update the accounts. Her sister opened the door to her and it was apparent that she was going out judging by her attire: a simple but tasteful plain black long-sleeved shift dress made of velvet, its hemline finishing just below the knee, a single string of cultured pearls around her neck worn with matching clip-on earrings, and on her feet a pair of low-heeled black court shoes. True to form she wore not a trace of make-up. Her dark hair was styled in its usual severe French roll.

Despite the fact that she still looked to Rica like a prim old maid, there was a radiance about her sister tonight. This told Rica that her plan to repay Fran for all her kindness, by bringing her together with the man she obviously had feelings for, had worked a treat. The way she managed to control her own joy and relief was a credit to Rica. She just hoped that should Reginald Moffett not secretly share Fran's feelings already, then hopefully this evening spent with her would open up his eyes and help him to see her in a new light.

As she entered the flat, Rica said casually, 'You look nice, Fran. Off out?'

'Yes, I am, so I can't offer you a cup of tea. I have to catch the bus in a few moments.'

Rica handed over the books and said, 'Oh, that's all right, I'm wanting to get home myself and put my feet up. It's been a really busy day. So where are you going tonight?'

'To the De Montfort Hall, to see an operetta.'

'Oh, which one?' Rica asked with a show of interest – as if she didn't already know.

Fran looked at her as if to say, You've never shown the slightest enthusiasm for operetta, so why now? Regardless she continued, '*The Pirates of Penzance*. And I really ought to be going.'

'Oh, you've plenty of time.' Then Rica looked her in the eye before adding, 'It's not like anyone will be waiting for you and you'll be leaving them standing, is it? Well, unless you do have a date and just haven't told me?'

Fran replied evenly, 'I don't wish to risk missing the start, Rica.'

She was obviously not going to confide in her sister about her date with Reginald Moffett, courtesy of a 'mystery benefactor'.

Rica knew that Fran was nowhere near as calm as she was pretending to be. She leaned over and gave her sister an affectionate peck on her cheek. 'I do hope you enjoy yourself tonight.' Then she couldn't resist adding, 'You never know, you might find yourself sitting next to the man of your dreams.'

CHAPTER SEVENTEEN

The shop was exceptionally busy during the two weeks before Christmas. It seemed a good proportion of the population of Leicester plus shoppers from outlying areas were wanting to buy their nearest and dearest something different as a present in these affluent times, thought a camera fitted the bill and that Dunmore's was the place to purchase it. Cheap instamatics and sundries for them were flying off the shelves, and the affluent customers were snapping up the more sophisticated cameras and accessories to go with them, money no object. It seemed that the rest of the population wanted to commission family portraits to be given to relatives as presents. Good news for her profits, but Rica herself was paying the price for all the hard work that went into achieving them. After arriving home in the evening, she tried to soak away her fatigue in a hot bath, and then, sometimes too tired to cook herself a meal, settled for a hastily made sandwich.

Thankfully her constant questioning of Jason and vigilant study of the way he dealt with customers had paid off, and she was confident enough now in her knowledge of the stock not to keep constantly calling upon him to help her. The administrative side of the business was not quite such a mystery to her either. She was adept at stocktaking, ordering new supplies and filling in sales sheets, but the accounts were another matter. As far as Rica was concerned,

Fran hadn't yet made any complaint about doing them, so she would let sleeping dogs lie.

Rica was working hard to get her photography up to an acceptable standard. She carried a camera with her at all times and would take it out at any opportunity she had, snapping shots of anything and everything. Then when the shots were developed – under the pretence they were for a customer as she didn't want Fisher knowing what she was doing and sniggering behind her back at her failures – Bill would examine them and offer her his advice on how she could have improved them.

Getting her shots in focus was something she mastered quickly. Far more difficult for Rica was learning how not to under- or over-expose a shot; getting the light right and then knowing how to judge the right moment to snap the shutter. A moment too soon or too late made a dramatic difference, especially when photographing anything that moved, such as people or wildlife. She was aware now of just how to draw the eye into a photograph by including an intriguing detail – a shadow on a wall, the angle of a branch, light on water – and also how different the aspect could become by taking the same pose or scenic view from several different angles.

And her sister had announced that there was nothing more to taking a photograph than pointing the camera at the object in question and pressing the shutter!

Rica was extremely grateful that having so much to concentrate on was helping to keep her mind off the approaching festive season. She was dreading the day itself, knowing that it was going to be an extremely difficult time for her on top of what she was already dealing with. By way of helping herself she did her best to avoid looking in shop windows at the festive displays, and tried not to notice the building excitement among her customers. Regardless, though, there were times when she had no choice but to acknowledge it, such as when she couldn't put off any longer following the other shop owners' lead and giving the premises a festive feel, with colourful decorations along with a Christmas tree. Or when customers came in seeking a present for their loved ones and, while she was wrapping the item and taking the money for their purchase, would insist on relaying to her their Christmas plans and then asking hers.

With a practised smile on her face Rica had a stock answer ready, which backed up what she had told Jason to excuse the absence of her son when the topic of Ricky's whereabouts had come up between them when they had been going about their work. Rica said that hopefully Simon's sick uncle would have rallied enough for him to make the journey home from Devon with their son, whom he had taken with him so that his aunt could take care of the child, leaving Rica herself free to run their business while Simon was looking after his uncle's. If he did get back it would be a traditional family Christmas for them; if he didn't then her plan was to make the best of it and celebrate doubly next year. At her long-winded response, she could see the recipient's eyes glaze over in disinterest long before she was halfway through her story.

But she hadn't withdrawn herself from what was going on around her so much as not to notice that Jason had become very quiet and subdued. About three weeks before Christmas he had arrived one morning looking as though he had something on his mind that was deeply disturbing him, and his usual pleasantness was forced. He also seemed to be carrying himself very stiffly, and she could see he was having difficulty bending down or reaching over to pick up anything. After three days had passed and there was still no change in him, her womanly sympathy for the young man got the better of Rica.

She waited until they were on their own in the shop and

then told him of her concern for him. His response was disconcerting. An unmistakable look of alarm flashed across his face, to be quickly replaced by a forced smile. He told her he had just slept badly and had a crick in his neck. She had no choice but to appear to accept his explanation. She wasn't fooled, though. She'd suffered from a stiff neck herself and there was more than that wrong with Jason.

She wanted to probe futher but the arrival of Mr Pointer, the professional photographer she had hired to attend to the studio sittings, interrupted her talk with Jason. Mr Pointer was a very tall, gaunt, dour man who always dressed completely in black. Rica felt he only needed a dog collar to be mistaken for the fire-and-brimstone sort of vicar. By the time she had politely said good day to him and given him the list of people he would be seeing that session, Jason was attending to a customer and another was waiting to be dealt with.

Her next opportunity to approach her assistant came just after dinnertime that day. After her direct approach had failed, Rica had decided to start a casual conversation with him, in the hope that she could steer it towards the reason for his malaise.

She was re-hanging ornaments on the Christmas tree. A customer's wilful child had pulled them off while waiting to have a photograph taken by Mr Pointer. Rica casually said to Jason, as he was engaged in putting packets of developed photographs into the collection drawer, 'I've lost count of the number of times I've had to put ornaments back on this tree after a child has pulled them off.' Then she paused momentarily as a memory returned to her of Ricky at only eight months old, lying on the carpet in the lounge this time last year. He was gazing mesmerised at the twinkling fairy lights on their tree.

Rica felt a vice-like grip begin to squeeze at her heart. Her eyes prickled with tears. She gave herself a mental shake, using all her inner resources to suppress the memory. The place for giving in to her emotions was in the privacy of her home, not here in front of her staff and possible customers.

Sucking in a deep breath, with forced cheeriness in her voice, she continued, 'Still, before I know it Christmas will be all over and we'll be packing things away until next year.' She paused for a moment before she asked him, 'What does your family do for Christmas, Jason? I mean, do you all spend it at home or with relatives?'

He turned and looked at her for a moment, seeming to be thinking carefully about his answer. Then he said blandly, 'We just do the usual, Mrs Dunmore.' And turned back to carry on with his task.

There was no excitement in his voice and Rica hoped it was her imagination that Christmas didn't come across as being a special time for him. Her mind whirled then, searching for something else to say that might elicit from him the information she was seeking. But again she was thwarted by a customer entering, and for the rest of the day they never seemed to be on their own long enough for her to start a conversation again. This state of affairs continued right up until closing time on Christmas Eve. Jason's subdued mood never lightened during this time.

Christmas Eve fell on a Tuesday so both Jason and Sid Fisher had already received their Christmas wages the Friday before. Fran and Rica had had a heated discussion over what they should pay as a festive bonus, both to the shop staff and to Bill. There was no real dissent about Jason, who clearly deserved a few pounds extra after all the trouble he had taken to introduce Rica to the running of the shop. Fran felt Bill was adequately rewarded already and not, after all, an employee, but Rica insisted he was a special case and his kindness to her should not go unobserved.

Sid Fisher was the real cause of their altercation. Fran was adamant he didn't deserve a penny extra due to his despicable attitude towards his new female boss and the way he had alienated himself from them all. Rica half agreed with her, but her own better nature got the better of her. Regardless of his manner and the deplorable way he was acting, for which he would be replaced as soon as she could find a suitable candidate, she couldn't find anything to complain about in the quality of his work. In respect of that, she felt he deserved a bonus, even if it wasn't the same as he would have got had he not been acting so badly. When all was said and done it was Rica's business, so Fran finally had to concede defeat and agree with her to give him an additional one pound ten shillings. They knew Fisher would see this as an insult, not realising he was lucky to be getting anything at all.

Rica hoped he would see it as a sign his attitude wouldn't be tolerated and would decide to change his ways and work with her instead of against her, saving her the trouble of searching for his replacement. Fran told Rica she could live in hope, but she couldn't see it happening herself.

Jason was handed his bonus at lunchtime in case he wanted to spend some on presents for his family – or even a new suit. The look on his face on seeing the £5 bonus inside the wages envelope left Rica in no doubt how overjoyed he was to be receiving so much. Then, to her bewilderment, a flash of regret sparked in his eyes and he spun on his heel and made for the door leading to the back, muttering that he needed to go to the toilet.

She put Fisher's envelope in the film-processing box outside the dark-room door. She had no wish to come into contact with him and witness his hatred for her blazing from his eyes while she presented him with money she would much rather have put in the church poor box. Thankfully she had been spared having to quiz him a week or so back over the extra processing chemicals they seemed to be using, as the next order he'd requested was back to its previous levels. Why the sudden increase for that week still remained a mystery.

Bill's last job for Rica had taken place the previous Saturday evening when he'd taken photographs of the twenty-first birthday party of the daughter of a local barrister. After dropping in the films he had taken to be developed by Fisher, he collected his payment for the job and handed Rica back the keys to the car. When he had a job he would drive his van over to her house, swap it for the car, then swap back again afterwards. She hadn't seen him since. She hoped he found a reason to call in before she closed up on Christmas Eve, so she could give him his bonus and wish him a Merry Christmas.

Much to her delight he called in mid-afternoon on Christmas Eve between jobs, to buy films and batteries for his flash gun to see him over the festive season. As his present to them he'd brought with him half a dozen shop-bought mince pies which were gratefully received, particularly by Jason. He virtually gobbled two down, one after the other, seeming ravenous, which surprised Rica considering he had told her he didn't get hungry during the day.

She asked Bill if he'd a minute as she'd like a private word with him in the office. He looked utterly confounded when she then gave him an envelope containing his Christmas bonus of £10. Rica could tell the thought he might receive a bonus from her hadn't even crossed his mind. She could also tell he was about to protest about accepting it, and stopped this by quietly reminding him that it was considered bad manners to refuse to accept a gift. He couldn't argue with that. She then wished him a very Happy Christmas and hoped he spent an enjoyable day with his family.

At these good wishes she was surprised to notice him glance away for a moment, but it happened too quickly for her to work out what it signified. Then he smiled at her and told her he hoped she managed to spend an enjoyable day too, considering she wouldn't have her husband and son to share it with. Then Rica realised what his strange behaviour had signified moments before. He had been about to wish her the same as she had him, a happy day with her family, until he had remembered that she had told him last week it looked unlikely they would be together, giving him the same fabricated reason as she did everyone else to cover Simon's desertion of her. She had not at all liked so blatantly lying to anyone, especially the man she considered to be her saviour, but wasn't ready to tell the truth about her situation until she had fully accepted it herself.

As she locked up on Christmas Eve after letting Jason out – Fisher had done his usual trick of skulking out the back way without bothering to wish either Jason or herself a Happy Christmas – Rica was glad the day she'd been dreading was finally upon them, so that she could get it over with.

Her parents had always made Christmas as special as they were able to. When times were hard they might not have had the means to give their children the presents they would have liked to, but what they did provide was given with love. Iris always managed somehow to put a traditional dinner together. The family would play games such as Charades, Draughts, and Snakes and Ladders, and when the girls grew older card games were introduced. To make these more fun they'd bet for matches. On Rica's marriage the tradition of gathering in the Derwent house continued, only now the party had increased to include Simon and his widowed father. After Richard Dunmore's sad death, and Owen Derwent's, the family still continued their tradition of Christmas at the Derwents' until Iris's illness started to show itself and the venue for their Christmas Day gathering was switched to the Dunmores' home.

As a child Fran had looked forward to Christmas as eagerly as any other little girl, but right from an early age she'd found that she dreaded the times when games were announced. Let the others enjoy themselves that way, she would have much preferred to sit by herself in a quiet place and read a book. Her parents' view, though, was that everyone should join in, so Fran was left with no choice but to do so too. When she reached the age of fourteen and left school to begin her life in the grown-up world, it was her opinion that she should be treated like a grown-up too – and that meant no more doing things she did not enjoy. Top of that list was participating in the games playing on Christmas Day. Since then, when the time had come for the games box to be taken out from the cupboard under the stairs and wiped clean of its year-long layer of dust, she would make her excuses and go up to her bedroom. On acquiring her own flat at the age of twenty, when games time arrived Fran would take her leave.

This Christmas, understandably, Rica had no motivation whatsoever for marking the holiday in any way. She felt she had nothing to celebrate. Just getting through the day itself was going to be a huge struggle for her. In her mind's eye she was seeing her husband and son opening presents around a tree in another house, with more than likely another woman fussing over them, while she herself would be no sort of company. She had thought Fran would be delighted to be given the opportunity for the first time ever of spending the day as she wished to and not feeling obliged to spend it with her family. Or what was now left of her family.

Rica had told Fran of her plan to spend the day alone this year on the Saturday before Christmas Eve when she took the shop's books round.

To Rica's surprise, Fran was not at all pleased to hear this and snapped brusquely, 'Well, of course, I can fully understand why you've no mind to celebrate this year, Rica, but then that condemns me to spend the day by myself too. That's hardly fair, is it?'

'Well, yes, but I thought you'd be relieved. You've never really enjoyed Christmas Day in the past, have you?'

'I haven't enjoyed the mandatory games playing and was relieved when I reached an age where I could get out of it, but the rest I enjoyed.'

Rica looked stunned. 'Oh, really? You never looked like you did. Anyway, I really won't be good company, Fran.'

'Well, we'll both sit quietly and read then.'

Rica sighed. Her sister was quick to brand her as selfish sometimes, but *she* was the guilty one this time. Rica's mind raced, trying to think of a good reason for Fran to spend Christmas without her this year. Then an idea struck. She had no idea whether her sister's evening with Reginald several weeks ago had gone so well that they had arranged another night out as Fran had not mentioned a word about it to her. It was typical of her to keep her private life to herself. But maybe if she were having more than a boss/ employee relationship with Reginald by now, then if she had no other commitments on Christmas Day he would ask her to spend some of it with him. Rica said to her, 'Isn't there someone else you'd like to spend the day with? Someone who'd be better company than me?'

Fran frowned at her, taken aback. 'Such as who?'

Rica gave a nonchalant shrug. 'I don't know. You never really talk to me about your friends. But you must have one you could invite to spend the day with you or who'd invite you to spend it with them, if they knew you were on your own?'

'So are we settling for traditional, like always?'

It was Rica's turn to eye Fran, taken aback. 'Traditional what?'

'Dinner. Don't worry if you don't feel like cooking, I'll do it.'

Rica inwardly groaned. Fran had simply refused to acknowledge what she was saying, intent on spending Christmas the way she always had. It seemed Rica wasn't going to be allowed to spend the day by herself but would have the pleasure of her sister's company, whether she liked it or not. She said tartly, 'I'll leave that for you to decide. And you can shop for the food too as I've no inclination to do that either.'

Fran might not have let her get away with being on her own on Christmas Day, but at least Rica had Christmas Eve to do as she pleased. The shop had been busier than ever that day and she and Jason had not stopped dealing with a steady stream of customers, buying their last-minute presents and stocking up with photographic sundries so they could capture their loved ones enjoying the special day. There had been a moment when she had worried they would run out of some items of stock even though, following Simon's lead in previous years, they had ordered triple of everything, not wanting to send a customer away disappointed or, just as bad, know that their shop's loss of profit was another shop's gain. Any of the over-ordered stock left would be sold later in the January sale, albeit at a reduced profit but a profit nevertheless.

Rica arrived home that night still with the sound of the till ringing in her ears, looking forward to soaking her aching muscles in a hot bath, accompanied by a large gin and tonic. But as soon as she shut the front door behind her and began to take off her coat, the silence and the empty feel of the house hit her. What she had feared would happen, did. The imaginary box in her mind where she had locked away all her memories and emotions burst open and they came tumbling out. The numerous visions of happy times with her son and husband danced tormentingly before her, indescribable misery filling her being. Her coat slipped from her hands to lie crumpled on the floor and she followed

188

immediately after, doubled over, wrapping her arms around herself, rocking backwards and forwards, fat desolate tears pouring down her face.

It was the knocker rapping on the front door that jolted her out of her emotional outburst. Sitting bolt upright, she wondered who her caller could be as she wasn't expecting anyone until Fran arrived tomorrow. It was probably a neighbour making their way around the area, calling to wish her a Merry Christmas and hoping to receive a warm welcome and be plied with drink and mince pies in return. If that was the case then they had called at the wrong house. Then Rica realised that as she hadn't put any lights on and the house was in darkness, whoever was at the other side of the door would think no one was in, and if she remained still and silent she wouldn't tip them off otherwise.

Then she jumped as the knocker was rapped again, harder this time. The caller was growing impatient with receiving no response to their summons. Still she remained statue-like, straining her ears for the sound of footsteps heading back down the path, telling her that the coast was now clear. Rica shuddered. It was so cold in here. She hadn't put the central heating on yet or lit the gas fire.

Then the rapping of the knocker came again, only this time it was more of an annoyed bang that resounded from it. It was obvious that her caller was getting very annoyed now at being ignored. Her mind screamed, Oh, please, go away! Please, just leave me alone. If she willed it hard enough maybe they would.

Then a thought struck her. Could the caller possibly be the one person in the world she would do anything to open the door to, holding in his arms the only other person she would do anything to see right now, and take into her own, and hug so tightly she would never again let go?

Her heart began to hammer in her chest. Without another thought Rica got up, turned the knob on the Yale lock and yanked open the door. On seeing just who her visitor was, the hopeful, expectant expression on her face vanished, to be replaced by one of acute disappointment. And it wasn't just a passing visit the caller was making to her either, considering the suitcase parked by their feet on the doorstep.

If Fran noticed her sister's apparent state of distress she made no comment, just said, 'Help me with these bags, Rica, and let me get inside, it's freezing out here.' She thrust out two overflowing brown carrier bags, which Rica automatically took, then Fran picked up a small case from the step and squashed herself past Rica to get inside. As Rica herself made no attempt to follow her, having put her case down by the stairs, Fran took her arm and pulled her in also, then shut the door, shivering, and said, 'It's nearly as cold in here as it is outside. Haven't you put any heating on yet? Oh, maybe you haven't had time if you've just come in yourself. Actually, I'll do it. You looked absolutely whacked out. Must have been a busy week for you, especially today. You could do with a long soak in the bath. I've already eaten but I'll make you something ready for when you come back down. What do you fancy?'

Rica was still trying to get over the huge disappointment she'd just experienced. She felt physically sick at the thought of food but knew that Fran would insist she had something should she find out that Rica hadn't eaten since one o'clock.

She lied, 'I've already eaten too.' And just in case Fran enquired what she'd had and when, fabricated further. 'I called in at the fish and chip shop on my way home and ate them out of the newspaper.'

Fran made no comment that she thought eating food anywhere but at a table bad practice, but just said, 'Well, a cup of hot chocolate is what you need then. Great for helping you to relax is hot milky chocolate.'

Rica sighed. It was a double . . . triple . . . gin and tonic she needed, not a milky drink.

Fran ordered her, 'Take those bags through to the kitchen and put the kettle on while I warm this place up, then you go off upstairs for your bath. I know there'll be hot water as you always keep the immersion on permanently at this time of year, to stop the pipes bursting. So don't try and tell me otherwise.'

A hot bath certainly did beckon, if only to get Rica away from her sister for a while. She wondered how she could sneak herself the gin and tonic that she craved, and which she hoped would go some way towards insulating her from the misery she felt. If Fran saw her pouring herself one, though, she would be subjected to one of her sister's accusing looks and a lecture on the demon drink.

Having taken the carrier bags into the kitchen, Rica tried to go into the lounge to sneak herself a drink from the sideboard, but found Fran kneeling down by the gas fire, trying to ignite it but failing as she didn't have any idea that the igniter that sparked the gas was temperamental and needed to be depressed several times in rapid succession before it would eventually yield a spark. Annoyed that her sister's presence in the room was preventing her from getting a drink, Rica decided to leave her to it and let her work it out for herself.

By the time the bath was full of hot water, Fran had figured out how to light the fire and made the hot chocolate, which she brought up to Rica to drink while she was soaking. Rica stayed in the bath far longer than she normally would have, periodically topping it up with more hot water, as it was preferable to sitting downstairs and being subjected to the dirge-like music which Fran was bound to have put on the radiogram. Thankfully the heat from the water, along with the aroma of roses from her foaming bath lotion, had worked its magic on Rica. She was now feeling a little better than when she had first got in.

With no other distraction apart from watching the steam

swirling while she sipped her mug of hot chocolate, she'd been able to rationalise her outburst, understand why it had been so intense today. There was something about this time of year that made people heal rifts, settle arguments, get in touch with those they hadn't seen for a while, and Rica realised her subconscious had been hoping Simon would realise he had made a mistake and be waiting for her to get home that evening, in order to beg her forgiveness. On finding the house empty and cold, those hopes had been dashed for good. Wherever Simon was now, he was obviously happier than he had been with Rica.

Admitting this was like a turning point for her. It was time she put the past behind her and, like Simon obviously was, got on with making a new life for herself.

Right now, though, she just wanted to sleep and be released from her whirling thoughts. The trouble was, though, she didn't think she would be able to still them long enough for sleep to work its magic. The gin and tonic she had promised herself earlier might do the trick. She'd just have to wait until Fran retired to bed and she was free to help herself without fear of recriminations.

Rica was drying herself off when to her surprise tiredness suddenly overcame her and she started to yawn. By the time she had completely dried herself and slipped on her nightie, she was hardly able to keep her eyes open. She just about managed to make her way down the stairs, wish Fran goodnight, go back up again and collapse into bed. And that was when the reason for Fran's arriving tonight and not in the morning hit her. She had known it was unlikely Rica would be able to get off to sleep, considering it was Christmas Eve, and had made it her business to make sure she did by once more slipping a sleeping pill into Rica's hot chocolate!

Rica awoke the next morning feeling refreshed. She could tell by the light in the room that dawn had long since broken, and turned her head to look at the alarm clock on her bedside cabinet. She was surprised to see that it was getting on for nine-thirty. She had never slept this late since being a teenager. The appetising smell of cooking bacon assailed her nostrils. Her stomach started to rumble. She tossed back the covers and got out of bed, slipping on her dressing gown and slippers.

She found Fran downstairs, peeling potatoes at the sink. On one plate on the stove stood the frying pan with the sound of sizzling coming from it. On another was the kettle with a steady stream of steam coming from the spout. In comparison to the cold empty feel of the house last night, the kitchen was now warm with a cosy, homely feel to it.

On hearing her enter, Fran turned her head and said, 'I hope you're hungry, I've bacon cooking for you.' She was drying her hands on a tea towel. 'Sit yourself down and I'll bring it over for you with a cup of tea. I hope you slept well?'

'Well, you made sure of that, didn't you, Fran?' It was an accusation, but not an angry one. Rica was in fact grateful for what Fran had done. She could not deny feeling better, both mentally and physically, this morning.

Fran obviously wasn't going to admit her guilt. Looking at her blankly, she asked, 'One sandwich or two?'

Rica asked for one, then changed it to two, both with a dollop of HP sauce.

Fran told her, 'When you've finished your breakfast and got yourself washed and dressed, I thought we could take a stroll around the park to help build our appetites. Then it's back here to put the dinner on, and when we've eaten and cleared away, we can get the games box out, or see what programmes interest us on the television, or just read if you want to.'

Rica was staring at her open-mouthed. Fran voluntarily playing games and watching television! She knew, though, that this was her sister's way of showing she cared for her, keeping Rica's mind and body busy to help her get through the day, even if it involved activities Fran herself detested. Suddenly Rica was glad that her sister had insisted they should spend the day together. As Fran came across to the table and put a plate holding her bacon sandwiches in front of her, Rica caught her arm, looked up at her, and in a voice filled with affection, said, 'Thank you for all you're doing for me. I couldn't wish for a better sister than you, could I?'

Fran responded matter-of-factly, 'I totally agree with you. Now eat your breakfast before it gets cold.'

Against the odds, Rica actually enjoyed the day Fran had mapped out for them. The walk after breakfast, although damp and chilly, blew the cobwebs away. It wasn't easy for her, witnessing families out together, happy children testing out their new toys, roller skates, scooters, bikes, Frisbees and the like, but she knew that she couldn't go through the rest of her days avoiding such scenes and had to harden herself against them.

The dinner they cooked together and cleared away afterwards was delicious, albeit the bought pudding couldn't compare with her usual home-made one. Fran was true to her word and it was she who actually fetched the companion box of games from where it had been stored since it was last used. Although it wasn't in Fran's nature to whoop in delight on winning a game, there was a hint of smugness about her when on a roll of the dice she won a game of Snakes and Ladders, and she appeared a little miffed when she lost to Rica in a game of Ludo. In the early evening, while Rica watched a couple of light-entertainment programmes on the television with the sound down low, Fran read her book. Rica was aware of Fran's dislike of television so did not feel it fair to subject her to any more than an hour or so, considering she had already participated in another activity of which she was far from fond. And, after all, the day was supposed to be enjoyed by her too, so after turning off the television Rica tuned the radio into a station playing the sort of music Fran liked to listen to, and settled down to read a book herself. To Rica's surprise the light classical selection the station was playing was quite pleasant.

There was only one thing that was upsetting for her that day. After dinner she tried to order a taxi to take her to visit her mother in the home, only to find that the couple of firms that were working that day had no cab available until later that evening, at a time when the staff would be getting the patients into bed. Rica had no choice but to order a cab to take her on Boxing Day instead.

When she went to bed that night she didn't need any help from Fran to ensure she slept.

CHAPTER EIGHTEEN

It was two days before New Year's Eve and Rica and Jason were checking through all the stock that was left over from Christmas, to decide what was going to go into their January sale.

Rica hadn't a clue how to organise a sale but Jason came to her aid. He informed her that he had learned from Mr Dunmore that sales were a good way to get rid of excess stock from Christmas, shop-soiled items and slow-moving ones, but also there needed to be items included that enticed in bargain hunters, which meant cutting the profit margin on some of the more expensive items.

Although Jason's 'crick in the neck' seemed to have righted itself, he still hadn't regained his spark, still seeming to carry the weight of the world on his shoulders. Rica wondered if it was her imagination that he also appeared to be very awkward around her, and when they did converse, didn't seem able to look her in the eye.

He was now answering a question she had put to him on which cameras from their exclusive range he felt would draw in a crowd. Gesturing to the camera he was holding in his hand, he said, 'If it was me, Mrs Dunmore, I wouldn't put this camera in the sale as it's our best-seller in the top-of-the-range bracket. The people who can afford to buy one won't be worried whether we've knocked a few quid off.'

She took the camera from him and put it back in its place

in the glass counter cabinet, saying, 'I value your opinion, Jason, so this isn't going in. Now we've been through all the cameras, what's going in the sale and what's not, shall we tackle the sundries? We've two hundred Magicubes left over from Christmas so what do you think . . . reduce by a third . . .'

She was cut short by the jangle of the shop door announcing someone coming in and automatically turned her head to see that it was Bill. Rica smiled at him welcomingly, although it struck her that it was most unusual for him to be calling in at this time of a morning. As he made his way over to the counter it struck her that he wasn't sporting his usual smile either, but seemed pensive.

She asked him, 'Is anything wrong, Bill?'

He looked bemused that she should be asking him that. 'No, no, nothing is wrong. I was passing this way on my next job so thought I might as well pop in instead of making a special journey when I break for lunch.'

His response was more than plausible but regardless she had a feeling he wasn't being entirely honest with her. It was his manner when he had insisted that nothing was wrong. It was just a little too insistent.

He was saying to her, 'So . . . everything all right with you?'

He seemed relieved when she said it was.

Bill then nodded a greeting to Jason. 'All right, lad?

Jason gave a mumbled, 'Yes, thank you.' Politely leaving Rica to deal with Bill, he went over to the collection drawer and began to put developed photographs away.

Bill whispered to Rica, 'What's to do with him?'

She whispered back, 'He's been in a strange mood for a while now, but whatever is bothering him he's keeping very tight-lipped about.'

Bill thought about this for a moment before he said, 'As my old gran used to say, *It'll be something and nothing when it comes out in the wash*.' He pulled out a packet from the inside pocket of his work-worn donkey jacket and put it on the counter, telling her, 'The films from the Boxing Day Quorn hunt that I took last Sunday. I should have brought them in on Monday but . . . er . . . I've been up to my eyes and never got a chance. Same went for yesterday. I am sorry about that, Rica. I know you're on a deadline to get them developed and down to London for *Horse and Hound* magazine. I'd hate you to lose the contract with them to do all their equestrian photography in Leicestershire just because I was late bringing them in.'

She assured him, 'Don't worry, Bill, we have until Friday. I'll put a note with them asking Fisher to develop them as a matter of urgency, and we'll get them in the post to the magazine's photographic editor tomorrow. I appreciate that this time of year must be your busiest.'

He gave a loud exhalation of breath. 'It is. From now up until the weather gets warmer, nearing the end of March, I never get a let up. I shouldn't complain about being over-loaded with work, though, should I?'

She was eyeing him with concern. 'Well, you mustn't fail to tell me if ever you can't manage . . .'

He cut her short. 'I've told you before, if I've made a promise to do something, I'd have to be on my deathbed ever to let you down. Anything in for this week yet?'

'No. You're busy next Sunday, though, if you remember, photographing the charity event.'

'I do.'

'And just to check, you still have no objection to my joining you on these commissions, so I can learn from you?'

'There's not much else I can teach you, Rica. You just need to remember what you've learned and put it into practice. I'll pick you up on Friday night at seven when I come to swap the van for the car.' He then looked at her awkwardly and again asked, 'So . . . er . . . everything all right then?'

She frowned at him. 'I've already told you it is, so why are you asking again?'

He blustered, 'Oh, no reason, just asking. I'd best be off then.'

Rica watched as he went out through the door. She mused aloud to Jason, 'Do you think everything is all right with Bill? Only I get the impression something is . . . well . . . bothering him. He's definitely not himself.' When she received no response, she turned and looked over at Jason who appeared not to have heard her, standing with his back to her, continuing with his task of putting away packets of developed film. Rica tutted. A little bit stupid of her to be asking one man she was worried about what he thought of another. She went back to work, busying herself with the forthcoming sale.

Rica followed Simon's habit of advertising their sale in the *Mercury*. Saturday was the first day and she had expected a few bargain hunters to be waiting for the doors to open at nine o'clock, but did not expect to find a queue of a dozen clustered around the door, stamping their feet and banging their gloved hands together to ward off the bitter cold. Especially not when practically every other shop in the city began their sale today too. She slipped in the back way and boiled the kettle for a cup of tea for herself and Jason. The kettle was warm so she knew Fisher was in and had already mashed himself a brew. It was a good thing that she had made that tea as by the time twelve o'clock arrived there had not been a moment when their help was not in demand, the shop never having less than eight people waiting to be served. There were at least a dozen now, and Rica hoped no more came in as she was desperate for a sit down, even for five minutes, and a cup of tea. She had no doubt Jason felt the same.

A customer she was serving was dithering over whether

to take a Kodak Instamatic S-10 or S-20 when she became aware of grumbles of discontent amongst the queue behind the two people being served by herself and Jason. She looked up to see what was causing the murmurs of displeasure and saw a woman barging her way through the other customers to the front. Rica was about to tell her that she would have to wait her turn and go to the back of the queue when recognition struck her. It was Bill's wife, Freda. Rica wondered what she was doing here. Whatever it was about, she wasn't very happy, judging by the angry scowl on her face. Then an awful thought struck Rica. Had something happened to Bill?

As Freda arrived at the counter, before Rica had a chance to open her mouth and enquire, the other woman demanded, 'I want to talk to my husband.'

'He's not here, Mrs Simpson. When he does call in to check on what work we have in or to buy anything he's in need of, it's usually around one.'

She snapped back, 'Well, I'll need your address then.'

Rica frowned at her quizzically. 'Why?'

'I need to talk to him. You tell him that I'll be around tonight after he finishes work – and he'd better be there. We've things to sort out. Of course, that's unless he no longer has to work, if you're keeping him? In that case, I'll go and see him now.'

Rica looked taken aback. 'I beg your pardon?'

Freda sneered at her. 'Oh, you should be begging it, lady, but I'll not pardon you for stealing my husband off me. Never.'

Rica was gawping at her in astonishment. 'You think Bill and I are having an affair!'

'I don't think, I know. Now give me your address so I can go and sort stuff out with him. He needn't think he's leaving me high and dry with no money to pay the bills . . .'

Rica was acutely aware that all the customers, Jason too,

were riveted on what was going on between her and this woman openly accusing her of adultery. 'Would you care to come into the office, Mrs Simpson, and we can talk there?' she suggested.

Freda barked, 'No, I wouldn't. I think your customers should know what kind of establishment they are buying from . . . that the owner of it is a slut! Your husband is away looking after his sick uncle, isn't he? Does he know what you're up to behind his back?'

Now it was Rica's turn to snap, outraged by what she was being accused of. 'Nothing is going on behind my husband's back, Mrs Simpson. Your husband is just doing work for me, for which I pay him.'

Freda gave a scoffing laugh. 'Oh, pull the other one! Every spare minute he has he spends with you, either supposedly on a job or telling me he's popping over to yours for an hour, to have a look at the photos you've taken, so he can give you his expert opinion on how you can improve. I've heard some excuses in my time but looking at photos takes the biscuit! Every time he does a job for you, you go along as well. You two have been having an affair for ages and now you've enticed him to move in with you. Don't insult me by denying it.'

Rica cut her short. Her tone was angry. 'I *am* denying it. We are not having an affair, and we are not living together. How dare you suggest we are? Now would you please leave?'

Freda gave a snort. 'I'm not going anywhere until I've spoken to my husband and found out what provision he's going to make for me. He needn't think he's going to be living in luxury in your big house, with you the owner of a business, while I try and survive on the crumbs I earn from my part-time job.'

'I hardly live in luxury. My house is a semi-detached three bedroom, hardly the mansion you're insinuating. I live in it . . .' Rica suddenly remembered that as far as everyone else was aware her marriage to Simon was as solid as it ever had been, and that he was only away temporarily. She quickly added, '. . . on my own at the moment until my husband comes home with our son. If Mr Simpson has left you, it has nothing to do with me. Now, if you don't leave, Mrs Simpson, I shall call the police and have you forcibly removed.'

Freda opened her mouth to stand her ground but saw the look in Rica's eyes and knew she meant business. She wagged a warning finger at her and hissed, 'Don't think you've heard the last of this. No one makes a fool of Freda Simpson and doesn't pay the price.'

As she watched Freda weave her way back through the crowd to the door, Rica's thoughts were racing round her head. She didn't at all like what they were telling her. Bill must have known his wife was going to come into the shop and accuse her of having an affair with him. He'd asked her twice if everything was all right and seemed to be very relieved when she'd answered that it was. Was he, though, having an affair but covering up the woman's real identity by allowing his wife to think it was Rica he'd been seeing and was now living with? She couldn't believe it of him, not the Bill she knew and had grown to like very much over the months he had been helping her. But the facts seemed to be telling her he was not the decent sort he had made out.

She would tackle him tomorrow when he called for her for the charity shoot, let him know how hurt and angry she was that he had used her in such a way. She'd demand he tell his wife the truth. Of course, this would also be the end of their association. Rica couldn't and wouldn't work alongside, or be on friendly terms with, someone she knew had acted so despicably. Mixed with her anger there was a great sense of sadness. She had become very fond of the

Bill she knew, and to her shock realised she would miss him.

Someone was addressing her. It was Rica's customer, apologising for taking so long to decide but now he had he wanted to make his purchase. He had obviously been so intent on making his choice he hadn't been aware of the altercation that had just taken place. He was the only one who had not.

Rica found it very difficult to be outwardly pleasant and helpful afterwards to her customers while feeling so humiliated and upset by what had transpired, but she did her best and hoped no one noticed. Jason never mentioned a word to her about it. As the apprentice he wouldn't feel it his place to, and as his boss she wasn't obliged to explain herself to him. Regardless, she hoped that he didn't believe Freda Simpson's accusation as she didn't like the thought her employee would see her as a slut.

By the time Bill arrived to swap over vehicles and collect her on Sunday evening, Rica had reasoned with herself that to tackle him before they attended the event could prove foolish. She risked compromising the quality of the photographs, and at such short notice there was little chance of replacing Bill with someone else, especially on a Sunday evening, so she had no choice but to leave it until after they had done their job. It was going to be difficult for her to act like nothing had happened in front of him, but she was just going to have to.

Their attendance at the shoot went on for far longer than she had believed it would. When it had originally been booked, Rica was under the impression that all the event organiser wanted them to do was take photographs of the guests as they arrived in the foyer of the Grand Hotel and ad hoc ones during the auction after dinner. It transpired, though, that they were being expected to take photographs of the guests dancing too, after the auction had ended, which was very annoying when all she wanted to do was leave and get things over with. It was difficult for her to appear outwardly her normal self with Bill when inside her emotions were in turmoil. She couldn't help but be stilted towards him whenever they conversed. Although Bill said nothing, he must have been aware something wasn't right due to her shortness with him. He, too, was far from his normal self. He made none of his usual jokey comments, was very subdued and looked pale and drawn. The other shoots they had tackled together had been so pleasurable; this was far from that.

It was after eleven when Bill switched off the engine at the kerb outside her house, to begin the process of swapping vehicles, and said to her, 'I'll drop the films and equipment into the shop tomorrow dinnertime as usual.'

Rica's nerves were jangling now and she couldn't help but snap back, 'Thank you.'

He flashed a look at her. 'Are you all right, Rica?'

She replied abruptly, 'You must be blind and deaf, asking that. I know it's late and you have to get up early for work in the morning, but I need to talk to you. Not here. Will you come inside, please?

He looked at her blankly for a moment before an expression of acute horror filled his face. He let out a despairing groan and uttered, 'Freda has been to see you, hasn't she?'

Having it confirmed that he had known his wife intended to visit her and brand her what she had came as a devastating blow to Rica. She said icily, 'Yes, she did. It's a pity you never thought to warn me so that I was prepared. I don't like to think what the customers or Jason think of me, now I've been branded an adulteress.'

With that she got out of the car and marched up the path, leaving the front door open for Bill to follow her inside.

When he joined her she was sitting in an armchair in the

lounge and, although she had left the heating on so the room was cosy, she still had her coat on and was shivering, not with cold but with hurt and anger. She had poured herself a large gin and tonic but did not offer Bill one. She didn't want him in her home or in her life in any way now she had discovered what sort of man he was. The sooner she got this interview over with, the sooner she would be rid of him.

Bill sat down in the armchair opposite her. Raking his hand through his shock of black hair, he looked over at her, his face etched with deep regret. 'I'm so very sorry for Freda's visit to you yesterday, Rica. She'd threatened to pay you one but I didn't believe she'd actually carry out her threat.'

'Well, you obviously don't know your wife as well as you think you do. Same goes for me, doesn't it? I don't know you, Bill. You're nothing like the decent man you made me believe you were.'

Bill's head reared back and there was defiance in his eyes. His voice was firm and filled with conviction when he told her, 'I *am* the person I've shown you I am. Nothing more, nothing less.'

He looked so sincere, sounded so genuine, that for a moment Rica believed him. Maybe he hadn't been playing a part, using her to cover up the real identify of his lover and fool his wife. But the facts were telling her otherwise. 'You can't be. A decent man would not let his wife believe that he was having an affair with one woman in order to keep secret the identity of his real lover. I want your assurance you will do the honourable thing and put your wife straight as to who the woman is you are having an affair with, so I don't get a repeat performance in the shop. Then you can leave and I don't ever want to see you again. You can leave the films and equipment here with me tonight; I'll arrange to get them to the shop.'

Again Bill's voice was firm and full of conviction. 'I'm not having an affair with anyone, Rica.'

She glared at him and demanded, 'Aren't you? Your wife seems to think you are, and with me. She must have her reasons for believing that.'

He gave a heavy sigh. 'Freda knows the truth, that you and I are not involved with each other in any way other than as work colleagues and friends . . . I've come to regard you as a friend, a good one, and I hope you have me . . . it merely serves her purpose to make out that we are more to each other.'

Rica frowned, bewildered. 'I don't understand. What purpose?'

'Blackmail.'

'Blackmail? Your own wife is blackmailing you! But why? How?'

'It's a long story.'

'Huh! I don't care how long it is, I think I deserve to be told it, considering I've been accused in front of witnesses of doing something you now tell me my accuser knows damned well I'm innocent of.'

Wringing his hands, Bill took a deep breath. 'You're right, you do deserve an explanation.' He seemed visibly to shrink before Rica's eyes. His shoulders sagged as he slumped back into the chair and sighed. 'It's Freda that's been having an affair and it's been going on for a long time, although I only found out recently. With a man, Peter, who for fifteen years I thought of as my friend, who'd not hesitate to call on me if he needed a hand with anything, and vice versa. A man I'd go to the pub with now and again and whose wife considers herself my wife's best friend. Poor Susan will be devastated when this all comes out, just like I was.'

He paused for a moment. It was apparent that relaying such a personal story to Rica was proving very painful as well as humiliating to Bill. His voice lowered as he continued,

'Freda and I were very young when we got married, had to as our son was on the way, but we were very much in love and would have married eventually. I was only on apprentice's wages at the time so we moved in with my parents. It wasn't an ideal way to start our married life but it wasn't that bad as my parents are kind-hearted, easygoing people and Freda never seemed anything but happy all the time we lived with them.

'Kevin was two and Paula on the way by the time I'd finished my apprenticeship and could afford to rent us a house of our own. It wasn't up to much but Freda made it a home for us. We moved several times in those first ten years of marriage, each time to a better property, and five years ago, having started up on my own a couple of years before that, business was doing well enough for us to save a deposit and afford a mortgage on a house of our own, which is the one we're in now.

'Freda had never been one for going out without me except to her knitting circle once a week, which she joined when the children were just babies. I had no problem with that. To my mind, she needed to have some time away from the kids and I would always make sure I never worked late on her knitting circle night, so I could look after them. Then, about five years ago, out of the blue, she announced to me that she'd joined the W.I. and was also going to start going to the bingo hall with a woman she'd become friendly with from her part-time job at the florist's. She'd taken it when our youngest child, Paula, left school to go to work. Again, I never begrudged her having a bit of a life by herself, but I have to say now that when the kids were out themselves with their mates every night, I found it very lonely in the house on my own those three nights a week Freda was out too.

'I think that's why I started to take my hobby more seriously and learned to develop the photos I'd taken, as a way to busy myself on those nights. Freda encouraged me, said

207

it was good for me to have a hobby. That was until she realised it was costing money she felt she could find a better use for. I pointed out that I was spending no more, probably less in fact, than she must be on her nights out. It was about this time that we stopped going out together as we usually did on a Saturday night, meeting up with Peter and Susan down the local. Freda said she didn't enjoy their company any more as she found them both boring, and would I mind if we knocked our get togethers on the head? I quite enjoyed our Saturday nights and couldn't understand why she found Peter and Susan boring as I didn't at all – good company I thought they were – but I agreed, to keep Freda happy. I'd just go for a pint myself if I felt like one. I'm not what you would call a boozer, but I like a drink now and again.

'Freda always used to go to town about once a month, on a Saturday afternoon, but she started going *every* Saturday afternoon. She told me she was meeting a friend for a coffee and then they'd browse the shops together.' He stopped and looked at Rica, his eyes filled with shame. 'How blind can you be to what's going on under your nose, when you don't notice your own wife is dolling herself up like she would for a night out, just to go to town and the W.I. and bingo hall?'

As Bill's story was unfolding it was becoming increasingly uncomfortable listening for Rica. Because Simon was always at home when he wasn't at work, she now realised that his illicit meetings with the woman he'd eventually left her for had to have taken place during his working day . . . with him slipping out of work on a supposed errand . . . and at times when he'd told her he was off on a shoot, he must have been with her. This meant he must have told Rica numerous lies to cover up his infidelity and she'd believed every one of them because she'd had no reason not to. She couldn't answer Bill's question because she herself had been in the same boat, not seeing what was happened under her own nose either.

He heaved a sad sigh before he continued. 'And how gullible I was when I found a bank book in her name, hidden behind all the cleaning stuff and toilet rolls in the cupboard under the sink in the bathroom. Freda was out at the time and I was having a wash when the sink became blocked. I cleared out the cupboard to get to the U-bend, and that's when I found it. I could see she'd opened it the year before. There was nearly fifty pounds in the account, but I believed without question her explanation for it. When she came home, I confronted her. Freda burst into tears and snatched the book from me, accusing me of spoiling the surprise she'd had for me. She told me she'd been saving up for us to go on holiday abroad, to Spain, not to a cheap hotel but a five-star one, and not just for a week but sixteen days, and have plenty of spending money too so we could go on all the trips while we were there. She'd managed to put the money away by shopping for bargains and watching what she spent on her nights out. She'd only started going to the bingo, she said, in the hope of getting a big win so she could spring her surprise on me even quicker.

'She told me she was doing it because she felt I deserved such a treat after all the years I'd worked so hard, making sure our family never went without. I was overwhelmed that she wanted to do something like this for me. I told her I really appreciated it and would look forward to the holiday. She said that now I knew, if I chipped in with any spare cash I had, she'd add it to her savings and then we'd have the money for the holiday all the quicker. I told her I would. What she was doing, though, got me to thinking that maybe I could plan a surprise for her. I'd no idea as yet how I was going to get the money.

'Then only a week later you offered me a way to earn some extra, covering your commissions, and the real bonus to me was that it was doing something I enjoyed doing. It was decent money you were offering me and, if I saved up,

I could do something really special for Freda. I had the very thing in mind. Her sister had emigrated to Australia with her family several years ago on the government ten-pound scheme. I knew Freda missed her as they were very close. She would give anything to visit Australia. We're not exactly on the breadline, but the kind of money a trip like that would cost was usually out of the question for the likes of us. Now maybe it wasn't. I decided to open my own bank account and put all the money I earned from you into it.

'After I'd done my first job for you, Freda made it clear she was expecting me to hand her my earnings so she could put them in the bank along with her savings. She wasn't at all happy when I just gave her a few shillings and told her I was following her lead and saving up for something special for her. She demanded to know what. She didn't like it when I told her she'd have to be patient and wait and see. I realise now she was hoping it would be something she could sell and get cash for, like jewellery. I hid my bank book in my van so she wouldn't find it.' Bill ruefully shook his head and his voice was gruff with emotion when he added, 'I feel such a fool now, remembering that at the time I was so excited about my plan to do something special for her. I couldn't wait to see her face when I handed her her ticket for Australia – when really all she wanted was the cash to help fund her new future with Peter.'

He ran a hand wearily over his face, then looked down before carrying on. 'It was the Saturday before Christmas when I found out what had been going on behind my back. It's not the sort of Christmas present you expect to get, finding your wife has been cheating on you . . . bad enough when it's with a stranger, but doubly when it's with someone you considered a friend. And it wasn't an overnight affair either but had been going on for over five years.

'I'd still be none the wiser now if my van hadn't broken down on my way back from seeing a customer. Peter is a mechanic, has his own business, just a one-man-band in a back street but, like my business, it brings in enough to keep his family well looked after. When I went into business myself it was taken for granted that I'd use Peter to maintain my van. That Saturday I'd had a busy morning, it was coming up for two and I was on my way home. We'd no shoots that afternoon so I planned to have a soak in the bath then take myself off to snap some photographs of my own. As I was nearly home the van suddenly stopped with no warning. Lucky there was no other traffic near me or it could have caused an accident. Thankfully I was only a couple of streets away from Peter's workshop. I knew he'd be there as after he shuts at one on a Saturday, he'll spend a couple of hours catching up with paperwork. Or so myself and Susan were led to believe. I now know that what he was catching up on was definitely not paperwork. I was hoping it would be a minor repair that he could do on the road otherwise we'd the task of pushing the van back to the workshop and me having to do without it while he got it going again.

'When I arrived at the workshop I knew he'd have locked the roller shutter door so immediately went around to the door at the side. There's a window just before the door and as I passed I automatically looked through it. It was grimy but still possible for me to see into the garage. I stopped short in shock at what I saw. Peter had a woman with him. She had her back to me, but I knew it definitely wasn't his wife. They were by the tool bench at the back of the garage and . . . well, I'll leave what they were doing to your imagination, Rica. But the surprise of catching him with another woman, doing what they were, was nowhere near as shocking to me as what I realised when the woman turned her head and I caught her profile.'

He shut his eyes at the memory of what he'd seen. 'My world fell apart. I just froze. Couldn't tell you how long I stood there, blindly staring through that window, seeing Freda and Peter so intimately together. I can't describe to you how I was feeling. It's the worst thing that's ever happened to me. Maybe if I'd suspected there was something going on between them it might not have hit me so hard, but I didn't as neither of them gave me any reason to. I hated to think what it would do to Susan when it all came out. I knew I should be a man and go into the garage and confront them both, but call me a coward, I just couldn't bring myself to. I wanted to go home and try and get my head around all this. So that's what I did.

'Freda came back a couple of hours later. I heard her come in and start to make her way up the stairs. With the van not being parked outside, I expect she thought I wasn't home and was going to have a bath or wash to get his smell off her before I came back. I was in the lounge and called out to her. I couldn't see her but I could picture the shock on her face, realising she wasn't alone in the house. It was several moments before she came into the lounge with a smile on her face, breezily telling me she wouldn't have stayed in town for as long if she'd known I would get finished earlier.

'I told her that I was nearly home when the van broke down and that I'd gone to Peter's garage to ask him if he'd come and have a look at it. Only, when I got there, I saw he was already busy. My look told her I knew what he had been busy doing, and with whom.' Bill gave a forlorn sigh and said bitterly, 'Freda never even bothered to deny it, make out that I'd been seeing things. She never even looked ashamed or the least bit guilty. She just told me that I was going to find out one day, but she would have preferred it if it had been when Peter and she had got enough money between them to start a new life together. She didn't even seem concerned when I asked her how she thought our children would react to this state of affairs. Just said that they were old enough to understand that marriages break down.

'It was then it hit me like a ton of bricks that there never was going to be a surprise holiday for me, that it was just an excuse she'd used to cover the fact she was saving to run off with Peter. I wondered if he was doing the same behind Susan's back, squirrelling money away.

'Up until then I was praying that what I'd seen was just a one off, and that when I confronted Freda with it, she'd break down and say how stupid she'd been, that what she felt for Peter was just infatuation. That it wouldn't happen again. Beg me to forgive her. I would have done, I loved her enough to do that. I asked her what Peter had got that I hadn't. Obviously there was something about him that she needed and that I lacked. She said if I really wanted to know, he was far better in bed. Not really what a man wants to hear, and she didn't show any remorse for making me feel so inadequate. But if she hadn't cut me deep enough already, she then insisted on telling me that almost from the moment she'd met Peter, it was apparent to both of them that there was a spark between them. They used to flirt a bit when we all got together and me and Susan weren't looking, but that was all. But about five years ago, on New Year's Eve, they were both a bit the worse for drink and Freda wasn't sure how it happened but they ended up together at the back of the outside privvy. She didn't need to go into any details for me to know what they'd got up to while Susan and I were inside the house, enjoying the party, unaware of what our *better halves* were doing behind our backs.

'She then really put salt on my wounds when she told me that if I gave her all the money I'd earned from my work for you, Rica, she would pack up her things in the morning and be out of my hair and never bother me again. I couldn't believe what she was asking of me. I didn't recognise this woman who was acting so coldly with me, treating me like

213

I didn't matter at all. She definitely wasn't the lovely girl I'd married twenty years ago. I told her I might be blind enough not to have noticed what was going on, but I wasn't daft enough to hand over my hard-earned money for her to set up home with her fancy man. She confounded me again, then told me that if I didn't she would make our children believe I'd been ill treating her for years. I told her that she could tell them what she liked, our children knew I was not capable of hurting any woman, let alone their mother. I'd had enough by this time, just wanted to get away from her and try and get my head around all this. I had no idea where I was going but I didn't care as long as I got away. That morning I'd gone off to work thinking I was a happily married man, wondering what to buy my wife for Christmas that she would like, looking forward to having the family all around me on Christmas Day, looking forward to me and Freda fussing over our first grandchild in a few months' time. And there I was, only hours later . . .

'I got up and went upstairs to pack a few things. She followed me up, shouting out her threat that she would manage to turn our kids against me. When she saw me packing she demanded to know where I was going. I told her that after what she'd done, what I did in future was none of her business. When I got back down the stairs she tried to stop me from leaving unless I handed my savings over to her. She was blocking the front door bodily. I did manhandle her then. I took her arm and dragged her away from the front door and pushed her over to sit on the stairs.

'As I was heading down the path to the front gate, she ran after me and grabbed my arm. She was shaking with anger and that was when she threatened to come to the shop and accuse you of enticing me away from her. I never thought for a minute she would carry out her threat. I just thought she was clutching at straws, trying anything to get me to change my mind and hand my savings over. I shook her hand off my arm and went off, hearing her screaming after me . . . just what she was screaming, I've no idea. I'd closed my ears to her by then, wanting to put distance between us. I went to my parents' and that's where I've been staying since.'

He looked at Rica for several long moments before he said in all sincerity, 'I've never tried to make out that I'm anything other than what you see before you, Rica. What I will admit to, though, is being stupid enough to have trusted my wife so implicitly it never crossed my mind she'd deceive me in any way.'

Rica was feeling both mortified and desperately sorry for Bill. Mortified that she had been so quick to believe the worst of him before she had asked him for his version of events, and sorry for the terrible way his marriage had come to an end. On top of all the other emotions he would be experiencing, she didn't like the thought that he was accusing himself of being stupid because of misplaced trust in his own wife. Without thinking she said, 'You're no more stupid than I am, Bill.'

He narrowed his eyes, bemused. 'What do you mean by that?'

Rica realised just what she had said and tried to make out that she hadn't meant anything in particular. But then she remembered that on Christmas Day she had finally accepted the fact that Simon had left her, and made a promise to herself to stop dwelling on the past and make the best of what the future held for her. She wouldn't be doing that if she was still hiding the truth of her situation from the outside world, would she? And who better to come clean to about her broken marriage than someone who would be understanding because they were facing the same situation?

She looked Bill in the eye and told him, 'Because I didn't see what was going on under my nose either.' She took a deep breath before she continued, 'Bill, my husband isn't looking after his sick uncle's business. Simon has left me and taken our son, and I have no idea where they are.' She then told him the whole story.

By the time she had finished, Bill was looking both shocked and sympathetic. 'Oh, Rica, I don't know what to say. I thought it was bad enough discovering my wife was cheating on me, planning to leave me and with whom, but to find out your husband had left you and never even had the guts to tell you, just went out and never came back, taking your child . . . well, what kind of man does that make him?'

'I've had a terrible job to accept it. It's three months since Simon went and it's obvious by now that he's not going to come back, so I have no choice but to accept it. If you had told me that Simon was going to do this, right up to the day he left I would have laughed in your face.'

'Same with me over Freda.'

'Are your children aware of what's gone on?' she asked.

He nodded sadly. 'They found out on Christmas Day. It's always been a tradition that we spend it at my parents' house. It's usually such a fun affair, but this year it was far from that. I wasn't ready to face them with this news, needed time to get used to it myself, but my mother told me that it was something that shouldn't be put off. The kids needed to know in case they went to the house and found I'd left and Peter had moved in. That wouldn't be at all fair on them. And, of course, immediately they arrived they'd want to know why their mother wasn't there. I wasn't prepared to blacken her in their eyes . . . Freda had always been a good mother to them. If they were going to find out the truth of why we had broken up, then it wasn't going to be me who told them.

'It was awful, nearly as dreadful to me as catching her with Peter. Of course, they both knew something was up when they arrived to find their mother not there. I made some lame excuse that she'd a headache and was resting, would be along later. In the end I just couldn't tell them, so their granny did. She told them what I'd told her to. That me and their mother had decided to go our separate ways as we weren't getting on any longer. I could tell Kevin was shocked and upset, but he never said anything. Paula was a different matter. We couldn't stop her crying for ages. She won't accept what has happened between me and her mother, just insists we're going through a bad patch and we'll sort it out and get back together. She'll have to accept it eventually. I just hope Freda feels some remorse for the pain she's caused her kids.'

He then eyed Rica apologetically. 'I don't know what Freda hoped to achieve by coming to the shop and doing what she did. I can only think that she was fuming so much because I wouldn't give in to her demands for money, it was her way of paying me back. She knows how much I enjoy our photography shoots and that they were giving me good experience and the confidence to do weddings and special occasions for friends and neighbours who can't afford to hire a professional. By causing bad feeling between us, I think she was hoping you'd not have me work for you any longer.'

Rica said with conviction, 'Well, if that was her aim, Freda hasn't achieved it.'

His eyes glinted. 'She hasn't?'

Rica smiled. 'No, she hasn't.'

'Oh, Rica, I wasn't sure, even though I've explained my side of the story, whether you'd still want to be associated with me or not.'

'I'm just so sorry, Bill, that I'd had you hung, drawn and quartered without even waiting to hear your side of things first. I was seriously doubting my own instincts, again after they failed me over Simon . . .' She smiled warmly at him before she added, 'They didn't as far as you're concerned.

217

You are the decent man my first impressions told me you were.' She swallowed back the last of her drink before she asked him, 'I expect it feels strange being under your parents' roof again? Will you stay with them until Freda moves out of your house to start afresh with Peter and you can move back in?'

He sadly shook his head. 'I'll never go back to live there, Rica. That house holds far too many memories for me. One of my mother's neighbours' kids took a letter from me around to Freda the day after I left. In it I told her I would go to a solicitor in the New Year and have the house signed over to her. She could have everything in it except for my personal possessions, which I would have someone go and collect for me. I told her that was all she was going to get out of me so there was no point in trying for anything else. I haven't heard a peep out of her since so I assume she's happy with that. If she's any sense, she'll realise it's more than she deserves in the circumstances. This has devastated my parents – they both thought the world of Freda – but both of them have told me that it goes without saying I can live with them for as long as I want to. I will get my own place some time, but I must say I'm rather enjoying having my mum fussing and faffing around me. If she had her way, she'd be tucking me into bed at night.'

They both managed a chuckle at the vision that conjured up.

Bill continued, 'The only downside to living back at my parents' is that the house is only a two-bedroomed terraced, so no dark room for me.' He heaved a sigh. 'Not that that's a problem to me as at the moment I've no real interest in anything including photography. I'm not sleeping at night, and it's a struggle for me to get up in the morning. I haven't been to work since this happened. I apologise for lying to you and telling you I was up to my eyes with work and would be until March. All the jobs I had lined up, I've passed on to my mates in the trade until I feel up to returning. If anyone has telephoned the house asking for me then Freda hasn't let me know . . . I know my parents, my mam in particular, are worried about me, but I can't seem to pull myself together.'

'But you managed the shoot tonight, Bill?'

'I wouldn't have, Rica, if I could have got someone to cover the commission for me, but as I don't know anyone who could, I forced myself. I told you before, I'd have to be on my deathbed to let you . . . anyone . . . down after I'd promised to do something.'

She knew only too well just what it had taken him to muster the motivation to wash and dress himself, let alone mix with over a hundred and fifty people and be polite and charming to get the best shots of them, coming over as though he hadn't a care in the world when in truth his life was shattered and all he probably wanted to do was crawl into a hole and die. She had to fight back tears of gratitude that he'd made such an effort for her.

'Oh, Bill, thank you. I speak from experience. This pain you're in will ease, but it'll take time and it won't happen without help from others. I'd probably still be in bed wallowing in self-pity myself but Fran had other ideas. It was she who made me see that what I was doing to myself was not achieving anything. If Fran were here now, she'd be telling you that the best way you can help yourself is to keep yourself busy. I know that, the way you're feeling now, it's easier said than done, but it worked for me. It might for you too, Bill.'

He looked at her thoughtfully. 'Well, if what your sister suggested worked for you, maybe it has some merit. I have to say that for a while tonight, while we were working, I forgot what was happening in my personal life because I was concentrating so hard on what I was doing. I won't make promises I have my doubts about keeping, but I'll do

219

my best to give it a try.' He looked at her searchingly for a moment. 'You and your sister are not at all alike, are you? Unless you had introduced her as your sister, I never would have thought for a minute you two were even related, let alone closely.'

Rica smiled. 'No, we're not at all alike, in looks or personality. Our mother used to say that we were like cold and hot tea – totally opposite from each other. I used to wish that we were more alike, like my best friend when I was a young girl, Helen, and her sister were, and like them we'd do things together and tell each other our secrets. But, no, instead I had an old-fashioned, stick-in-the-mud, bossy, know-it-all of a sister.

'I still felt like this about her until the business with Simon. That's when I became so thankful that Fran is like she is. She never shows her feelings and won't talk about them. She keeps herself very much to herself and has no sense of humour, whereas I'm the opposite. I once found her very hard to understand, thought she was a cold fish.

'I'd never needed her before in the way I did when Simon left me. It was a shock to me to discover then how caring and unselfish Fran actually is, beneath her austere surface. If she hadn't bossed and pushed me into picking myself up and making a future for myself, then I'd probably still be in bed now, wallowing in self-pity.'

'Well, I have to say that on the occasions I've met her, she's frightened me to death,' Bill mused, then realised he had spoken without thinking what he was going to say first. 'I'm sorry, I didn't mean . . .'

Rica was laughing. 'It's all right, I know exactly what you mean. She frightens me sometimes. It's a pity that she doesn't show her softer side more often, but I've learned now to accept her as she is.'

He looked wistful. 'I envy you having a sister, whatever she's like. I've always wished for a brother or sister as I'm an only child. My parents wanted a big family and tried to give me a few of each, but after Mam suffered several miscarriages they made do with just me.'

Rica's heart went out to his mother. She knew what it was like to want a child in vain, but at least she had had one. She felt the need for another drink, and felt guilty now for not offering Bill one.

'Would you like a drink?' she asked him.

'I would but it's past one,' he said, noticing the time on the star-burst clock. 'My mother won't be able to sleep until I get in.' He smiled at her warmly. 'Thank you, Rica.'

'What for? I haven't done anything.'

'Oh, but you have. By telling me what you did, you've made me realise I'm not the only one to have had the rug pulled out from under them. I know there's still a future for me, but I have to make it for myself, like you did.'

'Well, don't expect to get up tomorrow and have put this all behind you. As I said before, it does take you a while to come to terms with it all. We've no more bookings now until into the New Year and you've a note of those, but if you find you're not up to doing any, just let me know and I'll ask Mr Pointer or the man Simon used to use, if he's fit and well now. They can cover them until you feel better in yourself.'

'Thank you. I really appreciate that. But hopefully you won't need to call on anyone else, I'm going to work hard to see that doesn't happen.'

He got up and Rica saw him to the front door. As she let him out, a thought struck her and she said, 'Bill, when you feel up to taking up your own photography again, you can always use the dark room at the shop to develop your shots.'

He looked delighted. 'Really? Oh, Rica, thank you. But wouldn't Mr Fisher have something to say about that . . . someone else using his dark room?'

'He can say what he likes, it's not his dark room, it's mine.

I'll be the one to say who can use it or not. Anyway, it's not likely you'll cross paths, is it, as you'll be using it in the evenings or on a Sunday. I'm sure you'll leave things as you found them so he need never know.' She cocked an eyebrow at him, eyes twinkling. 'Now you might have withdrawn yourself temporarily from society and can lie in bed all day tomorrow if you want, but some of us have to get up at the crack of dawn and go to work. So goodnight, Bill.'

Rica watched him head off down the path and get into his van. She gave him a wave as he drove away before she returned inside the house, locking the door after her. She felt desperately sorry for Bill, knowing what he was now going through, but then unlike her own case at least he knew at once that there was no hope of repairing his marriage. The healing process would start quicker for him than it had done for her.

Although he had no Fran bullying him into putting on a brave face and making a future for himself, she hoped it wasn't long before Bill launched himself back into the outside world as, to her surprise, Rica realised she would miss his cheery face coming into the shop, and their working together on the photographic commissions meanwhile.

CHAPTER NINETEEN

A week later, a thoughtful Rica was just about to start clearing away after her dinner. She hadn't really enjoyed the meal, as she didn't like eating alone. But it was Fran who was occupying her thoughts at the moment.

Rica had not been looking forward to New Year's Eve, having never before spent it on her own. She believed that it was a night to be spent with family and friends, enjoying a drink or two and at twelve o'clock all toasting a welcome to the arrival of the New Year. Before Ricky had come into their lives, Simon and Rica's New Year's Eve parties were legendary, and even after he appeared and parties had ceased she and Simon would still sit up and toast the New Year in together. Rica knew that spending such nights on her own was the way of things in the future and, not wanting to allow herself to become morose, had made a plan to herald in the New Year with a gin and tonic and the television for company.

But it seemed Fran had other ideas. She told Rica that she would be coming over to see in the New Year with her. Rica hadn't had the heart to tell her sister that she would prefer to spend it the way she had planned, not after all that Fran had done for her recently.

The fact that Fran wasn't otherwise engaged on New Year's Eve did, however, suggest to Rica that her own plan to get her sister and Reginald Moffett together had not led to a relationship forming between them. Had it gone the way she had hoped, then surely Reginald would have wanted to spend New Year's Eve with Fran? This realisation saddened Rica. She had felt instinctively that her sister and he were made for each other. It appeared she'd been wrong, and they weren't. The chances of Fran meeting another man were not high, in Rica's opinion. She felt it a shame that her sister might never experience what it felt like to be loved and cared for, held tightly by a pair of strong arms, and be at the centre of someone else's world. Her own relationship might have ended badly, but at least she had experienced all of those things.

Despite Rica believing that New Year's Eve with Fran for company would be a sombre affair, it turned out to be quite the contrary. To Rica's shock, Fran turned up with a small bottle of cherry brandy in her overnight case. She told her speechless sister in her matter-of-fact manner that when Rica toasted in the New Year with her gin and tonic, Fran would do the same with a drop of the brandy as she had found out recently she had a taste for it. Finding her voice, Rica had curiously asked her how she had come to find she had a liking for cherry brandy, considering she had never before known any form of alcoholic drink to pass her sister's lips. As usual Fran had been very tight-lipped, just responded that she had forgotten and made it clear the subject was not open to further discussion.

As was the case on Christmas night, they listened for a while to the radio and then had the television on while Rica watched a variety show and Fran read her book. Periodically during the evening Rica would catch sight of her sister out of the corner of her eye. Fran was looking wistful and Rica wondered why, but knew it was a waste of time asking her. She would only find out if Fran chose to tell her, and it didn't appear she was going to. All things considered, Rica actually enjoyed the evening. Whether Fran did or not she kept to herself, but she did thank Rica for a nice time before she disappeared into the guest bedroom.

The next Friday evening Rica was wondering again what could have been the reason for Fran's contemplative mood on New Year's Eve when a loud rap on the front door made her jump. She groaned inwardly, hoping it wasn't a visitor in the form of a friendly neighbour. A couple of them had taken to dropping in on her, word having now spread that she had been abandoned by her husband. Although she appreciated their concern for her, she wasn't in the mood for making chit-chat tonight. It had been the last day of the sale today and the shop had been mobbed from opening to closing with last-minute bargain hunters. There hadn't been that many bargains left and most of the shoppers had gone away empty-handed, but they'd still had to be dealt with and she was tired and had planned to have a hot bath and an early night to refresh herself for tomorrow.

With a plan in mind as to how to get rid politely of a well-meaning neighbour, Rica went to answer the summons. On seeing who her unexpected caller was she smiled, genuinely pleased to see them.

Before she had time to give Bill a greeting she was asked, 'I'm not disturbing you, am I? I can always come back another time.'

'Only stopping me from washing up my dinner dishes, and they can wait.' She stepped aside. 'Come on in.'

Seated in the cosy lounge, sipping gin for Rica and Scotch for Bill, she said to him, 'I hadn't expected to see you for a while.' She quickly appraised him. 'You look well.'

He grinned. 'You mean not so haggard as the last time you saw me. I probably look better on the outside than I feel inside, though. I did take note of your sister's advice. I could either spend months pitying myself or cut out that stage and take charge now. I decided on the latter. It's not easy, is it? But I've made a bit of progress. I risk losing my business if I don't get back soon, so I'm aiming to start next Monday.'

Rica was looking impressed. 'You should be very proud of yourself, achieving what you have already.'

He looked pleased by her praise. 'Well, this afternoon I took myself off down the canal to take some photos. Not usually the sort of day I'd choose . . . very misty, cold and damp, and the light wasn't at all good. I doubt I've snapped anything of merit, but then you never know just what exactly you've taken until the snaps are developed, as you've seen yourself.'

Only too well. There had been many times when Rica was really excited, believing she taken a shot that was going to cause a sensation in the world of photography, only to cringe in embarrassment on viewing the developed negative. Times too when she had thought a roll of shot film wouldn't prove to be worth the expense, only to be surprised by how well several shots had turned out.

She said to him, 'And I gather you'd like to take me up on my offer of using the dark room?'

'If the offer is still open, yes, please.'

'Of course it is. I'll go and fetch you my keys. I will need them returning tonight, though, so I can get into the shop in the morning, but I'll send Jason to the ironmonger's to get a back door key cut for you tomorrow and then you can come and go as you please out of hours.'

She made to get up to fetch the keys but Bill stalled her, saying, 'Well, I was thinking, Rica . . . You're keen to learn the developing process and it's not likely Mr Fisher is going to oblige. Even if you ordered him to show you, the way he's been behaving I've my doubts whether he'd actually do it properly anyway. Hopefully you will find a replacement for him soon and then you'll be rid of him for good. Anyway, I'd be happy to show you. It would be like a thank you from me to you for allowing me to use the dark room.'

Bill had just solved a huge problem. Rica did need to learn that side of the business and Sid Fisher was not prepared to help. 'You don't need to pay me back for using the dark room, Bill, I'm happy to let you use it,' she said. 'But I will take you up on your offer to teach me the ins and outs of processing. Let me know when you're up to having a pupil along with you.'

'There's no time like the present, is there? Unless you've got something on tonight. We could make it another time if you have?'

Rica's plan to have a hot bath to ease her aching muscles was suddenly forgotten in her excitement at finally being shown the part of the business that still remained a mystery to her. 'No, I haven't.' She jumped up from her seat. 'I'll fetch my coat along with the keys.'

As they entered through the back gate of the shop premises, Rica was surprised to see a light shining through the kitchen window. She pulled a face and mused, 'Oh, I could have sworn the last thing I did before I locked the door behind me tonight was switch off the kitchen light.' She gave a laugh. 'Must be going doo-lally in my old age.' Immediately she stepped into the kitchen she noticed that the kettle was humming over a low flame on the old gas cooker. She frowned and said, 'Well, I know I wouldn't have left that on.'

Bill looked knowingly at her and said, 'Someone's here.'

She had realised that too and nodded in agreement. Looking concerned she said, 'Fisher was off as usual tonight before I'd locked the front door and turned over the sign, and Jason left the same time as I did. One of them must have come back, and obviously not just to collect something they left behind, considering that boiling kettle.'

With that she went over to the door leading to the rest of the premises and stepped into the corridor, Bill following behind. The corridor wasn't lit but both of them could see lights shining from under all the doors except for the main shop. She made to head for the office first as no one was allowed in there usually except for herself or Fran. If someone was in there now they had to be up to no good. She stopped abruptly, Bill almost colliding with her, when the door to the studio opened and a young woman came out. She was young, about seventeen, and very attractive although her face was caked with a thick application of make-up. Her blond hair hung past her shoulders. She was wearing a well-worn skimpy short robe in bright garish colours, it being apparent there were no clothes underneath.

She too stopped short on finding she wasn't alone in the corridor. Clasping her hand to her chest, she declared, 'Bloody hell, yer didn't half gimme a scare!' She looked Rica over, eyes mocking. 'Well, yer far too old ter be the new gel that's starting tonight.' She then looked at Bill and laughed sardonically. 'And you definitely ain't her. Yer must be after seeing Maurice about summat. If yer know 'im, yer'll know he dun't like being disturbed when he's setting up a shot so you'd better wait in there for him,' she suggested, pointing at the office door. 'I'll tell him he's got people to see him when I get back from the lavvy. Excuse me, I gotta dash or I'll wet meself!'

With that she shoved past them both and rushed off in the direction of the back of the premises.

Both Rica and Bill were staring blindly after her, minds whirling.

It was Rica who spoke first. 'She was naked under that flimsy robe.'

He nodded. 'That was what I was thinking. She said this Maurice chap is in the studio setting up a shot?'

Rica nodded.

'I don't like the sound of this,' Bill said to her in a worried whisper.

Her face was grim. 'No, neither do I.'

Rica made to head for the door leading into the studio but Bill caught her arm, pulling her to a halt. 'Best you stay in the van while I go and find out just what is going on in there.'

Normally she would have readily done what Bill told her to since, if any possible danger lurked, then men were usually the ones to make it safe, but if what she suspected was going on, then the business – her son's inheritance – could be in serious jeopardy and Rica wasn't prepared to go and sit in the van and leave Bill to deal with it alone. What really concerned her, though, was that there had been no sign of a forced entry. Did this mean that Simon had given his permission to Maurice, whoever he was, to use the premises before he went off to begin his new life?

Before Bill could stop her, Rica marched over to the studio and went inside. She had prepared herself for a shock but had not expected to feel so angry at what her business was being used for.

Inside she was confronted by the sight of a skinny, tall man, wearing extremely tight red velvet trousers which left hardly anything to the imagination around his crotch area, a frilled white shirt, matching red velvet waistcoat and scuffed black Cuban-heeled boots. His hair was down to his shoulders, and looked greasy and straggly. His face was long and narrow, features sharp. A hand-rolled cigarette hung from one corner of his mouth, a thin spiral of strange-smelling smoke wafting from it. His back to Rica and Bill, he was leaning over the camera sitting on a tripod, focusing its lens. The camera was aimed at a chair. It was one of the wing-back ones from out of the shop with a long strip of gold silky material carelessly draped over it. Behind it was a backdrop of a Victorian living room.

Hearing the door open and someone coming in, he said, 'Right, I've got the shot lined up so get into position, Gina, and hurry up about it. I've another session to do tonight after you.' When he received no response, he turned his head and looked across at the door, straightening himself up when he saw two strangers had entered. 'Who the fuck are you?' he snapped aggressively at Rica and Bill. Before they could respond, he carried on, 'Actually, I don't care. I won't be disturbed in the middle of a shoot, so whatever it is yer want me for, yer'll have to hang on 'til I've finished with Gina. Wait in the office.'

Rica found his rudeness offensive and snapped back, 'You won't be taking any more photographs of Gina or anyone else in this studio, Maurice, or whatever your name is.'

He took another nonchalant drag of his cigarette, blowing out a thin stream of peculiar-smelling smoke before he responded. 'And who the hell are you to be telling me what I'll be doing and what I won't?'

Bill said darkly, 'The lady is the owner of this place, that's who she is, and I don't appreciate the attitude you're showing her.'

Maurice laughed. 'I don't know what yer game is, the pair of yer, but I know who the owner is as we've a deal going on. And it certainly ain't *her*. It's a him – and he's in the dark room right now.'

Rica froze. Simon was in the dark room! It was as if an explosion had gone off inside her head. Her heart raced so thunderously she wouldn't have been at all surprised had it burst out of her chest. 'He's here, Bill,' she uttered. 'Simon's here.' Her mind was racing too. This was her chance to get the answer to why he'd left her. As she rushed out of the room, she bumped smack into Gina.

'Oi, watch where yer going,' the girl angrily exclaimed, not bothering to pull back into place her robe, which was exposing her bare shoulder and most of a breast.

Rica had far too much on her mind to apologise to her. Bill was close behind when she turned the knob of the dark-room door, shoved it open and charged inside. She stopped abruptly in shock at the busy scene that met her eyes. The room was bathed in red light. Fisher stood at the bench with a metal developing tray in his hands, gently rocking it backwards and forwards. Jason was pegging up wet developed prints to dry on a line. Both men had their backs to the door. At the moment the two people in this room and what they were doing were not of any consequence to Rica, she could deal with them later. There was no sign at all of Simon, and finding out where he was was all that mattered to her.

She demanded, 'Where's Mr Dunmore?'

Intent on what they were doing, neither Sid Fisher nor Jason had heard anyone come in. At the unexpected sound of her voice, they both swung around. Confronted by Rica, Sid Fisher slopped chemicals down himself and on to the floor. Jason's eyes filled with horror, his face paled alarmingly and he slumped back against the sink, sliding to the floor in what seemed to be a faint.

Sid Fisher was glaring at Rica. He snarled nastily, 'Now look what you've done, you stupid woman. You've ruined these photos! You know you should never come in here without my say-so.'

Knowing how deplorably Fisher had treated Rica from the moment she had taken over the shop, and seeing how contemptuously he was behaving towards her now, Bill's temper boiled over. He emerged from behind Rica and lunged at Fisher. He hit the tray the man was holding out of his hands, grabbed him by the shirt front and pulled him up so they stood eye to eye.

In the gloom, Fisher hadn't at first seen Bill and yelped in shock at this sudden attack upon his person.

His voice low and full of meaning, Bill hissed, 'And we don't need to look at the photos Jason is pegging up to know they aren't the sort you show your wife and kids, do

231

we? How dare you speak to Mrs Dunmore in that way, you nasty little man? Now, Mrs Dunmore asked you a question and it's only polite to answer.' Then he pushed his face even closer to Fisher's and whispered, 'Maybe your family might like to see just what you've been doing in the evenings when they more than likely think you're playing darts.' He then released his hold on the man and returned to stand beside Rica.

Fisher was glaring at them both contemptuously. His manner was as condescending as always when he said, 'How the hell should I know where Mr Dunmore is? She . . .' he saw Bill's expression and quickly added '. . . Mrs Dunmore told us he was down in Cornwall, looking after his sick uncle.'

Rica erupted, 'Don't lie, Mr Fisher. You *do* know where Simon is. The man in the studio said he'd done a deal with the boss here, and if we'd a problem with that to speak to him in the dark room . . .'

She stopped as the truth of the matter suddenly struck her. 'Oh, I see how it is. The man in the studio believes it's *you* that's the boss of this place, doesn't he, Mr Fisher? He takes the photographs, you develop them, and you both split the profits when they're sold.' The look on his face told Rica she had hit on the truth of the matter. She was mortally disappointed that Simon wasn't here and that she wasn't after all going to learn the truth about his disappearance with their son. The disappointment made her want to beat her fists against the door until her knuckles bled, but she wouldn't let the obnoxious Sid Fisher see her reduced to such a state. She took several deep breaths before saying, 'I suppose if the police had got wind and raided this place, you were going to tell them that you were working for me and just doing as you'd been told, for fear of losing your job?'

Fisher looked at her, saying nothing, but she felt sure there was a smirk in his eyes.

Rica then accused him, 'I can't believe you even had the nerve to use Dunmore's equipment for your illicit activities.'

'We bought all our own films and developing chemicals,' he said, in a tone that implied he felt Rica should be grateful for that.

A memory struck her. 'Not at the start, you didn't. Not the developing chemicals anyway. That was the reason for the sudden increase in our use of them when we weren't any busier than normal. Well, I suppose at least we've solved that mystery.' She eyed him darkly. 'I'd like you to collect all your personal stuff and leave.'

He sneered at her, 'You can't sack me. I work for Mr Dunmore. It's him I take orders from. When he comes back, I shall deny I had anything to do with this. It'll be your word against mine. I've worked for the family for over thirty years and never given him any cause to complain, so he'll believe me.'

At his insolence Rica's temper rose. Before she could stop herself, she blurted, 'Mr Dunmore *isn't* coming back. It's me who owns the business and runs it now, so it's me you work for – and I'm sacking you. Now get out!'

Fisher's mouth was opening and closing fish-like. 'But . . . but . . . Look, listen. These photos sell like hot cakes, and for a lot of money. We could cut you . . .'

She erupted, 'You seriously think I would willingly become involved in producing pornography? Get out. I never want to see your face again.'

'But I've wages due . . .'

Rica couldn't believe his cheek. 'Whatever you're due after we've deducted the cost of the extra chemicals and anything else you've used that we haven't noticed, I will make sure you get. Now please go.'

When he still made no move to, Bill spoke up. 'You heard Mrs Dunmore, Fisher. Collect what's yours and leave. Eh, and be warned. I shall be watching to make sure you take nothing that doesn't belong to you.'

Rica and Bill stood and watched as the furious man snatched his coat and haversack off the hook on the back of the door, but not before he'd pulled the dried photographs off the line and also picked up the pile on the developing bench. He put them all in his bag. Before he stormed out of the room, he shot Rica a murderous look and snarled, 'You'll regret this.'

At his threat Bill immediately shot after him, waiting until Fisher was in the kitchen and about to open the back door before he caught his arm, pulled him around to face him and told him in no uncertain terms: 'If the slightest thing happens to Mrs Dunmore or this business, it's you personally I'll come after, is that understood? Is it, Fisher?'

His eyes were mocking. 'Attack an old man, would you?'

Bill grinned. 'I wouldn't sink so low, Fisher. Remember what I said earlier. You've a wife, kids, grandkids. What do you think they'd say if they found out what you'd been up to in your spare time?' He was gratified to see the other man visibly pale, his eyes filling with alarm. Bill released his hold on the man's arm, leaned over and pulled open the back door. He was just about to tell Fisher to get out when another thought struck him and he held out his hand. 'Key,' he demanded.

It was apparent Fisher was hoping the fact he'd a key to the back door had been overlooked. Eyes black as thunder, he fumbled for it in his coat pocket, pulled it out and slapped it angrily into Bill's outstretched hand. With that he stormed out of the door and Bill watched as he passed through the back gate, slamming that too behind him.

Bill arrived back in the dark room a few minutes later to find Rica leaning over the bench, resting her head despairingly in her hands.

She became aware of his return when she felt his hand on

her shoulder and heard him say, 'Fisher's gone. I've got his key off him so he can't let himself back in.'

She hurriedly wiped away tears with the back of her hand before righting herself and turning to look at him, giving him a wan smile. 'Thank you, Bill. I know he's an old man, but I'm still worried he'll pay me back somehow.'

'I'm positive he won't, Rica. The slightest thing happening out of the ordinary to you or the shop and Fisher has been warned that he'll find out exactly what his family think of his way of making extra money.'

She gave him another grateful smile. Then she took a deep breath and scraped back her hair from her tear-stained face, saying, 'I dread to think how much longer this would have gone on, had you not forced yourself to go out today and take some snaps.' She took another deep breath and added reluctantly, 'Well, I suppose we ought to go and deal with those two in the studio.'

'I've already dealt with them, Rica. They've gone, and taken their belongings with them. I made sure they didn't take anything that belongs to you. That Maurice fella tried to hide the camera under his coat but I had my hawk eyes on his every move. I've never seen two people scarper so quick when I threatened them with the police.' He peered at her searchingly. 'You look like you could do with a drink.'

Rica nodded. 'Not just one . . . several. There's a pub up the road, fancy joining me?'

'I certainly do.'

A small, worried voice spoke up then. 'But . . . but . . . what about me?'

Rica and Bill both spun their heads to look over towards the sink. Jason sat on the floor beside it, looking back at them both, clearly terrified.

'Oh, I'd forgotten about you,' Rica said to him. 'I have to say that finding Fisher up to no good somehow didn't surprise me. But you . . .' Her eyes filled with hurt. 'I thought you were a trustworthy lad. I really liked you, Jason. You've been very clever, pulling the wool over my eyes. Just get your things and go.'

He eyed her imploringly. 'Oh, but I need you to know, Mrs Dunmore, that I didn't want to do what I was.'

'But, regardless, you did,' she snapped at him. 'Was it your cut of the money that swayed you?'

'I . . . er . . . didn't get any money.'

She frowned at him, puzzled. 'So what did you get out of it then?'

His head was hanging and he was wringing his hands. 'Nothing.'

'No one risks what you were for nothing, Jason. You must have got something out of it,' Bill challenged him.

He vehemently shook his head. 'I never, honest. I had no choice but to help.'

'So Fisher blackmailed you into helping him, is that what you're saying?' Rica asked him.

'I was blackmailed, but not by Mr Fisher.'

'Who was it then?' Bill asked.

Jason raised his head and stared across at them blankly for a moment. The red glow from the developing light made his acne-pitted face look grotesque. Reluctantly, he said, 'Me dad.'

Rica exclaimed, 'Your father! But how is he involved in all this?'

'He's not.'

'You're not making sense, Jason,' she snapped at him.

Bill told him harshly, 'Stop beating about the bush and tell Mrs Dunmore just how your father comes into this.'

Jason gulped, looking mortally embarrassed. 'When Mr Dunmore went away and you took over, Mrs Dunmore, Mr Fisher told me his idea for making money by coming back at night and using the studio to take those . . . well, rude photographs, to sell around the pubs and clubs. He said he knew a photographer that'd jump at the chance of earning the kind of money the photographs would make him. He would get the models, and Mr Fisher and me would develop them and packet them up.

'I told him that it wasn't right going behind your back, Mrs Dunmore, and risking the good name of the business if the coppers found out. I liked my job, didn't want to risk jail if we was caught, so I didn't want any part of it. He said he couldn't do all the developing by himself, and if I didn't help him he'd tell me dad, who'd make me. He knew me dad wouldn't miss a chance of getting his hands on more beer money. Fisher knows me dad as they both use the same pub, and he's seen me meeting Dad there on a Friday after work, to hand my wages over to him. Dad doesn't work. Well, not what you'd call legal work. But what he earns from his deals plus my wages keeps him in beer and fags for the week.'

Rica was looking appalled. 'Your father takes your wages off you?'

Jason nodded. 'All but thirty bob. I have to make that do me for everything I need. I'm saving for another suit, but by the time I've paid my bus fares and bought my food for the week there's not much left for saving.'

She gasped, 'So *that's* why you go without lunch? Not because you aren't hungry but because you can't afford to buy it. And what about your Christmas bonus?'

'I had no choice but to hand it over to him. He knows that each year since I've started working for Dunmore's I've had a bonus. He couldn't believe his luck when he saw how much you gave me this year. I could have bought a new suit and a couple of shirts with that . . . I know I look shabby in this old thing. Just before Mr Dunmore left he had a word with me about getting myself a new suit and I said I would, even though I knew it'd take me a month of Sundays to save up for it from the bit Dad leaves me with. I've been worried since you took over, Mrs Dunmore, that you'd tell me to smarten myself up, and when I didn't, ask me to leave.'

Rica and Bill shot a look at each other. They were disgusted to hear that Jason's father gave him back so little from his pay each week, out of which he was expected to feed, clothe and pay for any entertainment for himself while the rest of his hard-earned wages disappeared over the bar of his father's local.

Jason was telling them, 'I have to meet me dad every Friday night at six on the dot outside the local pub. If I'm a second late, no matter what the reason, he gives me a leathering. Even with the threat of that, I still couldn't bring myself at first to help Mr Fisher develop those disgusting photos. I never thought he would do as he'd threatened anyway, just find someone else to help him. But he did go and see me dad. Dad was fuming at me for refusing to earn some extra, and he battered me with the poker until I screamed at him to stop and agreed I'd help.'

Rica was looking at him, horrified. 'Was that when you told me you had a crick in your neck? Were you really suffering from being beaten up by your father, Jason?'

There were tears in his eyes when he nodded. 'I was lucky he only cracked a couple of ribs. I've never been in so much pain in all my life. They still hurt. I hated lying to you when you asked what was troubling me, but if I'd told you the truth you'd have wanted to know how I injured my ribs, wouldn't you?'

Rica was looking even more horrified. 'Why hasn't your mother got the police to him before now?'

He gave a shrug. 'She doesn't know what's happening half the time, she's too drunk, and when she's not, all she's bothered about is getting the money for more drink. She doesn't care about what's happening to me. I'm just glad I haven't got any brothers and sisters to worry about.

'It hasn't always been so bad. Mam's always liked a drink and Dad's always been handy with his fists, but when I was little my Aunt Dot, Mam's sister, used to keep her eye on me. Well, it was her that looked after me really, made sure I was fed and clean, and I'd sleep at her house most nights in a proper bed, not on the smelly flock in the corner of the kitchen. I dread to think what would have happened to me when I was young if it hadn't been for my Aunt Dot. She wasn't married. Used to tell me that I made up for her not having her own little boy. She died, though, when I was thirteen. I still miss her terribly. Since then I've had to fend for myself.'

Rica's heart ached with sadness at the tale Jason was telling. No wonder he had a sad air about him. Who wouldn't with the life he'd had? She was grateful now that she hadn't got around to tackling him about upgrading his work attire as that would only have served to add to his burdens. And no wonder he'd never had a girlfriend. No girl in their right mind, no matter how much they liked Jason, would voluntarily get involved with him considering the family he'd been unfortunate enough to be born into.

Rica said to him, 'I know it would be hard to manage on an apprentice's wage but there must be lodgings you could afford, even though they wouldn't be up to much? They'd be better than living with your parents, surely.'

He gave a miserable sigh. 'Oh, I tried that. When I was fifteen and first got the job with Mr Dunmore . . . me dad wasn't happy about that either as he wanted me to get myself set on as a labourer in a factory or on a building site, said it'd pay more money than what I earned as an apprentice, but I didn't want to settle for a dead-end job just to keep me dad in beer and fags. I was really keen to learn the photography business, then maybe have my own shop one day or be good enough to become a freelance photographer. So I made out to me dad that I was trying to get set on as a labourer, but each interview I went to, I made sure I was the last lad they'd take on. In the end Dad was relieved Mr Dunmore offered me the apprenticeship as at least I was earning something to hand over to him.

'Anyway, two weeks after I started with Dunmore's, I also got myself lodgings with an old lady just down the road and didn't tell my parents I was moving out. Mrs Vance was really kind but she was also a bit batty. She'd do things like make a sponge cake and put gravy on it for my dinner, and she'd boil potatoes but not peel them, but she did her best to look after me which is more than me mam ever did. At night we'd sit by the fire and Mrs Vance would smoke her pipe while we listened to the comedy shows on her old radio. She hadn't got a telly, couldn't afford one. The week I lodged with Mrs Vance was the happiest I've been since Aunty Dot died. I don't think either of my parents would have noticed I'd gone had it not been for the fact I didn't meet Dad outside the pub on Friday night after work with me wages.

'He found out where I was living and came round, bellowing and shouting and frightening Mrs Vance to death. He said he didn't care whether I lived at home or not, he wanted *his* money as he called it. He threatened I'd get what for if I didn't meet him outside the pub the next Friday night to hand him his dues, and before he'd leave I had to hand over all the money I had left to last me that week. I couldn't afford to live with Mrs Vance then so I had no choice but to go back home. I know she wasn't happy about seeing me go, but she was also relieved that she wouldn't be getting another visit from me dad.'

Defiance glinted in Jason's eyes then and he said fervently, 'When I'm twenty-one, though, I'll be legally allowed to do as I please and live where I like. Dad won't see another penny of my money then, and there'll be nothing he can do about it.'

He unravelled his long thin limbs and struggled to his feet. His expression guilt-ridden, he said to Rica, 'I know I should have told you what was going on, Mrs Dunmore, but I was scared of what me dad would do to me if he found out.'

It was apparent he wanted to apologise for his cowardly behaviour but obviously felt nothing he could say would excuse it. Looking like doom itself, he left the room.

Rica and Bill glanced at each other. They each seemed to know what the other was thinking. It was Bill who said, 'I know you want to offer him a place with you, but your husband has just left and if you move a young man in . . . what's that going to look like to the neighbours, not forgetting your strait-laced sister? Best he comes with me. My parents will take him in. They'll love having a youngster around again. I'll fetch him back.'

When he returned with an extremely worried-looking Jason, Rica had made a pot of tea and was leaving it to brew for a few moments while she put milk and sugar into three mugs. No one said a word while she poured out tea then handed them each a mug. A bewildered Jason accepted his silently.

Leaning back against the old pot sink, Bill told him, 'I hope you like porridge because my mother will insist you have a bowl every morning before you set off for work. And if you go out at night just make sure you're in on the dot at the time you've agreed else she'll be out in her coat over her nightie, looking for you. Oh, and you might think about getting a book on fishing out of the library. My dad's partial to casting a line down the canal on a Sunday morning, and you'll be his friend for life if you accompany him now and then.'

Rica was having a hard job not laughing at the comical expression on Jason's face.

His desperate need for clothes reminded her that Simon's

still hung in the wardrobe at home. Although she had acknowledged to herself that he wasn't coming back for them, up to now she hadn't been able to bring herself to do anything with them. It would be extremely thoughtless of her to allow those clothes to hang about accumulating moth holes when there was someone here who could put them to good use. Simon and Jason were roughly the same height, and a few of Bill's mother's nourishing home-cooked meals would soon bulk Jason out. She knew it would be painful for her, seeing him in Simon's clothes, but she would just have to keep reminding herself that the clothes were now his and not her husband's.

Before she could change her mind she bewildered Jason even more by telling him, 'I've some clothes of my husband's that he no longer requires. I'll get them packed up . . .' she looked at Bill '. . . if you would be good enough to collect them in the van whenever you can.' She then turned her attention back to Jason, who was now opening and closing his mouth without speaking. 'Don't feel obliged to wear any of them you don't like, but some of them will tide you over until you've got enough money together to go and fit yourself out. The charity shops can have what you don't want.'

He stammered, 'But . . . but . . . why are you asking if I like porridge and telling me about the clothes? I thought . . . well, that you'd come after me and made me come back because the police were on the way to arrest me.'

Bill leaned over and slapped him on his shoulder, saying in all seriousness, 'If a term in prison is preferable to living with me and my parents, then Mrs Dunmore will go through to the office now and call the police to come for you.' With a twinkle in his eye he added, 'Mind you, should you decide to come with me instead, you might end up wishing you'd opted for a jail sentence. If you upset my mother, it's the stony-faced treatment you'll get from her . . . and in my opinion that's far worse than any spell in solitary confinement.'

It was several moments before Jason found his voice and uttered, 'I can come and live with you? You really mean that?'

Bill nodded.

'But what if me dad . . .'

Bill cut in, 'Listen, son, he's bound to find out what's gone off tonight as he drinks at the same pub as Fisher. It's my opinion he'll automatically assume that you've been sacked same as Fisher, and when you don't come home, he'll think you've run off as you're scared the police will come knocking for you. Should he find out that you haven't been sacked and are in fact living with my parents, just let him try and get his hands on your wages because he'll have me to deal with! And I'll tell you now, if he pays our house a visit when either me or my dad aren't there, my mother is no shrinking violet. She'll scream that loud the neighbours will soon come running – but not before she's took the poker to him herself. Oh, and just in case he decides to lie in wait for you to come out of work on a Friday evening, I'll make a point of taking you back and forth in the van.'

Jason's face lit up like a beacon. Tears of happiness sparkling in his eyes, he blurted out, 'Oh, I've prayed for this day! Every night I've got into bed for as long as I can remember. I can't believe my prayers have been answered. I don't know what to say . . . how to thank you.'

'By never making us regret what we're doing for you,' Bill told him sternly.

Jason said with great conviction, 'Oh, I won't never . . . ever.' He then worriedly said to Rica, 'But aren't you going to sack me for what you caught me doing?'

She assured him, 'If you had voluntarily helped Fisher then I would, but you were blackmailed into it which is entirely different.' She smiled and patted his arm. 'Besides, I can't run this shop without you, Jason. You're my right hand.' She frowned. 'Of course, I have to find a replacement for Fisher, but I've been trying for a while and had no luck.'

'I could do it for you, until you get someone with the experience you're looking for,' Jason told her.

Rica was taken aback. 'You know all about the developing process then?'

'It was the first thing I learned when I started here. Until Mr Dunmore went away, I used to help Mr Fisher out when he was busy. I'm not as quick as he is, he's been at it a lifetime, but I'm not slow either. I like developing, but I prefer taking photographs.'

She exclaimed, 'You can take photographs too?'

He looked surprised that she should be asking. 'Yes. I'm not as good as Mr Dunmore yet but my photos aren't that bad, if I say so myself. Mr Dunmore was a good teacher, very patient. Before he went away, I was doing quite a lot of the studio portraits by myself as he said I was more than good enough. I never had any complaints from the customers whose photos I took.' Jason pulled a rum face. 'I wasn't keen on doing the babies, though. You have to have the knack of getting their attention so they'll keep still. It's not easy waving a teddy bear or a rattle at them and taking a photograph at the same time.

'I used to go with Mr Dunmore on the outside shoots when they were after shop hours. He used to line up all the shots and focus them while I'd watch, and some of them he'd let me actually take. But I still need lots more practice to get myself up to professional standard. When we weren't busy, Mr Dunmore would send me out with the camera to shoot a roll or two, and then after they'd been developed, same as Mr Simpson does with you, Mrs Dunmore, we'd look at them together, and Mr Dunmore would point out where he thought I could have improved. I started my apprenticeship three and a half years ago, only got six months left to do before I'm fully qualified, so really there isn't anything in the trade I don't know.'

Rica felt guilty. She had been so consumed with learning

the business inside out herself that she hadn't considered that Jason was already far more knowledgeable, having learned from Simon for over three and a half years. Had she not been so self-absorbed, he could have taken on the role of studio photographer or developer, which would have meant she could have got rid of the despicable Fisher as soon as it had become apparent he wasn't ever going to respect her as his boss.

Rica exclaimed, mortified, 'Jason, why didn't you tell me what you were capable of?'

'You never asked, Mrs Dunmore.'

She blustered, 'I'm so sorry. I realised when you showed me the sales side of the business just how much you knew, but it didn't cross my mind how much else you were skilled at. How stupid of me to be paying the likes of Mr Pointer to come in and do the studio shots when you could have taken care of them, Jason. Well, from now on, you will. When I'm competent enough, we'll do them between us. And when we're not busy, you need to resume the habit of going out and snapping a roll or two of film. We'll take it in turns.' She looked at Bill. 'Would you be willing to give Jason's handiwork your expert opinion, the same as you do with mine?'

Bill told them he'd be only too happy to, and that he'd also, if needed, come in a couple of evenings a week and help Jason keep the developing side under control until a permanent developer was found.

Jason had a look on his face like he'd heard he'd won ten shillings only to discover it was in fact a hundred pounds. But it was also possible to tell that he was still deeply worried he was in the middle of a dream and that any minute now he'd be waking up to find himself still stuck in his old miserable life, with no seeming escape route until he reached the age of twenty-one.

Bill resolved that by giving his arm a pinch, to which

Jason gave a yelp, then laughingly telling him, 'If you were dreaming, that pinch wouldn't have hurt. Now it's my bet you haven't had a hot meal tonight. I'm sure my mother will happily warm up what was left of the stew we had for dinner. There won't be any potatoes but I'm sure you won't mind making do with bread.'

Mind making do with bread to soak up the gravy? Discounting Mrs Vance's efforts, the last proper home-cooked meal Jason had had was when he was thirteen years old, before his aunt died.

Bill had not exaggerated his parents' generosity. When he had requested them to give Jason a roof over his head for the foreseeable future, Nell and Jack Simpson were sitting in shabby but comfortable-looking armchairs opposite each other by the fire. She was knitting, he was reading the local evening newspaper, with the radio blaring out a musical variety show.

Nell didn't even listen to the reason her son gave for asking them to take in the young man until he was in more of a position to fend for himself. All she saw was a skinny waif of a lad with an unloved air about him. Her maternal instincts rose to the fore. Long before her son had finished his tale she was out of her chair, the remains of the stew reheating on the stove, cutting thick slices of bread and liberally buttering them. Jack, the newspaper he had been reading crumpled in a heap at the side of his chair, was setting a place at the table for Jason while listening to his wife shout instructions from the kitchen for him to go upstairs immediately he had finished that task and clear the small box room of what she termed his 'junk', which in fact was his fishing paraphernalia, so she could freshen up the bed with clean linen and give the room a dust ready for its new occupant. Jack did, but not before he had told Jason that if he fancied coming with him to the canal on Sunday for a spot of fishing, he had a spare rod and would enjoy the company.

As his parents bustled around in their efforts to make the young man feel welcome in their home, Bill looked at Jason and asked, 'Do you think you'll be happy living here for the time being? My mam does tend to fuss.' Aware of what kind of life he would have here compared to the one Jason had described, Bill's question was asked tongue-in-cheek.

The light in Jason's eyes gave him his answer.

Just then Nell came in, carrying a steaming plate. She ordered her new lodger, 'Sit yerself down, son, and get tucked in before this goes cold.'

Jason did not need telling twice.

CHAPTER TWENTY

'You can't mean that?'
'I don't say things I don't mean.'
Rica looked at Bill sceptically. 'Do you think you might be exaggerating then?'
He laughed and shook his head. 'No.'
'But I've only been at it for just over five months.'
'Well, as I told you when you first set out, some people pick it up quicker than others – and you are one of those. Don't forget, this isn't just a hobby for you. You've had good reason to get yourself up to speed. I think you have that extra something too, though.'
'Oh, what's that?'
'Natural talent.' Bill then asked Jason, 'What's your opinion?'
He glanced again at a couple of Rica's shots out of the dozen or so spread out before them on the counter top.
Jason was no longer the thin, gangly, shabbily dressed young man with the sad air about him he had once been. Over the last eight weeks, under the nurturing care of the Simpsons, a dramatic transformation had taken place in him. Nourishing home-cooked food had filled him out; the hideous spots that had disfigured his face had dwindled down to the odd one. Knowing people actually cared for him had built his confidence. He looked smart and fashionable in Simon's cast offs, albeit they were still a little on the

248

big side for him. His own parents would have had to look at him twice to recognise their son. Rica knew for a fact that the transformed Jason had caught the eye of the pretty young shop assistant in the chemist's, who hadn't seemed to notice him at all before. Now, every time Rica went in to buy something, while the girl served her she always made a point of bringing Jason into the conversation somehow. His confidence still needed building up a bit for him to have the bravado to ask a girl he fancied out on a date, but Rica was sure it would happen if the girl had patience for a while.

It had been sad to see it confirmed that Jason had not been exaggerating in his account of his parents' lack of concern for him other than for what he was worth to them in monetary terms. The next Saturday after Jason had moved into Bill's parents' house, after he had not kept his usual date with his father at six on Friday to hand over his pay, Stanley Pickles paid a visit to the shop.

Jason was in the dark room at the time, ploughing through the dozen or so rolls of film customers had brought in, and taking advantage of the shop being empty, Rica was looking through several applications for the replacement member of staff she had advertised for in the *Mercury*. A couple of candidates appeared promising and she would invite them in for an interview as soon as possible. When she heard the bell on the door jangle, she automatically looked up, prepared to welcome her customer. Despite never having met Jason's father before or been furnished with a description of him, instinct told her that this was he.

Mr Pickles was around five foot eight inches tall, and thickset, though the muscles he'd once sported many years before had now turned to flab. A large gut hung over the top of his trousers. He wore his formerly dark hair long. His jowled jaw had not seen a razor blade for at least two days, possibly longer, and it was apparent he'd not been near soap and water today. The brown suit he wore was of forties style, double-breasted and with wide lapels. It looked as if it had never been cleaned since it had first been bought from the second-hand shop by Pickles. Under the jacket, all he had on was a grubby string vest. His large bulbous nose and the web of spider veins over his face showed that this man had a less than healthy liking for alcohol.

As she watched him lumber his way over to the counter and fix his bloodshot eyes on her, Rica had to fight down the fury that was raging within her for the life of misery this man had led his son. She wondered what he was after. As far as he would be aware Jason had been sacked along with Fisher so he wouldn't be expecting to see him here. Maybe he thought she might have an idea where Jason had gone. She prayed to herself that he would not make an appearance while his father was present.

Rica forced a smile to her face and said cordially, 'Good morning. What can I do for you?'

Mr Pickles placed his fat hands flat on the counter. As he opened his mouth to speak, she caught a waft of his stale alcohol-tainted breath. 'Me son's sent me to collect his dues. Too embarrassed to come and fetch 'em himself, see, after being caught helping that Fisher produce them vile photos. I'm disgusted with the boy meself. Believe me, I'd have knocked the little fucker's block off had I known what he was involved in.'

Rica wasn't blameless herself of using the odd swear word, but they were mild compared to the profanities this man was using. He obviously had no respect for women what-soever as he wasn't even trying to curb his language in front of her. But that aside, she couldn't believe the gall of him. If there was a penny to be gained from his son, he obviously felt it was his right to claim it. She fought to keep from him the disgust she felt, answering tartly, 'I can't imagine why Jason is of the opinion that he's owed anything, considering it was my facilities being used to carry out his and Fisher's illegal money-making scheme.'

'Well, that's for you to take up with Fisher. My son was just working for him. In fact, Jason told me that Fisher blackmailed him into it. Said if he didn't help then Fisher would tell you some cock and bull story about him, and leave you with no option but to sack him. It would be Fisher's word against Jason's, and Fisher would be believed being's he'd worked for the firm for so long with not a stain on his character. My lad is still wet behind the ears. He felt he had no choice as he knows we need his wage to survive. His mother can't work, she's a cripple, and I can't due to an accident at work a couple of years ago.

'Now, me son worked a week in hand, and a couple of days last week he wasn't paid for so it's that I'm here to collect.' He then looked at her meaningfully and, whilst cracking his knuckles, added, 'You're here on yer own, I gather, being's you've no staff at the moment.'

A surge of temper rose in Rica then. She was damned if she would hand over money that was not his to claim, knowing as she did it would only end up over the bar of his local. Two could play the blackmail game. She was about to inform him that he was getting no money from her, and should he attempt to force it off her then she would immediately summon the police, when out of the corner of her eye she saw the door leading into the back opening. Besides herself there was only Jason on the premises so it had to be him about to come in.

Very loudly she said, 'Mr Pickles, would you like to take a seat while I deal with your request?' Out of the corner of her eye she saw the door pulled to by Jason. She wouldn't breathe a sigh of relief, though, until she had got rid of the man himself.

Stanley Pickles snapped, 'Could yer just get on with giving me what I came for? I've somewhere I should be.'

It was coming up to eleven so that would be the pub, she assumed. 'Well, I will have to take a guess at just what the amount due is as the person who sees to the wages isn't around at the moment. Is that all right with you? Unless you'd like to call back another time and then I will have the amount correctly calculated and waiting for you.'

His eyes glinted with impatience. 'I've already wasted my time, not forgetting bus fare, coming here. Just calculate it.'

Rica went to the till and, mindful of the temperamental drawer, stood to one side as she opened it. Jason's wage at the moment was fifteen pounds, seventeen and six a week. So that amount for the week in hand plus the three days he had worked last week . . . Maths had never been her strong point and in her anxious and angry state she couldn't even work out this simple sum. So Rica just took a stab in the dark, thinking twenty-five pounds should do it. She took out five £5 notes, then a thought struck her. Pickles seemed the kind of man who would never accept a first offer, so she put a fiver back, shut the drawer, returned to the counter and handed the notes over to him.

She was right. Pickles took them then flicked his finger through the notes again. He looked at Rica and said, 'I think you've calculated a bit low. Another fiver seems about right to me. Oh, and I think the least yer can do is refund the two . . . three . . . bob it cost me in bus fare coming here.'

This man was beneath contempt. Rica risked losing control over her emotions and telling him exactly what she thought of him. But she needed to get rid of him before that happened, and she must not put Jason at risk. She returned to the till, reopened it and took out the £5 she'd just put back plus three shillings in change. Back at the counter, she handed it to Pickles.

'I believe I've given you more than Jason is due, Mr Pickles, but I'm not about to split hairs with you as I am in no doubt that you and Mrs Pickles are deeply distressed after finding out what you have about your son.'

Jason's father was putting his ill-gotten gains safely into the inside pocket of his shabby jacket. 'Well, yer do yer best to raise 'em proper but yer can't blame the parents for 'ow they turn out, can yer? He's proved to be fucking useless as a son. Couldn't even get himself a decent-paid job in a factory or on a building site, so he could help me and his mam out a bit more. He had to settle for this poxy one here 'cos that's all he got offered. Now he's not even got that. I expect the selfish little sod's not gave me or his mother a thought, wherever he's hiding his ugly mug, 'cos he's terrified you've reported all this to the police.

'I don't know how we're going to manage now as the bit we took off him each week for his board, he knew fine well made the difference between life and death to us. Mind you, I heard from Fisher that you weren't going to bring charges, so he'd no real reason to go on the run, brainless little twerp! Jason hadn't even the guts to come and tell us himself about all this, just never came home. I hope he can live with himself. He's broke his mother's heart and left us in dire straits.'

Rica felt sick to her stomach at this man's vile lies about his son. A thought had struck her, though, about something he had let slip during this tirade. She said to him, 'I haven't made my final decision yet as to whether or not I will bring charges, so Mr Fisher was wrong to inform you of that. I didn't realise, though, that you knew him?'

Pickles eyed her in alarm. It was obvious he was angry with himself for his slip, and now worried that he could be seen as implicated in Fisher's scam and thus in trouble with the law himself. He shot back, 'You never heard me right. I never said it was Fisher who told me about you not pressing charges, just some crony of his that has a pint in the same pub I do.'

Rica gave him a tight smile. 'Oh, that explains it then. I'm sorry I accused you of being an associate of his. But you did tell me you haven't seen Jason since that night?'

'Not hide nor hair of the little bleeder.' He then eyed her suspiciously. 'Why, have you? Only if you have, it's your duty to tell me what you know. He might think he's the big I am, but in the eyes of the law he's still a minor and under his parents' care until he's twenty-one.'

'No, I haven't seen him either.' Rica told the lie with no shame whatsoever. She added in a casual tone, 'It's just that you said Jason had asked you to come and collect what he was owed. Only now you're saying you haven't seen him, so he couldn't have. After all, what I gave you is Jason's money. I'm not sure I should have handed it over to you without some sort of proof of his permission for you to be collecting it on his behalf.'

Aware his lies had caught him out, Pickles was glaring at her darkly. 'I'm his father. I don't need proof of anything I do on his behalf.' With that he turned on his worn-down heels and hurried out.

As soon as the door closed behind him, Rica let out a huge sigh of relief before saying out loud, 'It's safe now, Jason, he's gone.'

It was several moments more before the door opened just enough for an eye to peep through. On seeing for himself that only Rica was in the shop, Jason fully opened the door and came in. His face was bleached sheet-white and contorted with fear. He said to Rica, 'I'm sorry, it's not that I didn't believe you that he'd gone . . . just that I was feared my dad had threatened you and forced you to make me show myself.' Fear then turned to sheer panic and he blurted out, 'Does he know I'm here? How does he know? He must have been watching the shop. Seen Bill dropping me off? He's going to make me hand over my wages to him again, and if I refuse he'll threaten me.

'He'll hurt not just me this time but Mr and Mrs Simpson and Bill . . . or you even, Mrs Dunmore. He would be no match for Bill in a proper fight, but my dad doesn't play fair. He's the type that'll hide in the dark with a length of pole and jump out on whoever he's after . . .'

Rica came out from behind the counter, went to Jason and grabbed both his arms. She shook them hard, telling him, 'Your father has no idea you still work here. He has no idea where you live. He thinks you're on the run from the police. You're safe, Jason, believe me. He's not looking for you.'

On hearing this his shoulders sagged in relief and a little colour returned to his cheeks. 'So what did he come for?' he asked finally.

Rica would have given anything to have been able to tell him that it was because his parents actually did care for him, and had come to check if she had an inkling where he could be. There was no way of covering the truth up, though, so she told him it as it was.

When she had finished, he was appalled. The little colour that had returned to his cheeks faded again. It was apparent he could find no words that would go anywhere near to apologising for his father's despicable behaviour to her. Jason didn't seem hurt at all by the man's lack of regard for him, though, and Rica wondered if this was because his father had hurt him so much in the past, not only emotionally but physically, that Jason had become immune to it.

Finally he found his voice and told her, 'Whatever me father wheedled out of you, I will pay back, Mrs Dunmore.'

She patted his arm. 'We'll discuss that when you've made a name for yourself in the trade and your bank balance is overflowing. Now, I could do with a cup of tea to rid me of this nasty taste in my mouth. If you'd be good enough to oblige, Jason?'

He couldn't get to the kitchen quickly enough to make one for her

That was eight weeks ago and since then Jason had concentrated on what the future held for him now that his parents were no longer there to hinder things.

Having been asked his opinion of the latest shots Rica had taken, Jason pulled a face and said, tongue-in-cheek, 'Well, of course, they aren't up to the standard of mine . . . but they're not bad, I suppose.'

Rica slapped him playfully on his arm. 'You cheeky thing! You wait until it's time for us to scrutinise your latest efforts.'

Just then the door leading into the passage opened and a middle-aged man wearing a long waxed apron over his trousers and shirt, the sleeves of which were rolled up to his elbows, came in, carrying a pile of packets in his hands. This pleasant-looking man had been chosen as Fisher's replacement out of the eight people interviewed. Rica had roped both Fran and Bill into helping her make the choice, as she didn't feel she had enough experience yet to tackle this on her own. She most certainly did not want to end up with another type like Fisher. She was after someone who was not only an expert at his job, but was the amiable sort who made an effort to get on with his colleagues. And, of course, they had to be honest.

Jason's part of the interview process had been to relay back to Rica the impression he had formed of each candidate as he passed the time of day with them while they waited in the shop to be summoned through for interview. Everyone unanimously agreed that Harold Baker had all the qualities being sought, and from the moment he'd joined Dunmore's he'd given none of them any reason to regret their choice.

Rica smiled at the new arrival and asked him, 'Come and give me your opinion of these photographs, Harry.' Then she whispered to Bill and Jason, 'Harry's appraisal will be unbiased as he has no idea it was me who took them.'

'Yes, of course, Mrs Dunmore,' Harry responded politely, immediately coming across to join the three of them at the counter. Rica still couldn't persuade him to address her by her Christian name. He was the old-fashioned sort who could not bring himself to address her in any other way but by her title, out of respect for her as his boss. He was a devoted family man, having been married to his wife for over twenty years, and had four children, three girls and a boy. He had worked in the photography business since leaving school, for the same small family business on the other side of town. Rica's requirement for a skilled developer had coincided with him losing his job on the death of his aged employer.

Harry first handed the packets of processed films he'd brought in with him to Jason to be put away before casting his eyes over the dozen or so snaps spread out over the counter. He said, 'I recognise these. I processed them this morning. Very sharp and clear. An unusual choice of subject matter, to my mind, people shopping in the market, but very interesting all the same.' He then looked askance at Rica. 'Am I supposed to be looking for anything in particular, Mrs Dunmore?'

'No. I just wanted your overall expert view, that was all.'

'Oh, I might be an expert at processing negatives and enjoy what I do immensely, Mrs Dunmore, but as you know photography itself holds absolutely no interest for me.'

'You still know a good photo from a bad one, though.'

'Oh, indeed I do. The ones you've asked me to look at are in my opinion very good, obviously taken by someone who knows what they are doing. Now, is there anything else you need me for, only I need to mix up some solutions before I start on my next batch?'

She smiled at him. 'No, that's it, Harry, thank you.'

After he had disappeared Bill said to Rica, '*Now* do you believe that you've reached a good enough standard to take on some of the studio and outside shoots by yourself?'

She still looked dubious. 'Mmm, I suppose so, but whether I've got enough courage yet is another question.'

'Well, just a suggestion, but the next wedding we've got booked, why don't you take the lead? I'll be by the side of you, ready to take over if you suddenly get cold feet.'

257

She thought about that for a moment, then smiled. 'Yes, I'm willing to have a go.'

Bill noticed her glance at the clock on the wall opposite for at least the tenth time since he'd called in less than half an hour ago. Cunosity as to why she was clock-watching got the better of him and he asked her, 'Just why the interest in the time, Rica? Am I outstaying my welcome or is there something you need to be doing?'

She smiled. 'You'd never outstay your welcome, Bill, but I have got an urgent appointment that I don't want to be late for. In fact, I'd better go and get ready.'

As she made her way to the office to collect her coat and handbag, Bill mused to himself, 'I wonder who her important appointment is with?'

He had spoken loudly enough for Jason to hear. 'I've not got a clue. Mrs Dunmore hasn't mentioned anything about having an appointment until now. Mind you, come to think of it, she has been jittery for the last couple of days, and more so today. If she goes out anywhere during work hours she usually tells me where to, but not this time.'

'Very cloak and dagger,' Bill said. 'Right, I'd better get off myself. Got a drain to unblock . . . and, believe me, I'm not looking forward to it. Be prepared for me to be stinking to high heaven when I pick you up this evening.'

'Well, I've been giving that some thought,' Jason told him. 'There's no evidence me dad is watching this place in case I show up here for any reason, so I think it's safe to be making my own way back and forth now. I know most of the time it's well out of your way to drop me off and pick me up.'

'It's no bother, but if you feel you're ready to travel by yourself then that's fine by me.' Bill slapped him playfully on the back. 'You're old enough and ugly enough to know your own mind. I'll still drop you off and pick you up when I'm working in the vicinity, though, as it wouldn't make sense not to. My drain job is just around the corner so I'll stop by for you tonight.'

As Bill got into his van and started the engine, he caught sight of Rica coming out of the shop and heading off down the road. She definitely had an anxious look on her face and this only served to heighten his curiosity.

CHAPTER TWENTY-ONE

Bill arrived back to collect Jason at just after half-past five that evening. As he pulled up in his van, he was surprised to see Rica's husband's Humber, the one he himself had been driving back and forth to commissions, parked at the kerb outside the shop.

Jason was just straightening the shop after the day's business, ready for tomorrow. He looked mortally relieved to see Bill and told him, 'I'm glad you're here. Mrs Dunmore has something to tell us. She came back from her appointment and told me that, as soon as you arrived, we were both to go into the office. I've been driving myself nuts wondering what it's about but she wouldn't say a word until you came. Whatever it is, she seems very chuffed about it. She's in the office waiting for us to go through.'

Rica was sitting behind the desk reading a letter when they both arrived.

She looked up at them, smiling. 'Oh, good, you're here.' She then picked up the letter, got up and walked around the desk to join them. 'I've got some very good news to tell you. When I returned from my errand this afternoon, I thought I'd only one bit of news to tell you but it seems now I have two. This letter was waiting for me, you see, must have come by the second post . . .'

Bill couldn't stand the suspense any longer. He urged her, 'Rica, just get to the point, please.'

'Oh, sorry, of course you'll both be wanting to get off home for your dinner. Well, it's like this. A few weeks ago I received a telephone call from one of the buyers of a company that Simon has sold a few of his photographs to. As they hadn't had anything from him for a while they were enquiring if he had anything he was thinking of submitting, as they were planning the production of next year's catalogues.

'With a bit of skulduggery on my part, I . . . er . . . procured a few photographs by each of you, hoping neither of you would notice them missing, and sent them off. Today I received this letter informing me that they are very interested in three of the shots. Two of yours, Bill, and one of yours, Jason.'

Both men were staring at her, speechless.

It was Jason who found his voice first. 'A company wants to buy one of my photos? Really? You're not having me on?'

'I would never joke about something so important, Jason. And it's not just any old greetings card company that wants your work, but none other than Marcus Ward and Company.'

Jason gawped. 'Marcus Ward! Even I know they're the biggest in their line. And they're after a photo of mine!' he uttered, astounded.

'It's the one of the pair of swans you took on the River Soar that frosty morning, with the mist swirling on the water. It's a beautiful photograph and it would have been such a shame just to let it sit in a drawer, gathering dust. Anyway you're both being asked to make an appointment with the chief buyer, a Mr Leader, to negotiate a price for your work and to take along with you any other photographs you think they might be keen on considering. Of course, once you've sold to them, it is then common practice for you to give them the first option on any future photographs you wish to submit, before you send them off to anyone else.'

Rica's eyes sparkled in delight. 'Just think, now you can claim to be published photographers. And the pay for desirable snaps is not to be sneezed at, I understand. This can only be of benefit to the business as well. We can truly claim now to have professional photographers on our commissions, can't we?'

Bill hadn't said a word up to now and his silence was worrying her. This was the sort of news that any budding photographer could only dream of hearing, like a writer having their work published. It was him she was primarily addressing when she asked, 'You're not annoyed with me for going behind your backs, are you?'

'I ain't, not at all,' Jason told her. Then said, 'Not that I would ever dream of it, but what I'd give to tell me dad this and see his face . . . considering he was always telling me I'd never amount to 'ote as I was about as much use as a bucket with a hole in it!'

Bill was looking at her blankly. He should be extremely annoyed with Rica, since she was well aware that he had already suffered greatly from what a woman had got up to behind his back, but instead he was very relieved that the news she had just imparted to them was not what he had thought it would be. He would miss his work here very much if she ever hired a full-time photographer, as he had feared she was about to tell them. To have work of his reproduced on thousands of greetings cards, or wherever the firm proposed to use it, his own name as photographer printed clearly underneath for all to see . . . He was just as thrilled about this as Jason, but before he could celebrate there was something else. Rica had told them she had two bits of news for them, and this other announcement could well prove to be what Bill most feared.

'No, no, I'm not at all mad about you submitting my shots. It's terrific news, really it is. But what is this other news you have to tell us then? Is it something to do with the appointment you were anxious about attending earlier today?'

'Yes, it is, but I wouldn't exactly say I was anxious about going to it . . . okay, well, yes, I was. But then, weren't you nervous when you were about to take your driving test, Bill?'

'No, I wasn't anxious. I was terrified that I was about to fail! I was twenty-one and usually quite cocky . . .'

Then like a thunderbolt the significance of what Rica had just told him registered, and a tremendous flood of relief washed through Bill that once again he'd been spared hearing the news he dreaded. He exclaimed, '*That* was your appointment this morning, to take your test?'

Her eyes lit up. Like an excited child, she clapped her hands together in delight. 'Yes. And I passed!'

Bill stood staring at her, his face a blank mask so that it was difficult to tell what he was thinking.

Jason blurted out, 'Blimey!'

She looked at him and said with a twinkle of amusement in her eyes, 'I hope that's not a shocked *blimey* because a woman has passed her driving test, Mr Pickles?'

He hurriedly exclaimed, 'Oh, no, not at all, Mrs Dunmore. Definitely not. It's just that I didn't even have a clue you were taking lessons.'

'I decided not to tell anyone as I didn't want the continual questions about how I was getting on. I did think I had failed, though, as I misjudged the kerb when parking and the front tyre hit it. Also, when we got back to the test station I couldn't answer two of the *Highway Code* questions . . . I did know them, that book has been my bedtime reading since I started taking lessons four months ago. I've studied it over and over, from cover to cover, until I was sick of the sight of it. But for the life of me I couldn't recall the answer to those questions. Well, you can imagine my shock and joy when the examiner finally told me that I'd passed!'

Bill couldn't imagine Rica's euphoria was any greater than his at this moment. It seemed his time at Dunmore's wasn't at an end after all. Such was the extent of his relief that he forgot himself, threw his arms around her and gave her a hug, exclaiming, 'Congratulations . . . and well deserved!' It was then that he remembered himself and released his hold on her as quickly as he would have dropped a hot coal.

Rica hadn't perceived Bill's spontaneous action as anything other than that of a friend showing his delight at her success. She was pleased he was so glad for her. 'This means I can come and pick you up for the shoots from now on, instead of you coming all the way across town to collect me.'

'Well, I can't wait to learn to drive,' piped up Jason, it being apparent that in his mind's eye he was envisioning himself zipping at speed down country roads, a pretty girl in the passenger seat . . . not that he could afford to buy a car in the foreseeable future.

'Well, I'm glad you can't wait because you don't have to,' Rica responded, then told him, 'Your Monday dinner hour in future is spoken for. Mr Pearson will be calling to collect you at one on the dot.'

Jason was frowning at her, non-plussed. 'What for?'

Rica tried not to laugh at his blank expression. 'Mr Sidney Pearson is the owner of Cobb's Driving School and he's just got me through my test. I went to him as I was told he was the best in Leicester.' While Jason stared at her confounded, she hurried back around the desk to take a book out of her handbag, then retraced her steps and held it out to him. 'This is now *your* bedtime reading.'

He took the *Highway Code* from her and clutched it to him, as if it was the most precious gift of all. 'Oh, I will read it. I'll go to bed early from now on and read it for an hour every night before I go to sleep. I'm really going to learn to drive? Really?'

Now she did laugh. 'Really, Jason. Then, when a customer

requests a home sitting, you'll just be able to throw all the equipment in the boot and off you go, instead of lugging it all on the bus. Your having a licence will come in really handy in future, I have no doubt.'

He was too overwhelmed to speak.

Bill asked her, 'So when are you going to take us for a drive then?'

Rica looked at him aghast. 'Well, I do need to get used to driving on my own and . . .'

He cut in, 'Come on, no time like the present. You can give us a spin around the block.'

Sidney Pearson had told Rica before they had parted company that once she had passed her test, that was when she would really learn to drive. Other drivers made allowances for learners, but she wasn't a learner any more so would receive no such consideration. She would no longer have him sitting beside her for support if she found herself in any difficulties, so she had to be extra-vigilant. His advice had been for her to get out and about as much as possible, on busy roads during busy times, in order to build up her confidence. She'd decided to follow his advice and had driven herself to the shop. But driving passengers . . .

'Don't you need to get home for your dinner, the pair of you? You know your mum isn't happy if you're late and the food is cold, Bill. I can take you on a drive another time.'

But he wasn't going to allow her to wheedle her way out of this. 'Oh, we've a few minutes to spare. Come on then.'

Jason sat in the back, Bill beside Rica. Although he didn't seem the critical type to her, it had crossed her mind as they locked up and got in the car that, as a seasoned driver himself, he might be on the lookout for any faults he deemed she'd made. She was nervous about that but need not have been. On the short journey round several nearby streets, Bill made not one comment but seemed to be content to be driven for

265

a change instead of doing the driving. When she dropped him and Jason back at his van, Bill got out of the passenger seat and said, 'It's not true what's said . . . that men make the best drivers.'

Rica knew then that his insistence on her taking him and Jason for a drive had been Bill's way of letting her know that he trusted her with his life, and that meant a lot to her.

Throughout the car ride all Jason could think of was that soon it would be him behind the wheel, something that before his employer's benevolence had been just wishful thinking.

Rica waited until they had driven off in the van before setting off herself, but she wasn't aiming to go straight home. She was going to visit Fran, to surprise her. Her sister didn't usually get home until about half-past six so Rica proposed to take the long way round and arrive just after her.

As it was she got lost several times during her journey to Fran's, a couple of times finding herself in a maze of unfamiliar terraced back streets and then, in complete contrast, leafy areas full of gabled properties she hadn't known existed. It was getting on for seven when she finally pulled up at the kerb before the large three-storey house where Fran had her flat.

Rica was already planning the excursions they'd be able to take, now that she could drive. Fran never had anything else to do on a Sunday afternoon except read or listen to the radio. They could go to Bradgate Park first, eight miles away. After a pleasant stroll, Rica would treat them both to tea and homemade cake in the cafe. That was one of the places she and Simon used to go on a sunny Sunday afternoon, for a blow of fresh air. She knew it could resurrect painful memories for her, but then she couldn't spend the rest of her life avoiding places Simon and she had frequented or she'd be housebound.

She knew Fran was home because the heavy red chenille

curtains that hung at the bay window of her flat were drawn. Rica dashed up the four steps to the communal front door, which was unlocked, then hurried upstairs to the first landing. She rapped purposefully on Fran's door. After waiting a minute and receiving no response, she knocked louder. She had knocked four times all told before eventually, from the other side of the door, she heard Fran call to her, 'What do you want, Rica?'

Her eyes widened in surprise. 'How did you know it was me?' Then she realised the odds were not high, considering that the number of friends Fran had could be counted on a fingerless hand. 'Just let me in, Fran.'

She replied, 'I'm just about to start making my evening meal.'

'Well, you can carry on doing that while I tell you what I've come for. Now let me in, will you?'

'Look, Rica, I've had a tiring day. I'm not in the mood for visitors.'

'I'm your sister, Fran, not a common visitor,' she snapped, offended.

'A very annoying sister at the moment, Rica. I'm really not in the mood for any callers tonight. We can have a chat if you still want to when you call on Saturday evening to bring me the books. Goodnight, Rica.'

She frowned. Whatever was going on with Fran, it was obviously something more serious than her being tired and not in the mood for callers. Her sister had some funny ways, but rudely talking to someone through the door was not usually one of them. She rapped on the door again and called out, 'You're hiding something from me, Fran, I know you are. Now open this door.'

She snapped, 'I'm not hiding anything from you, Rica. Now go away, will you?'

'No, I won't go away. I've known you not be in the mood for a visit from me before, a few times in fact, but you've always opened the door to tell me so to my face. So until I see for myself that nothing is ailing you, I'm not going anywhere. In fact, I'll bang on this door until you *do* open it, and it won't be just me you'll be letting in but all the neighbours come to complain about the disturbance!'

There was silence for a moment while Fran obviously mulled over what Rica had told her. 'Wait a moment,' she called.

It seemed to Rica that she was standing there for an age, waiting for Fran to open the door to her. She couldn't think what her sister could possibly be doing. Fast losing her patience, Rica was just about to rap again when she heard the turning of the Yale lock and the door opened to reveal Fran on the threshold. At a quick glance she looked perfectly all right expect that her eyes were puffy and rimmed with red and her skin tone was unusually pale. Rica knew that it was nothing to do with tiredness. Fran had been crying. *That* was what she'd been doing while she kept Rica waiting out on the landing – swilling her face with cold water, hoping to disguise the fact.

Before Fran could make a protest, Rica pushed past her and into the small hallway, where she turned to face her and demanded, 'What are you so upset about that it's made you cry, Fran?'

'Oh, don't be absurd. Crying is for babies. I told you, I'm tired. Now you've seen for yourself I'm fit and healthy, you'll respect the fact I wish to be left in peace.'

'Fran, stop treating me like I was born yesterday! I know when someone else is hurting.' Rica heaved a deep sigh and placed her hand affectionately on Fran's arm. 'I just want to help you, like you did me, and I can't if you won't tell me what's wrong. If I go home now, I'll only spend the night worrying about you and then I won't sleep myself and will be neither use nor ornament at work tomorrow.'

Fran stared blankly at her for several long moments before she said, 'I had an altercation with an annoyed client. There,

I've told you. Now you can go home and sleep peacefully.' She positioned herself next to Rica, took her arm and tried to herd her towards the still-open front door.

Rica, though, stood firm, wrenching free her arm from Fran's grip and laughing scornfully. 'You expect me to believe that having an exchange of words with an irate client has been enough to reduce you to tears? Well, I don't. Not for a minute. Now tell me the truth, Fran. I meant what I said, I'm not budging from this spot until you do.'

She heaved a sigh. 'All right, if it means you'll go. I did have an altercation but it wasn't with a client, it was with Mr Moffett. Now you're well aware I'm not at liberty to discuss this further as any company business is confidential, so please don't offend me by asking me to.'

Rica stared at her blankly. Some women would have sobbed hysterically after receiving a dressing down from their boss, but Fran always kept an iron grip on her emotions. Admittedly it was in privacy that she was letting her guard down, but even so Rica felt strongly that it would take much more than that to reduce her to tears. What exactly would it take to reduce Fran to tears? Then a probable reason came to her. Was it that after all her years of worshipping her boss from afar, any hopes she had had of him noticing her had finally been dashed as he had met and fallen for someone else? This seemed a more likely scenario than the one Fran had offered. Rica's heart cried out for her. Poor Fran. She was obviously devastated. Before she could stop herself, she had flung her arms round her sister and was hugging her tightly, whispering in her ear, 'I'm so sorry, Fran. So very, very sorry.' She then went to add that there were plenty more fish in the sea, though for the likes of Fran that seemed very unlikely. Letting go of her sister, Rica said, 'I appreciate you want to be left alone, to grieve for your loss.'

Fran frowned at her, bewildered. 'And what loss would that be?'

Rica sighed with frustration. True to form, Fran was deter-mined to keep her private business to herself and not expect any help at all with it. Rica was upset herself now that her sister wouldn't allow her to return the favour after all she had done when Simon and Ricky left. She said, more sharply than she'd meant to, 'Have it your own way, Fran. You know where I am if you change your mind. I'll go now and leave you in peace.'

'You still haven't told me what you came for in the first place,' Fran said crisply.

'Only to tell you I'd passed my driving test this morning.'

Fran said matter-of-factly, 'Well done.'

Rica was aware that she could wait for ever before she received any more praise than that. 'Well, I'll see you Saturday night when I drop off the books. And then, hope-fully, I might be asked in for a cup of tea.'

With that Rica stormed out of the flat.

Fran did ask her in for a cup of tea when she dropped off the books, but flatly refused to be drawn into divulging to Rica any more about the cause of her distress than she had already. Not one to bear grudges, Rica had put her sister's rebuff behind her by then. She asked Fran if she'd accom-pany her the next afternoon on a drive as she didn't like the thought of going so far by herself. Fran told her that of course she would, and they arranged for Rica to pick her up at two.

If Fran was nervous that her sister was in reality still a novice driver then she did not show it. She seemed to be enjoying the scenery on their drive into the country. Dropping her back at the flat before she headed off home herself, Rica thanked her for a very pleasant afternoon and suggested they should go out the very next Sunday, weather permitting. She would study some local maps to find inter-esting places for them to go.

CHAPTER TWENTY-TWO

A couple of weeks later Rica arrived for work one morning and was surprised to find Jason not in the shop as he usually was. Putting his delay down to a problem with public transport, and thankful that she did not have that to contend with any longer now she could drive, she took off her coat, put on the kettle, and said her good mornings to Harry who arrived not long after her.

A short while later she was standing at the counter, her face screwed up in worry over the contents of a letter she was reading, when the shop door burst open and Jason charged breathlessly in. Automatically Rica lifted her head to see who had entered, and was glad to see it was finally him. It struck her immediately that he was looking worried. 'Has something happened, Jason?' she demanded.

'Not half, Mrs Dunmore!' he responded as he stripped off his coat. 'That's why I'm late. I'm sorry, but I just had to go to the hospital myself, find out how he was and check that Mr and Mrs Simpson were all right. They'd been there all night with him. I missed them, though, as they'd already left to go back home.'

The *him* Jason was referring to could only be Bill. She exclaimed, 'Bill's in hospital? Was he suddenly taken ill? Has he suffered an accident?'

Jason shook his head. 'We think he was attacked.'

Eyes wide and with her hand clasped to her mouth in

shock, Rica said, 'Attacked! Oh, my God! Is he badly hurt? Jason, how bad is he?'

'I don't know, Mrs Dunmore. I'm not family, am I, so the hospital wouldn't let me in by the bed. They said I'd have to wait for news of Bill's condition from his parents, if they wished to tell me. All I do know, Mrs Dunmore, is that last night Bill and his dad went down the pub for a quick half and Bill must have decided to come back home before Mr Simpson did. It was his dad who found him, lying unconscious in the gutter, and an ambulance was called to take him to hospital. Mr and Mrs Simpson went with him. That was at half-past nine last night.'

Rica's face was ashen. She felt faint. It was then she first realised how much Bill had come to mean to her as a friend. The thought of losing him was unbearable. She needed to find out his exact condition for herself and couldn't wait until the news was delivered to them. Much to Jason's bewilderment, she dashed off to fetch her coat and handbag from out of the office.

'Hold the fort, I'm off down the hospital!' she cried.

He called after her, 'But you ain't family either, Mrs Dunmore, so the staff won't tell you 'ote or let you in to see Bill until visiting time at two. That's if he's well enough by then to have visitors.'

She paused at the door and turned back to face him. Jason had a point. She still wasn't prepared to endure a worrying wait for news of Bill's condition, though. She told Jason, 'I'll think of something, don't you worry. I'm seeing him.'

It was apparent he was in a great deal of pain but Bill's eyes told Rica he was pleased to see her when, an hour later, she slipped through the gap in the curtains pulled around his bed. He was in a seemingly never-ending ward lined with numerous other beds all filled with male patients, many of them with plaster casts on their limbs; a few of them looking mortally uncomfortable, with plastered limbs suspended in traction. Rica had imagined Bill having suffered all sorts through his accident, the worst of all and the one that terrified her most being that he had died from his injuries, so to find him propped up on pillows, looking enormously sorry for himself, was a sight for sore eyes to her.

She had to admit, though, he did seem to have just cause to feel sorry for himself. His well-muscled torso was tightly bound in crepe bandages which disappeared under the bedclothes around his waist. Several places on both of his arms were covered with surgical dressings. She couldn't see his legs, but considering how the rest of him looked, couldn't imagine they'd escaped injury. His swollen, bruised face looked as if he'd had a fight with a rampaging silverback gorilla whose favourite mate Bill had been trying to steal.

As she sat down in the chair by the bed, he said in a laboured voice, the effort clearly causing him pain, 'Not that it's not nice to see you, but how on earth did you persuade the staff to let you in out of visiting hours?'

Rica grinned. 'Got the gift of the gab, me.' Then her face became serious. 'I just had to find out how you were, Bill. We . . . Jason and I . . . didn't know whether you were alive or dead. All he could tell me was that you were found unconscious in the gutter outside the house by your father, and brought here in an ambulance at about nine-thirty last night. The poor lad is worried sick about you. On my way out, I'll telephone the shop to put his mind at rest.'

'I shouldn't worry about that. I sent my parents off home about half an hour ago as Mam was dead on her feet, having insisted on sitting with me all night to satisfy herself I wasn't about to die on her, and of course Dad had been adamant that he would stay too. Mam's not happy either as Dad is still determined to go into work, despite having been up all night and half the morning gone by the time he gets in, but Dad's the old-school type that goes into work whatever, unless they're on their deathbed. They were bickering about it as they went off down the ward. Anyway, Dad promised to get the taxi driver to stop by the stop to update Jason and you before they went home.'

Bill winced then as he temporarily forgot the state he was in and attempted to hoist himself up more comfortably against the pillows.

'Do you want me to fetch a nurse?' Rica offered.

He shook his head. 'There's nothing more they can give me to relieve the pain. I'm doped up to the eyeballs as it is. Nothing is broken, I'm just severely bruised. I feel like a herd of bulls has stampeded over me, if you want the truth. If I weren't suffering from a mild concussion, which means they need to keep an eye on me for twenty-four hours in case I have a relapse, I could have gone home this morning to recover there.'

'So what happened to you, Bill? Were you attacked by a mugger?'

'I was run over. By my own van, would you believe?'

She looked at him, stupefied. 'I don't understand. How on earth did you run yourself over with your own van?'

'I didn't run myself over . . . whoever was stealing it did.' He paused for a moment while another wave of pain passed before he continued. 'I'd been for a pint with the old man and he got roped into a game of dominoes with a couple of the other regulars. They tried to rope me in too but I wasn't in the mood, so I told Dad I'd see him back at home. The van was parked by the front door. I was a few yards away when I realised fumes were coming out of the exhaust, which meant the engine was ticking over. Well, as it wasn't me in the driver's seat, nor Dad as he was down the pub, that meant someone was in the process of stealing it.

'Then the van started to pull away and, stupidly I now realise, I decided to play Superman and stop the thieves. I ran around to the front of the van and put my hands on the bonnet, trying to bar the way . . . as if that would have stopped them! The next I knew, I was flying through the air and landed in the gutter like a ton of bricks. I can remember coming round in the ambulance feeling like hell on earth, my mother leaning over me, sobbing her heart out, begging me not to die.'

'Well, thank goodness your injuries are no worse. So what are the chances of the police catching the thieves and getting your van back for you? Oh, and your tools! You keep them all in the back of your van, don't you?'

He sighed heavily. 'There's no point in getting the police involved. By the time the theft is reported and they start a search, the two lads will either have wrecked my van or set fire to it, and either left the tools inside or sold them on. After he finishes his shift tonight, Dad is going to have a scout around our area and see if he can see the van. Or what's left of it.'

Rica was wide-eyed. 'But you must get the police . . .'

He cut in, 'Forget it, Rica. Same as I told my parents when they were pushing me to, I'm not wasting police time on this. Please just accept that, the same way they have to.'

But Rica couldn't let it go. 'Bill, if you don't report this and give the police a chance of catching the culprits, then they'll be free to do it to someone else. Their next victim might not be so lucky as to escape with a few cuts and bruises like you did. I can't understand why you're refusing to report these mindless thugs . . .' She stopped as something he had just said registered. 'You said something about two lads? You saw it was two lads who were trying to rob you. Maybe if you try and think hard you might recall what they looked like. Then the police will have something to go on and . . .'

He snapped, 'Rica, please, I asked you to forget it. I'm not taking this any further and that's that.'

She stared at him in bemusement for several moments, trying

to understand his reasons for not wanting the culprits to pay for what they had done. Then she realised why and said to him, 'You've got an idea who these two lads are, haven't you, Bill? In fact, I'll stick my neck out and say you know exactly who they are.' Then a horrifying thought struck her and she exclaimed, 'Oh, Bill, please tell me you're not going to go after these thugs yourself when you're better and . . .'

He cut in, 'Those lads aren't thugs, Rica. They've never done anything like this before, and I doubt they will again. It's my guess the pair of them have been simmering since it all came out in the open, and last night . . . well, it's only a guess but I think they couldn't control their hurt and anger any longer and decided to take it out on someone who was connected with it all. I was the unlucky one they picked on.' He suddenly stopped talking and let out a small cry as a wave of pain caught him unawares. Rica sat looking on helplessly. When the spasm had passed there was sweat on Bill's brow. Had they been more than friends, she would have mopped it with a cold flannel for him.

'Could you pass me a drink of water, please, Rica?' he asked feebly.

She was out of the chair before he had finished speaking. She poured him the water from a jug set on his bedside locker. While he slowly sipped it, she returned to her seat. When he had had his fill Rica relieved him of the glass. Cradling it in her hands, she said, 'Just who are those two boys, Bill? Why are they so hurt and angry that it made them . . . well, almost kill you?'

He opened his swollen mouth to respond, but was stopped by a pretty young nurse putting her head through the gap in the curtains. She addressed Rica. 'I did say a couple of minutes, Miss Simpson, and you've been here at least ten. Now say goodbye to your brother as he needs his rest.'

'Just another five minutes, please, nurse,' Rica urged. Then added another 'please' for good measure.

She looked at Rica for a moment, tutted and told her, 'Be thankful Sister Rogers isn't on duty. She'd only have allowed you two, not the fifteen I have . . . I have to go and collect the prescriptions from the pharmacy. I'll be gone for no longer than ten minutes. Please make sure you are not here when I get back.'

Gratefully she said, 'Thank you, nurse.'

Rica returned her attention to Bill and saw he was looking back at her with one eyebrow cocked. 'Well, they only let relatives in out of hours, don't they? Good job I wasn't asked for proof. So, just who are these two boys?'

He looked at her for a moment before sighing and telling her, 'Susan and Peter's sons. Darren is fifteen, Roland seventeen. Rica, if I report them they'll end up with a criminal record and then they might as well kiss goodbye to ever having a decent future. They're both good lads at heart. I've no doubt that right now they are deeply sorry and guilty for what they did last night. They both know I recognised them. I will make a point of catching them on their own as soon as I'm able. I'll tell them I understand why they did what they did, and to rest easy as the matter is closed as far as I am concerned. But I will also warn them that I won't be so accommodating again. I trust what I've told you will go no further than these walls . . . well, curtains, Rica?'

'I won't breathe a word, I promise.' She stared at him for several long moments before she said, 'You really are a good man, William Simpson.'

'Not good enough to keep my wife happy,' he said sardonically.

She shook her head and said gravely, 'What a mess. All the suffering that's been caused through other people's selfishness. So are you able to replace your van and tools? You can't do your job without either, can you?'

His face grim, Bill shook his head. 'Not right this minute, no, I can't. Not with the amount that I need. I could pick up a Transit easily enough for about fifty quid but the tools are a different matter. I built up all I had over twenty-five years in the trade. Some of them I'm sentimentally attached to as my parents set me up with the basics when I first started my apprenticeship; the rest I added to as money allowed. I've a few pounds left still, I can buy the bare essentials, then I think my only option is to approach other plumbers in the trade and see if one of them has an opening to take me on as an employee. Hopefully I'll get a works van thrown in. The fact I do have a number of jobs, a couple of big ones, outstanding on my own books means I could maybe give any possible employer an incentive to take me on. I reckon if I can get myself set on as soon as possible, then in roughly a year or just a little longer I might possibly have got enough saved to start again on my own.'

While he had been relaying his plans to her, Rica's mind had kicked into action. She told him, 'Well, I might have a way you can earn enough to be able to afford to replace your tools and van a lot quicker than that.'

He eyed her sharply and snapped, 'I would have thought you knew me better by now than to think I would ever accept charity, Rica.'

She said sharply, 'I wasn't going to offer you charity, Bill. I was going to offer you a way to replace your van and tools.'

He looked shamefaced to have accused her of something of which she wasn't guilty. He said gruffly, 'Oh . . . well . . . that's different. I take it you've had an influx of weddings and parties in since I last saw you?'

'Not quite, but a big job at any rate. I received a letter this morning from the Education Department of Leicester Council, advising me that Dunmore's tender to take all the junior-school photographs this year . . . that's individual children as well as class groups . . . has been accepted. Simon must have tendered for the job before he went off.' Her face screwed up in thought she said, 'You see, that's odd, isn't it? Why would he tender for such a big job when he knew he was planning to leave? It doesn't make sense to me. Anyway, until I dig out the tender and take a proper look at it, I'm not sure how many schools are involved, but the job is to include all the junior schools right up to the boundaries with the Shires, so it'll be quite a few. The sessions start at the beginning of May and run over a four-week period, that's in two weeks' time – hopefully long enough for you to be back on your feet by then.' She then looked at him pleadingly. 'Bill, you'd be doing me a big favour if you took this job on for me, as it would save me the headache of finding the right sort of freelance photographer to take on a job like this. I'm not sure how Simon proposed to handle it. I presume he intended to do it himself, and possibly get a temporary assistant in to man the shop while Jason saw to the studio bookings. Whatever rate for the job Simon put in for will of course be yours, Bill, less the cost of the films and processing, of course. I just hope that Harry and Jason between them can cope with all the extra processing, Jason is kept busy enough as it is, but I'll cross that bridge when I come to it. So what do you say, Bill? Will you help me out by taking on this job for me – and help yourself at the same time?'

He was looking thoughtfully at her. The job Rica was offering him was like a gift from God, and in the circumstances he'd be a fool to turn it down. The difficulty was that for him photography was the process of capturing subject matters that were of personal interest to him. He preferred to take an unusual slant on his subjects, capture them in a new light. But line-ups of school children, individual child portraits . . . there was only one way to approach them and that was straight on. Regardless of the money he'd earn, it was a mind-numbing prospect.

But then, should he turn her offer down, that would leave

Rica with the problem of finding someone else to take it on. Bill's conscience pricked him. A friend was in need and he was in a position to come to their aid. And Rica was not just a friend to him . . . he had grown very fond of her after the night they had bared their souls to one another after the charity shoot. He was full of admiration for this woman who had had her world ripped apart through no fault of her own. It was apparent to him that her wounds ran deep and were far from healed, yet regardless she was throwing herself into learning the business her husband had abandoned and had kept it thriving meantime. If Dunmore's reputation was damaged through any failure to honour the Council contract, Rica would suffer. And he couldn't bear that. He knew that he was going to have to accept her offer, despite the fact he didn't want to.

'Of course I'll do the job for you,' Bill told her.

His acceptance was made with no show of enthusiasm and Rica had a strong feeling that he didn't want to do it, but was only agreeing because she was asking him as a favour. She could be wrong, his lack of eagerness might be due to the pain he was suffering. There was no point in her quizzing him now, though. And she knew that Bill never went back on his word.

She leaned over to touch his hand with her fingertips, afraid to cause him any further hurt. 'Thank you, Bill. Now I'd better make myself scarce before that young nurse returns and manhandles me out.'

That evening while Rica was busy washing up her dinner pots and pans she was thinking of Cyril Jackson, the private detective on whom she had pinned such high hopes as a means of discovering her son's whereabouts. Since Cyril had delivered her the upsetting news that he had absolutely no leads left to pursue, he had telephoned her twice as a courtesy. He'd asked after her health and reassured her that during the course of his work he was still keeping an ear out for any snippet of information that might lead them to Ricky. After this long with no news, though, the chances of the whereabouts of Simon and her son coming to light accidentally were very remote.

It was with reluctance that she had decided that the next time Cyril telephoned her, she would tell him that she'd at long last resigned herself to the fact that when the time came for Ricky and her to be reunited, it would be because Ricky himself had instigated it. She would release Cyril from his promise to continue looking out for her husband and son when he should in fact he giving all his attention to those investigations that clients were paying him for.

The kitchen sparkling by now, she had just hung her apron on the back of the pantry door when there was a rap on the front door. It would be Mrs Craig, come to collect her donations to the forthcoming church fête, which she hadn't yet put together. Rica opened the door, ready to apologise to Mrs Craig for her laxness and tell her that she would deliver her donations herself as soon as she had sorted them out. To her surprise, however, her visitor wasn't her neighbour but Fran.

Standing aside to allow her entry, Rica said, 'What a nice surprise, Fran! Come in, I'll put the kettle on.' Then it struck her that her sister never visited during the working week, nor was she the type to call just because she fancied a general natter, so something must be wrong. 'What is it, Fran?' Rica demanded as she closed the door behind her.

Fran was taking off her coat. 'Nothing as far as I know,' she said, hanging it on the coat rack.

Relieved to hear that, Rica went off to the kitchen, Fran following behind. While putting the kettle on, she asked her sister, 'So why are you here? Not that it's not good to see you, but you don't usually . . . well, I can't remember when you have come over for a visit on a workday evening. And nor do you visit me without a reason. Oh, you've not come to tell me that you've changed your mind about going to Hunstanton for the day next Sunday, have you? I'm really looking forward to it.'

By now Fran had taken a seat at the kitchen table. 'I haven't come to break our arrangement for Sunday. For as long as you feel the need for my company, I shall be there for you, Rica.'

'I do still need your company, Fran. I've never been any good at going places by myself . . . having no one to share things with. It gets you out, too, doesn't it, to places you wouldn't normally get to visit? Instead of sitting alone in your flat. I bet you're really glad I learned to drive. If there's any place you'd like to go, you must tell me. Oh, of course, you've probably come to enquire how Bill is doing?'

Fran looked at her strangely. 'Is there any reason I would make a special visit to you to do that?'

'Because of his accident last night.'

'I didn't know he'd had an accident. How could I? The only time I have anything to do with Bill is when I'm at the shop at the same time as he is, and that's not been for a while since I returned to my own job. So what happened to him? Is he badly hurt?'

'It could have been a lot worse. He was run over by his own van. Last night he was nearly at home after going for a pint with his father when he saw the van, about to be driven off. It had all his work tools in the back. Bill remembers making a dash and getting round the front of the van in an effort to stop it driving off, but his sudden appearance must have shocked the driver as he revved up and drove away like a bat out of hell. Next thing Bill knew he was in an ambulance, feeling like he'd gone ten rounds with Henry Cooper. Luckily he's suffered no broken bones, just severe bruising all over his body, and mild concussion. They're letting him go home tomorrow.'

'How awful for him. Did he get a look at the culprit so he can give a description to the police?'

Rica was thankful that the kettle chose that moment to announce it was boiling, so she could attend to filling the teapot and not be looking directly at Fran when she lied. 'He said he never got a chance as it all happened so quickly. The chances of whoever it was being caught are remote. Bill's of the opinion that the van will either be found a complete wreck or burned out, and that his tools are long gone.'

'Has he the money to replace his loss? He won't be able to do his job without his van and tools, will he?'

'No to both. But as the saying goes, one man's misfortune is another's good fortune.' Rica proceeded to enlighten her sister about the letter she had received that morning from the Council, her worry as to how she was going to honour it, and the fact that because of what had happened to him, Bill was free to do the work for her.

Rica then asked her sister: 'So, if you didn't come to check on Bill as you didn't know what had happened to him, why did you call to see me, Fran?'

'Nothing sinister, I can assure you. I wanted to find out how you are.'

'But you saw how I was two days ago, on Sunday when we went out for the afternoon to Belvoir Castle. I'm fine.'

'I can see with my own eyes that you're physically well, Rica, but we haven't discussed for a long time how you're feeling emotionally.'

In the middle of collecting the tea things together, Rica turned round to eye Fran. Now she knew there was something wrong. Fran never took it upon herself to probe into the personal life of anyone else, her own sister included. As far as she was concerned, their private business was theirs, just as hers was her own. There had to be some reason behind Fran's uncharacteristic behaviour, but it was doubtful she would divulge it easily.

Rica waited until they both had a cup of tea in front of them before she said, 'Well, I think I'm coping extremely well, considering I didn't want to live any longer after Simon went off with Ricky. Don't you?'

'I do. I think you're doing remarkably. It's all right me thinking that, though. I wanted to make sure that you were.'

Rica said in all sincerity, 'I appreciate that, Fran. I won't lie to you and say I'm completely out of the woods yet. I still have my moments when a memory catches me unawares and the pain I feel then is as acute as it was when it first happened. But I'm getting better at dealing with those setbacks, and as time passes they're getting fewer. You pushing me into running the business has been my salvation, Fran. It keeps me physically busy and my mind occupied. I'm so tired most nights I fall asleep before I have time to dwell on the fact that I've not got Simon to cuddle any longer.'

She leaned over and gave her sister's hand an affectionate pat. 'But it's nice to know you're always available, should I ever sink to a low point and need you to bolster me again. Now, let's talk about our plans for Sunday. We need to set off early if we're going to enjoy a few hours there. It's a good three-and-a-half-hour journey, I understand . . .

Her eyes suddenly glazed over and she said in a regretful tone, 'Mum would have been beside herself to see me driving, wouldn't she? You remember how much she looked forward to the days out we used to have as kids? Every July fortnight shutdown, she and Dad both saved so hard to take us away. It would have felt good to treat her to a few days out. She'd have felt like the Queen, being driven about in her own car. I know you think I'm stupid to, but I tell her all about our trips, every last detail, when I visit her each Wednesday. Anyway, shall we take a picnic lunch on Sunday or shall we eat out? Oh, hold your answer for a moment, I must dash to the loo.'

She had just got there when she heard the telephone shrilling out. Rica immediately thought it would be Jason calling from a telephone box to update her on Bill's condition after visiting him with his parents earlier that evening. Then the ringing suddenly stopped and she could hear the muted tones of her sister's voice.

A couple of minutes later she made her way back into the kitchen and was about to ask Fran to relay the news of Bill's condition when she stopped short, seeing her sister standing in the middle of the room, her hands clasped together, her face grave.

An icy fear filled Rica then. 'No, he can't be dead!' she exclaimed. 'Please tell me that Bill's not died, Fran? He can't be . . . the hospital are sending him home tomorrow. His injuries weren't bad enough to kill him. So . . .'

Fran cut in, 'It's not Bill the call was about, Rica. It was the home, about Mother. It's Mother who's died.'

Four days later, clutching Fran's hand tightly for support, a bleak-faced Rica held back tears as she watched the pall-bearers lower her mother's coffin into the wet ground. A light drizzle was falling and the rest of the mourners were creating a canopy with their umbrellas, a couple behind doing their best to shield herself and Fran as well as themselves. Rica was grateful for their thoughtfulness and hoped she'd remember to thank them after the service was over.

She wasn't surprised by the number of old neighbours and friends of her mother who had turned out to pay their respects. Mary, the nurses' aide who had done her best to make Iris's life as pleasant as she was able to, had taken time off to attend, and the home had sent along their office clerk to represent them. Before illness had struck, Iris had been a popular woman and it warmed Rica to witness how during her time in the home she hadn't been forgotten by those whose lives she had touched.

Her mother's death, although expected sooner rather than later, had still hit Rica hard. She knew Fran viewed the funeral as just a formality, the burial of an empty vessel, as to her the essence of their mother had departed her body a long time ago after the relentless disease had killed her brain. But Rica always preferred to believe that somewhere in the depths of her being, her mother had still gained some comfort from her visits, still been aware to some extent of what was going on around her.

Although she had not voiced it, Rica knew that Fran was concerned that this latest devastating blow would cause her to suffer a setback. She had offered to move back in with her, temporarily, to do her best to make sure that didn't happen. Rica was very grateful for Fran's concern but had assured her that she wouldn't allow herself to sink into despair and take to her bed as had been the case when Simon had absconded. She was now responsible for the welfare of Jason and Harry through the wages she paid them, and more importantly considered herself to be the caretaker of her son's inheritance. She was adamant that she was going to do her best to make that inheritance worth having when it was time for Ricky to collect it.

In an effort to keep her mind busy and off her recent loss, she felt that this was a good time to throw herself into learning the last important part of the business, that was still as mysterious to her now as it had been when she had first taken over.

CHAPTER
TWENTY-THREE

'I give up! That's got to be the hundredth time I've attempted to do this and still I get it wrong. I just can't get the hang of it. I haven't got what it takes to master developing, have I, Harry?'

He said diplomatically, 'Well, it's not an easy job to learn. It's not only a matter of getting the mixing of the developing chemicals right, but also the timing spot on for how long you allow the negatives to soak at each stage. But let's not give up, Mrs Dunmore. Maybe I haven't explained the steps clearly enough. Why don't we start all over from the very beginning?'

'A five year old would have understood the way you've explained each step to me, Harry. I've been spending a good couple of hours a day here for the last four weeks, as if you aren't busy enough processing all the rolls of film for the schools contract. You've been so patient, trying to teach me the techniques of developing, but however hard I try, I just cannot get to grips with it. It's as if what you explain to me goes in one ear and straight out the other. By now I should be helping to ease your workload at busy times like this, not adding to it.'

'With due respect, Mrs Dunmore, you seem to be expecting

to master a trade in hours when it took me at least a year to learn just the rudiments of it.'

'Harry, I doubt that in a year I'd manage to learn any more than I have now. Maybe that's because I don't actually like doing it, if I'm honest. I consider it monotonous. I know you might find that difficult to understand as you obviously enjoy what you do, but I'd much sooner be out in the shop dealing with customers or taking the actual photographs themselves.' Rica heaved a deep sigh. 'I think I ought to be a wise woman and concede defeat on this one.' She took off the large protective apron and hung it on a hook at the back of the door just as someone knocked on it.

Harry called out, 'It's safe to come in, Jason.'

The door opened and Jason popped his head around, eyes seeking Rica. 'I'm sorry to disturb you, Mrs Dunmore.'

'That's all right, Jason. I was just on my way back into the shop anyway. What did you need me for?'

'Mrs Donaldson is asking to see you.'

Rica looked surprised. 'Has she decided what prints she wants copies of and how many of each already? You only delivered the proof shots of her daughter's wedding to her this morning. Well, I hope she doesn't want them in the next couple of days . . . we're snowed under at the moment as it is, with this big school job on. Tell Mrs Donaldson I'll be right with her, thank you, Jason.' As his head disappeared and the door closed she turned her attention back to Harry. 'Thank you for what you tried to do. I'm only sorry I wasn't a very good pupil. It must have been very frustrating for you.'

'Not at all, Mrs Dunmore. It was a pleasure.'

She laughed. 'A very diplomatic answer, Harry. And I do wish you'd call me Rica. It's only right that Jason still addresses me by my title as he's an apprentice, but you're not, Harry.'

'I'm afraid I was raised to respect my peers and I'm the sort who finds old habits hard to break, Mrs Dunmore.'

'Then I'll concede defeat again. Mrs Dunmore it is. I'd better go and deal with Mrs Donaldson. Thanks again, Harry. Oh, and don't forget to give us a shout if you find you need Jason's help at any time today.'

Harry took a quick look in the tray of films waiting to be processed. 'I should be all right, thank you, but I won't hesitate if I see I'm falling behind.'

She smiled warmly at him as she left the room, thinking how much the atmosphere in the shop had changed for the better since Fisher had been sacked and the very congenial and highly skilled Harry had replaced him. The last she had heard of Fisher was when Bill had caught sight of him a few weeks ago, selling newspapers from a kiosk in the town centre. Rica couldn't believe he was still working as he was seventy at least. He had obviously been under the impression that Dunmore's would keep him employed until the day he dropped dead as apparently he hadn't put away any of his wage or his ill-gotten gains to supplement the few shillings' government pension he received. What he was doing now was a huge comedown from the job he'd had here, but then he'd lost it through his own greed so Rica felt no sympathy for him.

Mrs Donaldson was a woman in her late-forties, slim and attractive still. It was evident she had been very pretty when young. She was dressed in good-quality clothes as befitted her husband's ownership of a successful electrical whole-saler's business.

As she approached her, Rica held out a hand in greeting and said, 'Hello, Mrs Donaldson. I didn't expect to see you quite so soon. Have you decided which of the photographs you'd like?'

'That's not what I've come for, Mrs Dunmore.'

Rica felt sure that her client was very upset

about something and assumed she wasn't pleased with the photographs for some reason, which surprised Rica. She had carefully checked through them after they had been processed by Harry, paying particular attention as this was the first assignment where she had taken the bulk of the shots herself, with Bill by her side for support. She had been on tenterhooks to see the results of her efforts, and on viewing the end result was astonished by the quality of them. So much so that her belief in her own abilities had soared. She felt that if the results were as good on her next couple of assignments then she'd feel confident enough to manage the shoots by herself. Now worry niggled at her that Mrs Donaldson didn't share her views.

'Are you not pleased with the photographs for some reason, Mrs Donaldson?' Rica tentatively asked.

'Oh, I'm more than pleased, Mrs Dunmore. You and your assistant photographer couldn't have done better, in my opinion. You somehow manage to capture the radiance that was pouring out of my daughter that day. I wouldn't hesitate to recommend your services to anyone.'

Rica was glad Bill wasn't here to hear himself being referred to as her assistant.

Mrs Donaldson went on, 'It's just one photograph in particular that has upset me.' She opened her handbag and pulled out one of fifty-odd proof copies that she'd received for her approval that morning, and handed it to Rica.

She looked at it searchingly. The shot was of the bride and groom posing with their chief bridesmaid and best man at the reception. They were all smiling happily, holding champagne glasses in their hands, and the photograph itself didn't seem to have any developing flaws. But then, she would have been surprised if it had as Harry would never send anything out of the dark room that he didn't feel was as good as he could get it. She was obviously missing some detail that Mrs Donaldson had spotted. Rica went behind the counter where the light was better, to study it again. As she was giving it a closer scrutiny she realised that Jason was by her side, giving the photograph a close look too.

Rica finally addressed Mrs Donaldson. 'I do apologise, but I can't find any fault with the photograph itself.'

'Neither can I. It's actually rather a nice one. Only it's marred for me by what was captured in the background.'

Bemused, Rica and Jason both looked at the photograph again, concentrating on the background this time instead of the group in the forefront. Then Rica spotted what had caused Mrs Donaldson to become upset. The shot was of the bride and groom and two of their guests raising glasses in a toast, and had been taken at one side of the large room where the reception was being held, in front of a long table covered by a white cloth and holding a selection of bottles and glasses.

Because of the clarity of the photograph, it was possible to make out what lay beyond the table. In the corner of the room the management had put up an ornate screen in order to hide several hostess-type trolleys that the waiters and waitresses were putting the dirty plates and glasses on. Thanks to the angle Rica had shot the photograph from, there was a clear view of what the screen was meant to be hiding. But at the moment the shutter was pressed, the trolley loads of dirty pots were not the only occupants of the space behind the screen. There was also a man and a woman, both obviously thinking that they were safely concealed from public view and totally oblivious to the fact that yards away a camera was about to capture them in an intimate situation. Rica knew that it wasn't just the fact that two of the guests had been caught acting indecently in what was tantamount to a public place that bothered Mrs Donaldson; it was just who the man in the shot was. Mr Donaldson.

She lifted her head and looked across at the client, mortified. 'I'm so very sorry that I didn't notice what was going on when I looked through the viewing lens to check the shot before I took it.'

Jason suddenly exclaimed, 'What are that couple up to behind the screen? It looks to me like they're . . .'

Rica glared at him, which made him blush and immediately clamp shut his mouth.

Addressing Mrs Donaldson again, Rica said to her, 'I really can't apologise enough for my carelessness. Would you like me to destroy this photograph, along with the negative?'

'Oh, no, definitely not.'

Rica looked at her, taken aback. 'Oh! So what is it you wish me to do? I don't see what else I can do to put this right . . .'

'Oh, there are certain people I *do* want to see it. You see, I've suspected that my husband has been carrying on behind my back for years. Nothing concrete, just a sixth sense . . . A woman knows when her husband is up to no good, doesn't she?'

Not this woman, Rica thought, as she'd never suspected her own husband was planning to leave her.

Mrs Donaldson was going on, 'You can best help me by helping me obtain my freedom from that detestable man.'

Rica was frowning. 'I don't see how.'

'By getting me the sort of evidence that makes it impossible for him to deny his infidelities. This one photograph is not enough. He could somehow explain it away, say he was drunk or something and didn't know what he was doing. The woman with him in the photograph, by the way, is the wife of his golfing partner. Her husband adores her and will be devastated when his wife's secret liaison is made public knowledge in the divorce court. I am deeply indebted to you, Mrs Dunmore. I had despaired of ever coming up with a way of getting the evidence I needed to end my marriage, and now you've given me an idea how to do it, with that photograph you innocently took.

'My husband's nights for visiting his floozy are Wednesdays and Fridays, when he tells me he's off to his club. I can't check he's actually there as women aren't allowed past the doorstep and the staff are so loyal to their clientele they wouldn't divulge any information . . . even if you stuck a red hot poker up their backside! What I want you to do is follow my husband this Wednesday evening, tomorrow in fact, and take photographs of where he goes and who he meets. Get shots of them together . . . or, even better, in a compromising situation.'

Rica was looking at her, astonished. 'But, Mrs Donaldson, it's a private detective you need to consult, not a photography studio.'

'That is out of the question. A private detective needs money up front as a retainer and Robert has tight control of all our finances. He settles the bills. I have a set allowance to manage on each month. I do have a little bit of money of my own, though, and with it I'm commissioning you to take some photographs for me. Isn't that what all your other customers ask you to do for them, take photos? I can't see why you're reluctant.'

An excited Jason blurted out, 'I'll do it, Mrs Donaldson. I've always fancied being a sleuth. I watch all the detective shows on the telly, so I know what to do, and I take a decent photograph, if I say so myself. Mrs Dunmore will back me on that. I've got black trousers and a poloneck, and Bill's got an old macintosh . . .' Then abruptly he stopped his excited babble, his face fell and he exclaimed, 'Oh, of course, it will mean following Mr Donaldson by car and I haven't got one.' Then his face lit up again. 'Oh, but you can drive, Mrs Dunmore. You could do the driving and I'll take the photos. We could be a team like Steed and Emma Peel in *The Avengers*.'

Rica exclaimed, mortified, 'Jason, what on earth has got into you? Your suggestion is . . .'

'Perfect, young man,' Mrs Donaldson cut in, a delighted

smile on her face. 'My husband usually leaves the house at eight so best be parked ready at ten minutes to, just in case he decides to leave early. I'll call in on Thursday afternoon to find out if you had any success.' She smiled and said gratefully, 'Thank you, Mrs Dunmore. I so appreciate your agreement to do this for me. You're my saviour, you really are. You too, young man.'

With that she took her leave.

As soon as the outer door closed Rica spun round to Jason and exclaimed, 'But I didn't agree to do this, did I, Jason? You roped me into your hare-brained scheme when you realised you couldn't carry it out by yourself. If you'd be happier working for a detective agency, then I won't stand in your way.'

He gawped at her in horror. 'Oh, I wouldn't, Mrs Dunmore. I just got carried away by the thought of all the excitement. Do you want me to go after Mrs Donaldson and tell her I spoke out of turn and we're not agreeing to do it after all?'

Rica raked one hand through her hair and heaved a despondent sigh. 'That poor woman thinks she's finally found a way to catch her husband cheating on her after years of suffering in silence. I can't bring myself to disappoint her like that and leave her in her awful marriage.' She then angrily added, 'If we land up in the slightest trouble for this, I will hold you entirely responsible. In future, Jason, keep your suggestions to yourself unless I specifically ask you for them. Is that understood?'

Face red with embarrassment, he muttered, 'Yes, Mrs Dunmore.'

'Right. Well, let me know when you've made your plan as to how we should go about it tomorrow night. Should be easy for you to come up with one, you being an authority after all.'

* * *

The next evening at a quarter-past eight Rica was praying she was driving a good enough distance away from Robert Donaldson for him not to become suspicious. At this moment in time she was seriously regretting that she had ever learned to drive. She very much hoped that they were successful tonight and didn't have to repeat this as she didn't think her nerves could stand it again. Sitting beside her, Jason was checking for the umpteenth time that the camera was all set up correctly to take night shots. Periodically he would take a snap through the window, just to be sure. In contrast to herself, she could tell that he was enjoying every minute of this assignment. At the moment Robert Donaldson was leading them through the backstreets of a rundown part of Leicester. Rica would never have thought that a man like him would associate with the likes of the working-class types who resided in such an area.

With her nerves frayed as they were, Jason's periodic clicking was very much irritating her and when he did it again, she snapped at him, 'For God's sake, will you stop that or you'll have no film left.'

'I was only checking that the camera was working, Mrs Dunmore,' he explained.

Having followed Robert Donaldson through several more narrow terraced streets, they emerged on to a main road and Rica realised he must have been taking a short cut to wherever it was they were heading. A short while later they were cruising through a leafy suburb of the city where the likes of bank managers and accountants chose to live. Rica slowed right down when they saw Donaldson had pulled his car to a halt outside a semi-detached house several yards ahead. Before he got out and spotted their headlights, Rica pulled her car in and switched off the lights. From here they had a good view of Donaldson who was now getting out of his car and heading towards the semi.

Rica said to Jason, 'Right, looks like this is it. Are you still sure you're up to doing this?'

Now he was actually faced with it, the enormity of what he was about to do hit him like a sledge hammer and his nerve began to go. Those television detectives made what they did look so easy, even laughing and joking as they made their way to arrest a vicious villain. But Jason wasn't laughing now. He had no one to blame but himself for landing up in this situation. And, worse, dragging his boss into it too. But if he backed out, it could result in Mrs Dunmore's reputation being tarnished and in damage to the business. And she'd been so good to him.

He said to Rica, 'Yeah, I'm ready.'

They both looked across the road. Donaldson was fumbling with the gate of the house he had parked his car outside, and it looked as if he was carrying a bottle of wine in one hand. Jason knew it was time for him to make a move or else he'd miss his chance of getting a photograph of his quarry going into the house, including whoever it was who was letting him in.

It would have been impossible to say who was the more anxious: Jason as he slipped out of the car and stealthily crept across the road, or Rica, back in the car, taking a long look at the houses facing them and hoping she wasn't going to spot anyone looking out and observing Jason's antics, for fear they might call the police. Thankfully all the curtains at the windows she could see were drawn tight. She then checked for pedestrians who might see what was going on. Thankfully there were none. She then returned her attention to the house Robert Donaldson had gone into, expecting to see Jason making his way back to the car as by now Donaldson must surely be inside . . .

Panic mounted in her when she couldn't see any sign of Jason at all. Her eyes darted up and down the street but still there was no sign of him. Where had he gone?

Then it struck her that he'd obviously been accosted by a neighbour or, worse, Donaldson himself. He'd have been frogmarched into the house while the police were called to deal with him. But Rica couldn't let him face a criminal record. When it really came down to it, Jason might have come up with the idea but it was she herself who'd brought them here. She would have to convince the authorities that as his boss she was responsible, and face the consequences.

Then movement across the road caught her eye and, to her tremendous relief, she saw it was Jason sprinting back towards her.

Yanking open the passenger door, he almost threw himself inside. Before she could ask him how he'd got on, he was begging her, '*Please* just drive away from here as quick as you can, Mrs Dunmore. I can't be positive I wasn't spotted. I don't think I was, but I can't be sure.'

Taking only long enough for a quick check that the road was clear, Rica put her foot down on the accelerator and sped off far faster than the legal speed limit, too anxious to put a safe distance between them and the house Donaldson had entered to worry about it. It wasn't until it registered with her that she was finding it difficult to see where she was going that she realised in her panic to make a getaway she had not put on the headlights.

For the tenth time in ten minutes Rica checked her rear-view mirror, mortally relieved to see that they were not being followed. She said to Jason, 'Doesn't seem like you were spotted. There's no one following us at any rate.' She cranked down the window and listened for a moment before winding it back up and adding, 'I can hear any police sirens.' She flashed a quick look at him. He was sitting slumped in the seat, the camera clutched tightly in his hands, staring blindly ahead. She demanded, 'Are you all right, Jason?'

'Eh? Oh, I'm fine. I can't believe what I've just done. Oh,

Mrs Dunmore, I was so scared but excited at the same time. I've . . .'

She interjected, 'Jason, please put me out of my misery and tell me that you got what we came for, so we don't have to go through this again? I couldn't face it. My nerves are shot as it is.'

He swivelled himself round to face her and began, 'Well, I couldn't believe it when I arrived at the hedge to see a hole in it right before my eyes. It was big enough for me to get the lens of the camera through and then just about see what I was aiming at. The front door was open by this time and I had a clear view of the person who'd opened it. It was a woman and I heard her tell Mr Donaldson that she wasn't expecting her husband back before eleven, so they had plenty of time together. But, Mrs Dunmore, you should have seen what she was wearing! It hardly covered her and I swear I could see through it . . . I don't think she had anything on underneath.'

Rica didn't comment on that. Instead she demanded, 'Please tell me you managed to get a picture of the woman and Mr Donaldson together?'

'Three of them. I shot them off as quickly as I could, one after the other. I was so worried they'd hear the cogs turning when I rolled the film on after each shot. Thankfully I didn't need to use the flash as the porch light was on and the light in the hallway as well. The woman was facing my way and if I had needed to use the flash, she wouldn't have missed it. Then you'd have seen me run like I've never run before, believe me!'

Rica said, relieved, 'So you got three photographs? Surely one of them will come out clearly enough for what Mrs Donaldson needs . . . Let's hope that along with the one I took at the wedding, that will be enough evidence now.'

'Oh, but I didn't just get those three photographs. I got

another three of them . . . really together this time, if you understand me?'

She flashed a look at him. 'You did . . . But how?'

He cockily explained to her, 'After they'd gone inside, I was about to come back to the car when I thought to meself, Now what would Paul Drake . . . you know, the detective Ironside off the telly uses . . . do now? Well, he wouldn't stop at just getting three photos and hope it was enough for Ironside's needs. He'd try and get some more.

'Do you watch *Ironside*, Mrs Dunmore? Mrs Simpson loves that programme and never misses an episode, that's how I got into it. We watch it together as neither Mr Simpson nor Bill can stand it. While it's on they find something else to do. Actually that's why Bill and Mr Simpson went off down the pub the night he got run over by the cretins who stole his van and tools . . . because *Ironside* was on.'

Three months ago it was difficult to get more than two words out of Jason unless they were business-related. Now, having been liberated from his despicable parents, he'd come right out of his shell and definitely seemed to be hell-bent on making up for lost time as he never seemed to shut up. Rica scolded him, 'Jason, right this minute the only thing I'm interested in is what you did after you'd taken the shots of them at the front door?'

'Oh, yes, sorry, Mrs Dunmore. Well, I slipped through the front gate and tiptoed my way round the side to the back of the house. I thought that if I could get around the back I might be lucky. So long as the curtains weren't drawn, I could see what was going on inside . . . unless they'd already gone up to the bedroom, of course, then I'd be snookered. But I was hoping they hadn't, if nothing more than to get a couple of shots of them together in the house, sitting talking or watching the television.

'Did you know, Mrs Dunmore, that you can take really good pictures through a window into a lighted room at night as there's no glare on the window panes? Oh, except when there's a bright moon, which thankfully there isn't tonight.'

She snapped, 'No, I didn't, as I've never had cause to take any snaps in the dark into a lighted room. Will you please get on with it!'

'Oh, yes, of course, sorry. Well, someone up there . . .' Jason said, pointing upwards . . .' is looking out for us tonight because the lady had drawn the curtains, but she hadn't actually shut them properly. There was a gap in the middle big enough for me to see through. I bet she was in the middle of drawing them when Mr Donaldson disturbed her by ringing the doorbell.'

Rica urged him, 'And through the window . . . did you see anything worth taking?'

He exclaimed, 'I bloomin' did, Mrs Dunmore! I caught them kissing again, but really passionately this time. Then one of them taking each other's clothes off. Then another of them . . . well . . . at it on the sofa.'

Rica gasped. 'Really? Oh, they're just the sort of photographs I know Mrs Donaldson was hoping to get. All we have to hope now is that they turn out okay.'

Jason lapsed into silence for several long moments before he said, 'Mrs Dunmore?'

'Yes, Jason?'

'Do you not feel excited at all, by what we were doing tonight?'

She flashed him a look as though to say she thought he was mad. 'Excited! No, I definitely do not. I've never felt so nerve-racked in all my life, especially when I thought you'd been caught when I couldn't see you. And if this is your way of asking if I'd agree to do it again if another customer should request it, the answer is no. NO. You got that, Jason?'

'Mmm,' he muttered, disappointedly.

CHAPTER TWENTY-FOUR

For obvious reasons, Harry was not going to be given this particular roll of film to develop and, not being able to stand the anxious wait until he vacated the dark room to go home for his lunch at one o'clock the next day, Rica drove straight to the shop to get Jason to develop them now. To her utter dismay, they arrived to find a power cut in progress, with no telling how long it had been going on for or how long it would last. She had no choice after all but to wait until next day.

She had little sleep that night, and could not remember a morning ever going by so slowly despite a number of clients keeping her busy and a couple of sales reps popping in, hoping to talk her into buying from them. Finally the moment arrived when Jason came back into the shop with the developed photographs. It was obvious that the results far exceeded the quality he'd hoped for, judging by the triumphant expression on his face, but Rica wanted to see them for herself before she could breathe a sigh of relief.

She accepted the pile of prints from Jason while he informed her that he had left the dark room as he'd found it just as Harry returned from lunch. Harry had asked him to kindly let Mrs Dunmore know he was finishing off the rolls of film Bill had dropped in last night after his latest school shoot.

By this time Rica wasn't listening to him as she was confused as to why there seemed to be at least fifteen photographs when Jason had told her he had only taken six, until she remembered he'd been snapping away on the journey there, to see if the camera was working correctly. She flicked through the early photographs until she came to the ones that were of interest to her, meaning to discard the ones that weren't, when one of the prints slipped out of her hand and dropped on the floor.

Automatically she bent to pick it up at the same time as Jason did. Rica beat him to it. In the time it took her to straighten up she gazed at the photograph – and then stood staring at it, frozen in disbelief.

This particular shot had obviously been taken by Jason when she had temporarily stopped the car at a junction or crossroads to check the way ahead was clear before following after Mr Donaldson. The photograph was in focus, with no sign of the blurring that would have occurred had they been moving at the time. It wasn't, though, the quality of the photograph that Jason had managed to take that was riveting all her attention, but its subject matter. It showed the back view of a woman entering a corner shop. Just the window and the door of the shop were visible. The woman was dragging along with her a young boy, of no more than two, who at the time Jason had pressed the shutter happened to be looking his way.

Rica's heart began to pound so violently she thought it would burst, her legs threatening to give way beneath her so that she had to grab hold of the edge of the counter for support. She might not have seen him for seven months now, and children changed a lot at that young age but, regardless, she knew her son when she saw him.

Jason was about to ask Rica why she seemed so interested in a photo of a shabby-looking woman and child when the look on her face registered with him. 'Mrs Dunmore, whatever is the matter?' he enquired worriedly. Rica didn't appear to hear him so he repeated himself, but louder this time.

Finally she did respond. 'This photograph, Jason, just where were we when you took it?'

He gave a bemused shrug. 'I don't know, Mrs Dunmore.'

She demanded, 'But you *must* remember, it's imperative that you do. Now think, Jason, think!'

Just then there was a knock on the shop door and Jason said, 'Oh, we haven't opened up and it's well past two. Shall I . . .'

To his shock, she told him, 'Leave it, the customer can wait for a moment. I need you to concentrate on where you took this photograph.'

He looked at it closely for a moment then said, 'Well, I obviously took it when we were travelling through that area of rundown terraces, but I can't remember which street it was. I wasn't paying that much attention, I was so excited about getting where we were going and playing the part of a private dick. That was, until we did get there and I nearly bottled it but . . .'

'Jason!' Rica snapped in frustration. 'I need to know where this photograph was taken. Try retracing the journey in your mind. Something might occur to you.'

The waiting customer was also growing frustrated at not being let in, and knocked on the door again to remind them he was still there.

Jason said, 'Shouldn't I . . .'

'I said, leave it! Now get back to doing what I asked you to, please, Jason. I can't stress enough how important this is to me.'

He looked back at her, shocked. Mrs Dunmore had never shouted at him before. Why was this photograph so important to her? There wasn't anything about it that stood out to him. Fixing his eyes on it again, he cast back his mind to last night, from the moment they were sitting outside Mr Donaldson's house waiting for him to come out.

While Rica looked at him, willing him to do her bidding,

it suddenly struck her that she was so desperate for the boy in the photograph to be her son that there was a danger she was deluding herself. She really ought to seek a second opinion before she found herself in the very awkward situation of accusing an innocent women of kidnapping her child. There was only one person who was familiar enough with Ricky to confirm Rica's belief that the boy in the photograph was him, and that was Fran.

To Jason's surprise he suddenly found the photograph snatched from his hands by his boss. As she hurried into the back of the shop, she called to him, 'I have to go out for a bit. I can't remember if I've any studio sittings this afternoon. If I have, just tell them an emergency came up and I've had to go out. You can rearrange the appointment. Or else shut the shop up while you do it . . . I'll leave it to you. And meantime, keep racking your brains about where you took that photograph.'

'But, Mrs Dunmore, remember . . . Mrs Donaldson is going to call in and see how we got on last night.'

'Well, just give her the photographs.'

'But we haven't checked them yet.'

Rica erupted, 'You are quite capable of checking them by yourself, aren't you? I'm sure they'll be absolutely what she was after.'

'What shall I charge her?'

'Ten pounds. And you can keep it yourself towards saving for a car when you pass your test as I can't really put it through the books, can I? Ten pounds received for sleuthing! Now I have to go. Oh, and for God's sake, open up and let that customer in before they have a heart attack!'

The building where Fran worked was situated on Rutland Street, in the centre of town. Rica managed to park not far away. On the ground floor of the building a pair of shops stood either side of an entrance that accessed the upper two floors and the attic via an old-fashioned gated lift or the stairs. All the rooms were occupied by different businesses, from a dentist's to a wine importer's. Moffett's Accountancy was on the second floor.

To Rica's dismay, a sign taped to the lift announced it was out of order. Desperate to ask Fran's opinion about the boy in the photograph, Rica dashed up the stairs to the second floor and had to stand still for a moment while she caught her breath. She was on the landing now, beside the stairs leading to the attic. In front of her were two half-glazed doors. She entered the one on the right.

Apart from Rica herself there was no one else in the outer room. The receptionist had obviously been sent out on an errand. In their respective offices, neither Fran nor Mr Moffett could have heard her arrive as neither of them had come out to investigate. She wasn't sure how to announce herself. Just go straight into Fran's office, whether she was disturbing her or not? It wasn't the done thing to visit friends or family during working hours; it was against the rules of most companies, unless of course it was a matter of life or death. But the reason Rica had come to see Fran was as important as that to her.

In her urgent desire to hear Fran's thoughts, Rica made her way across the room towards her sister's office – only to stand rooted to the spot on hearing two voices inside. Fran and Reginald Moffett were deep in conversation, but that wasn't what had stopped Rica in her tracks. What had surprised her was the fact that she had heard her own name mentioned and wondered why Fran and her boss would be talking about her. She had nothing whatsoever to do with Moffett's business. The reason for her visit was temporarily forgotten as she stood and listened. What she heard was astounding.

'Oh, Reginald, since we realised that we both felt the same about each other, the night we attended the Gilbert and

Sullivan performance, I've wanted nothing more than to become your wife,' Fran was saying.

Rica was jubilant to learn that her plan to bring Fran and her boss together had worked. She'd been right all along. They were made for each other and it seemed they had already got to the stage of discussing marriage. How typical of Fran not to share this news with her! But what her sister said next kept Rica rooted to the spot.

'When I do become your wife, you will come first with me as is only right and proper. A wife should support her husband to the best of her ability. But how can I give you my all when my sister still needs my support? I made her a promise that I would be there for her whenever she needed me, for how ever long she needed me. She has no one else to help her through this awful time. I can't break my promise to her, Reginald, I just can't.'

'I appreciate that at the time her husband went off, your sister needed all your support, my dear, but I understand that she has made good progress since.'

'It's true she's managing the business and has learned to drive. She doesn't need the type of close support I was giving her when her husband first left, but that doesn't mean she's out of the woods. I can't let her down.'

Reginald soothed her. 'I appreciate that you can't just suddenly abandon Erica but doesn't she have any friends she could take with her on her weekend drives, instead of commandeering you all the time?'

'Unfortunately all the friends she and her husband had fell by the wayside when their son came along. Rica had been so desperate for a child for so long that she wanted to devote all her time to being a mother to the new baby, and Simon was quite happy to go along with that. Rica will make new friends, I've no doubt, but only when she is ready to. You do understand, don't you?'

He sighed. 'Yes, of course I do. I'm just being selfish, my

dear. After all those years I hid my feelings from you because I never believed such a woman would look at a man who was older than her, but I now want to spend every minute I can with you. I just wish you hadn't promised your sister that you'd go on trips with her every Sunday! If it was every other Sunday instead, then at least we'd have one whole day a fortnight to do something together. And it's not as though you enjoy the sort of places you go with her, is it? You just let her believe you do, to please her. Don't you think that if you at least told her about us, she would understand that we need to be together outside working hours?'

Fran issued a heavy sigh. 'Oh, Reginald, I want nothing more than to tell my sister about us. I know she will be shocked, but also very pleased for me. I just can't bring myself to be ramming my happiness down her throat while I know she is still in grief over the failure of her own marriage and the way it ended, despite the brave face she puts on to the world. I will tell her, though, as soon as I feel the time is right. I know this is a lot to ask of you but . . .'

Fran suddenly stopped talking for a moment then resumed. 'Do you hear that, Reginald? Someone is crying. It's coming from reception. It'll be Valerie. Something must have happened to her on the errand she was sent on. I hope she hasn't mislaid the documents she was delivering. I'll go and see to her.'

Fran was most taken aback to find it was not their young receptionist in distress but her own sister, sitting on one of the high-backed chairs, hands covering her bowed head, sobbing uncontrollably. Fran thought she knew why.

She went over and sat down in the chair next to her. 'You overhead the conversation I was having with Reginald, didn't you, Rica?'

Miserably, she nodded. Then, dropping her hands from her head, she threw her arms around her sister and buried her head in her shoulder, heedless of Fran's discomfiture at this emotional display.

'Oh, Fran, I've not been fair to you at all, have I? You've made all those sacrifices for me and not once did I stop to consider what you were giving up. I've taken you so much for granted. I'm ashamed of myself for being so selfish and wrapped up in my own affairs. I knew there had to be a reason you came round the other night to check on how I was. If I'd told you I was completely over Simon, then you would have told me about you and Reginald, wouldn't you?

'And I expect you were crying the night I came to see you unexpectedly because Mr Moffett had asked you to marry him, and you didn't feel you could accept until you'd seen me through this awful time. Oh, Fran, to think that you were willing to risk your chance of happiness with Mr Moffett for my sake!

'I don't deserve you at all. I used to believe you hadn't an emotion in your body, were born a cold fish, but how wrong I was to believe that, just because you don't show your feelings openly like I do. You have to believe that I do appreciate all you've done for me even though I haven't really shown it. I'm just so glad I managed to do something good for you, Fran. I always knew you and Mr Moffett were meant for each other.'

Fran peeled Rica off her and said in her usual matter-of-fact tone, 'You're to forget what you heard. It wasn't for your ears anyway. And let me assure you that I'm not about to do anything that will mean I can't be there for you, whenever you need me. When the time comes and you don't need my support in the same way, that's when I shall marry Reginald.'

Rica shook her head and said with conviction, 'But I can't forget what I overheard, and I'm glad I did. I'm mortified enough about being responsible for keeping you apart from Mr Moffett this long. I'm not going to do it any more. You've seen me well on the road to recovery, Fran, now it's time for me to travel the rest of the way on my own. If you would show me properly how to do the books, I will take them over as soon as possible. And, Fran, just because you'll be putting Mr Moffett first in future, it doesn't mean I'm losing you altogether, does it?'

'No, of course it doesn't. I will still be there for you. Just not all the time . . . at the drop of a hat.'

'And you'll let me help you plan your wedding?'

A memory struck Fran then and she asked Rica, 'You said something earlier . . . that you were glad you had managed to do something good for me. That you always knew Reginald and I were meant for each other. What did you mean by that, Rica? Oh! It was you, wasn't it? You were the "grateful client" who sent us the tickets and brought us together?'

Rica gulped. She gave an attempt at an innocent shrug. 'I don't know what you're talking about.'

Fran huffed, 'I know it was you. I should have realised earlier . . . you're the only one who could have known that both Reginald and I were unlikely to refuse tickets to that performance. But how did you know how I felt about him?'

Rica grinned. 'Some things even you can't hide, Fran. On the odd occasion you talked about him, you didn't realise how your eyes lit up and you'd smile. That's how I found out that he was an opera buff as well, which came in very handy when I was trying to think of something nice to do for you, after all you'd done for me.'

'Well, as you know, I usually deplore anyone involving themself in my affairs . . . but in the circumstances, I can't be mad with you.' Then another thought struck Fran. 'Just what has brought you here this afternoon that couldn't wait until I got home tonight?'

Rica gasped. Considering how important it was to her, she couldn't believe she had forgotten the reason she had come. She picked up her handbag, which had slid out of her hand on to the floor by her chair. Opening it up, she pulled out the photograph and handed it to Fran. 'Take a look at this and tell me what you think?'

Frowning, Fran took it off her and looked at it. At first all she saw was the back view of a woman tugging a child with her into a corner shop. Then something familiar about the child drew her eyes. She realised why Rica had asked her to look at it, and mouthed, 'Oh!'

Rica urged her, 'Does that mean you think the boy could be Ricky?'

'Well, if it isn't, he has a double. He looks bigger and he's lost some of his baby face, but you still can't mistake him. That hair . . . Where did you get this, Rica?'

'Jason took it. I just happened to see it after he'd developed a roll of film. I instantly believed the boy was Ricky, but then I was worried that I was kidding myself because I so wanted it to be true. That's why I wanted your reaction before I took this any further. Now I have to hope that when I return to the shop, Jason will have remembered where he took that photograph.'

To her utter joy, when Rica arrived there he told her he did. 'Well, I'm as sure as I can be. I'm positive that this photograph was the one I'd just snapped when you told me that the clicking of the shutter was getting on your nerves, and to stop it. You'd halted at a junction to check the road was clear before you carried on following Mr Donaldson. I remember seeing the street name above the shop. It stuck in my mind because it's the same name as the company that makes my favourite sweets, liquorice allsorts. Bassett. It was called Bassett Street.'

Rica hadn't taken her coat off. She turned to go.

'I have to leave. It's unlikely I'll be back tonight before closing time so can you please do the honours with the locking up?'

And she was out of the door before he had a chance to make any response.

CHAPTER TWENTY-FIVE

The area where Bassett Street was located was rundown; not as dilapidated as the huge slum areas the council had just about finished clearing to make way for new housing, but the homes here would benefit greatly from some repairs and a few licks of paint. Rica was shocked that Simon had settled in a place like this after living in their smartly refurbished semi. She doubted many of the houses in this street even had a bathroom, and there were only tiny slabbed yards outside instead of gardens. He must love the woman he had left her for very much, to have walked away from his business and his home.

Not many people owned a car in this street. Apart from two rusting old bangers, one that had no wheels and was sitting on house bricks, and an old Transit van similar to the one Bill drove but in a far worse state, Rica's was the only other one. When she arrived at her destination she realised that to park right outside the shop or even on the opposite side to it could be dangerous as the woman could know what she looked like from Simon, have even seen a photograph of her. So she decided she'd be better placed in the middle of the street facing the shop. Rica was so consumed by desperation to see her son that it didn't strike her that should Simon come down the street he would immediately recognise the car, see her inside, and this would then put her plan to get her son back in severe jeopardy.

What did strike her, though, was that it was ironic that two years ago she had been outraged to be falsely accused of intending to kidnap a child, when now she was actually planning to do it.

So as not to look too conspicuous while she waited, Rica had had the foresight to stop off on her way there and buy a newspaper, so that should anyone take an interest in her it would look like she was waiting for whoever she was visiting to arrive home. With the paper now spread out before her, covering the steering wheel, her eyes were constantly darting over the top of it to snatch a glimpse of a young woman with a blond-haired child in tow.

When she had first arrived the street was virtually empty save for a gang of young boys at the other end playing football and three little girls sitting in the gutter with their heads together, reminding Rica of gossiping old ladies. Well over an hour later the street was becoming busier as residents were beginning to arrive home from work, looking weary from their day's labour. She had observed many of them going into the corner shop and guessed that quite a queue was forming. There was still no sign of the woman and the boy. She did realise that this might not even be the actual street they lived on. The shop here might be the nearest for them, so if they appeared from another direction she'd have to be ready to tail them on foot.

And what did she propose to do after that?

She couldn't very well knock on the door and demand the woman hand her son back. Simon was obviously not prepared to part with Ricky or he wouldn't have taken him away like that. She knew there was little point in paying him a visit once she knew his address and hoping he would be accommodating. But if she did manage to snatch Ricky back somehow and make away with him before she was discovered, she risked Simon doing the same in return. He knew where she lived after all.

It seemed to Rica in her desperation that there was only one option open to her. Immediately she got Ricky back, she would head off for pastures new and start afresh with him somewhere Simon would never find them. She would let him know by letter that their son was now back where he belonged, with her, and that he need not involve the police as she was the boy's mother and had as much right to have him with her as Simon had. There was money in the business account; not the amount Simon had taken from it when he had left, but hopefully enough to put a roof over their heads and keep them until she'd made proper plans for how to provide for them both.

Rica wouldn't tell anyone else about her plan, though. She didn't want them trying to persuade her that now she knew where Simon was hiding her son, the right course of action would be for her to approach a solicitor and take Simon to court, to fight for custody of Ricky. She wasn't prepared to take the risk that, when it came to the hearing, she was only awarded visiting rights. Ricky had been with his father for seven months, time enough for him to have stopped pining for his mummy and be looking at another woman in that light by now. A court might deem it not in his best interests to uproot him again. Then a horrifying thought struck her. What if Ricky didn't recognise her now? But she reasoned with herself that of course he would. Even if he didn't at first remember who she was then something about her would be familiar to him, surely: her smell, the sound of her voice, the feel of her lips on his cheek, the way she held him. She ought to prepare herself, though, for a period of adjustment while Ricky settled down with her again.

Her thoughts returned to her plan. After due deliberation she knew just how to proceed. She was still hopeful that she might discover where Ricky was living tonight. Tomorrow she could find a place where she could observe the house, waiting for the woman to take him out and then discreetly following them. The woman was bound to take her eye off him at some point when she was distracted doing her shopping, and that was when Rica would quietly grab Ricky and be away with him before the interloper had chance to notice. Hopefully they would be well out of the city before any alarm was raised over his disappearance. Tonight, as soon as she returned home, Rica would make preparations for her hurried exit. She would have a case packed ready in the boot with her belongings in it, including all the important documents, so that once she had Ricky she'd have no need to return to her house again.

She would miss her sister deeply; miss the joy of helping her to arrange her wedding and then of seeing her married, but once Rica was settled she would write to tell Fran where they were, so they could keep in touch. She knew that regardless of how much Simon badgered, pleaded or begged, Fran would never divulge where Rica had taken their son.

Rica would miss Jason, too; she had grown fond of the boy and it had been a joy to watch his transformation into a pleasant, easygoing young man who would one day make some lucky girl a lovely husband. She had no doubt he'd be a kind father, too, after his own miserable childhood.

It came as a shock, though, for Rica to realise that the person she would miss most would be Bill. She had thought him a pleasant ordinary man when she had first met him, but over the course of his helping her out and working alongside her she had slowly come to know him better as a person. Then when it came to light that they had both suffered a marital break up and they had bared their souls to each other, she had felt a kinship spark between them. When they had both had time to get over their pain, maybe something more might have developed between them. Rica would never know now. She hoped, though, that when Bill did eventually learn to trust again and found another woman to love, she would appreciate the treasure she had found in a man like him.

Thinking of Bill had temporarily taken Rica's mind off her task. She hadn't noticed someone approaching the car until an unexpected tap came on the driver's side window, almost making her leap out of her seat. She turned her head to see it was one of the young boys she'd seen earlier playing football. He was about ten years old, scruffily dressed and with a shock of unruly sand-coloured hair. He was standing staring at her.

Rica wound down the window. Before she could ask him what he wanted, he said to her, 'This your husband's car, lady? Boy, but it's a beauty, ain't it? My brother's got a car, not nowhere near as posh as this . . . in fact, it ain't got no engine in it at the moment as it blew up a few weeks ago and he can't afford another yet. But when it was working he wouldn't let his missus near it. He sez women ain't no good at driving. Will you give me a ride in it? Please, missus? Then I can brag to me friends that I've had a ride in a posh car, and won't they be jealous?'

Just for the cheek of him Rica would have liked to have obliged the boy, but while she was away she risked missing the woman possibly making a visit to the corner shop. Rica was about to let him down gently when through her wing mirror she caught sight of a woman emerging from an entry a little further down the road. As she approached the kerb to cross the street it became obvious she was heading for the shop as she had a gondola-type basket over her arm.

It wasn't the woman herself that Rica recognised as her back had been to the camera in the photograph, but her coat and headscarf were the same as the ones in the photograph. She didn't have Ricky with her, though. Where was he then? Had Simon come home from work and Rica been too distracted to notice? Or had she not missed his return at all and the woman had simply left Ricky by himself while she ran her errand? Or maybe she had children of her own and had left them minding Ricky?

Rica decided she may as well go home as she wasn't after all going to achieve her wish of catching a glimpse of her son tonight. At least she had discovered where they lived. At the crack of dawn tomorrow she would be back and waiting, ready to follow after them as soon as they went out. And if not that day then the one after or the one after that, until they did.

Then another thought struck her. Just what if Ricky had been left by himself? Then she would be missing the ideal opportunity to catch a glimpse of him through the window. From Rica's observations there was a queue of at least six or seven people ahead of the woman in the shop, so she should be away for at least ten minutes. It was a risky thing Rica was considering, but her desperation to see her son was far too great to ignore. Before she could do anything, though, she had to get rid of this boy. And she felt she knew just how to do it while making the woman's wait to be served even longer.

Rica snatched her handbag off the seat next to her, opened it up and from her purse grabbed a handful of change. 'I can't take you for a run tonight, another time maybe.' She then held out her hand to show him the money. 'Will this make up for your disappointment? You could get yourself some sweets.'

His eyes just about popped out of his head. There was at least ten shillings in change in Rica's palm, a fortune to him, and he was obviously having difficulty believing his luck. She thrust it all at him. 'Here, take it before I change my mind. If you hurry, you'll beat that woman who's on her way to the shop.'

In less than the blink of an eye the money had been snatched from her hand and the boy was racing off.

Fired up with excitement at the thought of possibly getting

316

to see her son for the first time in seven months, Rica immediately slipped out of the car, not even stopping to lock it, and hurried down to the entry she had seen the woman come out of. Two high gates faced her. She hadn't a clue which one the woman had used. Like the houses hereabouts, the gates were not in the best state of repair and both had holes in the rotting wood that she could look through. She chose the one to her left first. The slabbed yard was tidy, with nothing lying about that would indicate a child or children lived there. She then peeped through a hole in the gate to the other side. A child definitely lived here. Several toy cars were piled by the step and under the kitchen window stood a child's trike. From what she could see, there was no one in the kitchen.

Conscious that time was slipping away, Rica lifted the latch and pushed the gate open just far enough for her to squeeze inside. She shut it behind her, then flattened herself against the wall by the side of the back window for a second. She slid down on her hands and knees and crawled beneath the windowsill before gingerly raising herself just high enough so she could look over it. She had banked on it not being quite dark enough yet on this cool early-May evening for the curtains to have been drawn, and much to her relief they weren't.

The room she was peering into was furnished with shabby-looking furniture but was clean and tidy. From what she could see there was no sign of Simon or any children at all in the room. He must be working late and perhaps Ricky was already upstairs in bed.

Rica was about to stand up and return to her car when she spotted it at the back of the room: a playpen. Through the bars she could see movement . . . but she was too far away to make out the child inside. Who else could it be but Ricky, though? Just a wall and a couple of yards separated her from her son. She couldn't leave now, not without seeing him. Rica calculated that she still had at least five minutes left before the woman would return with her shopping.

Without any further thought she stepped across to the back door and let herself into the house. Before she entered the back room she took a peep through the open door, relieved once again to see no sign of any other occupant. There didn't seem to be any evidence at all of a man living here. No slippers by the fireside, no male items lying about, no coat or jacket hanging on the back door. She hadn't time to be wondering about that, though. She was halfway across the room, just about close enough to catch her first sight of her son with her heart hammering . . . when the unexpected sound of a voice made her freeze where she stood.

'Just what do you think you are doing in my house?'

Rica spun around to see the woman she'd just observed on her way to the corner shop standing glaring back at her from the back room doorway, the gondola basket still hooked over her arm. It hadn't taken as long for her to be served as Rica had calculated. Even in her shocked state, Rica found herself noticing that the woman Simon had left her for was much younger than she had assumed, no more than twenty-five or so, slim of build and just ordinary in looks, not at all the beauty Rica had envisioned.

'I asked what you are doing in my house?' she demanded again, her small dark eyes narrowed in suspicion.

Rica felt her legs beginning to turn to jelly. Her heart was thudding in trepidation and she couldn't seem to find any words to try and excuse her presence. Then an outburst of childish babble from behind her reminded her why she was here. Raising her chin, she boldly told the other woman, 'I'm here to collect my son.'

She seemed taken aback by the announcement for a moment before her eyes narrowed to two slits and she said, 'And why would you think your child was here? The only child here is mine.'

318

'That's not true,' Rica shot back at her. 'He's Simon's and my son. You're only looking after him now because you and Simon are together.'

To her surprise, the young woman laughed. 'Me and Simon together! That's what you believe, is it? I wouldn't have let that man near me if he was the last man on earth.'

Rica was eyeing her in confusion. 'But you must be together. I can't see Simon just leaving our son with a stranger and then going off.'

'No, you're right, he didn't leave the boy with a stranger. He left him with his mother.'

Rica eyed her incredulously. 'Look, lady . . .'

'Maisie Willett is my name. And you must be Mrs Dunmore. I can't say as I'm pleased to meet you, but carry on.'

'Look, Mrs Willett, I don't know what your game is, but *I* am Ricky's mother.'

'His name is Steven. And no, Mrs Dunmore. You might have played the part of Steven's mother for eighteen months, but I was the one who gave birth to him. I believe that makes me his real mother, wouldn't you agree?'

CHAPTER TWENTY-SIX

Rica was staring at her, stupefied by her revelation. 'But . . . but . . . you didn't want a baby. You signed the adoption papers giving him away.'

Maisie responded matter-of-factly, 'Now why would I sign papers to give away a baby I thought was dead?'

'What!'

'That's right. I believed my son was born dead. That's what I was told, and he was whipped away the minute he was born without me being given the chance to see my child's face. In fact, I wasn't even told whether I'd had a girl or a boy. I was assured I would get over its death quicker, the less I knew about it. So I was left to mourn my child, not being able to picture its little face or in my mind be able to give it so much as a name. A woman never gets over the loss of a child and I would have gone to my grave mourning mine, however many more came afterwards, had it not been for a deathbed confession from the midwife who delivered my baby. That's how I learned that my child . . . *my son* . . . wasn't dead at all, but very much alive and living with the couple my husband had sold him to!'

Rica couldn't believe the horrific story she was being told. She couldn't begin to imagine what torment this woman must have suffered. But what did it mean for her? It was obvious Maisie wasn't going to offer to hand Ricky, or Steven as she preferred to call him, back. Was she then expecting Rica to say her goodbyes to him and walk out of his life? She couldn't. The thought was unbearable to her.

While Rica gazed at Maisie, horrified and speechless, the young woman put down the basket of shopping on the well-worn oak dining table, took off her coat and scarf and hung them on the back of a dining chair. She then flashed a look over at the child in the playpen, satisfied to see he was playing contentedly with his toys, before she continued speaking.

'The old witch who'd attended me had the nerve to beg my forgiveness for what she had helped to do. Her excuse was that she was desperate for the money my husband bribed her with. She had managed to live with her guilt easily enough for seventeen months but, once she faced meeting her maker in a matter of hours, was petrified she would go to hell for her crime. She thought that if she was forgiven for it by the one she had helped deceive, that would secure her place in heaven.

'Well, I defy any woman to forgive such a crime committed against her. I led that old crone to believe that I would give her absolution, but only if she told me the whole story. And now I hope the vile creature is roasting in hell for all eternity! It's the least she deserves for what she willingly took part in.

'She told me that my husband had come to see her a couple of months before our baby was due. We'd been married for just over two years when I found out I was expecting our first child. Clive gave me no reason to believe he wasn't as thrilled as I was, but in truth that was far from the case. He told the midwife that he wasn't ready to become a father. In fact, he was unsure he ever did want to become one. Besides, he felt we couldn't afford a family yet anyway as we weren't earning that much between us and would really struggle when I gave up my job to look after a baby. The nearer it got to my time, the more worried he became about the poverty we faced. But still he didn't tell me what he was feeling.

'He was in the pub one night, brooding over his problems, when he found himself spilling his guts out to a stranger. But Clive wasn't entirely honest with him. He let the stranger believe that neither he nor his wife wanted the baby. The stranger said to my husband that if that was the case, then why hadn't we considered having the child adopted? And if we were to decide we would do that, then he and his wife would take it as his wife was desperate for a child but couldn't have any of her own. He gave my husband his business card and told him to get in touch with him if we decided to go down the adoption route.

'Before the stranger was halfway across the room, Clive had made his mind up. He called the man back and made a deal with him to hand over our baby as soon as it was born. He must be prepared to fetch it as soon as he was summoned. The midwife wasn't privy to exactly what the deal was that was struck between them, but she had no doubt money was involved. Clive offered her ten pounds to help him carry out his despicable deception of me.

'I'd already got my own midwife lined up, but he persuaded me that he'd heard rumours about her he didn't like the sound of and said that I really should go to this other woman as it was better to be safe than sorry. Like a lamb to the slaughter, I changed my midwife to the one he wanted me to use. When Clive disappeared straight after the midwife had wrapped up what I thought was my dead baby, he told me later he'd been sitting in the garden, smoking and crying for his child as he didn't want me to see how upset he was. Of course, I now know he'd gone to meet your husband, to hand over my baby, and far from being upset, he was more than likely rubbing his hands in glee.

'After damning that old crone to hell, I left her with a vivid vision of what she faced in hell for all eternity, and went home hell-bent on making my husband pay for what he'd done to me. It's amazing how quickly love can turn to pure hatred. As soon as I got home after seeing that woman, I searched the house for evidence of what Clive had done. In a little two up, two down there aren't too many places to hide things. It didn't take me long to find where Clive had kept hidden the money he'd been paid for our baby, though by then it was just a few pounds. One thing I did know about my husband, though, was that when there was money to be made, he would stick out for the highest price he could get. I had no doubt that he'd received a small fortune. I wasn't to find out exactly how much money my baby was worth until a while after, but I'll come to that later when I get to that part of my story.

'I found out who he'd sold our baby to as, stupidly, Clive still had the business card he'd been given tucked into the inside pocket of a jacket. While I planned my revenge, I gave my husband no idea that I was aware of what he had done. I meant my plan to have no comeback on me. I'd get my child back and didn't want to be living in fear that I could be hauled off to jail for murder at any time.'

Rica gasped and exclaimed, 'Murder! You *murdered* your husband?'

Maisie Willett's voice was icy, her eyes hard, when she responded. 'That was the least he deserved after what he'd put me through. I would have much preferred to have made him suffer before I finished him off. I could think of many ways to inflict such pain on him he would have been begging me to kill him. It still would not have been anywhere near the level of pain his selfishness put me through. But I daren't risk it. The walls are quite thick between these houses, but I doubt they would have contained his screams for mercy.

'I had to live with that bastard for a whole month while I thought of my plan then put it into operation, all the time playing the part of the loving wife, having to fight to keep myself from vomiting while we had sex, and not to spike his food with rat poison. But my patience paid off. When I did come up with a plan, it was so simple. There *is* such a thing as the perfect murder, take my word for it. Pity I can't afford to brag about it really.

'It was an advert in the newspaper that gave me the idea. It was for a coach trip to a stately home one Saturday. I'd never been out of the city and I'd have really liked to have gone on that coach trip, but I didn't like the thought of going on my own and certainly couldn't stand the thought of sitting next to Clive for hours on a coach when just being in the same bed as him made my skin crawl and it took all my strength not to smother him while he was sleeping. Then it struck me that maybe I should go on the trip and take Clive with me . . . only it wouldn't be the real Clive as he would already be dead and buried. A bloke who resembled him would take his place, and I'd stage Clive's "desertion" of me. The more I thought about it, the more I realised the idea had potential.

'It wouldn't be hard for me to find someone who would do what I asked of them for a few quid, no questions asked. I only had to call in at our then local to find at least a dozen suitable types propping up the bar. It didn't take me long to find a man who, dressed in Clive's clothes, would pass for him. The bloke I chose didn't seem at all curious about why I was asking him to pretend he was my husband and come with me on a coach trip.

'I told him he was to sneak into my house in the small hours the night before, and sleep on the sofa until it was time for us to get ready to set off for the coach station. On the journey he was expected not to talk to anyone, but was to pretend to be asleep for the whole time, only appearing to wake up when the bus arrived. After making sure he was seen by at least two or three of the other passengers, he was to head out of the stately home and disappear, find

324

somewhere to lie low until it was dark. He was then to make his own way back to Leicester. I meanwhile would act distressed that my husband had walked away from me. I would give him half his payment up front and the other half when I was satisfied he had carried out my instructions to the letter.

'Just to make sure he didn't for any reason start wondering afterwards why I'd paid him to impersonate my husband, I told him I was playing a joke on Clive. A drinking buddy of his was moaning down the pub one night that his wife was making him go on a coach trip, and he didn't want to. My husband then bragged that there was no way his wife would make him do anything he didn't want to, and certainly would never get him on a coach trip, no matter how hard she begged.

'I said I'd got to hear about it and decided to get my own back so that I could go down the pub myself and let it be known we had just come back from a coach trip. When Clive tried to deny it, I told the man, I could say I had plenty of witnesses to prove he was with me as there were thirty other people on the coach with us, as well as the driver and courier. I had only to show any of them a photo of Clive and they would back me up. Then wouldn't he regret the day he'd made out to his cronies that under no circumstances was he under my thumb? He'd never be able to live it down. The bloke thought my plan of revenge was very funny.

'With that sorted it just remained for me to book the trip then find us a new place to live that had certain facilities. I found this house with not too much bother and moved us in two weeks later, with another two weeks to go before the trip. Plenty of time for me to do what I had to, so that I was all set and ready to go.

'I'll never forget the look of shock on Clive's face the night before the trip he had no idea I was booked on, when

I bashed him over the head with the spade, screaming at him that that was for selling my baby and making me believe he was dead . . . The sense of satisfaction I felt at justice done as I stood over him while he drew his last breath was well worth all the sleepless nights I'd suffered, going over and over my plan, making absolutely sure that I'd not forgotten anything. As well as having to be nice to him meanwhile.'

Rica was staring round-eyed at Maisie. She couldn't believe this woman had just casually confessed to murdering her husband. 'What he did to you was despicable, evil even, but you can't justify killing him . . .'

Maisie cut her short. 'You tell me then what other punishment would go anywhere near to paying someone back for a lie like that?'

Rica argued, 'I would want to kill them too . . . but thinking it is one thing, carrying it out is quite another. You didn't attack your husband immediately you discovered what he had done. You first thought up a plan and then spent time perfecting it before you acted. That makes you a cold-blooded murderer.'

Maisie shook her head at Rica. 'Well, let's just beg to differ on the way we both look at life, shall we? So, with Clive dealt with and the coach trip over, and the police convinced that my husband had left me when I reported him missing, I could then put the rest of my plan in motion. I wanted my son back where he rightfully belonged. I found a business card belonging to your husband that told me he owned a photography shop. If he had his own business, I was sure he would be able to lay his hand on a bob or two . . . I decided to pay the shop a visit under the guise of a customer to get an idea of how much money he was worth before I put the rest of my plan into action.

'As I arrived, I saw a card in the window advertising for a cleaner. If I were to work for him, I would have the perfect opportunity to learn more about how the business was faring. It was only two hours a day and I felt sure I could manage to be pleasant for a couple of hours while I found out what I wanted to. But I never got as much of a chance to be alone in the office as I had hoped I would, and although I did overhear several telephone conversations requesting quotes for jobs, I never had the chance to look through his accounts books. I couldn't keep up my act much longer, and I didn't want to risk Dunmore becoming suspicious of me. I worked a week in hand but I was damned sure I wasn't going to go back the following Friday and collect the wages I was due. It was a measly amount compared with the sum I was about to demand.

'When I did return it was late the next Thursday night. I let myself in through the back door after all the staff had left. What a shock Dunmore got to see me walk into his office as he was putting his coat on to leave. He thought I'd come with an explanation of why I had upped and left, and to collect the wages that were due. As if those paltry few shillings could ever make up for the pain and suffering he and Clive had caused me . . . What a picture his face was when I revealed who I was and that I had discovered he'd bought my baby from my husband, who had told me the child was dead. I told him that if he didn't come to my house with ten thousand pounds by the next day I would make it my business to let you know exactly how he had gone about getting you your child.

'I've never seen a man look so terrified. He said he didn't have ten thousand pounds. I told him he'd better find it by tomorrow and bring it to my house in cash, then in return I'd sign a paper stating that I'd willingly handed over the baby at birth as I knew it would have a better life that way. There was one stipulation. He was to bring the child with him so that I could see him just one last time.

'Of course, you know now that I never had any intention

of letting my son go back with him. And if any of the neighbours had seen him bringing in the lad, I'd just moved in, remember, and hadn't made any secret of the fact that a friend was looking after my son while I first settled in, then for a bit longer while I came to terms with the fact of my husband leaving me. If any of my neighbours saw Simon arriving here with Steve, then they'd think he was my friend's husband bringing my son back to me.'

Rica was still reeling with shock from all this. 'Simon handed you three thousand pounds, didn't he?' she uttered. 'All the money he could lay his hands on. Our life savings.'

Maisie smiled. 'I wanted ten, but three was more than enough to keep me and my son until he was old enough to go to school and I could go to work. I was used to being careful with money, after the paltry wages me and Clive bought in, so that wouldn't be a problem.'

Rica's mind was reeling. Simon . . . he hadn't left her after all because he'd met someone else and didn't love her any more, and nor had he abandoned the business either. She couldn't understand, though, why he hadn't come home and broken the news to her that Ricky's real mother had reclaimed him so they could mourn his loss together, or why he hadn't returned since. But she couldn't think about that at the moment. She was getting a terrible feeling that after she left this house she would never again see the child she'd thought of as her own and still loved immeasurably. The law could force Maisie Willett to return Ricky to her, as Rica herself was named as his mother on his birth certificate, but morally she would not be able to live with herself, knowing she was raising a child when she knew its true mother was pining for it. All children deserved to be raised by their own flesh and blood if possible. Only if not should they go to loving people who couldn't have children of their own. Her hope of getting Ricky back with her one day had served to bolster her as she made a new future for herself, but now it all looked as bleak to her as it had the day she'd thought Simon had left her and taken Ricky with him.

Maisie stood looking down at the playpen where the young boy was still playing contentedly with his toys. 'Do you know the most ironic thing about it all, Mrs Dunmore? My own son doesn't like me. I was expecting it to take a while for him to settle in when I first got him back, but he's only just recently stopped crying all the time for his mummy. I kept telling him that *I* was his mummy, not that lady who looked after him until he came back to me, but I just couldn't make him understand. He won't sit on my knee and let me tell him a story unless I make him. He holds his arms by his sides when I hug him, and never runs to me to comfort him when he's hurt himself. If I try to, he pushes me off. Most of the time he won't do as he's told. It's very strange, but tonight is the first time I've seen him play so contentedly as he is now. Do you reckon he senses you are here?'

Rica didn't know what to say to that. Ricky's behaviour with her had been totally the opposite to what Maisie had described. Then another thought struck her and she asked, 'Just how did you get my husband to leave Ricky with you after you had accepted the money you'd demanded from him?'

'Oh, Simon didn't leave. I can take you to him, if you like.'

Rica's mouth dropped open. 'You mean, he's here . . . living here? So you are together after all! But you've led me to believe that you hadn't met until the time you went to work for him in the shop. You're not making sense to me . . .'

But Maisie was already heading off towards a door set in one corner at the back of the room. Mystified, Rica followed her through it and on down a steep flight of stone steps, into the darkness below. The further she went down, the stronger the vile smell of damp and decay became in her

329

nostrils. Why were they coming down here? It was obvious this room could not be in use, and why would Simon be down in this awful cellar anyway?

Immediately Rica joined her at the bottom of the stairs, to her shock Maisie pushed her forward with such force that she shot forward several feet then stumbled over an unexpected rise in the floor beneath her, to come crashing to a halt against the wall. In the near pitch blackness, as she spun around to demand what on earth Maisie thought she was doing, she was suddenly temporarily blinded by light flooding the room and for a moment had to fight to accustom her eyes to it. The first thing she saw then was Maisie standing at the bottom of the stairs, looking back at her with an expression on her face that Rica couldn't read.

She took a look around her. The cellar was the size of the back room and front room above combined. All around her were strewn the piles of unwanted items most people store in cellars, just in case they come in useful at some time in the future. She could see no sign of Simon at all.

Bewildered, she demanded, 'So where is my husband then?'

'You're standing on him.'

Rica blankly looked down at the uneven stone slabs beneath her. She then raised her eyes and looked back at Maisie. 'I don't understand . . .' Then, like a door springing open in her mind, the terrible truth dawned on her and she felt her life's blood draining from her. Her legs threatened to give way beneath her and she slumped back against the dirty red-brick wall. She let out an agonising wail, like an animal's last death throe. 'No, no, you didn't . . . Oh, please tell me you didn't kill my husband and bury him down here? Please, please, tell me you didn't, I beg you?'

Maisie snarled, 'Same as my husband, it was nothing less than he deserved. If he hadn't flashed his money around and offered to adopt our child, my husband would never have come up with his despicable plan.'

Rica hysterically screamed, 'You killed my husband just because he offered to take what he believed to be an unwanted baby! You're mad . . . insane. Two men dead. Oh, my God, is your husband buried down here too?'

Maisie smiled. 'Clive didn't even know this house had a cellar. I dug his grave while he was out at work, and when he was home I kept the door locked, telling him it led into a cupboard under the stairs only the agent never gave me the key for it so I'd have to remember to get it off him, then we could use it for storage.

'The night I killed him it was so easy to get him to come down here with me, wanting to see the cellar I'd "discovered", and planning what he was going to do with it. Your husband was too polite to refuse when I asked him to help me by bringing a box up from here. While he was bending over to pick it up, I bashed his head in with the spade, same as I had done to Clive. Of course, this does mean I'm tied to the place until they carry me out in a box. But it's the price I was willing to pay, to make my husband and his accomplice pay for their wickedness.'

Rica cried, 'I can't believe you feel justified in what you have . . .' Her voice trailed away as it was then she saw what Maisie was holding in her hand. A spade. 'You're going to try to kill me now, is that it?'

'There's no "try" about it. You have to die. Well, you don't think that after me telling you all this I can let you go free, do you, to fetch the law on me? Apart from that, I can't let you live as I have no proof I gave birth to my own son. It's your name down on his birth certificate, so legally you are his mother. The law would make me give him back to you and then have me locked up for kidnap if you went to them. That's hardly fair to me, is it? Take comfort from the fact that you won't be on your own down here, though I can't say you'll be in good company. And please accept my apologies for the fact you know what's coming to you, whereas Clive and your husband never had a clue. Oh, and there's no point in screaming or hollering. No one can hear you down here.'

Rica froze in terror as she saw Maisie Willett raise the spade to head height and advance on her. She knew she'd be wasting her time begging to be spared, promising faithfully she wouldn't go to the police. There was no mad glint in Maisie's eyes, no manic smile on her lips. The woman about to murder her appeared to be calmly intent and purposeful. After all, she'd done it before.

A vision of Ricky occurred to Rica then, in the room above them, playing contentedly in his playpen. What were the chances of her coming out of this alive? Maisie had already killed twice and she was armed. Rica wasn't. She felt like her heart would break at the thought that she'd never hold Ricky again, never say her goodbyes to him.

Then determination surged within her. She couldn't let this woman take her life as if it was nothing. No matter what had been done to her, Maisie had had a choice: to kill or not to kill. She could not justify her horrendous crimes by blaming them on her victims. As long as Rica had breath in her body, she would fight to make sure she protected Ricky from his deranged mother.

Maisie was in striking distance of her now and Rica instinctively threw herself to one side as Maisie heaved the flat end of the spade at her, aiming for Rica's head. She wasn't quick enough to evade it entirely. The sharp edge caught her on her arm, slicing through her coat and the jumper beneath and deep into her arm. The pain was excruciating but she hadn't time to think how badly she was hurt. She needed to get herself back on her feet, having landed among a stack of old paint tins and sent them rolling all about. Maisie meantime was cursing loudly as she fought to wrench the shovel head out of a joint between two slabs where it had stuck when it reached the floor.

On righting herself, seeing Maisie was temporarily occupied, Rica prayed she could negotiate her way through the piles of debris and paint tins, and reach the stairs. At the top she would lock the cellar door after her and then run for help. And if she switched off the light at the bottom of the steps, then Maisie would take much longer to come after her because she wouldn't be able to see where she was going.

But to Rica's dismay she had not even managed to get halfway across the room when she heard the clang of the spade connecting with the wall beside Maisie as she yanked it free again. Shooting a glance over her shoulder, Rica saw Maisie come after her again, the spade raised in readiness. Rica's slashed arm was now throbbing relentlessly and she felt something wet seeping down the back of her hand. She knew it was blood. Rica started to step backwards, not wanting to look away from Maisie so she could anticipate the next strike and try to avoid it. She was conscious, though, that she could fall over an unexpected obstacle. She prayed she would not.

Desperate for a weapon of her own or at least for something to try and defend herself with, as she continued stepping backwards she leaned to one side to grab the first thing her hand encountered. It was a half-empty paint tin. Rica threw it at Maisie as hard as she could. It struck her on the side of the head before bouncing to the ground. Intent on murder, Maisie seemed not to notice the large gash it had caused and the spurt of blood from it.

Panic was flooding Rica now. She continued backwards in the direction of the steps, grabbing anything she could lay her hands on which she then hurled with as much force as she could at Maisie. Her efforts did manage to widen the gap between them as Maisie had to keep stepping sideways to avoid being hit. But by now Rica's strength was ebbing.

As she leaned over once more to grab anything she could, her hand closed around an object with something metal protruding from it. It was a screwdriver. It was no match for a spade, but better than nothing.

When Maisie saw Rica holding the rusting screwdriver like a dagger, she shot her a look as though to say, Are you mad to think that will save you? Now that she wasn't being bombarded with missiles any longer, she had managed to shorten the distance between them enough to be within striking distance of Rica again. Using all her strength, she brought the spade down forcefully, aiming for Rica's head. Seeing it, she again managed to dodge out of the way just in time. With nothing to break its momentum the head of the spade juddered against the slab where Rica had just been standing, causing it to be jolted out of Maisie's hands and fly through the air, the sharp blade missing Rica's right arm by no more than a fraction of an inch. The spade landed with a clatter in the corner of the room where Maisie had said Simon was buried.

Now that Maisie was unarmed, Rica seized her chance to inflict as much damage on her with the screwdriver as she could, hoping that it would debilitate her long enough for Rica to get to the top of the stairs and through the door, locking Maisie in before she could arm herself again. Rica made a desperate lunge at her but before the screwdriver made contact with its intended target, Maisie had grabbed hold of Rica's wrist and twisted it, causing her to drop the screwdriver. Maisie immediately bent down to snatch it up. Rica flashed a lightning glance around, searching for another weapon, but could see nothing of use.

Maisie was holding the screwdriver aloft now and Rica saw she was about to stab her with it. In utter desperation, she took Maisie completely off guard by kicking her hard in her shins as she simultaneously gave her a hard push. Not expecting this, Maisie lost her balance and stumbled backwards over a discarded crate.

Rica didn't wait around to see what damage she had caused

her assailant, but immediately made for the steps, just managing to avoid tripping over two old bicycle wheels. As she arrived at the bottom of them she reached for the light cord and gave it a pull. The room was plunged instantly into near pitch darkness, the only light coming through the gap in the doorway at the top of the steep flight of steps in front of her. There were fifteen of them to climb before she reached freedom, but at the moment they seemed like a mountain to Rica.

From the sounds across the room, Rica knew that Maisie had recovered from her tumble and resumed the pursuit. Of course, she would know this room like the back of her hand. The lack of light was not such a handicap as Rica had hoped. Fearing she could lose her balance in the dark on the slippery stone steps, Rica started to climb them.

She was almost at the top, only two steps between her and the doorway, when she gasped in shock then let out a cry of agony as an excruciating pain seared through the calf of her left leg. Her head spun around and the light from the doorway allowed her to see that at least an inch of the rusty screwdriver was embedded in her flesh, blood pouring from the wound. Then movement caught her eye. Maisie, a few steps below, stretching out both hands. Rica knew her intention was to pull her back down the steps by her ankles and finish off the job.

Rica did not intend to allow that. She must live, for the sake of the little boy only feet away now from her. Thinking of Ricky gave her the will to resist. She had no weapon so she did the only thing that was open to her. She drew her right leg up as far as the next step would allow, then with all the strength she could muster, thrust it out behind her. She felt her shoe make contact with Maisie's body, and a second later the sound of a thud.

This brief respite might be the only chance she had left of making her escape. It would only take seconds for Maisie

335

to haul herself off the floor below and come rushing back up the steps. With every bit of strength she had Rica tried desperately to haul herself up the remaining two steps, but before she could manage even the first of them her vision began to swim and her whole body went limp. She slumped down at the top of the steps, then everything went black.

CHAPTER
TWENTY-SEVEN

Ignoring her aching back, the stiffness of her neck, the continual throb of her still very tender wounds and the pulling of the dozen or so stitches keeping them closed, Rica gazed down with pure love at her peacefully sleeping son. She wasn't aware that she'd been staring down at him like this for well over two hours, afraid to leave him in case he disappeared when her eyes were off him. There was a gathering downstairs of Fran and Reginald, Bill and Jason, all of them wanting to see her settled back at home after being released from hospital. She was grateful that none of them had disturbed her while she'd been up here with Ricky. They seemed to understand that she needed to spend time alone with her son, to really believe that he was finally back home with her.

Mixed emotions raged inside Rica. She was euphoric to have her son back, and bereft over the loss of her husband. Simon had left her, not voluntarily for another woman but because he had been given no choice. He had paid a terrible price for seizing an opportunity to grant his beloved wife's dearest wish for a child of her own. She would make sure Ricky knew what a good man his father was; how much he had adored his son; all the plans he'd had for the many things they would do together, and his hope that Ricky would eventually follow him into the family business. As well as, of course, telling the boy about the terrible car accident that had robbed them both of him. Because the truth about the way Simon had died was too awful for her to tell their son.

For Rica it was like starting her grieving for Simon all over again. She was angry beyond measure with Maisie Willett for taking him from her; would never forgive the woman for the pain of that grief nor the years that lay ahead denied of her beloved husband, and Ricky of the father who had loved and wanted him. There was, though, a part of Rica that felt deep pity for Maisie after what her husband had done to her. If she herself had gone through mourning a dead child, only to discover eighteen months later that it was still very much alive, having been sold by its father, she had no doubt it would have unhinged her too. But, regardless, Rica knew she herself would never have resorted to murdering those she held responsible for her suffering.

It had been three days since she had escaped death at Maisie's hands. Rica remembered in great detail every moment of her ordeal down in that hell-hole of a cellar; could still feel the terror and shock of it all. The doctors had warned her that it could be a while before she stopped having nightmares. It was strange, but when she dreamed it was not about her fight for life with a crazed woman intent on killing her, but about Ricky. She was in a dark room with no windows or doors, and could hear him crying for her behind the walls. But she couldn't find a way to get to him, to comfort him, and would wake sobbing and sweating.

She had been told that she had come round in the ambulance on the way to the hospital long enough to ask after her son, lapsing into unconsciousness again on being told he was safe and being well looked after by a policewoman. When she woke again it was a shock for a moment to find herself in a hospital bed. Then memories flooded back. She had used the last of her ebbing strength to kick out at Maisie, convinced at the time that her feeble attempt would achieve nothing. It seemed, though, that Maisie had not been expecting Rica to retaliate. In her surprise she had lost her balance as she had before, but this time her fall was much more severe. The thud Rica had heard was Maisie's head smashing against an unyielding stone slab.

The blow did not instantly kill her; she lived for several minutes more as her life's blood drained from the dreadful wound at the back of her head. She would have been aware that she was dying. Rica derived no satisfaction from that fact, but neither did she accept responsibility for bringing about her death. She had only been trying to protect herself from a murderer.

It was a neighbour who had raised the alarm. She had heard Ricky crying but thought nothing of it at first. After an hour, when his cries became very distressed and his mother did not seem to be doing anything about it, she sensed something wasn't right and came around to investigate. She couldn't believe what she found. It wasn't until Rica had recovered enough to give the police her statement that the neighbour discovered that for the last seven months she'd been chatting quite amicably over the garden wall with a kidnapper and double murderer.

Rica's statement of events to the police hadn't been entirely truthful. Her version had been that seven months ago her husband had taken her son to the park and not returned home. Although the police believed he'd left her for another woman, she had hired a private investigator to try and uncover his whereabouts, but all his leads were dead ends. It was only through sheer chance that she had seen Ricky in a photograph, which had led her to Maisie Willett's house. On checking through the back window she'd seen her son in a playpen across the room. Obviously she should not have gone inside the house, but could not resist going in to check on his welfare since there was no sign of anyone minding him.

She had only got halfway across the room when someone had grabbed her from behind. Before she could do anything to resist she had been dragged down into the cellar, and the first time she had seen her assailant face-to-face, Maisie Willett was brandishing a spade, leaving Rica in no doubt what she intended to do with it. The injuries she had sustained had been inflicted by Maisie in her attempt to stop Rica from escaping. Maisie had sustained her own fatal injuries accidentally in Rica's struggle to free herself. She pretended to be repentant that her actions had led to the woman's death.

Rica maintained that at no time did Maisie Willett offer her any explanation for why she wanted her dead, and nor did she enlighten her as to why she had killed her own husband and Rica's, and kept Ricky while making out he was her son. Consequently Rica had no idea how Simon had met her, had come to take their son with him to her house, given her their life savings or why Maisie Willett had killed him. It was all a complete mystery to her.

Rica felt no guilt for withholding the information she had, and was prepared to go as far as perjuring herself in court in order to protect her son. There was no need for him to bear the burden of knowing what his real mother had done in her thirst for revenge against those she held responsible for her suffering. Rica wasn't prepared to take the risk of what such knowledge could do to him. All he need ever know was that she was his mother and Simon his father, who had met his end through an unfortunate accident.

The police had given her no indication that they doubted her story in the slightest. In the future, of course, there was always the possibility that someone would connect Ricky's name with the Willett kidnap and murders. If they did, then and only then would Rica tell him the same edited story as she had given the police. She meant her son to grow up to be a happy, well-adjusted member of society, and would do everything she could to ensure that.

The hospital had kept her in for three days, insisting that she needed to rest and regain her strength as she had lost a fair amount of blood. Rica was desperate to be discharged, intent on being reunited with her son. She couldn't bear to think how deeply worried he would be to find himself being cared for by a stranger for the second time in only a matter of months. She then learned that the ward had just received a telephone call from her sister. Fran had learned what had happened from the police and as next-of-kin had immediately gone to collect Ricky and taken him straight to Rica's house. She was looking after him there until her sister could come home and take over.

Despite her sister's lack of affinity with children, Rica couldn't think of anyone better to ensure Ricky's well-being at that moment, and was able then to concentrate on her own recovery in order to be allowed home as soon as possible.

The police had interviewed her in hospital and as soon as they had left she had fallen asleep. She awoke to find Bill by her bed, holding her hand gently in his, looking deeply concerned. The moment he realised she had woken he had whipped his hand away. Smiling, he told her he had got in to see her out of visiting hours by using the same ploy as she had after his accident. He'd said he was her brother. Later, when she had come to terms with it all and put it all behind her, Rica would laugh at this, but right at that moment she couldn't raise even a chuckle.

Bill did not probe her about her ordeal but it was apparent he knew about it. He chatted to her for a few minutes, to satisfy himself that she was going to be all right. Rica sensed, though, that his need to see her ran deeper than just checking a friend was on the mend. His feelings for her were plain to see. She knew for certain then that when they had both come through their grieving, and were ready to trust their emotions again, they would take their relationship further. Where that would lead, who knew? But Rica was willing to find out.

Now she had her son back, her days of personally running the business were over. She intended Ricky to have her full attention all day, every day. She had lost seven months of his life and didn't intend to lose any more. She would, of course, keep her eye firmly on the business by doing the books, which Fran had promised to teach her to do, and paying ad hoc visits. When the time came for Ricky to go to school it was possible she would return to working in the shop, but she had at least three years to decide about that. In the meantime, she would appoint a new manager to oversee things for her. Jason might only just be about to complete his apprenticeship and was still very young, but no one knew the business better than he did, and Rica felt strongly that he would make a good manager, one she could definitely trust and who would rise to the challenge and do his best to prove his worth. She couldn't see the affable Harry objecting to having Jason as his boss. More staff would need to be hired as well. The dent in her profits did not concern her. So long as the business provided her with enough money to raise her son in the manner she wished, that was all Rica cared about. She wasn't sure whether Bill would want to continue handling some of their commissions once he'd received payment for tackling the Council contract. She hoped so, but if not then she would just have to find a suitable replacement, though deep down she felt Bill was irreplaceable to her.

Ricky stirred in his sleep, momentarily opened his eyes and smiled at her before his eyes closed again and he fell back to sleep. Tenderness for him filled Rica. When she had arrived back home a few hours ago her sister had been in the kitchen, preparing a meal for him. Fran had looked at Rica in shock when she walked through the back door unannounced, not having been expecting her. All she had said was, 'He's playing in the lounge.'

Rica had leaned over and kissed her on the cheek, saying with deep feeling, 'Thank you, Fran.'

Her sister had swatted her away, saying, 'You'll need all your kisses for your son.'

Rica had needed no more telling. She'd arrived in the lounge to find Ricky with his toys all scattered around him. He had been concentrating on what he was doing and hadn't seemed to be aware that anyone had come in. She'd stepped over to within a couple of feet of him, then got down on her knees to be at his level. 'Hello, darling. It's Mummy,' she had said softly.

He had raised his head and looked at her blankly for what had seemed an eternity to Rica. Then a flicker of recognition had flashed in his eyes and he had stood up to take a tentative step towards her. She'd opened her arms to him and the next thing she knew he had run into them and they were hugging each other tightly. Her dreadful fear that he would have forgotten her had been unfounded.

Now his stirring disturbed the covers around him. Rica leaned over and one-handedly tucked them back around him protectively. She knew she could stay here all night just looking down at him, but he'd probably stirred because he had sensed she was there. It wasn't fair of her to be continually disturbing his sleep with her own selfish need not to let him out of her sight.

Kissing the end of one finger, she reached down again to touch it gently against his forehead. 'Sleep tightly, sweetheart,' she whispered before going downstairs to join the others.